Blue
MARGUERITE

LJ EVANS

BLUE MARGUERITE

THE PAINTED DAISIES
BOOK 4

LJ EVANS

That's What She Said Publishing,Inc.

This book is a work of fiction. While reference might be made to actual historical events or existing people and locations, the events, names, characters, places, and incidents are either the product of the author's imagination or are used fictitiously, and any resemblance to actual persons, living or dead, business establishments, events, or locales is entirely coincidental.

BLUE MARGUERITE © 2023 by LJ Evans

Published by THAT'S WHAT SHE SAID PUBLISHING

www.ljevansbooks.com

Cover Design: © Emily Wittig

Cover Images: © Unsplash | weston m, Deposit Photos | VadimVasenin and Dekues, iStock| Punnarong, and Shutterstock | Mike Mols

Content & Line Editor: Evans Editing

Copy Editor: Jenn Lockwood Editing Services

Proofing: Karen Hrdlicka

Sensitivity Editor: Liss Montoya

Library of Congress Cataloging in process.

Paperback ISBN: 979-8-88643-916-8

eBook ISBN: 979-8-88643-915-1

Printed in the United States

060823

Blue MARGUERITE

PLAYLIST

PROLOGUE WOULD'VE, COULD'VE, SHOULD'VE BY TAYLOR SWIFT
CHP 1 SOME OF US BY STARSAILOR
CHP 2 YOU'RE SUCH A BY HAILEE STEINFELD
CHP 3 CLEAN BY TAYLOR SWIFT
CHP 4 BAD BLOOD BY TALOR SWIFT
CHP 5 SAME OLD LOVE BY SELENA GOMEZ
CHP 6 EXILE BY TAYLOR SWIFT AND BON IVER
CHP 7 GHOST OF LOVE BY THE RASMUS
CHP 8 FIGHTER BY CHRISTINA AGUILERA
CHP 9 UNWANTED BY AVRIL LAVIGNE
CHP 10 DO ME WRONG BY THE HALL EFFECT
CHP 11 I LOVE YOU'S BY HAILEE STEINFELD
CHP 12 EVERMORE BY TAYLOR SWIFT
CHP 13 LOST AND FOUND BY THE HALL EFFECT
CHP 14 THIS IS ME TRYING BY TAYLOR SWIFT
CHP 15 STUPID GIRL BY GARBAGE
CHP 16 BEFORE I GO TO SLEEP BY THE MILLS
CHP 17 VIGILANTE SHIT BY TAYLOR SWIFT
CHP 18 ANTI-HERO BY TAYLOR SWIFT
CHP 19 TEMPT MY TROUBLE BY BISHOP BRIGGS
CHP 20 BATTLEFIELD BY LEA MICHELE
CHP 21 STYLE BY TAYLOR SWIFT
CHP 22 I SHALL BELIEVE BY SHERYL CROW
CHP 23 VBEST THING I NEVER HAD BY ALY STILES
CHP 24 ROCK BOTTOM BY HAILEE STEINFELD
CHP 25 SOMETIMES BY GARBAGE
CHP 26 WILLOW BY TAYLOR SWIFT
CHP 27 NOT ALONE BY THE HALL EFFECT
CHP 28 CHOKE BY THE HALL EFFECT
CHP 29 I CAN'T SAVE YOU FROM MYSELF BY ALY STILES
CHP 30 PEACE BY TAYLOR SWIFT
CHP 31 SURVIVORS BY SELENA GOMEZ
CHP 32 LEST WE FORGET BY THE BROTHERS BRIGHT / LEVI LOWREY
CHP 33 FALSE GOD BY TAYLOR SWIFT
CHP 34 LABYRINTH BY TAYLOR SWIFT
EPILOGUE YOU'RE STILL THE ONE BY THE MILLS

https://spoti.fi/3ynObKE

To those who needed a push to take the leap, may your fall into love be bright and beautiful.

To Liss for teaching me all the Colombian curse words that surprised the heck out of me.

PROLOGUE

WOULD'VE, COULD'VE, SHOULD'VE
Performed by Taylor Swift

SEVEN YEARS BEFORE
MOVIE SET
BURBANK, CALIFORNIA

RONAN: What the hell have you done to me? Every look you sent my way today had me ready to go off like a pubescent teen.

ADRIA: Looks? You're accusing me? What about that whole finger stroll down my neck?

RONAN: I had two minutes before my dad called action again, and I had to touch you.

ADRIA: You can't say things like that.

RONAN: Get over here, Adria. Get to the hotel before we both spontaneously combust without ever being twined together.

Twelve hours later.

RONAN: I woke and you were gone.

ADRIA: We have one last day in the studio. I couldn't be late.

RONAN: We need to talk.

ADRIA: We already agreed this was a one-time thing. We have lives that will never touch again.

RONAN: No one should lose their virginity in a one-night stand, Star. No one.

ADRIA: This is why I didn't tell you. You wouldn't have had sex with me, and we both would have combusted—your words. But that's all it was, Hollywood—sex.

RONAN: Liar.

FOUR YEARS BEFORE
BURBANK, CALIFORNIA

RONAN: Meet me at my place? Seven o'clock?

ADRIA: No.

RONAN: I can't go another day watching you from behind my camera while you beat on those drums with your skin glistening and those hot-as-fire blue eyes calling me home. I'll lose my goddamn mind. I need to be inside you.

ADRIA: Don't you mean Landry? Or Fee? Or Nikki?

RONAN: You're jealous? If I didn't flirt with them, they'd see right through me —us —and you told me you didn't want them to know.

ADRIA: So, your excuse for hitting on my friends and band-mates is so you wouldn't flirt with me?

RONAN: Yes. I did what you asked. Now do what I ask. Show up.

ADRIA: I'm not sure it's a good idea.

RONAN: Coward.

ADRIA: Excuse me?

RONAN: You're afraid. You're afraid you'll remember what making love really feels like. I'll ruin you, just like you've already ruined me.

ADRIA: ***Eye roll emoji*** Hollywood's Player Prince wants me to believe the best sex of his life was with a random virgin? I'm not sure what that says about you.

RONAN: Making love, Star. Not sex. Sex is just bodies finding release. What we did to each other left scars. Permanent marks. Gouges in my soul only you can fill, damn it.

Twenty minutes later.

ADRIA: I'm at the door. Buzz me in.

THREE AND A HALF YEARS BEFORE

NEW YORK CITY

RONAN: Can you leave?

ADRIA: What? Why?

RONAN: You know why.

ADRIA: Landry wants to take pictures with the VMA award front and center. She plans on sending it to that dick critic who told her to give up singing and become a phone sex operator.

RONAN: The award is pretty amazing. But you and me, skin on skin, that's unforgettable. Stars-bursting-into-existence kind of unforgettable.

ADRIA: I hate when you say shit like that.

RONAN: Because you FEEL the words. Your body knows the truth of us.

ADRIA: How many women have you used that line on, Hollywood?

RONAN: I don't need to use lines with anyone else, Star. Only you.

ADRIA: I can't leave the party yet.

RONAN: Fine. I'll meet you in my room in thirty minutes. But I'm not sure how long I can hold off....

Ten minutes later.

RONAN: *** Image of Ronan's bare upper body that ends just below the divots above his hips. His muscled torso ripples, and his arm extends past the edge of the photo, hand flexed, gripping something out of sight.

ADRIA: You fight dirty.

RONAN: Fighting is the last thing I want to do. Hurry.

THIRTY-FOUR MONTHS BEFORE

RONAN: I'll be at the concert tonight, and I'd like to see you after.

ADRIA: You're in Washington?

RONAN: I was meeting with a production studio in Vancouver.

ADRIA: The after-party will last hours. We're celebrating the end of the tour with the crew.

RONAN: Get me backstage. We can duck out as soon as you think Landry won't miss you.

ADRIA: Lan will notice no matter when I leave.

RONAN: She's not your mom or your boss. I know you've missed me as much as I've missed you.

ADRIA: ***Eye roll emoji*** Neither of us has been lacking in companionship in the year since we've seen each other.

RONAN: I've told you before, and I'll tell you again, Star. Sex is sex. What we do...you know it's more.

Fifteen minutes later.

ADRIA: I'll leave you a backstage pass at the will-call window.

Ten hours later, she'd barely joined him in the back seat of the SUV when Ronan's hand slid underneath the hem of her little black dress. His touch along her inner thigh was like an electric shock to her system, sending waves of hot desire through every molecule in her being.

She wasn't sure if she loved it or hated it.

What she did know was she had to stop this. It had gone on too long.

This had to be their last hookup.

She'd told herself the same thing the last time, and yet, here she was. He'd reeled her back in with a handful of swoony words.

She wasn't weak, damn it, but he made her feel that way. Needy and desperate.

Even now, when she was physically and mentally exhausted from being on the road for over a year with barely a break, he had her amped up and ready to go with a single touch. She should have gone back to the hotel and slept for a dozen days with their tour finally finished. Instead, she was here, letting him turn her body into liquid lust.

She was pretty sure Fiadh had finally caught wind that something was up between them. Adria had been able to keep whatever this was under all her friends' radars until Landry had noticed her ducking out of the VMA party.

When Adria had shown up at the airport the next day with beard burn on her jaw and neck—and down below where no one could see—Landry had said, "We need him, Ads. We need him so we can keep winning awards, so don't fuck it up."

Which was exactly why she shouldn't have agreed to meet up tonight. Because Adria was most certainly going to screw it up. The over-the-top satisfying release they found together was never going to be a relationship. It couldn't be. He was the heir to Hollywood royalty, slowly making his own mark in the industry. Adria was one of six women in a band whose fame and demand were rolling downhill and picking up speed. Neither of them had time for more when they were rarely on the same side of the country.

Even if she hadn't promised herself, ages ago, that she'd never be in a relationship like her parents, spending more time apart than together, she couldn't be what Ronan really needed. Someone who wanted love and happily ever afters. Someone who fit into his family's squishy, cuddly mold that looked like a 1990s sitcom.

As Ronan's long fingers flicked against her panty line, she had to clamp her mouth shut to keep herself from letting out a breathy moan. She glared at him, darting an eye up front to the driver and her bodyguard in the passenger seat.

Ronan just smiled. His sexy smile that was plastered all over the tabloids on a regular basis. He would have made it on the covers of magazines regardless of his mom being an Academy-Award-winning actress and his dad being an Oscar-winning director. He had those timeless good looks Hollywood adored. Chiseled, square jaw. Cinnamon-burnished hair, silky and thick, with just a hint of a wave to it. Intense, stormy, gray eyes that made you feel like you were the center of their universe. A nose that plastic surgeons put on the screen for others to choose from even though his had never seen the underside of a scalpel. And below that perfect face, the corded veins of his neck led to broad shoulders and sharply cut biceps and triceps. His entire body was sculpted as if an artist had carved it out of stone, all sinewy power.

Ronan leaned in, the tip of his nose barely skimming her jawline. His warm breath sent goosebumps over her skin, and her nipples hardened. His lips lightly caressed the side of her mouth. "Hello, Star."

Yet another thing she hated and loved—the nickname he'd given her the first time they'd ended up twined together. From the moment their fingers had collided on a soundstage, she'd been flooded with a desire she'd never thought possible. She'd been sought after, pursued by boys in high school, even men around the pageant circuit she'd been on, but she'd never had her body light up for someone. Not until him.

And now, years later, it still lit up whenever he was in the same room.

She ground her teeth together, knowing those kinds of thoughts were the ones that would damn them both. She grabbed his hand, pulled it from under her dress, and set it back on his thigh. The curve of his grin pushed against her cheek.

"Shy isn't your style," he whispered.

"Neither is banging some guy in the back of a car while my detail watches," she hissed.

He pulled away slightly.

"God, I've really missed that growl."

Her heart tugged at the idea of him missing her. Of anyone missing her attitude and snark. For most of her life, it hadn't been seen as a positive. Hadn't she lost more than one beauty pageant because she didn't say what the judges wanted to hear? Hadn't her mom begged her to soften her tone?

The car stopped at a back entrance of the hotel the band and Ronan were staying at, and he alighted first, extending his hand to help her out. All gentleman. It would disappear when they were in the room. He would be masterful and commanding but hardly polite, and it made her entire core clench. He was an addiction she couldn't stop feeding even though she knew it would end up with one or both of them broken. They'd give each other just a hair too much of themselves and never be able to get it back.

In the elevator, with her bodyguard at the front, Ronan tilted his head and kissed her temple while his hand slipped up the back of her thigh, under her dress, and squeezed a cheek left bare from her thong. Her insides convulsed. She was almost ready to explode from a handful of touches.

¡Díos! She was a lost cause.

A ding announced their arrival on Ronan's floor, her bodyguard cleared the hallway, and then Ronan held the elevator door open as she exited. His eyes strolled down every inch of her, his grin growing wider and wider.

The door to his hotel room had barely clicked behind them before he slid her dress off, and she ripped his T-shirt over his head. Hands, fingers, and tongues were in a battle to find every last groove and valley that they'd been without for over a year. Hot. Wet. Needy. His pants were gone, her bra and underwear were gone, her shoes flung somewhere, and he had her on the bed, hovering over her with his lean muscles straining. His mouth trailed down her body, and every single nerve ending burned as if a stick of incense was being dragged along it.

She was gasping, panting, craving exactly where he was going and the heaven he'd bring when he was there, and then suddenly—

He was gone.

Air and space between them.

"Fuck. Hold on," he said. He stared down at her, eyes dark and heated, before wheeling around and searching in a messenger bag thrown over a chair. She lifted herself on her elbows, breath uneven. Desperate longing beat through her veins as she waited for him to come back with a condom.

When he turned around, his boxer briefs were straining to contain him, and her heart hammered as she took in the entirety of him. His muscles rippled over his entire frame as he moved. Stomach. Thighs. It was the thighs that made the ache in her grow even more. She wanted them encasing her, pushing into her.

He sat on the edge of the bed, setting down the foiled wrapper she'd expected, but it was the other items that caught her attention—a key, a piece of paper, and a pen.

Confusion bled through the lust.

"This isn't how I wanted to do this," he said, rubbing a hand over his short, clipped beard. "I had plans of champagne and strawberries before we ended up skin on skin. I wanted to start with this and not the naked bodies." His lips twitched upward as he waved the key in her direction.

"What is it for?" she asked, reaching for it.

He bent toward her, nuzzling her jaw again, and it sent another fiery wave through her, blending in with the inferno already blazing. "It's a key to my condo—our condo."

Her heart tripped at his words. They had to be a mistake.

She pulled back, scanning his face, managing to get out a choked, "What?"

His smile faltered, and it pricked at her soul. This...this was exactly why she should never have agreed to meet up with him. Not tonight. Not the last time. Not any of the times after that first one.

His hand skated over her thigh, eyes soft and pleading. "Your tour is done. I'm between gigs and actually considering making a movie. I thought LA would be the perfect home base while we figured it all out."

She closed her eyes against a rush of tears. The word home...the idea of coming home to someone, or someone coming home to you...it was too much.

She pushed his hand away and picked up the document, and that was when a chill filled in behind the layers of desire and panic. It was a non-disclosure agreement. And not just the standard one the people who worked for The Painted Daisies signed. This one was deeply personal. It was them promising to keep all aspects of their relationship and their lives, from hygiene to food habits, confidential. Worse, it stated any arguments or disputes they had that couldn't be resolved directly between them would be mediated by his agent. His agent! And the coup de grâce was the paragraph where she agreed to remain on birth control until he signed a waiver agreeing she could come off it. Fury sparked as her eyes flicked to his signature already at the bottom, and her entire being iced over. Every last ounce of desire disappeared in one rapid beat of her heart.

She stood up, searching for her underwear, as her body shook with a sea of emotions. If, for some godforsaken reason, she'd even been willing to contemplate an actual relationship and sharing a home together, she wouldn't, simply because of the NDA. It was like saying, *I care about you enough to ask you to move in, but I don't trust you enough to not secretly get pregnant.* What kind of screwed-up way to start a relationship was that? Even more screwed up than her parents being married and never living in the same city.

"Star?" For the first time, there was a hint of concern in his voice. Confusion.

She couldn't have this conversation naked, but when she went to step into her thong, he was there, pulling it away. He put one hand on her waist and the other on her chin so she was forced to meet his beautiful, hopeful gaze.

"Talk to me."

"I'm not moving in with you, Ronan." She went with the simple fact because it allowed her to keep her emotions hidden just like she'd been taught to do for decades.

"Why not?"

"We've had a handful of one-night stands. I don't even know you."

"That's bullshit and you know it," he said. "We know each other."

"Do we?" She tried to pull away, and his grip tightened. She had to fight to keep her voice calm. "If you really knew me, you'd know I don't want any kind of long-term commitment, and you sure as hell wouldn't need to ask me to sign an NDA to know I'd never sell your underwear online."

His jaw ticked as he scoured her face, looking for the emotions she was desperate to hold back. "Is this really about the NDA, or is this about your parents?"

"Don't." One word was all she could manage. She jerked away from him and was finally able to put her bra and underwear back on all while he watched.

"Where are you going?" he demanded as she picked up her dress from where it had fallen. When she didn't respond, he continued. His voice was low with frustration carved through it. "I never thought I'd see the day the badass rock star ran chicken."

She tried to ignore his attempt at goading her, but it still pricked, and she tossed back a response before she could help it. "Just because you turned this into something I never agreed to, doesn't mean I'm chicken. You're too used to everyone pandering to you. Do you ever think about what someone else wants, or do you just expect them to fall in line?"

She'd struck a nerve, because his eyes narrowed, and he crossed his arms over his chest.

"You want it, Star. You want me, us, the whole shebang. This, what you're doing right now...it's not about moving in with me or being pissed that I tried to protect us both with an NDA. It's about you loving your parents, and them not being around long enough to show you how much they love you back. You think by not getting close to anyone, by walking out before they can, you can protect yourself."

It tore apart scars she pretended she didn't have. Her parents were good parents! They'd loved her. They'd said the words. She'd been hugged and held and kissed good-night...or goodbye. She and her siblings had everything they'd ever wanted. *Except them,* a little voice chided, but she shoved it away.

She wasn't sure what was worse, that he'd torn open her hidden wounds, that he was right about them, or that he didn't understand just how hurtful the NDA had been. Like a wounded cat, she struck back, nails and all. "Don't go all psychologist on me, Hollywood. Stick to what you're good at."

"And what exactly is that?" he demanded.

"Charming your way into people's panties and using Daddy's name to help you make a video or two."

His face reflected the pain her words had caused, and she regretted the words as soon as they were out. But then

13

again, she regretted everything about tonight. From acknowledging his text, to agreeing to meet, and walking into the unsuspecting trap he'd laid.

She pulled on her dress, shoved her feet into her spiked heels, and stormed to the door. She'd barely gotten it open an inch when he reached over her head and slammed it shut before she could escape. His arms caged her, and she flipped around to glare at him.

"Damn it. Don't leave. Not like this," he said, his tone a command and a plea all rolled together. "Fight with me. Tear up the NDA. But don't go until we've settled it."

"That's the problem right there. We have settled it. You just don't like the way it landed," she tossed back, and he was already shaking his head as if to disagree, which just frustrated her so much that she threw out another jab. "For heaven's sake, it was just sex! And not even that great."

His eyes narrowed, a flush of irritation coating his cheeks. They both knew it wasn't true. The sex had been off the charts. Addicting. A candy you couldn't turn down whenever it came within reach. Even her first time had been life-altering. Her friends all said losing their virginity had been so painful and awkward they'd barely been able to get through it. Not her. Ronan had ignited her until she felt like she was coming apart in the very best kind of way. Pleasure and sin wrapped in one heady package.

"Liar," he growled.

To prove it, he trailed a hand down over her breast hidden under the thin dress and flicked a finger over one taut tip. She had to bite her tongue before she let out a longing gasp.

"It was never just sex between us. If it was, you wouldn't still be wet and hungry for me right now. You're going to ache for days if you walk away."

"Any dick will satisfy me. Hell, even the toy in my drawer or my fingers will do just fine, and they won't ask me to sign a stupid NDA," she said, lifting her chin in defiance.

"Star," he growled out in a tangled mix of something like remorse but also a warning.

The nickname curled in her stomach, an ache for something she'd never get back. Not after tonight. But then, it had never truly been hers to begin with. It had been a mirage she'd let herself hold on to for a handful of hours whenever their worlds crossed.

"Don't ever call me that again."

She pushed his hand away from her chest, ducked under his other arm, and jerked the door open. He didn't stop her this time, and somehow, that hurt almost as much as walking away did.

"I hate to break it to *you*," Ronan's voice, full of condescension and anger, carried down the hall, "but putting someone else inside you, putting *anything* inside you, won't make you want me any less, Beauty Queen. Just like running chicken won't fix the hurt of your childhood."

His hotel room door banged shut, and she realized, with a flush of humiliation, that there was a little group of people at the elevator who'd just heard everything he'd said. They were all making a good show of not staring by darting surreptitious looks under their lashes. Her cheeks turned red, and she hated that almost as much as the fact everything he'd said was right.

One of the men in the group cleared his throat.

She knew he was going to ask for her autograph. A picture. Hell, maybe he was going to offer to try and fill the void Ronan had promised couldn't be filled. This godawful, mortifying moment was going to be all over the news. *Daisy Drummer storms from hotel in a cloud of sex-filled innuendos.* And if they'd recognized Ronan, it would be worse.

She whirled on her feet, heading for the stairs with her bodyguard on her heels.

She was already halfway down the flight of stairs when Ronan's new nickname for her hit her in the chest. *Beauty Queen.* He'd used it as a sneer when being a beauty contestant was hard work. It took talent and smarts, but he'd used it as a dagger. A way to strike back when he hadn't gotten what he wanted. And the Hollywood Player Prince always got what he wanted.

But he couldn't have her.

Not now and not ever again.

CHAPTER ONE

Ronan

SOME OF US
Performed by Starsailor

EIGHT DAYS BEFORE

Ronan rolled his suitcase out the door of the guest cottage on his parents' estate and headed for the main house. Skirting the infinity pool looking over the Hollywood hills, he let himself in through the back door and into the kitchen. It smelled like burnt toast, which meant they were between cooks again. Every other year, his mom, or his dad, decided they could make their own meals and let their private chef go. It would last maybe a month before they hired one back.

His mom looked up from buttering a piece of black charcoal. Born Gayle Benson, his mom had long ago legally changed her name to Greer Bennett after two of her all-time favorite movie stars. She was in her early fifties but didn't look much older than him. Ronan had inherited both her willowy frame and her cinnamon-colored hair and hoped he'd inherit her agelessness as well.

She looked up and smiled until she saw the suitcase. "You heading out again? I feel like you just barely got home," she said.

"Off to two more concert stops in Texas," he said.

"You ever plan on finishing the documentary?" his dad asked, walking in and kissing his wife on the cheek.

The question stabbed into Ronan's chest where an aching wound had long ago begun to fester. Two and a half years was an eternity to spend on any film, let alone a documentary on a rock band. But he never could have predicted that everything would go to hell weeks after he'd started filming. When he'd first pitched the exposé to Asher for the streaming service his best friend had kicked off for Ridgeway Media Industries, it had seemed like a cakewalk. A way of killing two birds with one stone.

Now, he couldn't let it go for more reasons than he could count.

He owed it to himself, to Landry, and all five of the brave women who were getting onstage every day to show the world they wouldn't let murder and mayhem stop them.

"I'm close," he said. It was only a partial lie. He had almost all the footage he needed, while at the same time, it didn't feel like he'd ever have enough.

His dad saw through him, raising a dark, bushy brow in his direction. Strong and fit for a man who'd just turned sixty, his dad had barely any white in his beard, but the wrinkles around eyes as gray as Ronan's made him look his age in a way his mom's face didn't.

"No matter how much we're enjoying a project, we still

have to call it quits at some point. Either the money or our energy will run out if you don't," his dad said.

Ronan would never admit how right his dad actually was. Just like he wouldn't tell him that the budget for the documentary had long stopped coming from RMI's cups and had been bleeding into his profits from his movie, *The Secrets Inside Us*. He was hoping to recoup the losses with a sequel to the film. The new movie was going to be the first thing the production studio Asher had bought and handed over to Ronan would make.

His gut flipped with anticipation, thinking about everything he was going to accomplish as president of Ravaged Storm Productions. With the scripts, the decisions, *and* the money fully in his hands at last, he wasn't going to have to listen to a sea of rejections before doing what he really wanted. He just had to finish the damn documentary, hire an assistant, and get to work.

"Is your head hurting?" His mom's concerned question drew him back to the fact he'd been rubbing the scar on his temple.

A flicker of panic ran through him that he'd gotten good at pushing aside. His injury hadn't truly hurt in months, but the nightmares and the waves of anxiety still threatened to pull him under on a regular basis. The powerlessness he'd felt the day of the attack would wash over him at unexpected moments, and he'd live through it all over again. He'd obsess over ways he could have prevented being cuffed, taped, and thrown into a tub by Paisley Kim's attacker. He was still working through it.

Therapy and hand-to-hand combat had helped.

"Not really," he told her.

Both his parents were staring at him with that look—the

one that said as much as they cared about him, they had some tough-love speech to deliver.

"We feel like the longer you stick around the band, the harder it's going to be for you to move on," his dad said gently.

Ronan didn't feel like he was ever going to move on. Not because of what had happened in Albany, but because of a blue-eyed, black-haired drummer who'd stolen his heart and never given it back. A woman he'd hurt and who hadn't let him close enough to her again to apologize.

He'd almost found a way in with Landry's help. They'd concocted a scheme that would have given him a fighting chance, but then she'd been murdered, and Adria's sister had been kidnapped. While Ronan hadn't felt the loss in the same way as Landry's family had, he'd still been shaken up by the events of that awful night at Swan River Pond long before the attack in Albany ever had impacted him. He'd considered Landry a friend, and when she'd died, he'd wanted to mourn her with the rest of the Daisies. But they'd scuttled into the woodwork. Adria had disappeared to Colombia with her mom, and Ronan had been forced to give up on any ideas of reconciliation.

By the time the band got back together earlier this year, he'd convinced himself he was finishing what he'd started only because it was what Landry would have wanted. She'd believed in the documentary. Believed it would bring them closer to the fans, allowing them to be seen as real people and not just vague, unattainable superstars. Every fiber in Ronan's being wanted to honor her and her wishes. But as soon as he'd seen Adria again, he'd known the truth. He'd needed to do this for much more than Landry. This was his last chance to apologize for pushing too hard and too fast. For the fucking NDA he hadn't even read until it was too late. It was his last chance to find the part of his soul that had shriveled up when she'd stormed out of a hotel room in Seattle.

A chance that still hadn't happened. He'd been with the Daisies for months now, and she continued to push him away—maybe even more than before everything had gone to hell in her world.

"Ro," his mom called to him, and when he looked up, her eyes were concerned, pleading with him. "What's really holding you up?"

A long-legged former beauty queen.

Ronan tugged at the beanie on his head. He almost hated wearing it these days. The image consultant he'd hired to convince the world he was more than just a pretty face, more than just his parents' son lucking into every open door in Hollywood, had insisted it made him look artsy and hip. But these days, it seemed to remind him of all his mistakes. With Adria. With Landry. With an attacker who had nearly killed him.

Worse, he couldn't get out of his head that if he hadn't gotten sidetracked by his grand gesture that awful day at the pond, he might have been able to save Landry's life. But he supposed the truth was that he might have wound up dead too. After all, he hadn't been able to save Landry's sister either. Paisley had all but saved herself while he'd lain useless in a tub with his hands tied.

His chest grew heavy, and his entire body felt weighed down.

Nothing good would come of reliving any of those memories.

Maybe his dad was right. Maybe it was time to call it quits.

His heart screamed in objection. His heart wanted what

21

it had always wanted—the wild connection he felt when he was tangled with Adria. They'd seen beyond the false faces they both presented to the world to the real people beneath. But it was the fact he'd seen the truth of her that had sent her scrambling in the first place. She was terrified of anyone actually seeing her, of wounding a heart that had already been scraped too many times as a child.

But he knew, with a certainty he could never explain, that what bound him and Adria, the ties that went all the way to the bottom of his soul...he'd never find that again with anyone else.

So, he'd go back on tour with them for one more concert.

But because his parents were right, because he had to stop at some point before his pride and his heart were completely obliterated, he'd make this his last effort. If she still hated him, if she still refused to even meet with him to finish her interview for the documentary, then he'd find a way to walk away. He'd put this part of his life behind him.

He crossed the kitchen to his parents, kissed his mom on the cheek and gave his dad a one-armed hug. "Thanks for looking out for me. I think this will be the last trip. I have a studio to pull together, after all. And a house to buy."

"You're moving out?" His mom's eyes grew wide. "That's not... You don't—"

"I've left the Oscar-winning actress tongue-tied," Ronan laughed. "I know. You like having me here, but it's about damn time I flew the nest, don't you think?"

"I like my nest full," she said softly.

She hugged him to her, and he hugged her back before stepping away.

He was so close to having all his dreams come true. It was missing an important chunk, but this trip would have to be his last attempt to fill it. The longer he chased after Adria, spinning his wheels, the more it jeopardized the other things in his life that mattered. Asher and Asher's dad had trusted him with the production studio, and he wasn't going to let them down. If he couldn't have Adria, he'd have to be satisfied with accomplishing his professional dreams and not his personal ones.

♫ ♫ ♫

By the time Ronan got off his flight in Arlington, he was antsy as hell. He'd had to play nice with his seatmate in the first-class cabin, listening to the man drone on about all the things Ronan's dad had gotten wrong in his *Stilleto* movies. The guy had acted like he was a spy himself and had been personally offended by the inaccuracies.

But more than his irritation with the guy tearing into his parents' films, what had bugged him even more was how the man had looked decidedly like the asshole who'd attacked him in Albany. Or maybe hadn't looked like him as much as there had been a vibe coming off him that screamed *unhinged stalker*.

So, once Ronan checked into the hotel, the first thing he did was change into his workout gear and head for the hotel's exercise room, hoping to find a sense of control through the martial arts moves he'd recently learned. The two men in the black uniform of Reinard Security at the door had him simultaneously wanting to beat his head against the wall and go storming inside to see which of the Daisies was in there.

"Gym's closed. Come back in an hour," one of the men said. The guy was new and didn't recognize Ronan. Or maybe he did, and he'd been given the "Don't let Ronan near me" speech.

Before he could respond, she was there, stepping up behind the bodyguards, looking like the pageant winner she'd once been, even with sweat glistening over her fore-head and dripping down her chest. She looked completely and deliciously hot and bothered. Just like she'd looked coming apart beneath him as they moved together in a sea of white sheets with her black hair spilled across the pillows. Her brilliant blue eyes had burned for him back then. They'd warmed him up like a fire that would never die —except it had. Now, as those lapis eyes landed on him, all he felt was ice.

Her tiny pair of workout shorts and sports bra showed off every line of her lean frame and every curve that bordered on being too much for her fragile bone structure. And yet, every piece of her was goddess-like perfection with naturally red lips, high cheek bones, and a classic oval face. She was an enchanting image that had haunted his dreams from the first time he'd seen her on set in a Burbank studio.

"I'm done, Red. Let the man in," she said, easing past her guards and into the hall.

Her hand accidently brushed his arm, and they both jumped as a shock wave rushed through them. It shouldn't have pleased him as much as it did that she still felt the same overwhelming rush, but he couldn't help it. He was sick. He had an addiction. He needed her. As if nothing in his life would truly be right if she didn't agree to be the person at his side.

It was ridiculous.

When the media had labeled him the Hollywood Player Prince, it had been for not needing anyone. For leaving a string of hearts behind him as he'd moved from one to the other. But the truth was, those past conquests...they hadn't really wanted *him*. They'd wanted the suave exterior the world saw as Greer Bennett and Quentin Hawk's son. The few people he'd let past the façade had been confused by the moody, sensitive artist they'd found there. Of all his friends and girlfriends, only Asher had stuck once he'd seen past the shiny surface.

Ronan watched as Adria moved down the hallway without a word in his direction.

"Nice to see you, too, Adria," he called after her, chest hammering and body aching.

What he got back was a one-fingered wave.

His jaw ticked. They'd both been at fault that night in Seattle. He'd pushed too hard and had stupidly not read the NDA ahead of time. But she'd also overreacted. Words had been said that they'd both regretted. The hard truth was, Adria didn't want him to apologize. She was still running scared. She didn't trust him to stick when that was all he wanted to do.

Her bodyguards followed her down the hall, and he entered the gym with yet another layer of frustration to burn off. He went to the boxing bag first, pounding on it for a few minutes, and then turned to the mat jammed up against the mirrors and worked through a sequence of punches and kicks.

"Jerome show you that move?" a quiet voice asked.

Ronan turned to see Nikki standing there dressed in workout gear similar to Adria's. As tall as her bandmate and with hair just as black, Nikki was the leaner of the two. Adria was toned and shaped with strong arms from pounding on her drums, but Nikki was defined everywhere. Ronan didn't think there was an ounce of her that wasn't muscle.

"He did," Ronan answered.

Jerome Barry was a former Green Beret who was a friend of Nikki's family. After the attack in Albany, she'd put Ronan in touch with the man, promising he'd be discreet. Barry had been more than discreet. He'd been a godsend. He'd helped rebuild Ronan's confidence in a shorter amount of time than he thought therapy ever could have.

"Feel like sparring?" she asked, closing the distance to face him on the mat.

He raised a brow and ran a hand over his beard before glancing toward the door where her bodyguards waited.

"They're not going to come after you for working out with me," Nikki laughed.

"Fine, but I'm not going easy on you because you're a girl."

She huffed. "As if."

Then, she swirled and kicked at him. He barely blocked it. He moved on instinct, batting each offense that she sent his way, but just barely. They moved around the floor in a dance that surprised the hell out of him. He'd known she was strong, but this was skill from years of practice.

When he finally ended up on the floor with her elbow up against his throat, she laughed. She rose and then offered him a hand. When he got up, she was still smiling—something he didn't see often in Nikki these days. She'd been quiet even before Landry had died. Not shy in the way Paisley had been, but just reserved. As if she saved all her words for when they really mattered. But now, she seemed to have a shell around her that was all but impenetrable, even by smiles.

"Barry teach you also?" he asked, uncapping a water bottle and taking a long drink.

"My dad and Jerome. These days, I mostly workout with my stepmom."

He frowned. "She's here with you?"

He had a vague recollection of a tall woman with plain brown hair and thick black eyeglasses who'd shown up at the farmhouse that awful night when Landry had died. But he didn't remember seeing her on the tour with them.

Nikki shook her head. "No. I just mean when we're together. She might be joining me for a few concerts stops, though. She's in between jobs."

"What does she do?" he asked.

"She's worked mostly as an executive assistant for a couple of CEOs and studio execs. But in the last two years, she's had some bad luck. Positions being downsized, that sort of thing."

"You know I'm looking for a personal assistant, right?" he said.

Nikki glanced over, wide-eyed. "No, I didn't."

He chuckled. "Serendipitous, then. When Asher fired the Ravaged Storm president and put me in his place, the guy's assistant took it personally and walked out. I need someone and soon. Have her send me her résumé."

He headed for the door, and Nikki called after him, "You're done? Was I too much for you, Hollywood?"

His chest tightened at the nickname, wishing with all his being it was her friend saying it instead of her. Nikki was beautiful, stunning even, but she wasn't Adria Rojas. She'd never be able to make his blood pressure spike and his groin ache. He didn't even have it in him to flirt with Nikki anymore. What did that say about the player prince? When was the last time that name the paparazzi had coined for him had even truly applied?

Years. Maybe since Seattle.

"I'm man enough to admit that if we kept going, you'd continue to whip my ass," he said, shooting her a hand wave as he left.

Her laughter followed him into the hall.

And just like he'd wished it was her friend's voice, he wished it was Adria's laughter. Wished he'd been able to share half as many words with her as he'd just shared with Nikki. Maybe then, his Star would finally hear and accept the truth. They'd both been wrong. But it wasn't too late to fix it.

CHAPTER TWO

Adria

YOU'RE SUCH A
Performed by Hailee Steinfeld

SEVEN DAYS BEFORE

Adria stood with her eyes closed, letting the noise of the stadium wash over her. The fans were filtering in. The laughter and chatter could be heard even over the music playing through the large speakers hanging from the rafters. They wouldn't be onstage for a while. Their opening act would play for at least an hour, but Adria loved the energy that was already filling the air. It was going to be a good show. She could feel it in her bones.

When she opened her eyes, they fell on a man in a *Goonies* T-shirt, beanie, and tailored jeans near the entrance to the stage. She hated the way her eyes and body still gravitated to him after all this time. You'd think that almost three years would be enough time for the humiliation and anger to have beaten every ounce of attraction out of her. And yet, her body was still addicted, still craving what her brain knew better than to want.

"I feel like we haven't left the stage in two weeks," Nikki said, and it was with relief that Adria turned her gaze to her friend.

"Just think of how many weeks we were on The Red Guitar tour without a break," she said with a shudder.

"I don't know how we did it," Nikki replied, pushing back the mass of onyx corkscrews that had settled around her face. Her high cheekbones, full lips, and perfectly arched brows over dark-brown eyes blended together into a painting of perfection. She would have done well on the pageant circuit, probably better than Adria ever had, because Nikki never riled anyone up. "Never mind. I do know how. It was all Landry. She infused us with some kind of magical, Energizer Bunny power."

Nikki's voice was sad and tired as she rubbed her temples.

Adria scanned her friend's face, looking for the telltale signs of a migraine, but she didn't see any. Nikki was just exhausted. They all were. Even though they'd had a few weeks off in September, the time hadn't been as relaxing as it should have been with Leya's disappearance and reappearance. They'd barely gotten her back before they'd moved on to the next six weeks of their tour without a stop, and they had at least six more to go before they got another break.

They'd be pretty darn shattered by the time the holidays rolled around.

Adria's eyes caught on Ronan again, sitting on an amp with his camera in hand. His strong thighs were spread wide, elbows propped on his knees. The pose showed off the muscles rippling beneath his snug clothes. Muscles that had never once faded in the years since she'd first met him. If anything, they'd grown bulkier, as if age had refined him, chiseling him further into a David-like statue to be worshipped and admired.

The mere sight of him was enough to send her heart knocking furiously against her rib cage. She loathed the fact the ache she'd felt leaving his hotel room in Seattle that humiliating night hadn't once been assuaged. The taunt he'd thrown at her like a curse as she'd stormed from his room had proven true. Nothing had ever made the craving for him go away. She'd tried to bang it away. She'd tried over and over again.

But the longing was still there. Just like every hurt and every humiliation he'd caused remained with her as well. None of it had lessened an ounce since that night in Seattle. Not even the pain of losing Landry and Tatiana had dimmed the torment she felt over Ronan. It was like all three of them had their own slice of her heart they twisted and turned on a regular basis. Some days, she wondered how it even continued to beat.

Nikki caught her watching Ronan, and her friend's lips tilted upward at the corner. "When are you going to put us out of our misery and tell us what happened with you two?"

Adria slid one of her drumsticks down the back of her blue leather tank top, securing it below her bra strap, then twirled the other one like a baton. Her mom had wanted her to use a baton for her talent in the beauty contests, and she'd adamantly refused.

Nikki's brow raised the longer she went without responding, but Adria was saved from replying as Leya joined them, asking, "Where are we again?"

"Arlington," Nikki and Adria both said at the same time.

"I swear it feels like one town just blends into another these days," Leya said softly. She pushed her dark-brown hair, shimmering with highlights, away from her heart-shaped face. She smiled, the edges of her lips pulling the cleft on her chin upward.

"That's because you've spent every waking moment when we aren't onstage locked in a bedroom with Captain Avenger," Fiadh said, coming up behind her.

Leya blushed beautifully, the soft pink spreading over her tan skin, and she flicked Fee on the shoulder. "You should talk. At least Holden hasn't pulled me from the stage and devoured me in the middle of a baseball stadium."

Fee's eyes danced as much as her deep-red curls normally did. Her lavender highlights were pulled partially back today, showcasing her ivory skin and the barely visible dusting of freckles that traveled over her cheeks and nose. "That was one time, and, to be fair, he had just asked me to marry him."

Her thumb twirled the almost Gothic-looking ring on her left hand.

Fee had been married now for almost seven weeks.

Adria's stomach turned at the idea of being in a long-term relationship, and yet, she couldn't stop her eyes from skittering over to where Ronan stood at the thought of the one that had been offered to her. She couldn't stop the "what if" that flew through her mind before she slammed it back into the black box she kept there. She'd glue the damn lid shut if she had to.

Ronan laughed at something one of the roadies said, and even from across the stage, the deep timbre of it hit Adria in the chest. He had the best laugh. Deep and full-bodied. It traveled through him, vibrating through every vein so you felt it too.

When she pulled her gaze back, Nikki was smirking again. "I'd probably be the only single one left if Adria stopped being ridiculously stubborn."

She snorted, heart clenching because her friend's words were so close to the ones she'd just stuffed away. "I'm not throwing away my freedom. Don't worry."

"Okay, you be the last single one. I'd happily trade places with you. I'd love to have a man devouring me with a gaze like that."

Adria's heart flipped, wondering if the look on Ronan's face now was like the one that haunted her in her dreams. She barely resisted turning her head to look at him again as she insisted, "There's no place to trade with, Nik."

Her friends all attempted to hide their smiles, and irritation drifted through her. Just because Paisley, Fiadh, and Leya had found love and pledged forever to the men in their lives, didn't mean she wanted it for herself. In Adria's book, the sacrifices her bandmates and their partners had made to be together weren't any better than the lack of sacrifice her parents had made. Love was fucked up. She didn't want any part of it.

She could almost hear Ronan calling her a liar and a coward.

It made her want to walk over and smack him in the chest and demand he leave. She was positive if he just faded out of the picture, she'd eventually stop wanting him. But then again, she hadn't seen him for almost two years after Landry had died, and it hadn't stopped every emotion from blooming back to the surface as soon as he'd walked in.

Instead of punching anyone, she did what she'd been trained to do from a young age and tucked every emotion away. She turned her beauty-contestant smile on them and said, "Looks like I'll be hitting the clubs as Nikki's wing-woman soon to find her the happily ever after she wants. Let's make a list of all the characteristics her man needs to have."

"I don't think a club is the place to find love," Paisley said with a grimace as she joined them. Her long, black hair was partially up, accentuating her sharp chin and large, round eyes. The star-shaped birthmark below her lashes was the only reminder these days of the shy little girl who'd first joined the band at eleven years old. Where once she'd barely been able to talk due to her shyness, now she had almost the same level of confidence Landry had once had.

The lights flickered in the stadium, and the crowd went wild. Screaming, pounding, clapping. Their opening act ran onto the stage from the opposite side. The heavy beat of a drum and the long strum of an electric guitar filled the air. Adria was itching to get onto the stage. She needed to pound away her frustration. She needed to get lost as she always did in the rhythms.

Adria's phone rang, and she pulled it from her pocket to see her brother's face on the screen. She slid the stick in her hand into her shirt to join the other as she stepped away from the band, ducking into the labyrinth of gray cement corridors backstage to find a quieter spot to talk.

"*Buenos noches,* Vicente."

"*Hola, hermanita.*"

They continued talking in Spanish, a soothing rhythm that was like being home, even though she was thousands of miles away.

"You're in Texas?" he asked.

"Yes, Arlington."

"Damn. I thought you were in Houston."

"That's our next stop. Why?"

"I need you to check in on Papá." The quiet, seriousness of his tone sent worry coasting through her veins.

"What's wrong with him?" she asked, finger sliding along the scar on her thumb. Most days, she forgot it existed, but for some reason, whenever she was nervous or upset, it called to her, almost aching, as if she could remember the pain of receiving it even though she had no memory of how it had happened. "Has he heard something new about Tati?"

Her stomach flipped thinking about everything her family had been through since the day her sister was kidnapped and Landry had been murdered. They couldn't take much more, and yet, they desperately needed answers. They needed to know the truth about what had happened to both her sister and her friend.

"Nothing that he's told me about. But that's just it... He's been really quiet," Vicente said. She leaned against the wall, hunching over slightly to ease the pain that rushed through her gut as it twisted with worry. "Normally, he's on my case daily about production and which contracts I'm working. But lately, if I don't call him, he wouldn't even know we have new business coming in."

She swallowed the lump that began to form in her throat. Her father had given up everything, including a regular life with his wife and children, to ensure Earth World Solutions was the number one provider of solar, wind, and hydrogen energy in the Americas. For him to not care who her brother was signing with...it was like saying he'd lost his will to live.

He'd taken Tatiana's disappearance the hardest of all of them. The guilt of his business being the reason the kidnappers had taken her had eaten away at him. He'd lost his full, portly shape and happy demeanor. Now, he was almost skin and bones with a sourness to him that never left.

"I was planning on staying with him anyway. I'll go straight there from the airport tomorrow," Adria promised.

"I wish he was still in California. At least there, he'd still have family and friends."

Unable to pass up the incentives Texas had offered, Papá had moved the corporate offices out of California several years before Tatiana had been taken. It had meant selling everything, including their childhood home, and moving him and Tati to Houston. These days, their father lived in a penthouse at the top of a high-rise all alone, as they and their mother drifted in and out even less than before.

A shimmer of awareness drifted over Adria's skin, and she turned her head to meet a pair of steel-gray eyes. Ronan raised a brow as if asking if she was okay, and that was when she realized what she looked like, hand to her stomach, almost doubled over. He started down the corridor toward her with a concern on his face she couldn't handle any more than she could handle the worry over her father.

She stood up, back going straight. "I have to go. The concert is starting, but I'll give you a call once I've seen him."

"Thank you."

"There's nothing to thank. I'm glad you called me."

"Have a good show, *pollita*," he said, a tease twisting through the nickname her siblings had used since she was a tween. The word reminded her of Ronan calling her the same thing for very different reasons. Vicente had called her a chicken because of the awkward growth spurt she'd had that left her torso perched atop spindly, skinny legs.

That was when she'd stopped winning pageants, and when she'd grown even snarkier and bitter, putting the judges off even more until, finally, she'd quit. That single action had sent their mother retreating even further from their lives.

At the time, she'd told herself it didn't matter. She'd always had her brother and sister. They'd been a constant in her childhood. They were so close in age most people thought they were triplets, but really, they were just best friends—the nerd, the drummer, and the fighter. Even as the youngest of the three of them, Tatiana had been the one who'd defended them to the world. It carved a bitter line through Adria's soul knowing they hadn't done the same for her. They hadn't protected her, and now she was gone. Taken... Lost... Who knew what horrible things had happened to her—may still be happening to her.

She shivered as dark images filled her mind before she pushed them away. If she let those thoughts take over, she'd never get onstage. She'd curl into a ball of nothing. She'd come to a complete stop like she had ever so briefly that horrible year when she'd lost first Ronan, then Tati, and finally Landry.

When Ronan got close enough to touch her, she side-stepped him, heading back toward the stage. But he was faster than she expected, shooting out a hand and surrounding her wrist in a loose hold she easily broke. She kept going, even as the fire from that single touch traveled its way up her arm and into her heart.

"You okay?" he called after her.

"I'd be better if you'd finish your damn documentary and left for good," she said without turning around. She didn't need to because she already knew he'd have one of two looks on his face. It would either be a straight-lipped annoyance or a taunting smirk. Both would make her wish she could wipe them off, and she had more important things to do, like plowing full throttle on her drums in a way that made her worries for her family wash away for at least a few hours. Then, she'd go see her father and ensure he wasn't going to fade away just like the other people she'd lost.

CHAPTER THREE

Ronan

CLEAN
Performed by Taylor Swift

Every inch of Ronan vibrated with a sea of frustration, regret, and craving as he watched Adria stalk away from him yet again. He wondered if he'd ever escape those emotions. He bounced from feeling like a fifteen-year-old burning with unrequited love, to wanting to punish her for every snarky look and comment. He wanted to torture her as she tortured him. And then he wanted to remind her how good they were together. It was the most ludicrous set of contradictory emotions he'd ever felt in his life. He blamed his study of philosophy for being able to see and feel all the sides.

When he'd walked into the corridor and seen her slumped over, his heart had fallen into his chest, wondering if she'd gotten even more bad news, wondering if they'd finally found her sister. But as always, as soon as anyone tried to give her comfort, she pulled on her tough exterior, shoulders going back an extra inch, turning right back into the badass drummer the world knew her as. She put on her armor that made her seem strong and powerful on the outside when he knew inside was a little girl who'd been wounded by the carelessness with which her parents had loved each other and their children.

To him, Adria was the embodiment of Betrand Russell's famous quote about how fearing love is to fear life. If she denied herself this important part of their humanity, she'd always live a partial existence, and that made his chest burn. She deserved a full experience. The entire gamut of human emotions. If only he could make her see she didn't need to be afraid of her feelings...or of him. They didn't have to end up like her parents.

But the truth was, it wasn't his responsibility to make sure she experienced any of it. Love. A full life. Not even forgiveness. She had to want those things for herself. He couldn't force it on her, and it was time he stopped trying.

"Finish the damn interview, Beauty Queen, and then I can leave," he tossed after her, knowing the nickname would irk her. And it did.

"You're not getting another piece of me, Hollywood."

His jaw clenched as she disappeared around the corner. It was more than time to be done. Being with her and the Daisies had nearly cost him his life. He was determined it wouldn't make him lose his soul too.

He pulled the beanie from his head. He was tired of the heat it kept in. Tired of holding onto something that was never going to fix the pain on his inside. He was done. He'd get in some more footage of the concert and the crowd tonight and then head back to California. He didn't need the one-on-one interview anyway. He knew her like the back of his hand whether she liked it or not. He knew what to say to the world about Adria Rojas.

As he walked by a trash can, he tossed the hat inside.

He wasn't the same man who'd stupidly handed her a key and an NDA he'd never read. Just like he wasn't the man who'd been held hostage in a bathtub, or a wannabe director, or the Hollywood "It" couple's son. He was the damn president of a production studio. He needed to leave this part of his history in his past, move on, and hope the nightmares remained behind with it. Hope that the gaping hole Adria had left in his soul would somehow, eventually, seal itself up enough for him to live his own full life.

♫ ♫ ♫

Ronan inched forward from his place in the shadows of the stage. He scanned his handheld camera across the crowd as the audience danced and screamed to the fast beats of "Riding the Green." Fiadh's lyrically lilting voice filled the air. There was a manic feel in the stadium tonight. No one was in their seats. Some people were actually standing on the chairs while others were sitting atop people's shoulders in order to get a better look at the fiery women onstage. The ushers and security folks were having a hard time containing the energy. It felt like one whisper would set a wildfire loose.

Ronan wasn't sure what had happened to cause it. Maybe the moon was full. Maybe Mercury was in retrograde. All he knew was he could feel the hint of chaos in the air.

The crowd grew even more frantic as the band moved into the next song, and the heavy cadence of "Wild in You" filled the stadium. Paisley's voice was almost a mimic of the steady rhythm of Adria's drums. At the end of the song, Adria had a drum solo, and without even being aware of it, he'd turned his camera from the crowd to her. Like the audience, he was mesmerized by the muscles on her arms and the way she bit her lip and closed her eyes, swaying with the movement of her sticks as they flew across the drum kit. The long layers of her hair were sticking to the sweat glistening over her face and neck, and his body grew hard at the image. She'd looked the same way when he'd been sliding in and out of her as they created their own personal rhythm.

Just as you thought the song would never end, the roar of her sticks came to an abrupt stop, and only silence filled the stadium. Even though he'd heard it dozens of times already, it still hit him in the chest. The suddenness of it. The almost brutal nature of the ending. The call of the wild that disappeared. The crowd went nuts. The thunder of feet and the scream of thousands of voices called Adria's name, and he twisted to capture it all again so he could show her through the documentary what she did to their fans...what she did to him. She filled him with a pulsing he'd never be able to replace. Music he'd never feel again. That thought tore through him as he realized he really was walking away just as she'd asked him to over and over again.

He shut off the camera and made his way backstage.

He should have felt jubilant, excited at having filmed the final piece of the documentary, but instead, he felt hollow. Powerless again. This time to stop her from destroying the beauty that had been them. He'd stitch together some of the frames from tonight to what he already had and be done.

But it would never feel like a win. This piece of work would always feel like things he'd lost.

Instead of waiting for the concert to be over like he normally did, he headed for the exit with his jaw tight. There was a part of him that despised throwing in the towel like this when he'd never been a quitter. But he couldn't continue this way forever either.

He walked out of the arena, heading through the park-like complex to the luxury hotel where he and the band were staying right off the stadium property. The air was crisp, on the chilly side, but the cold seemed to bring clarity with it. By the time he was strolling into his suite with a view of the arena he'd just left, he'd found the calm he needed to finish up.

He'd close this chapter with something memorable. A tribute to all of them. And then, he'd move on. He'd take up a mantle in Hollywood that had nothing to do with his parents and everything to do with him.

As if to ensure he kept his word to himself, he sent a text to Asher.

RONAN: This is the last night I'll be on the tour. I'm heading back to LA.

ASHER: You finally got Adria to do the interview?

RONAN: No, but I'm done trying.

ASHER: Whatever happened between the two of you must have been pretty messed up if she still won't talk to you.

He wasn't sure why he hadn't told Asher about Seattle. It wasn't like his friend didn't know everything else about him.

Maybe it was because of the humiliation he still felt. Or maybe it was determination to protect him and Adria both. To keep her soft underbelly a secret like she wanted it to be.

RONAN: It's water under the bridge now. I'm ready to close the door and dig into Ravaged Storm. I'll have it whipped into shape in no time. We're going to make beautiful films together.

ASHER: Is that a line from a movie? Am I supposed to know it?

RONAN: There's a version of it about music and not movies. I feel the need to send you a list of the world's all-time greatest movie quotes.

He turned away from his phone and started up the high-end laptop he never left home without. It allowed him to edit and cut films anywhere when, even a decade ago, he would have been stuck at a clunky desktop chained to a floor in an office somewhere.

His phone buzzed again, and when he read the message, a lump formed in his throat.

ASHER: Whatever happened with Adria, it was important enough that you asked me to make a damn documentary and stuck around for almost three years to finish it, even after what happened in Albany. Most people would have bailed by now. I'm here if and when you need to talk.

And this was why Asher was the only friend who'd stuck. Not only did they understand the demands the world placed on them simply because of their last names, but they understood that sometimes you just didn't want to talk about the shit that happened. You just needed someone to care enough to ask about it. To know they were there if you *did* need to unburden your soul.

Ronan connected the camera, downloading the footage from the concert and backing it up to the enormous cloud server at the production company. Then, he scrolled through what he'd filmed. When Adria's face appeared on the screen, his entire insides tightened. He wondered how long it would take before her blue eyes stopped haunting his dreams now that he'd finally decided to let them go.

He forced himself to focus on the footage with the objectivity and vision of his director's eye, picking out the plush scenes and assembling them together. A few hours later, he was almost done. He just needed a crowd scene from tonight to slide into place, and the last drum solo with those rapid beats abruptly stopping would be the perfect ending for the entire documentary.

He scrolled through the crowd shots, and his finger hit pause before his brain caught up to what he was seeing. Every last molecule of air left his body for so long that when he breathed again, it was sharp and ragged. He backed the video up, frame by frame, zooming in.

Fuck.

It couldn't be.

Maybe he was mistaken. Maybe it wasn't who he thought. Then, he looked at the frozen screen again and could see the similarity in the nose and brows and jaw. A shiver ran up his spine. Everything about what he saw felt wrong, and yet the proof was right there.

He reached for his phone, ready to call Asher. The police. The damn former Secret Service agent who'd attached himself to Leya.

But then, his fingers paused again.

She'd hate him even more than she already did if he told

anyone else first. As much as he'd promised himself he was washing his hands of her and their past, he couldn't let someone else be the one who told her this.

He glanced at the clock to see it was two in the morning. She'd be done with the after-party, maybe even asleep by now, but this couldn't wait. Hell, it might already be too late. He grabbed the camera and his keycard and rushed out of the room.

At the elevators, he doubted himself all over again. He played the video once more, pausing it again at the same place.

Fuck.

Two floors later, he approached her suite with trepidation dripping through him. It wasn't her primary bodyguard, Lennox, who stood outside her door, and that would either go in his favor or not. Lennox was very much aware of how things stood between him and Adria, and she wouldn't have let him in regardless of what he said.

"I need to see her," Ronan told the man.

The bodyguard shook his shaved head. "Sorry, she's sleeping."

"It's important," Ronan told him, a growl to his voice that rippled along the hallway a hair too loud for the quiet of the early hour. "Life-and-death kind of important."

Ronan's heart banged loudly as he said the words. Flashes of a gun landing on his temple and the cold ceramic of a hotel tub against his bound hands flitted across his mind that he pushed away.

The man hesitated. "Call Zia. Or Kent."

"This isn't something I can tell either of them, damn it. Just knock on the fucking door and let me in," his voice raised even further, and suddenly, the door was wrenched open.

"What the hell, Ronan?" Adria said with a scowl.

Relief flew through him. Then, he registered her barely-there pajama top and sleep shorts, and his body had an instant, primal reaction to her skin on display. A reaction that was wrong for more reasons than the message he was there to deliver.

"I need to show you something," he said, trying to keep his voice calm, but even he could hear the edge in it.

Her eyebrows raised, her eyes strolled over him, and then she said with perfect sarcasm, "I've already seen all you have to offer, and I'm not interested in a repeat performance."

The bodyguard's body stiffened. Ronan wasn't sure if it was from laughter, or if the man was getting ready to toss him down the hall.

"I don't want to be here either, believe me. But I need to show you something I filmed tonight." His gaze bore into hers, hoping she could read the importance in his tone. Hoping she still knew him as well as he knew her. He didn't want to have this conversation in the hall with a security guard he didn't know looking over their shoulder. Someone he didn't trust. "Star, seriously. You need to let me in."

She visibly flinched at the nickname but finally seemed to understand he wasn't there to try and get into her pants. She stepped back, and he brushed past the bodyguard.

The loud click of the door shutting resonated through the silence of the room as she led the way into the suite that was almost a mirror image of his. She stood by the couch, arms crossed over her chest. Her eyes were narrowed and guarded with a flicker of uncertainty inside them.

"I was editing, hoping to be done with the documentary—"

"About time," she interrupted, and he tried not to let it

piss him off. Her tone. Her attitude. Because what he was going to show her... it was going to put her in a tailspin.

"I was editing," he said, "and...damn, just let me show you."

He moved until he was right next to her. Their arms brushed, sending a zap of electricity through him so harsh it made the camera in his hand bobble. She stiffened, and he knew she'd felt it too, but he ignored it, turning the camera on.

He backed the video up some and hit play. After a few seconds, she made a disgusted sound and said, "The crowd?! You filmed the crowd and had to come and tell me at two in the morning?"

She started to move away, but he stopped her with a hand on her arm.

"Wait. Watch it again." He backed it up, zoomed it in, and hit play.

He could tell the moment she saw it, because she froze, inhaling sharply. Then, she grabbed the camera from him, hitting the pause button before rewinding it and playing it again, and pausing it once more.

He watched her face as excitement, relief, fear, and confusion strolled over it.

Everything he'd felt.

"What the hell?" she hissed, glancing up at him. The pain in her eyes was so vivid, so strong, so harsh that he felt it inside his own body, as if a knife had landed in his gut and was pulled up into his chest.

Mere hours ago, he'd thought he was saying goodbye and severing the connection between them, and that was what he still needed to do. He needed to escape her orbit for his own pride and mental health. But it was as if fate had laughed at his attempt to walk away, tightening the noose around his heart instead of loosening it.

He shook off the ridiculous notion. He hadn't been dragged back in. He'd be here for her while they showed the authorities the video, then he'd hand her over to her friends and be gone. A few more hours. A night at the most. And then he'd leave just like he'd intended.

CHAPTER FOUR

Adria

BAD BLOOD
Performed by Taylor Swift

Adria's entire body was shaking as waves of conflicting emotions swam through her, and a rush of tears hit her eyes. She touched the screen. The relief was so visceral it made her legs give out. Ronan's arm went around her waist, catching her before she could fall, lowering her to the couch, and sitting beside her.

Adria hit rewind again. She watched as a woman danced on a chair in the crowd, swaying back and forth to a beat that was completely different than the rhythm of the song. She wore jeans with wide hems and a halter top with broad stripes that ended above her navel, looking like some seventies show rerun. Her long black hair was in two French braids that went from the crown of her head, down to almost her waist. Her eyes were closed, a small smile curling her lips upward, and then suddenly, her lids popped open, and she looked directly at the camera. Her smile widened, and she held up a poster the fans weren't supposed to have. It read, "You have to decide," and then she slowly flipped it over to display the words, "which side you're on," in large black capital letters.

A handwriting Adria was achingly familiar with.

"*Dios mío.*" Adria's blood ran cold.

Like being unable to look away as an accident happens, she played the video over and over and over again, forgetting Ronan was even there. Forgetting anything but the pain and relief and confusion that settled over her veins.

"It's her, right? It's Tatiana?" he asked, breaking into her stunned silence.

She swallowed hard, trying to find her voice. But all she could do was touch the screen and the image of the sister she hadn't seen in two years, two months, and twelve days.

"I didn't want to tell the security detail or the cops until you confirmed it." Worry and confusion were evident in every word he spoke.

He reached for his phone, and her body finally broke free from its frozen state enough to stop him. She pulled his phone from his hand and held it as she rose and ran into the bedroom portion of the suite.

"Adria?" Ronan followed, his voice puzzled.

She dropped his phone and the camera on the bed as she reached for the closest clothes she could find. She tugged an oversized hoodie on over her tiny sleep tank before sliding her feet into canvas sneakers. He was watching her. She could feel it as she always could, but the awareness was dimmed, sitting at the back of her over-loaded mind as bigger, wilder, more concerning thoughts took over. Had it really been her or just a mirage? What the hell was she doing there? Looking happy. Alive. Mischievous. That was so not her somber, serious sister. Were they drugging her? Had she been brainwashed? Had she become some alternate version of the quiet but fierce girl who'd wanted to become a doctor?

She headed for the door at a sprint, and he grabbed his electronics from the bed before joining her.

"Where are you going?" he asked.

"Back to the stadium," she said. She frowned at the strange voice that had emerged from deep inside her, zombielike. As if she didn't have a soul. Maybe she was dead. Maybe she'd finally collapsed on the stage in a heap of heartache and loss.

"What? Why would you go back?" he demanded.

"There was another poster..." Adria put her hand to her chest. She was out of breath, and she hadn't even left the room. Her heart couldn't keep up with the physical demands her emotions were causing her body.

Ronan glanced down at the camera in his hands. "What? There was?"

"I need to know what was on the other one."

"It's probably gone by now. The cleaning crew will have swept it away."

"Or they're still cleaning."

She could read the doubt on his face, but she didn't care.

"We should call the police. Your detail. Anyone."

They should. She knew they should, but something was screaming at the back of her mind to not do it. Not yet. Not until she saw what was on the other poster.

"I don't have time to argue with you," she said and pulled open the door to almost run into the back of one of her detail. It was a guy she didn't know very well. It was probably for the best Lennox wasn't there, because she would have taken one look at Adria and known something was seriously wrong.

"I need to go back to the stadium. I lost something," she told the man.

He reached for his ear and his two-way mic.

"It's...embarrassing. I'd prefer you didn't alert the team. Can we just go?" Adria's eyes darted to Ronan standing next to her. "The three of us?"

The bodyguard hesitated. But it wasn't his job to stop her. It was just his job to protect her regardless of the stupid things she decided to do, so she headed for the elevators with both men following her. She shuddered as the doors closed. Normally, elevators didn't bother her, only dark spaces, but tonight, with her heart already pounding, it felt like the box from her nightmares closing in on her. She could almost feel the brush of the sides against her arms and feet.

Not now. Not tonight, she screamed to her subconscious as her finger rubbed the scar on her thumb. She needed her wits about her. She couldn't crumble at an illusion that had never been true while Tatiana was out there... Why was she here now? What had happened?

She tried to control the wild beat inside her as they moved silently from the elevator, to the lobby, and out onto the path leading from the hotel back to the stadium. When they got there, the parking lot near the employee entrance still had a handful of cars in it, and hope spiked that maybe they weren't too late. Her bodyguard found a security guard at one of the back doors who recognized Adria and let them in with a shy smile.

Adria hurried to the stage with Ronan at her side while her bodyguard talked to the man who'd let them in. Adria made a good show of looking for something near where her drums would have been, and then she went to the front of the stage, eyeballing the stadium and trying to visualize where Tati had been. Ronan brought up the video again, stopping at the image of her sister, and her heart stutter-stepped once more.

"There," he said, pointing. "By section 205."

She'd already jumped off the stage and gone over the barrier separating it from the crowd before Ronan joined her. The chairs were all gone now, loaded up on carts littering the stadium floor. A handful of janitors were sweeping up debris. Adria's heart banged harder in her chest. The men and women had started at the back of the arena, but they were getting close to the section her sister had been in.

She ran across the white plastic covering the grass, eyes scanning the ground. She could feel Ronan next to her, doing the same, searching for the poster with its black print.

A white rectangle caught her eye, and she ran to it with Ronan on her heels. Before she could pick it up, he stopped her. "You shouldn't touch it."

She shrugged out of his grasp and grabbed it anyway.

Below the larger poster they'd seen on the video was a second, smaller one. It was only the size of a sheet of paper. Her heart skittered again as she read the words, "I'll meet you at The Attic. Alone. No cops."

Chills coated her body. It was her. It was Tati.

"The Attic? What the hell does this mean?" Ronan demanded.

Adria's hand pushed into her stomach, and her legs wobbled. Ronan caught her just as he had back at the hotel. Her shoulder landed with force into his chest.

"It means...it's her."

For the second time, he reached for his phone, and for the second time, she stopped him. "She said no cops."

His eyes narrowed, jaw clenching. "You can't meet up with her, wherever the hell this is, without the authorities knowing. This could be a trap. They could be trying to get you too."

He twisted his phone from her tight grip, and she fisted his T-shirt.

"Please," she begged, eyes filling with tears. Tati had asked her to come alone. Had asked for no cops. She'd do anything...anything if she got to see her...hold her... More goosebumps erupted over her skin. Ronan was right. It could be a trap, because anyone who knew the slightest bit about her would know she'd be desperate to see her sister again.

"Damn it, Adria. This is serious shit."

She longed to lean into him more. To let his arms surround her and hold her up completely because she damn well needed someone else's strength to fill in the cracks she could feel splintering through her. But the heat of him, the sparks that traveled back and forth whenever they were together, were already burning in ways neither of them could afford.

So, she pulled herself back, eyes boring into him, willing him to understand. She had to meet the demands on the note. She had to do exactly what was said because if she didn't...if she didn't and her sister slipped through her grasp after all this time...*jueputa*. It wasn't even something she could consider.

She swallowed the lump in her throat and said, "The Attic is a club in Houston. We used to go there when I'd visit her and Dad after they moved. No one would know that,

Ronan. Sure as hell not some random revolutionary-wannabe guerilla force the authorities think took her."

"You have no idea what she's been through. She could have told them everything and anything about your lives."

She turned on her heel and headed toward the stage, tossing back, "I'm going. Without the so-called authorities who did nothing for Landry and almost got Paisley taken. The same authorities who also couldn't stop a hate group from coming after Leya or a stupid fucking punk musician from nearly killing Fee. They'll screw it up. And if you tell anyone..."

She couldn't even stomach it. If he told the cops or her detail and they messed this up for her, she'd never forgive any of them. Not even herself.

"You don't think I know how badly they've all fucked up?!" Ronan growled. "I was tied in a bathtub while that asshole put his hands on Paisley. I have a scar on my head to prove it and the nightmares to go along with it."

Adria stopped to glance back at him, guilt washing over her. Ronan had lived one of Paisley's worst days with her. He was the reason Jonas and Trevor had known something was wrong. If he hadn't set off his S.O.S. on his phone...

She hadn't known he had nightmares. Hadn't wanted to know.

But she remembered the strangled pain she'd felt when she'd first realized he'd been held hostage with Paisley, and the enormous relief that had filled her once she'd known he was okay. That twist of emotions was exactly what she'd felt minutes ago when he'd shown her the video of Tatiana dancing in the crowd. It was as if something she'd lost had been found again.

She'd gone to him that night in Albany, even knowing it was a mistake. She'd been both disappointed and thankful when he hadn't been in his room, because she didn't know what she would have done—if she would have let the feelings she'd stuffed into a box back out. She'd been relieved to find out he'd packed up and headed out as if the wolves were chasing him. If he had nightmares, they obviously were still haunting him.

She knew what it was like to wake with your body trembling and your blood running cold. Except, his were caused by things that had actually happened and not some imaginary event she couldn't shake.

Tears pricked her eyes again, but she couldn't afford for him to see her cry. Not him. She forced her feet to move toward the stage and the single bodyguard who was watching them with a frown on his face.

Ronan caught up with her. "If you go, then I'm coming with you."

"No."

"I'm obviously not a cop. Tatiana knows that."

Her sister knew all about Ronan. Adria had told her, and no one else, the entire pathetic Seattle mess. She and Tati had never had secrets. With barely eleven months between them, she and Adria had always been the closest of all of them.

"She said to come alone," Adria snapped at him.

He yanked her to a halt, his fingers squeezing into her arm. "You have two choices. You either let me come, or I tell the cops, the FBI, your detail, and every law enforcement agency in the area exactly what I saw tonight."

She jerked her arm, but he held on. She glared into his eyes and saw something close to panic flare before it dissolved into anger. It was an emotion he rarely showed anyone except her. To the world, Ronan Hawk was flirty and laughing, or cocky and commanding, or annoying and taunting, but never furious. She was the only one to see it when she pushed him like she was now.

"I'm serious, Beauty Queen. You try to go alone, and I'll be singing all about it from the rooftops."

She felt his resolve as if it was part of her own being. She wanted to rant and rave at him that he had no right to make demands or tell anyone anything, but she knew it wasn't true. Acid burned through her stomach and up into her esophagus not only at the thought of somehow missing Tati at The Attic but also at the idea of him coming with her. There'd be more secrets of hers he'd hold in his hands.

The need to see her sister again won out.

"Fine. You can come," she said through gritted teeth.

Relief flooded his face, and it tugged at the locks and seals she had on her emotions. She had to put some space between them before she collapsed. She jerked her arm away, and this time, he let her go, tagging after her as she moved toward the waiting bodyguard.

"Everything good?" the man asked, eyes skating between them and lingering on her arm where Ronan had held it.

"Everything's fine." Only the years of experience she had hiding her nerves kept the tremor out of her voice.

The walk back to the hotel was as silent as when they'd come, but the air was heavy and full. Expectations flitted through and around her as if it was a dark aura she couldn't quite shake.

But below it, one thought beat loud and clear—a drum-roll chanting out, *Tatiana is alive.*

CHAPTER FIVE

Ronan

SAME OLD LOVE
Performed by Selena Gomez

Ronan's mind was whirling as they made their way back to the hotel. His jaw was clenched tight, and his heart was beating like a fucking basketball being driven down a court. Every instinct in him was screaming at him to call the authorities—anyone who could talk Adria out of the ridiculousness of them meeting with a kidnap victim without backup.

He should at least tell his best friend. He and Asher had lived through each other's worst moments. It had been Asher who'd woken him from the first nightmare after Albany, sitting up late into the night with him while he'd drunk himself into oblivion so the gun and the blood wouldn't return...at least not that night. And it had been Ronan who'd sat at Asher's side after Nova had overdosed, and then again when she'd almost strangled Wren. He'd been at his side when Asher had almost lost his daughter. That night seemed to have cost Asher a decade of his life, and he had the gray hair at his temples to prove it.

But if he told Asher about this now, he'd convince Ronan to tell her security team and the FBI. Adria's tormented plea not to tell anyone hung over him like a cloak he couldn't remove. She was desperate to see Tatiana, which was something the kidnappers would clearly know. And yet, he also couldn't blame her for not trusting the authorities. The band had been through more than most people experienced in a lifetime. It was why he was showing off their resilience in the documentary—the courage it took to not just continue breathing but to take the world by storm, glowing and commanding and vibrating with life.

At the hotel, Ronan followed Adria into her room, shutting the disapproving bodyguard outside once again.

"How do you even know what day and time to meet her? The note didn't say," he asked, watching her as she paced in front of the couch.

"We always went on Mondays. It was open mic night and the one night you could be eighteen and get in."

"I don't like this. Seriously, we could be fucking up any chance the authorities have of getting her home safe and catching the bastards responsible for taking her. Plus, we could be putting you at risk."

Adria halted, turning tormented eyes toward him. Her hands fluttered as if flipping her drumsticks even though she didn't have them.

"I have to go on her terms. If I think she's being coerced, I'll call the cops right there from the club."

Ronan sat down in an armchair, leaning forward to put his elbows on his knees, hands clasped, body vibrating with adrenaline that hadn't stopped since the moment he'd seen Tatiana's face on the video.

"The FBI kept everything about her kidnapping under wraps. Are they certain that's what happened?"

"They left a note," Adria responded. "They said they were coming for me next."

His heart bottomed out. He wanted to demand again that she give up this stupid idea, but if he did, she'd lock him out. Instead, he forced his voice to be soft as he said, "Maybe they are. Maybe you're giving them exactly what they want."

She scoffed. "After over two years? I was in Colombia with my mom for a long time after that. They had plenty of opportunities to come after me."

That singular thought made the hair on his neck stand up. Made him want to wrap her in bubble wrap and stuff her in a closet where no one could get to her. His instincts were screaming at him that something was off about all of it. From the original kidnapping right down to what had happened tonight. He just couldn't put his finger on what it was.

"How do you expect to go to the club without your security detail knowing?"

"I'm staying with my dad while we're in Houston. I'll sneak out the same way Tati and I used to," she said with a casual shrug.

"How's that?"

Her lips twisted upward at some hidden thought. "That's my secret."

His eyes narrowed, but he didn't push. She pulled off the sweatshirt she'd thrown on to go to the stadium, and her tiny tank rose, showing off her taut stomach and the barbell bellybutton piercing his tongue had played with on multiple occasions. Heat soared through him, tightening his muscles and his groin. Her nipples pebbled under his gaze, the thin white cotton putting the dark circles on display.

He barely caught a groan before it escaped. Tortured thoughts about how perfect they fit with their bodies twined slammed back into him, and it pissed him off. He'd told himself he was leaving, shutting the door on this chapter of his damn life, and now he was being dragged back in. Instead of the one night he'd sworn to himself, he had another two at a minimum ahead of him. Maybe fate really was laughing at him.

Maybe he'd never escape the net she'd settled around him that very first day on his father's set in Burbank.

He stood and headed for the door without looking back, irritation bubbling through him. Not just at the situation but at the intense sexual frustration that still brewed after two years of wanting the one thing he couldn't have.

"Text me the details," he snapped. "I'll meet you at your dad's place."

When she didn't respond, he finally did turn around. Her dark hair tumbled around her shoulders, and her eyes shimmered with emotions she normally hid from everyone. She was upset and shaky, and yet still glowing with a stunning light like the moon goddess, Chía. The world couldn't afford to lose her. He'd be damned if it happened on his watch.

"Go to that club without me, Beauty Queen, and you'll regret it."

"Don't threaten me, Hollywood."

"Don't go without me, and I won't have to."

Then, he left before his feet and his dick led him back to the one place his body desperately wanted to be. Before he was reeled back in for much longer than a few nights and a screwed-up meeting with her kidnapped sister.

♫ ♫ ♫

It was just his luck Asher saw him as he was checking into the hotel in Houston on Monday. His friend's eyebrows raised in question before he leaned down to whisper something to Fiadh. She turned her head in Ronan's direction, her lips twitching as if seeing him was funny. It irked him that any of them might consider him a joke, but then, wasn't he? Wasn't he nothing but a court jester when it came to Adria Rojas?

Fee took Wren's hand, and they got into the elevator while Asher made his way over to him. His friend was wearing a pair of jeans and a sweater that were a complete turnaround from the expensive business suits he'd worn for half a decade. But ever since getting together with Fee, Asher's entire demeanor had softened. He smiled more, laughing even. The deep grooves between his blue eyes had eased, making him look younger while love practically dripped from him.

"I thought you were heading back to LA," Asher said, coming to a halt next to him.

"So did I."

Ronan hadn't thought through an excuse for still being there. He hadn't been able to think of anything besides this stupid-ass plan to meet up with Adria's kidnapped sister. Every single minute since they'd seen the message at the stadium, his feelings and thoughts had yo-yoed back and forth.

"Care to expand?" Asher asked.

Ronan took his key card from the desk clerk, grabbed

the handle of his rolling suitcase, and headed toward the elevators with Asher keeping pace.

"Adria agreed to do the interview," he said. He'd have to send her a text and let her know he'd used her as an excuse in case anyone asked. It wasn't quite a lie. She was the reason he'd stayed. Again. As always. He gritted his teeth.

Asher's hand rose to his mouth, but Ronan saw the smirk anyway. When they stepped into the elevator, Asher started to say something, and Ronan cut him off.

"Don't. I'll meet up with her this week, and then I'm out." He thought if he kept saying it to himself, he might still be able to make it true. He'd finally gotten the courage to move past this...past her...at least enough to set it behind him and concentrate on his career, and now it had been shot to hell.

When Asher didn't say anything, Ronan looked over and groused, "What?"

Concern had taken over his friend's face. "You look tired. More nightmares?"

He barely bit back the yes before it escaped. He'd had two nights' worth of them. But they weren't his normal ones. In these, it was as if his past became tangled with his worries about the future. He was in a tub, zip-tied, with his mouth duct taped just like what had really happened, except this time, Adria was with him, and she had a slit along her neck like the one that had killed her friend.

It had left him panicked and breathless.

He'd itched to call the authorities all over again. He'd wanted them to check every security feed at the stadium and around it. But instead, he'd watched the video of the concert on repeat. He'd gone through every frame. Not just the one where he'd caught Tatiana holding the sign, but every single second he'd had the camera facing in her direction. He'd wanted to see if she'd been alone or if there'd been people with her. It had been impossible to tell. All he knew for sure was that she hadn't seemed like she was in duress. She'd seemed relaxed…almost fucking happy.

And that had pissed him off because if she'd been off playing hooky while her family had been tearing themselves apart in grief and despair thinking harm had come to her, then she was a pretty shitty human being. He had a feeling Adria would never admit to it. She was too protective of her family. Look at what had happened when he'd had the audacity to suggest she was afraid of relationships because of her parents. She'd flipped out and stormed out of his hotel room.

Of course, the idiotic NDA he'd asked her to sign hadn't helped.

Fuck. If only he could take that one moment back.

Then, he shook the thought away. No, he'd moved past this. He was finally putting that night and her behind him. He just had to get through the meeting with her sister tonight, and then he could go back to LA and focus on what came next.

The elevator stopped on Ronan's floor, and he got off. Asher held the door so it wouldn't close and met his gaze. "I'm saying this not only because I'm your friend and I care about you, but because the Daisies are my responsibility now. Shit or get off the pot."

Annoyance bloomed through him because that was exactly what he'd been attempting to do. Get off this train. Get as far away from Adria as he could. But instead of saying that to his friend, he just joked with him. "Really? Shit or get off the pot?"

For a moment, Asher's lips also tilted upward before he sobered. "I'm serious, Ronan. This isn't healthy for you or her. Whatever went down, whatever is going on, fix it or leave it. Neither of you deserves to be caught in this antagonistic limbo. It isn't good for the band's vibe, and you deserve to be happy."

Ronan's jaw clenched because it was exactly what he'd been trying to do. He was two seconds from spilling everything to Asher when Adria's tortured face came back to him. He turned away, calling out over his shoulder. "I hear you. Vibes and all."

As soon as his hotel room door shut, Ronan sent a text to Adria.

> RONAN: *Asher just gave me the third degree about why I was still here when I'd said I was leaving. I told him you finally agreed to the interview.*

> STAR: *I don't need you here.*

His heart crashed down into the pit of his stomach.

> RONAN: *I'm not kidding. You go without me, and you'll regret it.*

He'd stake out the damn club from the moment it opened if he had to, but he sure as hell wasn't letting her go alone.

> STAR: *I hate that you feel like you can threaten me.*

> RONAN: *What time am I meeting you?*

While waiting for her response, Ronan set up his laptop, determined to get some work done.

STAR: Eight o'clock. Corner of Prairie and Fannin.

Relief flew through him, but he didn't respond.

Instead, he buried himself in the tasks that would move him into the next chapter of his life. He set up interviews for his executive assistant position, including one with Nikki's mom, ran through the latest changes of a script he was working on, and scoured listings for houses on sale near the beach. These were the dreams he'd always wanted—making movies, waking to the sound of the waves. They were all within reach. More than that, they were actually in the palm of his hands. He just had to close his fist around them in order to keep them from disappearing.

♫ ♫ ♫

It was dark when Ronan stepped out of the CarShare in front of a luxury condominium building near downtown. A bitter wind whipped through him, and he zipped up his olive-green ski jacket, wishing he hadn't thrown out every beanie he'd had in a moment of rashness. He shoved his hands into his pockets and walked to the intersection where Adria had told him to meet her. He cursed inwardly when he realized she wasn't there. If she'd gone without him, he was going to be furious, but it wouldn't stop him from showing up at the club.

His phone buzzed, and he pulled it out, thinking it might be her.

MOM: Harvey tells me you're looking at property in Malibu.

He snorted. He should have been pissed his real estate

agent had blabbed, but as the man was one of his parents' long-term friends, it shouldn't have surprised him.

RONAN: Just starting my search.

MOM: Have we been cramping your style and didn't know it?

In order for them to cramp his style, he'd have to have a love life to begin with. Ever since Seattle, starting something new with anyone had been far from his mind. He'd moved back into his parents' guesthouse because he couldn't even look at the condo he'd intended to live in with Adria without thinking of her. Then, he'd been so caught up in making *The Secrets Inside Us* he'd never had time to search for another place. When the movie had taken first place at the Avalyn Film Festival, his life had blown up, and he'd had even less time. He'd been overwhelmed with offers to direct and piles of scripts to review. The movies he'd really wanted to make had all been red-lighted by the money men, and he'd started to get frustrated until Asher offered the Ravaged Storm deal to him. Now, he'd get to pick and choose what he really wanted to do.

RONAN: It has nothing to do with you, and everything to do with me needing to feel like an actual adult instead of a quasi one camping in my parents' basement.

MOM: The guesthouse is hardly a basement. It's bigger than many people's actual homes. And I like having my family close.

The guesthouse was an eighteen-hundred-square-foot, two-bedroom, two-bath converted cottage that had his mom's style and grace stamped all over it. Some days, he wondered if he'd be better off actually living in the main house in his childhood bedroom. At least that felt like him —or at least some version of him that had once existed.

He looked up from his phone to see Adria emerging from the shadows at the back of the building. Her long stride and graceful lilt were clear even when it was too dark to see her face.

> RONAN: Got a meeting I have to get to, but I'm not moving to Japan. We'll still see each other.

> MOM: Promise?

> RONAN: Promise.

He stuffed his phone back away and noticed Adria was dressed nothing like her normal rock star self. Instead, she was in a pair of black leggings and a ski jacket similar to his. She had her long hair in a ponytail that was pulled through the back opening of a Houston Astros baseball hat.

When she eased up to him in her heeled combat boots and looked up at him from under the brim of her hat, her eyes were shadowed and tired. He itched to pull her to him and comfort her, and he fisted his hands inside his jacket pockets to prevent himself from doing it. From kissing her until she was senseless and had forgotten about this stupid plan. Until he'd re-embedded her into his soul instead of having pushed her out.

The breeze blew the scent of her his way. It was her signature perfume, Black Opium. She'd worn it for as long as he'd known her, and it had the ability to make him long for things they'd never shared, like late mornings in a hotel on the Riviera with the aroma of coffee, vanilla, and flowers

69

drifting in the open windows and the sounds of the sea surrounding them.

"We walking or getting a car?" he asked.

"Let's walk. It's only a couple of blocks from here."

As they headed down the street, he pushed her gently to the inside of the sidewalk in the way his dad had taught him, hoping he could protect her from more than random splashes of water. It was the unknown of what they were walking into that was making his stomach twist and turn in uncomfortable ways. He couldn't rid himself of the image from his dreams of Adria covered in blood.

His pulse was already pounding furiously, and they hadn't even shown up at The Attic. If whoever came with Tati had a gun, he was screwed, but if they ended up in a physical altercation, he'd have a chance. Barry had taught him a solid mix of offensive and defensive maneuvers. He was stronger than he'd ever been.

He sure as hell wouldn't be taken without a fight.

As the club came into view, he scanned the streets and the people. What he was looking for, he wasn't sure. Anyone and anything that set his nerves rattling. His instincts were all he had to keep them safe, and he promised himself he'd do that. He'd do it because the world needed her. He'd do it because Adria, her family, and her band had already been through too much hell to add more to it.

He'd do it because if he didn't, he'd have one more regret that had Adria Rojas's name tied to it, and he wasn't sure if he'd survive it.

CHAPTER SIX

Adria

EXILE
Performed by Taylor Swift and Bon Iver

FIVE DAYS BEFORE

Ronan was a talker by nature. Witty and philosophical. Charming and alluring. Even in the throes of passion, he liked to use sexy, sultry words. He'd even used poorly learned Spanish with her in a way that had only increased the ache inside her until she'd been shaking and trembling around him.

But tonight, as they walked down the street toward the club, he was silent.

Ever since seeing the note Tati had left, she'd debated the intelligence of letting him come with her. She hated relying on him, hated that they now had another shared secret, and hated there was a teeny-tiny part of her that was glad he'd shown up.

But it wasn't just her own pride and secrets she was putting in his hands now. She was placing her family's in them as well, and it twisted her gut in an unhealthy way.

When she'd walked into the penthouse today and seen the shadow of her father, the truth had almost ripped out of her in order to ease some of the torment inside him. In two years, he'd lost at least thirty pounds, and while he'd been on the portly side before, it was too much weight to have lost. His cheeks were sunken, the shadows below his eyes so dark they looked permanently bruised.

Growing up, her father had always been jovial and sparkling, bringing joy into the house whenever he popped in between his almost nonstop business trips. He loved what he did as much as his family, and it showed. As a driven, dynamic leader in the green energy field, he'd had an almost semi-permanent smile on his face, even after being targeted by guerillas and protest groups—even after being kidnapped once himself.

When Tatiana had been taken, he'd lost his smile, but he'd still been a fireball of energy, doing everything he could to find her, including paying the million-dollar ransom. After Tati hadn't been returned, he'd retreated into a stoic wall that was hard to penetrate, getting up and going to the office with shadows following him. But he'd still been conducting business, still been driving the entire industry forward. So, something had changed since Adria had last seen him in January. Something that had turned him into the skulking man she'd seen today, aimlessly watching television and pushing his food around on his plate. She was terrified she was going to lose him too.

It was the change in him that eventually held her back from telling him the truth. She had too many unanswered questions that only Tati could answer. Questions that had repeated nonstop ever since seeing the video until both her head and chest ached. Where had Tati been this whole time? Why did she look so damn happy? What had her kidnappers done to her? Was it even really Tatiana? She'd looked different somehow...the same, but not. If she'd been let out of captivity at the concert, why hadn't she gone for help? Any of the stadium security would have assisted her.

It felt like Adria had swallowed broken glass and the shards were ripping through her. At the back of her mind, in the dark recesses she kept trying to push back, she wondered if Tatiana had simply run away, if she'd just decided to no longer be part of their family. She'd been the one to complain the loudest that their parents were hardly around and more focused on their work than on their children. That their love felt like a thin layer of translucent paper, easily punctured.

But if she'd just run away, who had demanded and accepted the ransom?

None of it made sense.

As upset as Tatiana had been when it was their nanny or their cook who showed up at school events, she'd loved her siblings with a fierceness that bordered on violent. When Vicente had been teased for being scrawny and nerdy in high school, it had been Tati, two years younger, who'd defended him with fists. Adria had to believe her sister would never have done this to her and Vicente.

Music blared from The Attic as they approached—an electronic beat that grated on Adria's already torn nerves. The neon sign cast a sea of pastel colors onto the sidewalk, turning the people waiting in line into weird art forms, all one color. Adria and Ronan joined the queue, and he leaned in so she could hear him over the noise around them.

"It's not too late, you know. We can call someone for backup."

His warm breath coasted over her cheeks, mixing with the cold breeze and sending shivers up her spine. The woman in line in front of them did a double take at Adria, and her pulse picked up. The last thing she needed was to be recognized. She reached out and gripped Ronan's jacket, pulling him closer and tipping her head away from the crowd.

Ronan's eyes flickered, and his nostrils flared.

"No cops. No security, Hollywood," she said, lifting on her toes slightly so she could say it in his ear. In her heeled boots, he wasn't too much taller than her. Close enough to make kissing him easy. She'd always loved the way they'd fit, as if they'd been made to slide together.

Just that thought had her releasing him and stepping back, dipping her head to examine her boots and keep her face away from the crowd.

Unease drifted between them, dancing along the barriers she'd thrown up ever since that night in Seattle. There'd been many times she'd relived what had happened, wondering if she'd overreacted. Sure, she hadn't been looking for anything permanent, but she still suspected he'd been right when he'd said it had been the baggage of her childhood that had caused her to run. Then, she'd remember the humiliation of his words that a whole group of strangers had overheard, and her anger would return. He'd signed an NDA basically assuming he'd need protection from her scheming ways and that he'd have to use his agent to resolve their differences. He hadn't been asking for a partnership. He'd been asking for a play toy he'd eventually be able to throw out without consequences.

As her pulse spiked in hurt and rage all over again, she

stepped farther away from him. She didn't need these thoughts tonight. Didn't need them on top of what was really happening—Tatiana.

She was going to see her sister! That sent happiness spiraling through her before her mind spiraled into confusion again.

By the time they finally got to the door, she was a nervous wreck. The bouncer hardly looked at their IDs before giving them the nod to go on in. Ronan paid their cover charge, and they slipped into the darkened space. It had been ages since Adria had been to The Attic, but it had hardly changed. It still had a mishmash of furniture from wingbacks to counter-high stools thrown around an equally eclectic mix of tables in every kind of design from ultramodern to eighteenth-century ornate. A couple sitting at a Queen Anne-style table got up, abandoning the four chairs, and Ronan grabbed Adria's hand and slid in before someone else could snag it.

Adria's gaze scanned the room, searching for Tati's black hair and dancing pale-blue eyes. For years, Tatiana had kept her hair shoulder length at most, hating the time it took to do much of anything with it, but in the video, it had been down to her waist. What other changes to her sister could she expect? She'd always been practical and calm, almost to the point of unfeeling, and yet Tati had looked almost mystically happy in the concert video.

A waitress came by and took their order. She asked for a beer but knew she wouldn't drink it. She needed all her wits about her. Beside her, she could feel the tension in Ronan's body, a mirror of her own, just like she could feel the heat and electricity zapping between them as it always did. Hell, her hand still tingled from where he'd momentarily held it while directing her to the table.

The music had stopped as the bands switched up, but the club was still loud. Drunken laughter and chatter filled the air.

"Did you tell your dad?" Ronan asked.

She shot a look in his direction before returning her eyes to the crowd, finger sliding along her scar, wishing for her drumsticks instead. "He's a mess. I...couldn't tell him without knowing more about what was going on. Because what if..."

"What if it isn't really her?" Ronan finished.

"It was her..." But Adria felt another niggle of doubt she had to force aside. As different as she'd appeared, it had been her sister. Adria just had to understand what had happened before she got their dad involved. Plus, if she'd told him, her father would have insisted on coming, and that might have scared Tati away. If she ran, it might be another two years before Adria saw her again. Her heart and soul couldn't take that. To have her and lose her all over again.

Her eyes caught on a woman pushing through the crowd from the back of the bar. She couldn't see the woman's face yet, but she could see the black hair wound into a crown-like braid on top of her head. The audience shifted, and Adria's breath caught.

Tati.

They saw each other at the same time, and the woman smiled. A slow smile that seemed...almost disdainful. Haughty. Mocking. It curled Adria's nerves and sent dark thoughts creeping in where she had trouble pushing them away.

But *Dios*...it was her.

Her heart soared, and Adria jumped from her chair, covering the last few steps between them in a run. Then, she had her arms around Tati's shoulders, pulling her into a strong embrace. A sob lodged in her throat, and her body shook. Her sister's arms were loose as they returned the hug. Not anywhere near the fierce, unforgiving one Adria was giving her.

"You're here." The words were garbled and choked as tears flew down Adria's cheeks unchecked. She squeezed harder and tried to speak again. "H-how are you here? What the hell happened?"

Tatiana pushed out of her embrace, but Adria reached for her again, holding on.

"Please let go," her sister said, and it tore at Adria in a new way because the voice was so calm, so unemotional. Relief and terror and frustration took hold as images of what she'd imagined happening to Tati came back to her. Nightmares she'd had for years. There were so many things worse than getting your throat slit as Landry had...

Adria wanted to hug her again, but her sister backed away.

Ronan was suddenly there, arm around Adria's waist, pulling her toward the seat they'd taken. She was shaking, her entire body trembling violently as if she'd stood in a snowstorm for hours. Her fingertips felt numb, and she couldn't feel her lower extremities.

Tatiana sat across from them. She was in another pair of seventies-style pants, these wide, brown cords partnered with a gold lamé tank that was cut down the front almost to her belly button. She was stunningly beautiful and not anything like the conservative sister Adria had grown up with.

Tati's eyes narrowed on Ronan, who hadn't removed his hand from around Adria's waist. For the first time in years,

Adria was grateful for his touch, as the heat of it pulled at her frozen veins, keeping her fully present.

"How did you escape?" Adria asked. "Where have you been this whole time? How could you let us...me...think..." Adria's voice trailed away as another sob escaped her chest. She couldn't hold back the tears. Tati was there, and yet it still wasn't her sister. This woman felt stony. Distant. Far removed.

"I had my eyes opened, Ads."

Nausea rolled through her stomach. "¡Dios! They brainwashed you? What, are you part of them now?"

Her sister laughed, and it was exactly Tati's laugh—high pitched, almost a squeal that normally made Adria smile in return. But now, she just made her feel sick.

"I joined them long before I left college," Tatiana said with a careless shrug.

Adria's heart stutter-stepped, not able to keep up, not understanding. The joy of seeing her sister was twisted with fear as ugly truths she couldn't bear to consider came crashing in.

"I don't understand, Tati."

"You were behind it all along." Ronan's deep voice carried over the sound of a country band that had come onstage, a slow song about love and loss. Adria was reeling with both.

"No!" Adria insisted. Even though her thoughts had gone to the same place, she didn't want to admit it aloud. She looked from Ronan, with his brows drawn together in an almost scowl, back to Tatiana, whose smile still looked off. "Have they drugged you? Are you on drugs?"

Tatiana's only reply was a wider smile and a raised brow.

"What's wrong? Did the ransom money dry up? You need more now, so you've come after Adria? I won't let you take her." Ronan's voice was scathing. Dark and angry. Adria's brain was still reeling, trying to catch up.

Tati laughed again, and it was sardonic and cynical. "I won't need to kidnap her."

Adria inhaled sharply. "You were...you were going to let them kidnap me?"

"No. You'll join us of your own accord once you've learned everything I have about our father and Earth World. It's all a big chess game, Ads. He's working with the CIA to destabilize the entire region so the U.S. can put puppet governments in place and control the entire continent. The conflict with Venezuela? It's all been manufactured, and our father has helped them every step of the way—for decades."

Adria scoffed. "No."

"I was like you at first, too. I didn't believe either. But I have proof. Irrefutable proof."

Adria shook her head, trying to clear the haze the relief of seeing Tatiana alive had brought. What was Tati trying to say? That their father was some secret operative? That he was working for the government? It didn't make any sense.

"Think about it, Ads. He was gone all the time, traveling around the world, but mostly to South America. His company is the perfect front."

Adria heard the words, understood them at some level, but was still having trouble connecting the dots. Her sister thought her dad was trying to help the U.S. bring down... what? The world? It was the most ludicrous thing she'd ever heard.

"There's more, Ads," Tati's voice turned brittle. "It isn't just our father's treachery against Colombia that turned my gut. It's how he dishonored his family! The real reason Mama left us in the States was that she couldn't stomach the women he kept on the side. She threatened to divorce him, and he told her because she wasn't a U.S. citizen, she'd lose any chance of keeping us. She'd never see us again. She had to settle with a half-life in order to have us even part of the time."

Adria was shaking her head, and slowly the confusion was fading, being replaced with pain and anger at the lies Tati was spilling about their family. The people she loved. The father who'd done nothing but laugh and joke and love on them even if he was absent most of the time. And Mama... She wasn't someone easily cajoled or steamrolled. If Papá had threatened her that way, Mama would have struck back.

Adria finally found her voice. "What the hell, Tati? How can you? How can you say these things? How can you believe them? How could you let us all think the worst had happened to you just because someone has been filling your head with nonsense? Do you have any idea of the night-mares I've had about the horrible things they'd done to you—"

"If I'd gotten to you before Papá had sent you into hiding, you would have known all along."

"And Mama? And Vicente? Have you even seen Papá? He's some shriveled version of himself because he blames himself for this. For you!" Adria said, voice filled with indignation.

"He deserves worse than shriveling away. He turned his back on Colombia, on us, and on Mama. There is a price he must pay. Justice will be served."

"Do you even hear yourself?" she asked. "I demand to know who told you these lies! Who has been filling your head with these thoughts?"

Tatiana scoffed. "Which of us has the higher IQ, Ads? Do

you really think I wouldn't check my facts? Do you think I would act without proof?"

"I think you've been brainwashed!" Adria's voice started to rise, and people started glancing their way.

Tatiana didn't like the attention, and she rose from her chair. Adria stood, grabbing her sister's wrist, as panic filled her veins. She couldn't lose her again, not again. She had to find a way to fix this, to fix her family. "Don't go! I j-just got you back!"

Her sister ran a hand over Adria's cheek, and said softly, "I'll be back in touch, Ads. I'll send you the proof you need, and then we'll talk about what's coming next."

She pried Adria's fingers from her wrist and stepped back.

"Tati!" Adria called out.

"You have a decision to make, Adria. Whose side are you going to be on? Will you stand with the people of Colombia? Our homeland? Our mother? Or will you join Papá in his bid to spread the evil of the United States?"

She moved farther into the crowd, and Adria tried to go after her, but Ronan was there, holding her back with an arm around her waist. When he tried to draw her into his chest, she pulled away with a sob, mind whirling with everything she'd heard, a new sort of grief carving its way into her chest.

Tati hadn't been kidnapped, but she'd been brainwashed. Filled with hateful lies.

Ronan dropped several twenties on the table and all but dragged her from the club.

She was gasping, trying to get air into a chest that was wrung so tight she thought she'd never breathe again. It made her head spin, and she had to push at the darkness threatening to overcome her. She wouldn't pass out. She couldn't.

She barely registered Ronan's large hand around hers as he led her down the street. She stumbled, and he stopped, tucking her under the shadow of a lowered awning. The store was vacant. Dark and empty like her. She could barely see his face, and yet she knew it was stormy and concerned.

"Don't," she said. She'd break if he tried to comfort her. She'd get lost in his strength and comfort and never be able to find her own footing again.

"Forget it's me, Star. Just pretend I'm whomever you actually need right now. Your friends. Your mom. Just don't stand there trying to keep it together alone when you don't need to be."

His words struck at her very core because, as much as she hated the truth, she didn't have to pretend he was someone else. He was one of the few people she'd ever wanted to turn to. One of the few who'd ever seen past her forced smile and bad attitude to the little girl who'd wondered why neither of her parents were around enough to truly show her how to love and be loved. Had that been why Tati had turned on them? The haphazard way their parents had showed them affection?

It tore at her last remaining ounce of resolve, and then, she was in his arms, face buried in the crook of his neck, drinking in the heady scent of him and letting it center her. He smelled as he always had, like toasted caramel with the hint of a sweet cigar he never smoked. It was comforting in a way it shouldn't have been because, regardless of how much she might need him, no matter how much he saw the truth of her, they still would never work.

But in this god-awful, desperate moment, she'd let herself have it. Have him.

He rubbed her back in small circles while she trembled and fought against the tears. Fought against every single reality that she'd been bombarded with tonight.

Tatiana hadn't been kidnapped.

Tati was part of it. She'd ransomed their family for money. She'd let them think she'd been killed or worse.

What the hell had happened to her sister?

What proof could she possibly have to back up her accusations?

Who had done this to them? Because it had been a clear and concerted effort to destroy their family. Someone had known them well enough to pick at Tati's scars, to wheedle into the holes that had been left by their unconventional childhood. And they'd used it to strike at her father's reputation. To demolish the good he'd done for not only Colombia but all of South America. For all the countries laden by the heavy burden of fossil fuels.

That thought sent renewed shivers over her spine, and she twisted her fingers into Ronan's jacket, holding on to him as if he was a lifeline. Tomorrow, she'd despise herself for letting him comfort her, for acknowledging, even to herself, that there was a piece of her that needed him. But today, she'd hold on because she wasn't sure she had another option.

CHAPTER SEVEN

Ronan

GHOST OF LOVE
Performed by The Rasmus

Adria was trembling so hard he thought she'd crumble. She'd had all her beliefs about her family shaken to the core. Ronan's chest was tight with anger and grief. For her. For this beautiful, spirited soul who'd just found out there was something worse than a sister gone missing.

Footsteps clattered on the sidewalk coming from the direction of the club, and even though the street was busy, for some reason, these hurried steps raised the hair on the back of his neck. For the first time, he was glad he'd pulled them into the alcove of the vacant business. The striped awning had been lowered, allowing them to hide in the shadows.

The street beyond their hideaway was busy. Car horns honked and engines revved while people laughed and drunkenly sang their way down the sidewalks. The beat of the music from not only the bar they'd just left but the others along the block vibrated over the cement.

Hidden away in the dark space, he felt the first drops of tears hit his neck.

It unraveled him in a way none of her snark or anger ever had.

A soft sob escaped her throat just as a pair of male dress shoes and dark slacks came into view, stopping on the other side of the awning. Ronan put his hand over Adria's mouth so the sound of her crying wouldn't give them away. She started to protest, but then she froze when a man's hushed voice asked, "Do you have eyes on them?" Silence was followed by more quiet demands. "Find them. They didn't just disappear."

The man continued past their hiding spot. Ronan placed Adria behind him as he eased to the front of the shop, barely peeking out to watch as a large man in a suit and overcoat hurried down toward the stoplight. He searched all four directions at the intersection, scanning the crowd. When he turned back around, starting toward them again, Ronan shifted them into the darkness once more.

Fuck.

"Whatever you do, stay behind me," Ronan barely whispered. There wasn't enough light to see the reaction on her face, but her body stiffened, proving she'd heard and understood.

The man came to a stop in front of them again. He paused and then stepped below the lowered awning. Ronan didn't even hesitate. He swung, knocking the man sideways with a blow to his face. He hit him again, this time in the solar plexus. The man coughed and staggered into the windows behind him.

Ronan dragged Adria out onto the sidewalk and broke into a run.

Behind them, a choked voice hollered, "Stop! Wait!"

He didn't. He gripped Adria's hand, thankful her long legs and lean muscles could keep up with him as he raced down the street, zigzagging between people, and then darting through cars waiting at a stoplight to cross. The pace they were running had them bumping into whole groups who complained loudly, but he didn't slow down, not even once. As they approached another intersection, a dark-windowed Escalade skidded to a stop in front of them. A man and a woman in suits jumped out, searching the crowded street. As soon as their eyes landed on Ronan and Adria, they started toward them. Ronan wheeled around, yanking Adria back toward a pool hall they'd passed.

He crashed through the door, and it drew eyes. The bouncer stepped forward, but Ronan didn't give the man time to stop them. He hauled Adria through the tables and grabbed a pool stick from the wall before sprinting down the corridor to the bathrooms where a fire exit sign gleamed. He shoved through it.

The alley behind the bar smelled like stale alcohol, rotten food, and urine. They ran through it, heading toward the street. The Escalade roared into the lane, blocking their escape. Ronan pushed Adria against the brick wall, hiding her from the car. He held the pool stick in front of him like a *bō* he'd used in his training with Barry. It was smaller than the stick he practiced with, but it would do.

The emergency exit of the bar burst open, and the man and woman from the street appeared just as the passenger door of the Escalade opened to reveal the guy Ronan had hit in the face. The man tucked his hands into the pockets of his overcoat and said, "Get in."

"Not going to happen, asshole." Ronan had promised himself he would never be taken again. He'd die before it happened. He'd leave his mark on them and get them the hell out of this. He just had to focus on one of them at a time.

Adria tried to move around him, but he pushed her back.

The headlights lit up the alleyway, but there were plenty of dark, shadowy spots as well, and Ronan searched those recesses for another way out. There was a fire escape hanging down near a dumpster, but he wasn't sure they could get to it before one of the men grabbed Adria or him.

The man with the woman stepped forward, and Ronan lunged the pool stick in his direction. The man stepped back just in time to avoid being hit with the point.

"We don't have time for this," the guy in the overcoat said. "I'm CIA Case Officer Warren Times. These are my colleagues." He waved to the others. "We'd like to talk to you and Adria about the meeting you just had with Tatiana Rojas."

"CIA doesn't operate on U.S. soil," Ronan growled.

The man didn't smirk, but there was a decidedly humorous look to his gaze.

"We're working a joint case with the NSA."

Adria stepped to the side of him, and when he went to shove her back again, she pushed his hand away, sending a glare in the CIA officer's direction.

"You knew my sister was alive?!"

The man's face was impassive. "We'd like to discuss this in a more secure location."

He waved his hand to the SUV.

Adria stepped forward, and Ronan grabbed her arm,

hauling her back into him. "We don't know if what they say is true or if they're with Tatiana."

The pain and confusion radiating from the look she settled on him almost undid him all over again. "I need to know what's going on."

Ronan's gut was screaming not to get in the car. But she was already tugging away, and he knew once she'd made up her mind, there was little he could do to change it. Didn't he have three years' worth of proof? His only option was to follow where she went and hope to hell these people were actually working for the U.S. government.

He tried to convince himself it wasn't the same as being taken. He was going with them of his own free will, but it still churned in his chest uncomfortably as he let the pool stick slide to the ground. He tangled his hand with Adria's as they stepped toward Times.

"I guarantee we were caught on at least one security camera," Ronan said. "We'll be missed. All hell will break loose if we don't show up at the stadium for practice tomorrow morning."

"We'll have you back at the hotel as soon as we chat," Times promised. If it was an attempt at reassurance, it failed. Nothing but having Adria in his room with the locks in place would make him feel safe tonight.

As the man opened the back door of the SUV his overcoat shifted, and Ronan caught sight of the butt of a gun. His stomach fell, sickening memories flashing before him of the struggle with Paisley's stalker. The weapon that had smashed him in the temple. His reaction now was visceral, a fierce hatred for the cold metal and the man carrying it.

As Adria got in the car first, she started to slide all the way over to the other side, but he grabbed her hand and stopped her in the middle. He needed her close. Needed her up tight against him, so if they had to, they could bail out at a stoplight.

The driver met Ronan's glance in the rearview mirror. A woman. Hazel eyes. Dark hair. A decidedly Spanish arch to her cheeks and brow. After Times got in, she backed the SUV out of the alley to a flurry of honks before pushing the car into drive and heading down the busy street.

"Did she tell you their plans?" Times asked, turning so he could watch them.

"You...the government knew she was alive?" Adria asked, fury and irritation leaking into every word. "You knew and didn't tell us? We've been grieving...we've been a fucking wreck thinking of the awful things they'd done to her!"

"Did she tell you anything about *Grupo Nacional Vive Libre*? Who's in charge? What their next target is?" Times demanded, completely ignoring Adria's questions.

"Look, asshole, Adria just came face-to-face with the sister she thought was likely dead, so why don't you cut her some slack and cough up what you know before demanding anything," Ronan growled.

"Everybody calm down!" the woman in the driver's seat said.

"Who the fuck are you?" Ronan snarled.

"I'm an intelligence...analyst with the NSA."

Next to him, Adria shivered, long fingers coming up to scrub her forehead. "I don't understand any of this!" her voice rose in exasperation.

"Your sister is working for GNVL. We've received notification of a credible threat by the group against a target in Houston within the next week."

"GNVL?" Adria's brow furrowed. "Why would they be in the U.S.?"

"Who the fuck is GNVL?" Ronan demanded.

"Protest group," Adria said just as Times said, "Terrorist group."

The NSA operative blew out a breath and said, "They're a group who, on the surface, organizes rallies protesting on behalf of Colombia. They target anything from presidential laws, to mining companies, to unionization and health benefits. At a cursory glance, they don't appear to be a terrorist group, but we believe they've been behind several recent kidnappings and bombings in South America."

Silence fell in the car, and Ronan's gut twisted even more.

Adria shook her head. "I don't understand. Tatiana didn't even go to college in Colombia. She was at Bonnin University in Virginia. Where would they have even gotten to her?"

"You've all spent a considerable amount of time there with your mother," the NSA analyst said softly.

Adria shook her head, finger rubbing viciously over a scar she had on her thumb, and then her eyes jerked back up. "Wait. You think my entire family is involved?"

The two government agents exchanged a look, and Ronan's stomach screwed up even tighter.

"What did Tatiana tell you?" the woman pressed.

Ronan squeezed Adria's thigh, hoping she'd understand it meant to keep quiet as unease flew over him. Were they setting Adria up? Did they suspect she was working with her sister? Her family? She needed a lawyer. Someone to advise her against incriminating herself.

"Nothing. She told me nothing. Some ridiculous things about my father." She shook her head.

"Such as?" Times asked.

Ronan squeezed her thigh again.

"About him cheating on our mom. Which is absurd. Our

parents may not be the most conventional couple, but they love each other."

"Did she say she was going to contact you again?" Times asked, and Ronan noticed the NSA analyst almost roll her eyes at the directness of his approach.

Silence settled over the car, and Times's eyes narrowed. "I'll take that as a yes."

"She's our most viable lead," the woman said quietly. "We think their next target is related to Earth World Solutions."

That was a low blow, and Ronan let out a grunt of disapproval. Using her father's company against her was sure to propel Adria into helping them.

"We don't want any civilians to get hurt," Times added.

"I don't know anything," Adria said.

"But she'll contact you," the woman said, as if it was a forgone fact.

Adria shrugged.

Times handed her a business card that said Lakefront Appliances with his name and a phone number. "All we're asking is that you give us a heads-up about any meeting, and we'd like to listen in on any phone calls."

Ronan snorted. "Is that all?"

Times glared at him. "It's not your choice, Hawk. This has nothing to do with you."

Ronan didn't like that the man knew exactly who he was. He leaned forward. "If you think I'm going to let you steamroll her into handing her privacy over to the fucking CIA, I've got news for you."

"Don't let the little spy movies your parents make lead you into believing all the conspiracy theories about us," Times tossed back.

"Jesus. Can you both put your dicks away for about ten minutes?" the NSA analyst snipped.

Silence settled down in the car. They pulled up across the street from the hotel where Adria's bandmates and Ronan were staying.

The woman turned around in the driver's seat to take Adria in. "It's a credible threat, Adria. There might be casualties. People who work for your family...others."

Adria's shoulders sagged. Ronan couldn't even imagine what was going on inside her head. Just the shock of seeing her sister alive would have been enough for a single night.

"I don't know anything. I don't even know if I'll see her again, but if she gets back in touch, and I have anything to share, I'll let you know." And then, she pushed against Ronan, indicating he should get out.

He did, gladly. The breeze hit him as soon as he stepped out of the vehicle. Cold and fierce, it sent chills over him. Adria joined him on the sidewalk, and Times rolled down his window to look at them. "It would be better if we could monitor your calls."

"I'll let you know if I think that's necessary," she told him, and he frowned, jaw ticking, unhappy with the answer.

Ronan wondered if they'd do it anyway—or if they already had. They'd followed them tonight. They'd already known she was meeting up with Tatiana. If they hadn't had permission for a wiretap before, they did now after Adria had met with a suspected terrorist. They'd use it against her.

"You can't tell anyone," Times told her. "Not your parents. Not your brother. Not even your security detail or the cops. If you do, they'll start looking for Tatiana in Houston, and she'll skedaddle. Any chance we have of bringing down GNVL will go with her."

Adria didn't respond. She just turned away from the car

and headed for the crosswalk. Ronan jogged to catch up. His heart was pounding furiously as she practically ran through the intersection with him on her tail. She floundered at the hotel doors as if finally realizing she wasn't staying there with the others. He grabbed her hand and pulled her inside, halfway surprised when she didn't argue. They stayed hooked together that way as they rode the elevator in silence and walked down the hall to his room. Once they were inside, she finally jerked her hand from his before wrapping her arms around her waist and staring into nothingness.

She looked pale and shaky, but hell, who wouldn't after everything that had happened tonight? They needed a drink. Something strong to settle their nerves. Ronan went to the fridge, glancing inside and debating the full-strength whiskey, but then just grabbed two canned Moscow Mules, handing her one. She cracked it open and took a huge gulp. He did the same. It did nothing to calm him. He took another swig, fingers clenching the can so hard it indented.

Adria sank onto the chair at the table by the window. He sat down on the bed, and it brought them so close their knees almost touched. She took another long drink before putting it on the table.

"I don't even know what to say," she said quietly.

She didn't have to. Her eyes said it all. The relief she'd felt at seeing her sister tossed in with pain and frustration—rage, even. He wasn't sure if it was at her sister, or the group that had likely brainwashed her, or the government agents who'd chased them down. Maybe it was even directed at her dad, who may have been the catalyst for all of this in a very different way than she'd originally thought. Instead of being an honorable businessman, he could have been a cheating husband working against his country—although, which country was that?

"Was your dad born in Colombia or the U.S.?" he asked.

"The U.S. My grandparents immigrated from Colombia when *Abuela* was pregnant with him."

"You all have dual citizenship?"

Instead of answering, she asked, "Why do you ask?"

He was trying to put together the pieces. Who belonged to what country. Who would have the most to gain. But none of it really mattered. What did matter was the way he could feel her withdrawing, pulling back into herself. He knew it was only a matter of minutes before she forgot the comfort she'd found in his arms and remembered she hated him with a ferocity that was as palpable as the desire that thrummed through their veins.

She'd tell him to leave, and just this morning, he would have agreed. He had intended to do just that. But everything had changed in a matter of hours...minutes. As much as it smashed to hell all the promises he'd barely made to himself about flipping over a new page, he couldn't walk away. Not with her life crumbling and him the only one who knew why or how or what she'd been through. His entire being was vibrating with the need to protect her. Shield her from any more hits. To somehow ease the pain and turmoil bubbling through her. But he also knew if he said any of that, she'd run. She'd bolt and not look back. So, instead, he did the only thing he could, which was to keep her talking.

CHAPTER EIGHT

Adria

FIGHTER
Performed by Christina Aguilera

The alcohol had done nothing to numb the heartache cutting through her. Pain mixed with confusion in a way that was hard to wade through. She'd held Tatiana in her arms. Held her, smelled her, heard her laughter. And yet, the Tati who'd shown up was nothing like her sister. The fierce family defender was now the one striking out at them.

With the CIA showing up after Tatiana's big reveals, did it mean their father was really a villain like her sister had accused him of being? Was Earth World a front for the CIA? *Dios*, was Vicente working for them also? She should call her brother, throw all of this at him, just to hear his reaction so she would know if he was in on it. He wouldn't be able to hide from her. He never had.

Her chest felt uncomfortably tight, and she was terribly

close to breaking into tears once more. She had to pull herself together. She couldn't lose it with Ronan again. It had felt too good to be held. To have it be *him* who was holding her up. And where would that lead them? Right back to earth-shattering sex and him wanting more than she could ever give as their lives drew them in different directions. Look at the mess that had come from her parents' lives barely circling each other.

As if sensing her distress, Ronan slid onto his knees from the bed and pulled her up tight against his chest. Her face went to the crook of his neck as if it belonged there, just as it had in the shadows of the storefront downtown. His heat bled into her just like always, the slow, boiling desire unleashing itself, even when there was nothing sexual about his embrace. This was all tenderness. Caring.

She trembled from the effort of easing away from him rather than giving in to the temptation to hold on. But this was Ronan. The man who'd said he wanted to move in together and then simultaneously said he didn't trust her enough to not secretly get pregnant. So, she pushed him away.

When he tried to pull her back into him, she all but crawled over him to get out of the chair, storming toward the door. He didn't stop her as he had in Seattle. Instead, she stopped herself because where was she supposed to go? Back home to her dad's penthouse? To the man sliding away into nothingness? How could she see him and not ask the million questions that had been pouring through her brain since Tati had dropped her accusations like a thunderstorm?

She could go to Nikki's room. But what reason could she give for being at the hotel instead of at her father's? Could she whisper the truth? Tell Nikki she was afraid her family was responsible for what had happened that awful day at

Swan River Pond? That maybe it really had been Tatiana's friends who'd come for Adria and found Landry instead? Had there been a struggle? Had GNVL slit Landry's throat so she couldn't tell the world the truth, that Tati was involved all along?

Her stomach heaved.

She made a dash for the bathroom, slammed the door shut, and fell in front of the toilet just in time for the little bit of liquid she'd drunk to come back up along with the acid that had been pooling in her stomach for days. She sobbed and then put the back of her hand to her mouth to prevent another from escaping.

She got up, rinsed with the hotel-provided mouthwash, and stared at herself in the mirror. She looked almost as bad as her father tonight. Pale. Dark circles under eyes filled with a haunted expression.

A knock on the door was followed by Ronan's tortured voice, "Star?"

Her heart squeezed tight at the nickname, but if he continued to use it, she'd never pull herself back together. He needed to go back to the Beauty Queen taunt because at least then she'd be angry. She pulled open the door. He was leaning with one hand on the doorframe, blocking her path with eyes full of concern.

"No matter what fucked-up things happened tonight, you still don't get to use that name. Not ever again."

His jaw ticked, eyes narrowing. He didn't move. He didn't do anything but stare, trying to read the inner recesses of her soul like he once had. She couldn't let him. She couldn't add Ronan to the sea of unknowns rolling around her.

"Will you please back up?" she demanded.

"Where are you going?" he asked.

"Nikki's room."

"You can stay here," he said.

"No, I really can't," she retorted.

"Do you think I'd try something? You've made it clear there won't be anything between us again. Even if I wanted to argue with you about why I think you're wrong, I'm done trying."

"Maybe you need your agent to mediate it for you." It was out before she could stop, and she wanted the words back as soon as she'd said them. "Never mind. Just let me by."

"You never let me explain or apologize," he said, still not budging.

"You didn't need to. The NDA said it all."

"It didn't."

"Please move, Ronan. I can't do this with you tonight. I don't ever want to do it. I just want to lay my head down and forget everything that's happened in the last two days. Better yet, go to sleep and wake up with it being two and a half years ago, and Lan is alive, and I can tell her not to go jogging. I can tell Dad to make sure Tati is safe in her dorm…" She choked on the emotions, tears filling her eyes. She tightened her jaw, bit her cheek, and fought them back.

"How can you be so damn strong and resilient when it comes to everything in your life except us?" Ronan demanded, irritation filling his syllables, and all it did was make her angry.

"Us? There never was an *us*. There was a casual series of one-night stands you *said* you wanted to make into something more, but then disproved it with a damn contract," she tossed back.

"The only time you've ever been a liar was when it came to us. It shows just how afraid you were of what we had. What I was offering. But you didn't need to be afraid. Not back then and not now." He blew out a frustrated breath, dragging a hand over his short beard as if he was mad at himself for having said too much.

She wanted to throw it back in his face that he'd proven exactly why she had reason to be afraid. He'd almost broken her that night, and that was without ever having moved in with him. Without having tangled their lives together. What would have happened to her if they'd spent years with each other only to realize, just like her parents, they wanted completely different things? Would she have been able to pick up the pieces that were left of her? Or would she have let them become her parents, passing like ships in the night with the I love yous spoken and meant but not enough to stay? Would she be just another child doomed to repeat the dysfunctional cycles of their parents?

No way she'd let that happen. She didn't want him, or a relationship or complications.

All she wanted was to play her drums.

Bang away at skin and wood and metal and create music.

She raised her head and commanded every inch of willpower she had left. "If you don't step back, I'll show you just how little I fear you."

He didn't even hesitate. He just moved away from the door. It was what she'd wanted. And yet it hurt. But a man could only take so much before he threw in the towel.

Good, he'll finally leave, she told herself. But he was right. She was a liar.

She stepped around him.

"Go back to LA, Ronan. Go film your next movie and win another award and just move on with your life. I don't need you here."

"Are you going to tell your detail and your band what's

going on?"

"The CIA just told me not to."

"Fuck the CIA. Are you going to tell the people who are paid to protect you so they can do their job?"

"I just told you, no."

He glared, crossing his arms over his chest, widening his stance. "Then there's a fat chance in hell of me going back to LA, Beauty Queen. I'm not leaving you to face your sister and whomever she's working with on your own."

"You're not a bodyguard, Hollywood. Go put your crown back on, and leave me the hell alone."

She raised her chin, scowling back. Angry at him for reading her. Angry at her sister, her family, and the government. Angry at herself for wanting him to stay when it could break her or him or both of them. He could end up being hurt much worse than he had been when Paisley's stalker had immobilized him. Her heart and stomach heaved at the same time at the thought of anyone else being hurt... because of her family...*Dios...I'm so sorry, Lan...*

"I may not be a bodyguard," he replied, "but I was trained by a Green Beret after the attack in Albany. I know what I'm doing."

She narrowed her eyes. "Like tonight? When you pissed off a government agent, got us trapped in an alleyway, and then tossed your only weapon to get in a car with the people chasing us."

"Only because you wanted to! I will never be taken against my will again! I would have gone down fighting. I would have done serious damage."

She snorted. "With a pool stick?"

"It wasn't a bō, but believe me when I say I could have hurt them."

She stared at him in disbelief, heart pounding almost as

100

if they were running down the streets of Houston again. Panic settled in her veins as an image of Ronan battered and bloody appeared as if he had tried to fight off the group of government agents tonight. She wouldn't be the reason something bad happened to him.

"Stay. Go. I don't give a damn. Just keep the hell out of this."

She stormed toward the door, ripped it open, and stalked toward the elevator. She'd punched the up button before she realized he'd followed her.

"What are you doing?!" she growled.

"Do you even know what room she's in?"

She didn't, and that made her as mad as everything else tonight.

The doors opened, and she stepped in with him following her. He hit the button for the fourteenth floor. "How do you know where Nikki's room is?"

She expected a taunt...a tease...something to rile her further, but all he said was, "Her mom applied for the executive assistant position at the studio. I went to chat with Nikki about it."

Surprise traveled through her. Nikki hadn't said anything when they'd talked earlier. Or maybe she had, and Adria had been too preoccupied to hear it.

The elevator lurched as it took off, and it made her stomach sink. It was an old hotel, and the elevator was a small square box made of shiny, dark wood. With her emotions running high, it brought back her nightmare in vivid clarity. The overwhelming sense of sides pushing in on her. Hands pounding on the wood, trying to get out. It felt real today. More so than ever before. And yet it wasn't... It was just a dream...wasn't it?

She swallowed hard. Her body shook, and she almost

cried with relief when the doors slid open. If he noticed, he didn't say. He didn't even touch her again. He just led the way down the hall to a door where one of Reinard's body-guards stood.

Ronan didn't say a word as he turned to walk away. Guilt hit her. He'd done a huge thing tonight for her. He'd done many huge things over the last few days, starting with trusting her and not calling the cops when he'd first seen her sister on the video.

"Ronan," she called, and he looked over his shoulder, expression hooded. She swallowed, voice full of emotion as she said, "Thank you."

His jaw ticked, and he gave a curt nod before disappearing around the corner. Her body yearned to call him back. Maybe even a corner of her soul did. She ran a finger over her scar, fighting all of her internal instincts, and then turned back to the bodyguard who was watching everything with an impassive face.

"She's here, right?" Adria asked. He nodded and reached out to knock on the door.

It took a couple of minutes, and she was just about to have the man call the room, when Nikki finally appeared. Her eyes widened. "Ads? What time is it? What are you doing here?"

Adria stepped inside, fighting back wave after wave of emotion and the tears that accompanied them. The door shut, and she turned to face Nikki, who was in her pajamas, hair coiled beneath a silk wrap.

"C-can I stay here tonight?" her voice broke on the question.

And then she was in Nikki's arms, and the warmth of her friend eased the pain, anger, and frustration enough that tears leaked out. She couldn't hold them back. She cried as she had in Ronan's arms outside the club, and that just brought back more annoyance and wells of emotions she couldn't contain.

"You're scaring me, Ads. What's going on?" Nikki asked.

Adria pulled away and wiped at her face. She needed the space in order to pull herself together and tell a partial truth—one so far removed from the whole that it was almost a lie, but not quite. "It was just too much at the house. Dad is like this shell of the man I once knew. He won't tell me what's going on, but it's like there is something new…something different than just Tati's disappearance."

Suddenly, she wondered how much her dad really knew. Did he realize Tati was alive and working with GNVL? Maybe he hadn't when she'd first disappeared—Adria couldn't even think of it as being kidnapped anymore—and that was why he'd paid the ransom. But maybe later, he'd learned the truth. Maybe his CIA buddies had clued him in.

"I'm so sorry," Nikki said. "Let me find you some pajamas."

"Thanks."

She followed Nikki into the bedroom portion of the suite. Her friend rifled through the dresser and pulled out a pair of sleep shorts and a T-shirt, handing them to her. She changed and then joined Nikki in the bed.

Once upon a time, when the band was first touring as an opening act for Watery Reflection, Adria and Nikki had shared a bed a lot. If things were really tight, they'd slept three to a bed. It had been like a giant slumber party, night after night. Everything had been so new and exciting back then. Touring. Fans. Their first single working its way up the charts. Sometimes, with each of them assigned their own suite now, she missed those days. The camaraderie they'd built. The sisterhood.

That only served to remind her of her actual sister again and all the things she'd thought were true and weren't.

"You want to talk?" Nikki asked. She always asked. She understood sometimes you didn't want to say anything. You just wanted to be with someone so you weren't alone. Nikki had lost her dad when they'd been in high school in some random shooting at a gas station—a holdup gone wrong— just before the band had really taken off. Some days, Nikki had wanted to rant and rave about it, and some days, she'd needed to do anything but think about him. Some days, she'd needed to pretend she hadn't lost him at all.

"No." Adria couldn't talk about it. If she said any of it out loud, it would sound like some telenovela gone wrong.

Nikki squeezed her bicep and leaned over to turn off the light.

Soon, her friend's breathing had evened out, and Adria could tell she was asleep. But Adria's mind wouldn't stop whirling.

She'd held Tatiana in her arms tonight, and yet, it was like she'd lost her sister all over again. The grief...the pain... lodged inside her chest. The weight of it felt heavy and wrong. If her dad knew the truth, did her mom? Vicente? Was Adria the only one who hadn't known? No. Vicente would have told her. It had been the three of them against the world for so long. She knew he'd never hold something like this back.

And yet, here she was, doing that exact thing. Not telling him. Not telling any of them. Because some stupid CIA operative had told her she couldn't.

If she didn't hear from Tati again, she'd tell everyone the truth.

And if she did hear from her...well, she'd have to see what happened then.

CHAPTER NINE

Tatiana

UNWANTED
Performed by Avril Lavigne

TATI: She doubts me.

BLOCKED: You act as if I should be surprised by this.

TATI: I'm sending her the video.

BLOCKED: Make sure it can't be traced back to me.

TATI: Don't worry. I know what I'm doing.

BLOCKED: I told you all along you were going to have to choose. It's too late to turn back now.

TATI: I'm not turning back. Colombia deserves better than Salvatore Rojas. My mother and my family deserve better.

BLOCKED: We'll not stand by, cowering behind our rooks, while he tries to win with a slow game. Just don't give away our hand too soon, Tatiana. You are smarter than that, but you must be willing to sacrifice her for the checkmate.

CHAPTER TEN

Ronan

DO ME WRONG
Performed by The Hall Effect

Ronan couldn't sleep. He paced the floor, reliving every moment and wondering how Adria was doing...wondering if he'd done the right thing by keeping it all to himself. What he should have done was head back to LA after telling Asher, Kent, or any of her security team what had happened. But he knew he wouldn't, even when she'd basically thrown him out once again.

He'd stay, not only for the reasons he'd told her, but because he'd seen a flicker of the truth in her tonight. She'd thrown the NDA at him, not calmly but with a well of emotion behind it. There was only one reason why she would have that deep of a reaction to it after all this time. In spite of everything she said and did, she still had feelings for him. Feelings that continued to scare her and piss her off and made her want to run. It was the reason she'd clung to him tonight, searching for comfort, and then pushed him away. She was fighting herself as much as him. But she couldn't fight it forever.

From the very first time they'd come together, they'd marked each other in some way. A brand neither of them would ever be able to remove. For a handful of days, he'd thought he could walk away, but fate had slammed that idea out of him in one sweep of his camera. There was no chapter for him to move on to, no new fresh page, because it would always carry the watermark she'd left behind. So, he'd stand by her, and maybe in doing so, she'd see the truth —that one historically bad decision on his part couldn't hide the reality.

They were meant to be together.

He didn't know what it would mean for his career and his new job, for everything he'd built, but he'd figure that out after he was sure she was safe. After he'd earned back her trust—or really, earned it for the first time because she'd never truly trusted him to begin with. She'd never expected him to stick around. She'd always been waiting for him to leave, and when he didn't, she pushed him out the door to make sure it happened.

So, he'd earn her trust, inch by inch, minute by minute. First, by keeping what had happened with her sister to himself, no matter how wrong he felt it was, or how his instincts were screaming to do the opposite. It didn't mean he had to go into this blind, nor did it mean he'd just let Adria mosey through the next week with no one watching her back. He needed information, and he needed to be stuck to her side like glue.

He opened his computer and pulled up information on GNVL in the web browser. From what he read, it seemed like the group had only been around since the early 2000s.

In that time, it had been responsible for several significant incidents in Colombia. They'd been responsible for blockading shipments at the wharves and stopping government workers from getting into the capitol. There were suspicions they'd been behind several high-level kidnappings and car bombs targeting executives from the companies they felt were anti-Colombian, but none of it had ever been proven. None of the group's leaders had even been identified. Unlike other radical groups where the people in charge liked to be seen spouting their propaganda, this group was stealthy. Hiding in the shadows.

There was no mention of GNVL having taken any action within the States. Everything they'd done had been on Colombian soil. While Adria's family's company wasn't the only U.S.-based company on their unfriendly list, it had the most marks against it, which was confusing to Ronan since Earth World Solutions was trying to free the world of its dependence on fossil fuels. It should have been in the positive category as it wasn't depleting natural resources. But the GNVL cited multiple infractions against the company, stating it exploited its employees and stole contracts from local businesses.

Even with those marks against it, Earth World certainly wasn't the worst corporation listed. So, why had GNVL come at them so hard? It had to have been because of Tatiana's personal grievances with her father. Ones Adria hadn't believed, but Ronan had to admit were quite likely. Her parents were rarely in the same city, and it had been that way not for a year or two, but for over a decade. The likelihood of one, or both of them, having a lover on the side had to be high.

But then again, what did he know? Ronan wasn't even with Adria, and every time he'd tried to hook up with another woman over the last three years, his stomach had turned. Maybe time and distance didn't matter. Maybe all that did was the strength of the feelings you had for the person you were with.

He gave up on sleep around four in the morning. He worked out in the hotel gym, showered, got the largest espresso he could find, and then waited in the lobby for the band to emerge for rehearsal at the stadium. He was uneasy, and he knew that feeling wouldn't go away until he saw Adria for himself.

Slowly, the Daisies started emerging from the elevators. A mountain of bodyguards surrounded them—two different security companies plus the Secret Service. If Ronan hadn't known all the horrible events that had happened to these women in the last couple of years—many of which the average person didn't—he would have thought the volume of guards was overkill. Now, he wondered if it would ever be enough.

Not wanting to talk or explain why he was still there, he stayed halfway hidden behind a pillar as the group made their way out to the vehicles. Paisley was wrapped in Jonas, Holden was hot on Leya's trail, and Fiadh was by herself, which meant Asher was either working or spending the day with his daughter. The disquiet inside him grew stronger the longer it took for Nikki and Adria to appear. When Nikki finally did, she was alone, and his heart fell into the pit of acid that whirled in his stomach.

He stepped into pace with Nikki and demanded, "Where is she?"

Her eyes widened at his intensity. "Her detail took her back to her dad's earlier to change. She's coming to the stadium from there."

He ran a hand over his beard, his entire being vibrating

with frustration. She'd known he'd be worried, and she hadn't even sent a damn text. Nothing. The emotions must have shown on his face, because Nikki's face melted from surprise to a glare. She stepped closer to him and hissed, "What did you do to upset her?"

"Me? Is that what she said?"

"She didn't say much. Some crap about her dad that I knew wasn't the full story. I've never seen her so rattled, and believe me, we've been through enough shit that it's saying something."

"It wasn't me. I was there, but it had nothing to do with me."

Nikki looked like she didn't believe him.

"What the hell is going on, Ronan?"

He shook his head. They stared at each other for way too long before Nikki turned on her heel and headed for the door with her detail following her. Ronan was just about to do the same when the front desk clerk called his name. The lady hustled out from behind the counter with a small brown envelope.

"This came for you this morning, Mr. Hawk."

Ronan stared at it for a moment, gut squishing uncomfortably. He hadn't been expecting any deliveries. He took the envelope hesitantly. "Who dropped it off?"

"A courier service."

His heart pounded. He wondered if he should have even been touching it. Was it their new friends with the CIA? GNVL?

He thanked the clerk, shoved the package into his backpack with his laptop, and then hustled out the door to join Nikki and Leya in their SUV. He felt their eyes darting at him, unasked questions filling the air. He was supposed to be gone. Supposed to have met with Adria and scuttled back

111

to LA. But they were going to have to get used to him hanging around.

The ride was quiet, and his mind whirled with questions about what was in the envelope. He didn't dare open it with the others around him. Couldn't risk them seeing something that Adria wouldn't want.

He'd spent another entire night worrying about her, and she'd thought nothing of leaving to go back to her dad's place. Irritation welled. Her family's penthouse was the last place he trusted her to be. If Adria had been able to sneak out of it without her detail seeing, that meant Tatiana knew how to sneak in. How would Adria ever be safe there?

The back parking lot of the stadium held a smattering of cars, including another one of the Escalades their detail preferred. Ronan leaped from the SUV before it even came to a full stop. He was thankful Asher wasn't with Fee this morning because he would have read Ronan's distress in an instant.

He barely glanced at the stadium security as he stalked through the corridors, heading toward the green room. When he found her, she looked as put together as normal in a pair of skintight jeans with a loose-fitting T-shirt on and a pair of low-heeled Doc Martens. Her back was completely straight, poised, even with one of her drumsticks tucked behind her like a samurai sword while she flipped the other one in her hand.

He stalked toward her, ready to chew her out, but when her eyes glanced his way, the look in them caused his feet to stall. Haunted. That was the only way to express it. They were red-rimmed with circles below them so dark they looked as if someone had punched her.

Adria had always had a composure not many people could replicate. He'd rarely seen her not holding herself together. Not even at Landry's funeral. But now, the look on her face...it was as if the smallest gust of wind might make her come apart. It tugged at something deep inside him, tugged at something that wasn't muscle and bone but part of the very fabric of his soul.

He ached for her.

But he was also goddamn pissed. Some of it was at her for leaving Nikki to go back by herself, but mostly it was at her sister for putting her family through this. Ronan was an only child, so he didn't know what it was like to grow up with your best friend in the same house, but he knew he'd never allow his parents to think he was dead.

And that was what Tatiana had done.

Even if she hadn't trusted their father, even if she thought their father was an evil villain, she still should have reached out to Adria and told her she was safe. Told her she didn't need to worry. Instead, Adria had spent over two years imagining the worst.

Adria's eyes slid over him as he strode toward her. Her gaze darted to the side and behind him, as if waiting for the others, or maybe a way to escape, but he wasn't letting that happen. He closed the distance, catching her elbow and drawing her toward a single-stall restroom at the back before anyone else had even made it into the room.

"Ronan, not now. I'm trying to get myself together enough to play."

She tried to pull away, and he refused to let her. He got so close her scent enveloped him like a bubble. He didn't know if he wanted to kiss her, shake her, or stuff her in a car and send her to the ends of the earth so nothing could happen to her.

"We can either do this here"—he waved to the green room—"where everyone might hear, or we do it in private."

113

She scowled at him as if she thought one dark look would send him on his way. He glared back, gaze boring into her with a resolve he hoped she could feel, because he was deadly serious.

"Fine, but not the bathroom. If they see us coming out of there, they'll think..." she trailed off.

Jonas and Paisley joined them. The man towered above Paisley by over a foot, and yet they still seemed perfect together. You rarely saw them without a finger or hand entwined. It was as if they were symbiotically tied together. Paisley was lost in her phone, working on songs or words, or maybe looking at the band's schedule for the rest of the week, but Jonas's eyes had already settled on Adria and Ronan. His eyes narrowed almost imperceptibly. He and Jonas had gotten off to a rocky start that had never really progressed past mutual tolerance.

Adria huffed out a breath and headed toward the door. "I'm taking some of Ronan's questions. We'll be out in the stadium."

Her words drew Paisley's head up, surprise filling her face. Her friends were already suspicious. It was going to be impossible to keep this from them. Didn't Adria see that? She should have them at her side. She should tell them the truth.

Adria was already out in the corridor when Paisley's quiet but firm voice landed on Ronan. "Don't upset her."

He gritted his teeth. Why did everyone assume he was at fault for everything that happened between them? *Because they're her friends, not yours*, his conscience replied automatically. Of course, they'd take her side. And they had no idea of what had really gone down. Not back then. Not now. They just saw him pushing, pushing, pushing and her standing her ground with her middle finger all but raised in typical Adria fashion.

They had no idea what he and Landry had once planned. That he'd convinced their fearless leader of his good intentions and the depth of his feelings. If he'd convinced cynical Landry, he could certainly convince them —if only they'd give him a chance.

But the only person he truly needed to persuade was Adria, so he ignored Paisley's comment and jogged to catch up with her. Her long legs and stormy stride led them through the tunnels until they emerged into the stadium itself and found seats in the lower bowl.

"You went back to your dad's!" he snapped. "Even knowing she could sneak in? What were you thinking?"

"I'm not afraid of my sister."

"You should be. Have you looked at what's happening in Colombia with GNVL? The bombings? The violence?"

"It's my home! Of course I know what's going on! It's so much better than it was even a decade ago," she tossed back. "I was more afraid of the CIA folks last night than I was of my sister." Her chin was defiant, eyes flashing. He was so angry and frustrated he wanted to kiss her just so she'd be forced to at least pay attention to how he was feeling.

He grabbed the envelope from his backpack and showed her. "I got a package this morning. Couriered to me with no return information."

Her eyes flickered. "Just because you got a delivery, doesn't mean it has anything to do with me."

"I didn't want to risk opening it with the others around." He ignored her comment, tearing into it. A flash drive fell out along with a note. It had the same slanted writing as had been on the posters Tatiana had held at the concert in

Arlington. All capital letters that were straight and impersonal and yet feminine in some way.

Adria yanked it from him, and he had to lean in to read it. *Seeing is believing. I'll be in touch.*

"What the hell does that mean?" Ronan asked.

Adria looked at the flash drive as if it was going to explode. "Do you have your laptop with you?" she asked.

He nodded and pulled it out of his bag. He started it up, but then looked at the drive hesitantly. It seemed stupid to put it onto his computer when he had no idea what was on it. It could wipe everything or send some strange virus out into the world using his contacts. He had everything important backed up both on a cloud and an external drive, but there were worse things a computer worm could do.

"I don't think I should use mine," he said.

"*Dios!* Why even bother telling me about it, then." Adria stood up.

"I'll get a cheap tablet or something today. I won't connect it to any of my accounts, and we'll keep it offline. That way, we can limit any damage."

She moved down the aisle.

"Adria," he called her name, and she looked back, eyes blazing. "Don't stay with your dad. I have... I have a bad feeling about it."

She stormed back to him, shushing him. Her face turned toward the stage where the band was moving around, adjusting mics and instruments and getting comfortable with the layout of the stage. "What am I supposed to do, Ronan? I'm here, and my dad is a mess. He's literally falling apart. I can't just say, 'Sorry, Papá, I'm in town but I'm going to stay with my friends instead of you.'"

"Then let me come with you." He groaned internally as

116

soon as the words slipped out. It was a fucking disaster. All of it.

"What are you going to do that my security can't?" she asked.

"You haven't told them what's going on. They don't even know who or what to look for!" he insisted.

"You're not staying with me." She started to walk away again.

He stood, crossing his arms over his chest, and did the only thing he could think of, which was to taunt her. "Chicken."

She glared at him, and then she was waving a drumstick at him. "No! Absolutely not! You don't get to do that. You don't get to try and force my hand by challenging me."

"Why? Because it's the truth, and you can't seem to handle the truth these days?" he growled.

She was back again, poking him in the chest with the end of her stick. "What exactly do you think I'm avoiding?"

"The fact that Tatiana played you all. She's involved in something deep and shitty enough the U.S. government is crawling up her ass. She doesn't care what happens to you. She's using you as a pawn in some game we don't understand." The more he talked, the harder the wooden tip pressed into his sternum. Her eyes were flashing, and her breathing was rapid, chest heaving, and still, he pressed his luck. "You're afraid letting me help, letting me back in even the slightest, will open the vault you've shoved your emotions for me into. You're afraid of wanting me—or worse, needing me."

"You are such a narcissist! This isn't about you!"

He grabbed the stick and twisted it out of her fingers. "Prove it. I'll meet you back at your dad's tonight. We'll check out what's on the drive together and go from there."

When she tried to grab the stick back, he held on to it, and she made a sound that was half huff and half snarl. It landed in his chest and groin in a way it shouldn't have, given everything they were talking about...dealing with. And yet, he'd never been able to be this close to her, hear her sounds, without wanting to be tangled with her. It was twisted and wrong, but it was the truth.

"Bawk, bawk, Beauty Queen," he continued to dig.

"You're such an ass. Give me my drumstick."

"Agree."

She stared for a long time, shadowed eyes flaring with a wide range of emotions. Finally, her shoulders went back, her chin went up, and she said, "Fine."

He handed her the stick, and she whirled around, heading down the aisle.

Relief filled him. And hope he shouldn't have but did.

He wasn't sure what he'd do if the worst came at her with only him watching, but it was better than her facing it alone while her detail remained clueless.

CHAPTER ELEVEN

Adria

I LOVE YOU'S
Performed by Hailee Steinfeld

Adria stormed away from Ronan with her stomach clenched tight. She wasn't sure it had loosened once since seeing Tatiana push her way through the crowd at the bar. She was barely holding herself together. Wondering what was on the stupid drive and dealing with Ronan's taunts only threatened her composure more. She was cracking, inch by tiny inch, and he'd seen it, as he always did. Which meant she couldn't afford to be around him, and yet she'd committed herself to an entire evening simply because she'd let him goad her into it.

Nikki was waiting for her when she crossed the stage to her drums. She was glad they were practicing. Glad she'd be able to pound away at them for hours. She needed to lose herself in the rhythm. Things she could control. Forces she could manipulate so they had an outcome she could predict.

"Hey, you're worrying me," Nikki said quietly, shooting a look around and trying to keep the others out of it, which Adria appreciated. "Is he being an ass? Do we need Asher to send him away?"

Adria pulled her second drumstick from the back of her shirt and rubbed the two of them together like chopsticks. "I'm sorry I'm worrying you."

"Ads... What's really going on?"

Adria met Nikki's gaze. Her friend's eyes were a deep brown, so dark sometimes they looked black, and right now, they were full of compassion and concern. Adria took a deep breath. "I can't talk about it. Ronan found some stuff out about Tatiana. We're... figuring it out."

Nikki's mouth dropped. "What? Do the police know?"

Adria shook her head. "Not yet. There are some authorities involved though. But you can't say anything, Nik. Just know that, in his own screwed-up way, he's trying to help."

She swallowed hard as her own words settled over her. They were true. He was looking out for her, even after she'd pushed him away with enough attitude and snark to have sent him running ages ago.

"That's why he stayed instead of heading back to LA?" her friend asked quietly.

Adria nodded.

"Just know I'm here when you're ready to talk about it." Nikki squeezed her arm, compassion written all over her face that did nothing to help her contain her emotions.

Adria was grateful when Nikki turned and walked away without forcing her to come clean. After what happened with Fee, Asher, and Angel, the band had agreed they wouldn't keep secrets from each other anymore, but she couldn't tell them this. Not only because of the CIA telling her not to, but because she was terrified her family was why Landry was dead. The feeling of glass tearing her stomach lining returned. She didn't know what the truth really was anymore. Not about her family. Not about Ronan. Not even herself.

She wasn't a badass rock star. She was a quivering pile of emotional nonsense.

Adria took a seat at her kit and adjusted the rims. Just those simple actions and being behind the instrument she could play in her sleep felt like a reprieve. Here, for a few minutes, she was the one who would drive the pace. Everyone else would follow her lead. She may not be the one who wrote the songs, and she rarely sang more than backup, but she was the one who kept them on course. That was what she needed to do. Forget everyone and everything while she concentrated on the music.

♫ ♫ ♫

It was late afternoon by the time the band was done rehearsing. The next day, they'd play for another sold-out stadium, and then they'd be on their way to her hometown. When she'd first proposed a tour stop in Colombia and the band had agreed, she'd been overjoyed. She'd wanted to show her friends one of the places she'd grown up, and she'd loved the idea of playing for the people of Cadencia. Now, dread filled her because what would happen with Tati and GNVL while the band was there? If Adria didn't agree with her sister, would she come after her friends? They were staying with her at their family's estate, which meant Tati would know how to get to them. Would more horrible things happen?

Her stomach twisted.

But if she suggested canceling the show, her friends would want to know why. They'd want to understand the reason for coughing up a whole bunch of money to the venue and the ticketholders. Besides, Adria had other obligations this week other than just the concert. Teen Colombia was crowning their next beauty queen at the *Fiestas del II de noviembre,* and the girls she'd been mentoring were counting on her to be there. She'd been meeting with them virtually for months and in person whenever she was home. If she didn't show up, she'd be letting them down—and her mother as well. They were co-hosting the pageant together. There was no way she could leave Mama to pick up the pieces alone. Not when her mother and the pageant had helped her find her feet again after everything that had happened with Landry and Tatiana.

It was no wonder she was sweaty and clammy by the time she made her way to the dressing rooms to pick up her bag. She almost expected to see Ronan there even though he'd said he'd meet her at the penthouse. She tried to tell herself the feeling in her chest was relief when he wasn't in the green room. Tried to say she was rejoicing in having escaped his presence for a few more minutes, but she could hear his voice in her head calling her a liar.

As the band made plans for the evening, including dinner, Adria bailed out, saying she wanted to spend time with her dad while in town. They all nodded, but Nikki sent her a look that was full of concern. She gave her friend her signature wink, a flash of humor and reassurance, before leaving.

Lennox led the way to the SUV in silence. Her body-guard was still simmering with anger because Adria had ducked out on her the night before. They were friends in an odd sort of way, and Lennox had been hurt by Adria's actions. What she'd done had reflected badly on her body-guard, and Adria felt a twinge of remorse for how it had gone down. But she wouldn't change what she'd done even if she could.

She'd held her sister in her arms. It still seemed unreal.

Tatiana was alive!

Dios, did that hurt as much as it healed.

The quiet in the car was uncomfortable, but neither Adria nor Lennox broke it as they rode to her dad's condo. Her bodyguard stared out the window. The way she kept tightening the ponytail in her ash-blonde hair a tell that she was irritated.

They parked in the underground garage and took the elevator to the lobby. Adria rubbed her finger along her scar, holding her breath. She might have to start taking the stairs permanently if the feeling of being trapped didn't start to go away soon. Relief filled her when the doors dinged open.

As soon as she stepped out into the building's light-filled atrium, she felt Ronan's presence. Their eyes connected across the marble floor, and she realized he looked as tired and haunted as she did. He'd shouldered all of this with her without even hesitating. There weren't many people who would take on that kind of burden. It brought right back to the surface all the emotions she tried to bang away on her drums.

She watched as he stood, and the simple movement showed off the new layer of muscles he'd developed this year. He'd always been strong, powerful, but it was combined now with some secret maturity, a masculinity that sank right into her chest. He shouldered his backpack and headed toward them. Even exhausted and on edge, he was stunning. He would have easily captured and held her gaze whether or not his stormy eyes had locked on to her. His look was full of promises she couldn't afford. The cost would be too high. He'd find all the cracks in her veneer and fill them with his own fierceness, and when they drifted apart—when their lives pulled them in different directions—she'd be left with even more holes.

Adria could almost feel the questions reeling in Lennox's mind as he joined them and they silently made their way into the penthouse's elevator. Her bodyguard slid her key card into the slot, and the car jerked into motion. The tension in the air kept Adria from obsessing about the narrow walls, but she was still thankful when the doors opened to reveal the tiny foyer leading to the only doors on the floor. One of her father's security detail was waiting there. He gave a curt nod before letting them inside.

"Is Papá home?" she asked the man.

"Not yet."

As Ronan stepped inside, a new wave of apprehension hit Adria. Her family was wealthy, and their homes displayed it. Expensive art was hung on the walls, and hand-woven rugs rested on the polished wood floors. Furniture that cost more than some people made in a year filled the space. It bordered on being ostentatious, and some of her friends, boyfriends, and acquaintances in the past had either made snide comments about it or tried to use her after realizing exactly how wealthy her family truly was. And that had been before the Daisies had taken off and she'd earned her own piles of cash to go along with it. Even knowing Ronan had grown up in a Hollywood Hills mansion that was as equally flashy and dripping with money, it was still reassuring when he barely glanced around the penthouse before moving past her into the living room.

When Adria went to follow him, Lennox stopped her with a hand on her arm, leaning in to whisper, "I thought he wasn't allowed anywhere near you."

Adria rubbed her forehead and told another partial truth. "He's helping me with something."

Lennox stared at her for too long. "You look like crap."

Adria snorted. "Don't hold back."

"It's my job to make sure you're okay. So, are you? Really?"

Adria hesitated and then pulled on her beauty pageant smile, winked, and said, "Everything is fine, Lennox. There are lots of reasons for me to look tired."

"Bullshit." Lennox tossed aside the innuendo.

Adria didn't have another response she could give, so she simply turned away, saying, "We're in for the night, and I promise I won't duck out again, so you're good to leave me with Dad's detail."

"I'm not going anywhere," her bodyguard said before storming out the door and shutting it with a decisive bang.

Adria made her way to the floor-to-ceiling windows where downtown Houston glittered below them, lights starting to blink on as the sun sank low on the horizon. She felt Ronan assessing her again, and it made her chest ache, as it always did, but she didn't look away from the view.

After a couple of minutes, he asked, "You ready for this?"

She turned to see he'd set up a battered, ancient laptop on the glass coffee table.

"Where'd you get this?"

"Pawn shop."

She crossed the room to sit down next to him on the couch, and her stomach flipped nastily as he inserted the flash drive into a port on the computer. When the drive came up, there was a single file on it—a video file. As he double-clicked the icon, she wanted to scream not to open it but bit her lip instead.

Tati had said seeing was believing. Would this shatter her world even further?

It took her a minute to recognize the office. It was her father's old building in California. The Earth World Solutions logo was a blur on the back wall of a conference room. The angle on the camera changed, and the end of the table came into view, and Adria went completely still. There was a man and a woman twisted and tangled together there. It was evident from the motions and the sounds what was happening. The woman had her legs spread, her skirt up around her waist, and the man was thrusting between them. He was still fully dressed in a dark-gray suit that her father favored. The camera was behind him, so you couldn't see his face, but he was tall and broad-shouldered—as Papá had once been—with thick black hair.

Acid burned through her stomach lining. But you couldn't see who it was. There were plenty of men who worked for their company who wore suits and had black hair. Plenty of men in and out of the office with the same build and height and coloring. It was clear the woman wasn't their mother. Too young. Too blonde. But that didn't mean it was their father.

"What the hell?" Ronan muttered just as Tatiana's voice came over the screen.

"I know what you're thinking, Adria. You can't see the man's face. It could be anyone." Her breath caught. Her sister knew her so well. Knew every thought. "Look at the watch, Ads."

Adria's gaze flew to the man's arm with his palm face-down on the table. The suit jacket had shifted to reveal a watch with a glowing face. There were only two watches like it in existence. Exclusive, expensive, and easily identifiable. The gold and silver twined like vines around the face where a sun radiated, its rays turning into the hour lines.

"It isn't *Tío* Claudio," Tatiana's voice said, a lilt to it—a tease—as if she was right there and found Adria's thoughts humorous. "He wasn't even in the U.S. on that date."

Adria stood up, unable to look at the video any more. She was disgusted. Sick. Unable to even think about what it meant. Their father had cheated on their mother. In his goddamn office building. Like some cliché of a CEO.

As unconventional as their marriage had been, her parents had always said, "*Te amo*," with enough emotion you could hear it in each syllable. Even when they were apart, their calls were full of warmth and joy, and what Adria had thought was love. It was why it had always been confusing. How could they love each other so much without feeling the need to be together? But she'd never doubted they *did* love one another. To do so would have meant challenging the idea that they loved her and her siblings as well, because they were treated the same way—with words of love, hugs, and affection freely given when they were together, but with long spans of absences, without a pressing need to be at their side.

And now, there was this disgusting piece of evidence shattering more of her beliefs. She wasn't sure it would take much before she simply disintegrated. She looked out at the city, not seeing the lights or the orange and yellow twisting into the denim and gray of the evening sky. Only seeing the god-awful video.

Tatiana's voice filled the room behind her. "This is what opened my eyes first, Ads. I have more. More you need to see and hear and understand. But I can't come to you again in Texas. It's too dangerous for me. I have some things to finish, and then I'll see you in Cadencia."

Silence followed the voice, and when she turned back, Ronan was pulling the drive from the external port. His brow was furrowed together.

"Could it have been your brother in the video?" he asked.

It was a fair question. Vicente looked so much like their father that, even with their age difference, people sometimes mistook them for one another.

"Not unless he was wearing Papá's watch."

Adria hugged herself, wishing she hadn't put her drumsticks in her bag. Wishing she had something to hold on to. Her finger found the scar on her thumb, rubbing at it.

"What's the deal with the watch?" Ronan asked.

"Papá had one made for himself and another for Claudio when Earth World earned their first million dollars. He and *Tío* celebrated by taking a trip to Capri. Mama joined them. It was a big deal..." Adria's voice cracked, and she hated it. Hated every single moment of all of this.

"Is he your mom's or your dad's brother?" he asked.

"Neither, really. His family and Mama's family have been friends for generations. Mama grew up with him. It's how my parents met. *Tío* Claudio introduced them when he and Papá first started working together."

Her heart tugged, thinking of the rift that existed between them now. She thought of the man in the video again. It could easily have been Claudio, but Tati had insisted he wasn't there. Was her sister wrong? How could she so easily believe it was her father rather than their uncle?

Noise from the kitchen drew Adria's eyes. Dulce was working on dinner. Her father was going to walk through the door at any moment, and there was no way in hell she could face him. Not yet. Maybe never again.

She grabbed her bag from where she'd dropped it by the door and headed down the hall. Ronan looked at her, brows raised in question.

"I can't be here when he gets home," she told him and then continued along the corridor. It was only seconds before she heard the squeak of his sneakers on the floor behind her. She popped her head into the kitchen to see Dulce stirring something in a large pan with the smell of chilis in the air. The older woman looked up and smiled, brown eyes glittering with affection as Adria gave her a hug.

"I've hardly seen you since you got into town, *mija*. We have a lot of catching up to do before you jet away again."

Dulce had been more of a constant in her life than either of her parents, and she'd tried to fill the void their parents left behind. But Adria and her siblings had relied on each other more than any of the staff. Even still, Dulce had been one of the first people she'd texted when the Daisies had won their Grammy.

Ronan's presence behind her in the hall drew Dulce's eyes to him, and her lips twitched when Adria said, "I'm going to eat in my room tonight."

The housekeeper leaned in and said conspiratorially in Spanish, "I'd eat in my room also if I had him following me around."

Adria snorted. Dulce was old enough to be Ronan's

mom, or maybe even his grandma, and she had the gray hair to prove it.

"He's just a friend," Adria told her also in Spanish, quite aware Ronan was following the conversation with his intermediate knowledge of their language.

Dulce grinned. "I'll bring you a tray in a bit."

Adria kissed her cheek and then made her way in the other direction to the dual suites at the back of the penthouse. One of the suites had belonged to Tatiana...still belonged to her. No one had removed her belongings even after the FBI and their security team had been through it. They'd all been waiting for her to come back.

A shiver ran up Adria's spine. Tati was alive. And she had let them think the worst. She couldn't stop having one thought without the other.

Adria opened the door to her room. It revealed a small sitting area surrounded by three doors. One led to her bedroom, a second to her closet, and the third to an enormous bathroom with a sunken tub she used to love to linger in. For the first month after Tati had disappeared, Landry had died, and the band had fallen apart, she'd hidden herself in this room before her mother had dragged her to Colombia.

After another month of lingering in a well of nothingness on their family estate, her mother had forced her to go to work with her. That was where Adria found a purpose again, merging her childhood with her adulthood by becoming part of her mother's pageant world once more. Not as a contestant, but behind the scenes, helping her mother run Teen Colombia.

Adria could feel Ronan's gaze on her, but she was grateful he hadn't said more about the video. She needed time to process it. To figure it out. To disprove it. She threw her bag under a table by the door. It was loaded with pictures of her family, the band, and even some from her pageant days. It was all her mother's doing, and when Adria had laughed at her for the sheer volume of frames she'd stacked there, Mama had said, "Sometimes your purpose in life means you can't be with the ones you love in the way you want, but it doesn't mean they aren't in your heart and soul. If you keep enough pieces of them with you, you'll feel them even when they aren't there."

And Adria had thought it was true. Thought if she listened enough, texted enough, talked with them enough, she'd still have them with her. After all, it was how her parents had existed for the majority of their lives. Apart and yet together. But now, all she felt were the holes and not the ways the pieces were supposed to be filling them up.

Ronan left his backpack with her bag by the door and crossed his arms over his chest, feet wide. It was a stance that seemed all alpha male when she'd never considered him one. In bed, he'd been thorough and demanding, commanding even, and she'd been glad to give in because it had brought such beautiful pleasure. Such an intoxicating release. And when he was behind a camera, he was confident and sure. He had a vision only he could see until all the parts came together. But she'd never considered him a He-man type. Right now, he looked like he could give any of their bodyguards a run for their money.

He looked brave and strong. The exact opposite of how she felt. She was the chicken he'd always called her, not sweet and teasing like her brother, but with all the negative connotations shoved behind it. She was scared not only because of what she'd seen, what her sister had said, and what it all meant, but because of the way her body thrummed with him there. She didn't want to face any of it.

She wanted to stick her head back in the ground like an ostrich and just ignore everything.

"Was there anything else on the video?" she finally asked, needing to break the silence.

Ronan shook his head. "No. That was it."

She sat down on a blue-and-yellow, floral wingback chair, leaning her head against the back, closing her eyes. But that just made the video replay in her mind even more. When she looked up, Ronan was still watching her.

"Say something," she demanded.

He crossed over, sitting on the periwinkle striped loveseat. His knees were only inches from hers, and electricity wafted between them, eating up the air until it felt like she'd be drawn to him like a planet into a black hole.

"Both my parents have had people come at them with allegations of cheating," he told her. "There was even a video once of my dad. It had been filmed, without his consent, long before my parents had ever gotten together. But an old girlfriend messed with the date stamp and tried to say he'd slept with her after he was with my mom."

"That's pretty screwed up."

Ronan nodded.

"You think... You think maybe that's what happened here? Someone messed with the date? Papá had those offices before he ever met Mama." Her heart spun. Maybe it was all wrong. Maybe she could prove it and convince Tati that whoever had told her about their father was lying, trying to destroy them. Hope flooded her veins.

But would her sister listen to her? How would she even find her to convince her? Tati had said she'd come to her in Cadencia. She just had to have proof before then.

She'd need Ronan's help. She'd have to keep him around for a little longer.

Part of her rejoiced at that thought, and part of her groaned, but it was like those two pieces had switched places. The joy taking over more than the frustration. It freaked her the hell out because no matter what he said, no matter how their bodies felt tucked together, their worlds were as far apart as her parents' were. She could never allow herself to live the same way as they had. She couldn't because the marks their absence had made on her child-hood were too great to repeat in her adulthood.

CHAPTER TWELVE

Ronan

EVERMORE
Performed by Taylor Swift

FOUR DAYS BEFORE

Ronan saw hope flare in Adria's eyes and immediately wished he hadn't said anything. While he wanted the video they'd just watched to be false, he also knew the odds of what had happened with his dad being the truth here were slim to none. "I'm just saying, there could be lots of explanations."

"How did they figure it out with your dad?"

"We're in the film industry," he said with a small twist of his lips. "We know people who could dissect it. We can try with this video, too, but because your sister already altered it by dubbing her voice in, it will be more difficult. But I can send the flash drive to someone I know."

"There's no way I'm giving this to anyone," she said, voice firm.

"If you want to check its authenticity, I don't see how you have a choice."

She got up, pacing the room. "No. There's no way I'm risking that video getting into the wrong hands. Someone would splash it all over the media... My mama..." Her hands went to her stomach, and her face paled.

"It's already out there, Star. Do you think this is your sister's only copy? She could hand it to your mom, the press, whoever the hell she wanted. Which begs the question, if she's trying to discredit your dad, why hasn't she already done it?"

Adria's feet came to an abrupt halt, and her voice was pained as she said, "She doesn't want to hurt Mama."

"But she wants you to believe her."

"This is so fucked up," Adria said. "I don't even... I just can't."

She sagged, and in two strides, he had her in his arms. Just like the night before, she let him hold her for all of two seconds before she tried to push away. She kept forcing herself to be strong when she was almost shattering. Pretty soon there'd be pieces of her all over the place. He ached to be the one to help her hold herself together, so he loosened his grip but didn't let her escape completely. His hands settled at her waist, and the air between them thickened.

"I don't know what to do," she said, her voice a whisper, eyes large and pained. "About the video. About Tati. About my family. I'd be furious with Vicente if he knew and didn't tell us she was alive. We've all been mourning her, all while hoping she'd show up. What should I do?"

The agony in her voice shredded his stomach.

"If it was me, I'd tell them. To hell with what Tatiana or some damn U.S. operative told me."

"And what if...what if...Agent Times is right? What if—"

"I've been thinking about that. Even if it's true, even if GNVL is planning an attack here in the States, you telling your family you saw her won't change anything. If you were to do an interview and spread the news across the globe, maybe, but three people knowing the truth? Why would it?"

He could see the debate as it washed across her face. To his surprise, she rested her forehead against his chest, and his entire insides convulsed. Hesitantly, as if she was a deer who'd bolt at the smallest movement, he drew her closer. They stood there for a long moment, and he reveled in the feel of her against him.

His throat tightened. How long had he wanted to have her like this? If not relaxed, at least in a place to listen to him? It seemed like the wrong moment to bring up what had happened and yet perfectly right. If he was ever going to have her trust him—truly and completely trust him—they had to have the discussion. He had to tell her both why he'd given her the NDA and how he'd screwed it up.

"What happened to my parents...it's why our team of agents, managers, and lawyers always insisted on an NDA before we ventured into any kind of personal or professional relationship."

Her body stiffened, and she slowly raised her head, a frown appearing between her brows. She shook her head and choked out a strangled, "Don't."

"Please. Let me explain," he begged.

Her lids fluttered shut, and when they opened again, her eyes were glassy with unshed tears. It stuffed a knife into his heart because he was the one to have caused this round of pain. The first she'd suffered that awful year.

"I hadn't even read it, Star."

Her eyes rounded. "Wh-what?"

He shook his head in disgust at himself. "It was stupid of me. I just thought it was the normal agreement. I trusted my agent implicitly. I was so excited about giving you the key, so wound up in my own head about what it would be like to have you with me all the time, I didn't even think to read it. When you reacted like you did, when I actually took the time to see what was on the page..." His throat bobbed, remembering the way he'd wanted to throw up when he'd seen the lines about birth control and his agent mediating their disputes. "Just know I've regretted it every second of every day since."

She tried to pull away, and his grip tightened around her. "Don't go. Say whatever it is you have to say right here, to my face. No lies. No hiding. Just the damn truth."

"Even if I hadn't been humiliated, hurt that you thought—"

"I didn't think it."

She ignored him, continuing, "You went from us hooking up once a year or so to tying our lives completely together in one heartbeat. It was the last thing I expected walking into your hotel room that night."

"I know. I pushed too hard, too fast."

"Did you really expect me to agree?"

A sardonic laugh escaped him. "Yes. I was narcissistic enough, self-involved enough, to think just that. I was sure the overwhelming connection, the earth-shattering attraction I felt meant you had to feel it too. That it meant we belonged to each other. I never even considered you not wanting it."

Her eyes flickered with something he couldn't name. Was it regret? Agreement? Frustration?

He waited for her response, and when it never came, it made his chest ache. He tucked a dark strand of her hair behind her ear, and she swallowed hard, blue eyes meeting his gray ones with an intensity that made him burn from the inside out. His gaze dropped to her mouth, and it parted slightly, as if responding to a silent command. God, did he crave kissing her. He needed to feel the lightning and thunder that blew through him whenever they touched once more.

Her soft lips had always tasted just like she smelled, like coffee and vanilla, and they were merely a breath away. They could so easily be his once more. She watched as he slowly lowered his mouth. She didn't stop him, didn't tell him to back the hell away, and something unfurled in his soul—hope that he'd tried unsuccessfully to bury, and something deeper...something more. Emotions he couldn't even acknowledge to himself.

Just as their lips brushed against one another, the entire building shuddered and shook. It took Ronan longer than it should have to realize it wasn't from their bodies finally colliding.

Lights flickered, and a high-pitched squeal erupted.

Shock rolled through him that was mirrored on Adria's face. He whirled around, grabbed their bags, and threw them over his shoulder before reaching for her hand and pulling her out of the room. Their feet stumbled as the building rolled again. The entire building seemed to tremble.

As they hit the entryway, the chandelier above them swung dangerously, and Ronan pushed them against the wall, sliding along it to the exit. The front doors burst open, and Lennox and the other bodyguard who'd been on duty when they'd arrived raced in.

"We need to leave. Now!" Lennox commanded.

Adria yanked her hand from Ronan's and headed in the wrong direction.

He and Lennox both called her name, but she ignored them. "Dulce! *Dónde estás*?" she shouted.

They all hit the kitchen at the same time, where the Rojas housekeeper was standing, eyes fixed on the swaying drop lights.

"Dulce!" Adria said with relief. "We have to go!"

But the woman didn't budge, frozen in place as the alarms continued to shriek at them. Lennox grabbed the woman by the arm. "Let's go!" She jerked the housekeeper into the hall, and the older woman finally seemed to come to her senses, feet moving along with them as they fled back toward the front entry just as the wildly swinging chandelier let go. Instinctively, Ronan covered Adria with his body as it crashed to the ground, crystals flying like shrapnel. He winced as pain sliced through the back of his arm, but as soon as the layer of glass and metal settled, he was on the move again. Holding Adria's hand, he sprinted out the door after the two bodyguards and Dulce.

They flew into the emergency stairwell just as the building groaned again, and they all tilted into the brick wall. They'd only gotten down a flight before Dulce was panting, hand to her chest, and Ronan hoped she didn't have a heart attack. The blaring alarms were almost deafening, covering the sounds of their heavy breathing. Time seemed to slow and speed up all at the same time as they rounded the next flight.

More people poured into the emergency exit, and the lower they went, the more crowded it got, slowing them down. People were wide-eyed and worried, children were crying, but no one was talking. They moved in a weird, concerted effort, feet slamming along the cement as they tried to escape the building as quickly as possible.

He tightened his hold on Adria as the crush on the stairs kept threatening to pull him away. Their hands were clammy, bodies sweating, but there was no way he was letting her go. Not until they'd gotten out of this death trap. Not until he could be sure the whole thing wouldn't come tumbling down on them.

The sound of fire trucks and police sirens broke through the building alarms as they got closer to the ground floor. When they finally careened into the lobby, it was to find utter chaos. Residents poured from four different stairwells, some screaming and sobbing, most just rushing with children and pets toward the doors. Lennox led them outside, where emergency personnel directed them away from the building and farther down the block in case of a collapse.

As they merged with the sea of people streaming into the street, Ronan looked back at the building. An acidic black smoke billowed from the entrance to the underground garage. The gates hung awkwardly, torn off their hinges. The walls that had once held them were crumbled, rebar showing. It was like the images of bombings he'd seen on the news. Like being on a set of one of his father's films but with none of the safety precautions built in. It struck fear into his soul.

From the smoky hole that had been the garage, rescue workers emerged, hauling out several stretchers. Adria's feet stumbled next to him, and he realized she'd been looking at the scene as well. As they watched, an arm in a gray suit jacket fell off the side of the gurney, and then, she was using her entire force to pull away from him. Before he could stop her, she was running back toward the building, pushing against the crowd.

"Adria!" he hollered, following her, shoving his shoulders and elbows to make a path and receiving glares and complaints in return.

He barely heard Lennox as she commanded the other bodyguard to stay with Dulce, and then she was there beside him, fighting their way through the crowd to Adria.

"Adria, stop!" Lennox yelled.

But she didn't. She'd broken through the crush of bodies to where the firefighters were loading the stretchers into waiting ambulances and cried out, "*Papá!*"

Lennox lunged forward, grabbing Adria by the shoulders and forcing herself between Adria and the first responders. "Stay here, damn it. Let me check it out first."

She thrust Adria toward Ronan, and he wrapped his arms around her, pulling her against his chest. At first, Adria fought against his hold, and then she went still, body trembling as they watched Lennox approach the EMTs. It was then that Ronan noticed the watch peeking from the sleeve of his suit jacket. It was just like the one in the porn-worthy video.

"You don't want to see that, Star," he muttered in her ear.

"Fuck you. It's my dad. I need to be there."

"Let Lennox make sure."

But they both knew it was him. They'd just had an entire discussion about the damn watch.

Lennox whirled around, jogging back to them.

"They don't believe his injuries are life-threatening," Lennox told them, and Adria sank back into his chest. "I've got a vehicle coming to pick us up. We'll follow them to the hospital."

"I want to ride with him," Adria demanded.

"Let them do their job, Adria. Your dad's bodyguards... they're in worse shape. We'll meet them at the hospital."

Squealing tires had them jerking their eyes to a dark Escalade as it pulled up along the barricade the police had resurrected. Holden emerged from the passenger seat, stepping onto the running board and scanning the crowd. Lennox put her hand to her ear and said, "We're coming to you."

Then, she led the way through the chaos to the waiting vehicle with Ronan practically carrying Adria. She was trembling, shock and anger and fear rolling through her. Ronan cursed silently. He cursed Tatiana and GNVL because even though neither he nor Adria had said it, he was pretty sure they both knew the truth. This was exactly the threat Times had warned them about.

CHAPTER THIRTEEN

Adria

LOST AND FOUND
Performed by The Hall Effect

A dria was tucked up against Ronan in the Escalade as the SUV blew through lights and traffic in the wake of the ambulance taking her father to the hospital. He was alive. He was alive, but his bodyguards might not make it. *Jueputa!*

She was sick to her stomach. Thoughts of the CIA's warnings, the stupid video, and Tati's words filled her mind on repeat. A shiver ran through her, and she clamped her jaw tightly, trying once again to prevent tears from falling. What the hell had her sister done? How could she do this? It wasn't just her father who'd gotten hurt. An entire building full of people could have died.

It turned her blood to ice, shivers cascading through her.

Memories flooded her of their father's smile and the sound of his laugh. The joy he'd shown watching them tear through Christmas presents or galloping through the hills outside Cadencia on horseback. The affection she'd felt when he'd rubbed his knuckles through her hair or after he'd spent hours putting together her first drum kit. He was a good father. He hadn't always been there for them, even less so after their mom had moved permanently back to Colombia, but he'd shown his love and affection when he was there. He'd taken them to dinner to celebrate Vicente getting into Cal Tech, and he'd taken Tati to Hawaii for graduation. He'd sent Adria an enormous bouquet and a diamond tennis bracelet when the Daisies had won their Grammy. He cared. He loved them. He just showed it in ways that had left gaps in their childhood.

But that wasn't a reason to take his life. To take others' lives.

Acid burned her throat. The sour taste was as bitter and harsh as her feelings.

The driver pulled up in front of the ER where the ambulances had already unloaded. Holden and Lennox exited the car first, scanning the parking lot before pulling open the back so first Ronan and then Adria could slide out. Holden talked to the staff at the front desk, and they were directed to a waiting room that made both Lennox and Holden side-eye each other. There were too many people. Adria paced the hall, desperately needing to see her dad.

An army of men in suits joined her and her detail. These were all her father's men. They spoke quietly to the hospital staff, who had them wait along with Adria.

It felt like an eternity before they were allowed to go back to see him in one of the curtained-off sections of the ER. As soon as her eyes met her father's, the tears she'd been holding back broke free, relief and horror blending together. She was at his side, head pressed to his chest in a flash. His arm, skinny and so much smaller than the brawny one that used to surround her, draped over her shoulder, patting it.

"I'm okay, *mija*."

Adria stood back up, grabbing his hand and squeezing it as she assessed the damage for herself. His gaunt face had a slash down the side of it, and his left arm was wrapped from elbow to wrist. He was covered with dust and debris that made his black hair look gray. Someone had tried to clean it from his face, but it had only added streaks, making his face look even more haunted than ever before.

Her father turned to the sea of bodyguards behind them, asking, "Can you find out about Jorge and the others?"

One of the men headed for the nurse's station.

"What happened?" Adria asked.

"Backpack. Someone left it on the trunk of the car next to my parking spot. Jorge saw it, went to move it, and the next thing I knew, Miguel and Eduardo were throwing me to the ground as the entire world exploded around us."

Adria swallowed hard, eyes fluttering shut and then opening again to find Ronan watching her. She knew he was thinking the same things she was about Tati and GNVL. Knew he was waiting to see what she'd tell her father. The thought filled her with dread. What the hell had Tati done?

The bodyguard who'd left came back. "Jorge didn't make it. Miguel is in surgery, but it doesn't look good, and they're removing shrapnel from Eduardo's back. They believe he'll recover."

Her dad closed his eyes, a pained expression on his face. Adria squeezed his hand, hoping to give him some strength even though she felt like she barely had any to give. When his gaze opened again, his pale-blue eyes held a bit of his old spark and determination. "I want them found, Gregory. All of them. I want them to pay."

Adria's heart plummeted to her stomach, and sweat broke out along her neck.

"Excuse me," an attendant said, coming into the room. "We need to take Mr. Rojas in for X-rays. After, we'll be moving him into a private room. You can ask at the front, and they'll give you the number."

Adria leaned in and kissed her father's forehead. "I'll see you in a few minutes."

The crowd of people followed her out while a single guard remained with her father, and Adria suddenly felt claustrophobic. Too many bodies. Too many people hovering. The box closing in...darkness. As they passed a single-stall restroom, Adria opened the door, muttering, "I'll be just a moment."

She stepped inside, the smell of bleach overpowering the normal antiseptic scent that seemed to cling to all hospitals. She braced herself against the sink, looking in the mirror. Her hair had been sweaty from rehearsal, and now it was wild from the race down the stairwell and out of the building. Her eyes looked almost as bad as her father's—haunted and grim.

She splashed water on her face and washed her hands. They were shaking so bad it was hard to even do these simple tasks. What did she do now? Why had her sister put her in this position? What would Papá do when he found out Tati was behind it?

I need to know whose side you're on.

Everything was so fucked up...

More damn tears slid down her cheeks, and she brushed at them furiously. She could barely breathe her chest and lungs were so tight.

A knock on the door. "Star, your phone is ringing. It's Fee."

Ronan's voice was deep and dark and somehow soothing. Her heart tripped over the nickname she'd once loved, then forbade him to use, and now it felt like a saving grace. How was it, out of everything that had happened, he seemed like the only stable thing? If anyone had asked her a week ago—hell, four days ago—if she'd ever see Ronan Hawk as being the one to ground her, she would have laughed and then scorched them with a seething retort.

And yet, here he was, stabilizing her with just his damn voice through the door.

He'd called her a chicken. And she had been. She'd run. She'd put up every damn wall she could, and he'd just continued to crash through them. What he'd said tonight, about never having read the NDA, apologizing for so much more than a piece of paper...it just proved all over again that it wasn't really him who was the untrustworthy one. It was her. She didn't know how to do this. Couldn't do this.

If he'd died today...because of her screwed-up family...

It made her stomach rebel all over again.

Another knock. "Adria?"

It was a warning that screamed, *I'm going to burst through this door if you don't answer me.* While it should have pissed her off, all it really did was make her feel safe. Secure, in a way not even her bodyguards ever truly made her feel.

She opened the door to find him with his hand reaching for the handle.

His eyes were dark and turbulent again. He looked her over from top to bottom and back. Then, he handed her the phone that had been in her bag with the blue marguerite daisy stitched on it. She hadn't even noticed he'd had the foresight to grab their bags before they'd scrambled from the penthouse.

"I'm okay, Fee," Adria said as she answered it.

"Adria! Thank Jesus, Joseph, and Mary! What happened?" Her friend's voice was breathless, panicked. How many times had they all been this way just this year? It was as if the trauma that had bled into their lives that night at the side of Swan River Pond hadn't ever gone away. Instead, it had grown into a flowing river, with riptides ready to take them under at every turn.

"Someone left a bomb for my dad." She saw Ronan's jaw twitch as she said the words, his steely eyes meeting hers again.

"Feck," Fiadh said. "Is he...?"

"He's alive and awake. Minor cuts. They took him to X-ray, but I think he's going to be okay. But his detail...one of them didn't make it. Two others are in surgery," Adria said.

Voices chattered behind Fiadh where the other Daisies were demanding to know what was going on. Adria was surprised Leya hadn't already gotten an update from Holden, and it increased her respect for the man that he'd let her be the one to tell them what had happened.

"Look, I need to go. But I'll call you later."

"Paise wants to know if you'd like to postpone the concert," Fee said.

She couldn't even get her head around what was happening this minute let alone tomorrow. "I don't think so. I don't know. I can't even think clearly."

"Go be with your dad. Call us later. We love you, Ads."

She hung up, and a text chimed immediately.

NIKKI: Does this have anything to do with what we were talking about this morning?

Yes. But she couldn't say that because she didn't have the proof. In all honesty, she wasn't sure she wanted the proof. It would require her to do something. Say something. It would require her to turn on a sister she loved with all her soul.

ADRIA: I don't know.

NIKKI: Do you want me to come to the hospital?

She did, and she didn't. If Nikki was here, it would just be one more person who might discover what was really going on, and she couldn't risk it.

ADRIA: Ronan and Lennox are here. I'm okay.

NIKKI: Ronan was there? When the bomb went off?

She didn't have the energy to explain or answer, so she just shoved her phone in her back pocket. She went to push past where Ronan was leaning against the doorframe when she saw a trail of blood on the back of his arm.

"You're bleeding!" She reached for him as guilt rolled through her.

Ronan looked down, surprised. He twisted his arm to look at the back where a gash ran down from the sleeve of his shirt almost to his elbow.

"It's just a scratch," he grunted.

Adria turned to Lennox. "We need to see if this needs stitches."

Ronan put his hand over hers. "Adria, it's just a scratch." Their gazes locked. "Let's go see about your dad."

She rubbed her scar, wishing again for her drumsticks, anything to keep her hands busy. She nodded and let

Lennox and the others lead her back to the waiting room while one of the detail asked about her father's room. They were told they had a few more minutes to wait before they got him into his room.

Adria turned to one of her dad's detail and asked, "Where's Dulce? Do you know if she's okay?"

"She asked to be taken directly to the airport. She wanted to go be with her kids in California."

Why did that stab at her? Another person who couldn't stay. Who had other places to be. Adria sent Dulce a text, knowing she wouldn't get it if she was in the air but needing to apologize for what had happened. Adria let her know that they would give her whatever she needed. Money. Time. Escape from them. She didn't say the last part, but she meant it. She hoped Dulce knew it without her having to say it.

Trouble seemed to hover around them like a cloud. Papá had almost died! What would Mama do? What would any of them do? *Dios*! She needed to call her brother and her mother. She didn't want them to hear about this from anyone else.

She stepped to the side of the waiting room and hit Vicente's name in her contact list. When he picked up, she asked him to go find Mama so she could talk to them both. He hesitated, hearing the panic in what she wasn't saying, but did as she asked. Adria's voice was tight as she explained what had happened. If she'd ever doubted the love her mother felt for their father, the tortured cry Mama let out would forever prove her wrong. The sound rattled through Adria, scratching at her strung nerves, drawing them tighter until they might burst.

"I'll have the jet fueled. We can be there by morning," Vicente said.

"Wait until I have a chance to talk to Papá at least. I don't know what he's going to want to do," Adria said.

"Why the hell is this happening to us?" Vicente said, his voice full of frustration, sounding so much like their father's.

She swallowed hard, knowing she had to come clean, knowing she had to tell him. But she was afraid of what would happen when she did. He'd be so angry—with her and Tati. He'd feel betrayed, and rightly so, but she couldn't tell him like this, over the phone with people streaming around her. She'd tell him when she got to Colombia and hope by then she'd have more information...so she could say for sure their sister had or hadn't been involved.

"We'll figure it out," she said softly, hoping it was true. "I'll be there the day after tomorrow, and we'll figure it out together."

Going to Colombia seemed...dangerous. But maybe if their father was here and they were there, it would be okay. Or maybe it would be worse? She didn't think she wanted him alone in Texas with her sister hunting him. It seemed unreal. A ridiculous nightmare she was sure to wake up from eventually.

Finally, they were directed to her dad's hospital room, but when they got there, he was asleep. The nurse said it was just the pain meds they'd given him having kicked in, but Adria's heart still banged angrily in her chest. Fear. So much fear.

She scooted down in the chair next to the bed, resting her head on the back as she tried to decide exactly what she would tell him when he woke. She turned to look at Ronan who was half-sitting on the arm of a loveseat shoved against the wall. "You should go back to the hotel and get some rest. There's nothing you can do here."

"I'm not leaving you," he growled.

Her eyes darted to the door. Lennox and Holden stood just outside in deep discussion, plans being made without her say or input. Sometimes, she wondered if she'd ever have control of her life again.

"I have them," she said with a chin nod to the bodyguards.

Ronan closed the distance, squatting down so his eyes were level with hers in the chair. "This has nothing to do with keeping you safe physically and everything to do with the fact your father just barely survived a bomb attack instigated by—"

"Don't say it." Her eyes darted to the people outside the room. Her dad's detail. Hers.

"The authorities are going to come asking, and you know what the CIA will say."

"They still have to prove it," Adria told him. She didn't know why she was protecting Tatiana. Maybe because her sister had always been the first one to defend them, and it seemed only right they shield her as well.

She closed her eyes. A hand fluttered along her cheek, and then he was moving away, giving her space as if he inexplicably knew that was exactly what she needed in order to pull herself together.

"I'm going to get something to drink, for both of us, but I'll be right back," he told her. It wasn't until he called her name from by the door that she finally met his gaze. There was a look on his face that was a combination of fear and regret and hope she wasn't sure she could handle. "I'll be right back," he said.

When she didn't respond, he turned and left, and her heart tugged.

Her father moaned, twisting in his drug-induced sleep. "*Mija!*" his voice cried out in the throes of a nightmare before his eyes popped open. They looked troubled...scared. Then, they landed on Adria, and it wasn't relief but tortured guilt she saw travel over his face.

"I'm here, Papá."

She grabbed his hand, thinking how pale he looked, like a ghost, and his next words sent shivers over her spine as if she'd seen one too. "I see her, Adria. Since January, I see her all the time. In a crowd. In the reflection on a building. Sometimes even in the house. But when I turn, she's gone."

Adria's heart skittered. Was he actually seeing her real sister or a mirage? Before this week, she would have said it was a figment of his imagination, but now... *Dios*, maybe her sister was purposefully haunting him as a means of breaking him. It made her chest ache as she realized this was why he'd wilted away this year. Sorrow filled her. Then, she thought of her mother's tortured cry just now and the ugly, disgusting video, and it made her stomach ache as bad as her chest.

Who was right? Who was wrong? What the hell had happened?

Did she just ask? Did she tell him the truth?

"Papá—"

"Ms. Rojas," a deep voice said from the door, and Adria turned to see CIA Operative Times standing there. He looked just as he had the night before, as if he was a sales-man, briefcase and all. "Could I have a word?"

She looked back at her father and squeezed his hand. "I'll be right back."

His eyes were already drooping again.

He looked like such a pale version of the father she'd known.

A shadow.

She heard Tati's voice from The Attic in her head all over

again. *There is a price he must pay. Justice will be served.* Would she consider this enough? Would it be done? Or would she never be satisfied until he was completely destroyed? Until even the shadow that remained of their father had all but disappeared?

CHAPTER FOURTEEN

Ronan

THIS IS ME TRYING
Performed by Taylor Swift

As Ronan got out of the elevator, he saw Adria walking down the hall with Warren Times. His pulse raced, and he jogged to catch up. Adria looked up at him with a hint of relief, but Times's jaw twitched. Ronan tossed the two water bottles he'd picked up into his backpack and followed them into an empty patient room. Times shut the door behind them. It was dark in the room with only a single reading light above one of the beds turned on. Everything else was in shadows.

"Do you know if there was anyone else injured?" she asked him.

Times stared so long at her that it made Ronan uncomfortable.

"Luckily, the garage seems to have been empty except for your father and his detail. The main extent of the damage was to the parking area and the maintenance rooms above where the explosion occurred. A thorough inspection will have to be done to see if the building is safe, but the bomb was relatively insignificant."

"My father's bodyguard died. Two others may not make it. That's hardly insignificant." Her voice was icy, and Ronan's chest filled with pride. If Times expected her to fall at his feet, begging for his help because of this, he was going to be in for a shock.

"In light of what happened," he said dryly, "we wanted to remind you not to tell anyone about your sister."

"What?" Adria breathed out just as Ronan snapped, "Fuck that."

Times scowled. "The FBI and ATF will conduct investigations alongside the local authorities. We need them to be unbiased. We can't afford for their evidence to be colored by our operation in case it isn't GNVL."

"That's ridiculous!" Ronan scoffed.

Times ignored him, focusing his stare one hundred percent on Adria.

"Has she been in contact since last night?" Times asked. Adria visibly paled, and Times was quick to notice it. "Did she set up another meet?"

Adria looked away and shook her head.

"What did the note say? How was it delivered and where?" he pressed.

Ronan couldn't stand it anymore. "Back off. Can't you see she's been through enough already?"

A tense silence settled down between them.

When Adria didn't respond, Times pressed, "She's not the person in charge, Ms. Rojas. She's following commands. We're willing to offer her immunity if she gives up the people above her."

Adria snorted and then turned away from him, walking to the window in the room and adjusting the blinds to look out at the dark sky. "Do you know what my sister's IQ is, Mr. Times?"

"One-sixty-five," he said, and she glanced over at him, surprised. "Just like I know yours is one-forty."

Ronan's gut tightened. He'd known Adria was smart. Smart enough to skip a grade and graduate with Landry and the others when she was a year younger than them, but he hadn't known she was pretty much a genius.

"Being smart doesn't mean she's the one in charge. That just means the leader knows how to manipulate her," Times said when Adria hadn't responded.

"My sister isn't a follower. She never minded being on the outside. Almost preferred it. But she loved us all with a fierceness you've never encountered in your life. That's what makes it hard for me to believe she's behind this."

"Who else would be coming after your father?" he asked.

"Big oil. They hate that he's spreading green energy in oil-rich countries."

"They do hate him and what he stands for, but they aren't the ones behind this," Times insisted.

"How can you be so sure?" she asked, eyes shimmering in the darkness.

"He'd be dead. They would just send an assassin."

Ronan and Adria both looked at him with shock on their face. He shrugged. "They don't have a message to send. They just see him as a roadblock to be removed. Terrorists, protest groups...they want their message heard." When neither of them responded, Times continued, "We want you to meet with her again. We want you to set it up and allow us, at a minimum, to listen in and perhaps detain her."

Adria's finger rubbed at the space between her brows

with a shaky hand. "Even if she was going to meet with me again, it wouldn't be until Cadencia, and I don't know if I can do this... She's my sister!"

"Even if she was responsible for your friend's death?"

"Are you saying Tatiana killed Landry?!" Adria was back across the room in two strides, shaking now with fury instead of fear and frustration.

"Let's say, for the sake of argument, that GNVL goes to snatch you up. They find Landry on the shore, think she's you, grab her, and then she sees your sister or something that ties your sister to them... But by now they've realized their mistake, and..." he trailed off with a cold shrug.

"No! She wouldn't have killed Landry!"

"But she tried to kill your father today."

"You don't know that!" Adria all but screamed. Ronan was at her side, pulling her into his arms for what felt like the millionth time in several days. She buried her face in the crook of his neck, clutching his T-shirt in her hands.

Ronan glared over her head at Times, growling, "We're done. Get out."

"We need your help, Ms. Rojas. If you want your sister to live... If you don't want her to be collateral damage when the Colombian National Intelligence Directorate decides they've had enough and just takes out the entire organization, you don't have another option but to trust me."

Adria was trembling uncontrollably, and Ronan felt like hitting the man.

Times had a hand on the door before he turned back. "That number I gave you. It's available twenty-four seven, and I'll personally be in Cadencia with you."

Then, he was gone.

Ronan tightened his hold on her. Wetness hit his neck,

and he realized she was crying again. Strong and fierce and being shredded by circumstances. He hated it. He wanted the fierce, almost arrogant, Adria he knew. God, even at eighteen she'd been that way, commanding a room with her presence.

He rubbed her back, trying to give her even the slightest bit of comfort.

"Papá won't stop...not until he finds out who did this. And what happens when it's her?" she spoke between deep breaths as she corralled her emotions once again.

He put a hand to her chin, lifting it, searching her eyes. "Do you believe she did this?"

"I don't know..." She swallowed. "That woman who showed up at The Attic... She looked like Tati...had her mannerisms and her smile and her voice...but it wasn't my sister. Would Tati defend Mama and our country? Yes, absolutely! Would she be cruel to me to do it? Would she kill someone?" Adria shook her head. "I don't... I can't..."

He moved his hands to massage her shoulders, trying to ease the tension radiating from her.

"And Lan... He's wrong about Landry, right?" Her voice and her eyes begged him to agree with her.

And the worst part was, he couldn't. The scenario that Times had laid out could have been exactly what went down. Whoever was working with Tatiana could have come for Adria, and once they'd realized their mistake, and Landry had seen enough to identify them, they could have killed her. Someone comfortable with a knife and the human body had done it. While Tati might have had enough medical training to do it, Landry hadn't been some weak little thing, and he had to believe Tatiana herself wouldn't have been able to kill Landry without there being more of a struggle. The authorities had found nothing of the sort. Landry had no defensive wounds. It had happened too quickly.

"I don't think Tatiana killed Landry," Ronan said because he could say that much with honesty.

"But it could have been GNVL?"

"I don't know, Star. Maybe it was big oil. Maybe they thought killing you would be enough to derail your father and not draw an eye to them directly. Maybe it was GNVL. Maybe it was someone we don't even know about yet. They're still trying to find Angel Carter and determine his involvement. He has a knack for showing up at the worst times for the Daisies, so who knows."

She pushed away from him. "I want to go back to Papá."

He reluctantly let his arms drop away, and she stepped out of his embrace. She was at the door when she stilled, looking back at him. "Thank you," she said softly.

"I haven't done anything."

"Shy isn't your style," she said with a small twist of her lips that went straight to his heart. She remembered the words he'd said to her that night. The fact she did gave him another boost of encouragement he hoped wouldn't end up breaking him.

"I'm in this with you. I mean that. Whatever it takes, for however long it takes."

"You need to go back to LA and the studio. That's what Asher expects. I'll be on my way to Cadencia after the concert."

She was right. The last thing he needed was an unscheduled trip to Colombia. He needed to get back to LA and the pile of work waiting for him. He had a career that was just taking off and would only take a nudge to fall off a cliff. Worse, Asher and his dad were counting on him, and they were men he respected and would hate to let down. But then he looked at her—wide-eyed, shoulders back, the brief breakdown she'd had shoved away again—and he knew the truth. He couldn't leave her. It wasn't just about her. It was about him and the lifetime of regrets he already carried with him.

"I'm going with you," he said with not a hint of hesitation.

"Ronan—"

He crossed the room, hands going to her biceps and giving her the slightest of shakes. "*Ni una palabra más, cariño.* There's no way in hell I'm letting you deal with this on your own."

He wasn't sure why he'd used his poor Spanish or the term of endearment. Maybe to snap her out of it. Maybe to reach her on a different level, using her first language.

"Why? I've dealt with my sister and Landry and everything that's happened to the Daisies on my own, Ronan. So why now?" she challenged him.

He inhaled. What he wouldn't have given to have been there with her through all of it. His stupidity had made sure he couldn't. Instead of saying that, he asked, "Did you know Landry was helping me figure out a way to make it up to you?" Surprise washed over her face. "I told her the truth. I told her it was costing me a piece of my soul every damn day to be without you, and for whatever reason, known only to her, she believed me. She helped me concoct a grand gesture. That night...it was supposed to happen down by the pond. It's why I was late. She'd told me to go buy as many bouquets as I could find, and I'd spent the entire afternoon scouring every store and flower shop I could find for daisies. The van was filled with them."

His throat bobbed, thinking back to that night. The smell of the flowers that had filled the damn car. The rich, heady scent mixing in with the heat and humidity. The film crew had thought he'd lost touch with reality.

"When we arrived at the farmhouse and found out... God, all I could think was that if I hadn't stopped at the last grocery store to buy one more bouquet, I would have been there in time."

Her hand went to her stomach, pushing into it as if his words had wounded her. "I... What am I supposed to say to that?"

He shook his head. "Nothing. Just know that my life has been full of regrets when it comes to the Daisies. Landry... Paisley... You. So, the last thing I'm going to do right now is walk away. I'd never be able to live with myself if I did."

She did the last thing he expected. She fisted his T-shirt, leaned in, and kissed him. Fiercely. As if she hated what she was doing but couldn't help herself. And as soon as her soft mouth was pressed against his, the dam inside him broke, years of tortured longing escaping. He backed her into the door and devoured her, hands digging into her hips, pushing his tongue beyond her sweet lips, and groaning as the taste of her hit him. He was instantly hard, muscles coiled from top to bottom, ready to throw her down on the hospital bed, rip off her clothes, and remind her of just what he was capable of doing to her. Remind her of the screams and moans he'd brought out with his fingers and his tongue.

Her hands moved to his neck, nails biting into the skin. His palms slid under her shirt, gliding up until he could feel her taut peaks through a thin lace bra. He ran a finger and then a thumb over them, pinching, and she gasped in a way that did nothing but make him harder. He groaned, plunging his tongue deeper into her mouth, shifting so he could find every corner. She met every lap and lick with as much force as he gave.

He burned. His chest, his lungs, his insides. She rocked her hips into his, and he almost combusted. Almost lost it right there.

Laughter on the other side of the door from the nurses' station brought him back to where they were. To the anti-septic smell, the beeping of machines, and the fact her father lay two doors over, wounded. He pulled back but didn't let her go. He dropped his hands to her waist again, eyes meeting hers in the darkness, and he knew all over again that he was lost. Gone. There was never going to be anyone else in his life who would ever be able to do to him what she did. Adria Rojas was his future whether she was at his side or not.

CHAPTER FIFTEEN

Adria

STUPID GIRL
Performed by Garbage

Adria's eyes met Ronan's in the darkness, and her pulse fluttered at the lust in his gaze. Her breath was coming in small pants as she stroked the soft bristles of his beard. Her chin and cheeks felt slightly raw from them, and her body clenched tightly, remembering the way the rasp had felt on other body parts. Remembering the things his tongue and his teeth and his fingers had done to her repeatedly in the past. The way he, and only he, had ever shattered her and then put her back together.

Like he was right now. Not only carefully holding her broken parts but binding them together as if he was the glue she'd been seeking all along. And maybe he was. Maybe there would never be another person who could weld her together as he did.

Ronan Hawk was a narcissist. The world knew it. He

even admitted it. So this, right now, fit what he needed. Wanted. But what he'd told her...about Lan...about his regrets...about losing pieces of himself the longer he went without her... How could she push him away after that? Why would she want to?

She thought about her parents, the love they had and the miles that were between them. She'd been afraid of ending up like them, but what was to say that they would? Even as she thought it, she knew the truth. He'd want her to live in LA with him. But just like her mother, she now had professional and personal ties to Colombia that she didn't want to sever. If they were together, she'd end up hurting him as she flitted in and out like her parents had.

Worse, the even more horrific thought, was the one she'd had earlier. What if he got physically hurt if Tatiana came after them? He already had a bloody cut on his arm because of her and a scar over his eye from Albany.

She slid a lid over that thought, trying to regain some composure. To put up a flimsy wall Ronan could easily tear down, but he might recognize as what she needed to keep her shit together.

His hands dropped away, and the loss of his heat made her shiver.

He took another step back, and then she could only feel the energy that wafted between them and no longer his actual physical presence.

When she opened her eyes, she expected to find him watching her, but instead, she caught his profile. Jaw tense, nostrils flared. He was trying to regain his self-control as much as she was.

She should push him away. She should demand he leave her alone—if for nothing else, than to keep him safe. But she didn't know if she had the strength. She was so damn tired of being strong. How much could one soul bend before it broke completely?

She felt caught. Enclosed. Like she was in a damn box.

Stuck...unable to get out.

The wood was cold against her palms.

Lately, when she had the dream, instead of her being stuck in the box, it was Tatiana. But she still felt it as if it was her—the wood jammed up against each shoulder, touching her forehead when she leaned up, the sound of her fists pounding it, and her sobs as she cried for help. She could hear laughter just beyond the crate. Male laughter and a rat-a-tat-tat of a tapping along the box. A tease. A taunt. An incessant, unforgiving sound that was almost as bad as being in the box itself.

It was only a nightmare. It had always just been a dream, and yet, at the moment, she felt like she could almost grasp the image and sounds like an old memory resurfacing. What if, like she'd thought earlier, it had really happened? She shook her head. Whenever she'd had the nightmare, everyone had insisted it was just a dream. Vicente and Tati would squeeze into her bed, holding her, making sure she wasn't alone. On the rare occasion it happened when one of her parents was around, they'd sit up with her, watching movies until she fell asleep with her head in their lap.

Her head throbbed, the blood pounding in her ears as more panic settled over her.

She needed out. She needed air.

She threw open the hospital door and practically ran toward the elevator. She knew Ronan was following her even before she heard the squeak of his sneakers on the linoleum flooring. She heard Holden's deep voice asking what was wrong as she frantically pushed the down button.

"I just need to take a walk," she said, and her voice

sounded nothing like hers. It was shaky and unsure and weak. So damn weak.

"What did you do?" Holden demanded, and she looked up with a start to see him glaring at Ronan, whose jaw clenched tight in response.

"He didn't... It's not..." She inhaled deeply, trying to still her chattering nerves. "It's fine, Holden. It isn't Ronan. I just need to get some air. Put my head on straight."

The two men were still locked in some kind of staring contest.

"Really," Adria said, putting her hand on Holden's arm.

Lennox stalked down the hall from the bathroom. "I leave for two minutes! Two minutes, and you're already pissing her off?" Her bodyguard was also in Ronan's face.

"Stop!" Adria shouted, and the nurses glared in their direction, but it made the other three finally look at her. "I don't need this right now. I need to calm my nerves before I go back in and see my father. Ronan didn't do anything!"

She wanted to be alone. She wanted to peel back her thoughts and emotions and find the truth about everything around her, and she didn't think she could do that with any of them hovering, but she also knew none of them were going to allow her to go anywhere by herself. Not after today. Not after everything the band had been through.

The elevator dinged open, Adria stepped inside, and then she turned to put her hand out to the others. "Just Lennox."

Ronan looked hurt and angry. He'd just told her he wasn't leaving her, wasn't going back to LA at all, and now she was basically thrusting him away. She softened the blow by asking, "Can you stay with Papá for me? I won't be long. I promise."

His eyes narrowed, taking her in for way too long, and

then he gave a curt nod because he knew her, knew she had a trembling wall to resurrect and that this was her way of doing it. But maybe he also knew she'd be back for him. That thought squeezed her heart tight.

He turned on his heel and walked toward her father's room. She stepped farther into the elevator, and Lennox joined her without a word.

When the doors shut, she lost her breath again, the contained space bringing it all back. The box. The pounding. The need to get out. Once, the band's set designer had wanted them to emerge from a trap door in the stage using a tiny black elevator. She'd adamantly refused, and the band had moved on to other ideas.

She closed her eyes, inhaling and exhaling, thinking of the yoga meditations Leya had tried to get her to do. They weren't really Adria's thing. She much preferred a boxing bag she could beat the shit out of with her hands and her feet, or a road she could eat up miles on.

When the elevator slid open, she almost ran through the lobby to the doors. Outside, the brisk air hit her immediately, a shock to her system she urgently needed. She inhaled deeply, breathing in the scent of the city. Car exhaust from the busy street. Fast food from the restaurants on the other side of the block. The dank smell of asphalt as it cooled. She looked around, unsure where to go.

"There's a park just across the street," her bodyguard said. "I'm not crazy about going there at night, but it might be quiet."

Adria nodded, and Lennox led her down the sidewalk. They wove through the hospital parking lot and crossed the street to where a paved path wound through a small park not more than a block in width. The lampposts were tangled up in tree branches, deepening the shadows. The scent of pine and flowers along with fresh-cut grass hid the smells of the city. There was a dampness to the air that brought a rush of goosebumps to her skin. The temperature had dropped considerably, and she had on nothing but a T-shirt.

Her stomach flipped, thinking of the harrowing trip down the emergency stairs. The horror and fear she'd felt when she'd realized it was her father on the stretcher they'd pulled from the wreckage. What the hell was she going to do?

Her phone buzzed with an incoming text tone. She almost ignored it. She had come outside to be alone. To think. To clear some of the weight that was threatening to break her soul in half. But she didn't want anyone to worry about her either, so she pulled the phone from her pocket.

BLOCKED: I can't believe you ran to him. How can you care what happens to him after what I showed you?

Adria's heart pounded furiously.

ADRIA: Please tell me this wasn't you. That Jorge isn't dead because of you.

BLOCKED: Casualties of war, Ads.

Adria shivered, feet stalling completely. Lennox kept walking, not realizing Adria had stopped.

ADRIA: The sister I grew up with wanted to save lives! What happened to you? What did they do to you?

BLOCKED: I had my eyes ripped open. By that video. By the truth. What he's done to Mama and Colombia. I hate that you've chosen his side.

Adria's hand shook, and she swallowed hard.

ADRIA: I haven't chosen any side. I just need more than what you gave me. I'm not as easily swayed.

BLOCKED: You think it was easy for me to believe the worst of our father? You think any of this is easy?

ADRIA: I don't know anything about you anymore.

BLOCKED: When that asswipe came for Vicente, who took the hit? This is me taking the hit for the right reasons.

Tatiana had landed on her butt when she'd stepped between Vicente and a bullying jock in high school. She'd had a bruise on her cheek that had lasted for weeks. Vicente had been furious that she'd gotten in the middle of it, but they all knew he wouldn't have hit back. He didn't believe in violence. So, Tatiana had taken the swing that had broken the jock's nose.

They'd both been suspended.

Adria had never been sure any of them had been right—the jock, Tati, or Vicente. It was the same dilemma all over again with much steeper consequences. Wasn't there another way?

ADRIA: I need more than a faceless image on a sex video.

BLOCKED: I'll see you in Cadencia.

ADRIA: Where?

There was no response. Not even after Adria caught up to Lennox, walked completely around the small park, and headed back toward the hospital. She'd come for fresh air and perspective, and she'd gained nothing. Frustration brewed inside her that turned into anger.

"If we don't know everything that's going on, we can't protect you," Lennox said softly as they neared the parking lot of the hospital.

Adria glanced at her and away. "What do you mean?"

Lennox huffed. "Please don't act like I'm stupid. It does neither of us credit. Ever since Arlington, you've been uptight and upset. You've let Hawk in, whereas you hated him with enough force it vibrated out of you before. Now this. The only way I can help you, keep you safe, is if I know what's going on."

Adria knew it was the truth.

"The man at the hospital with the briefcase..." Lennox continued. "He's got the stench of a government operative all over him. I've seen enough of them to know. What did he want? Do they know who did this?"

Adria warred with herself, then she stopped, meeting Lennox's hazel eyes. "If I tell you, you can't tell the rest of the detail. Not Holden. None of the Daisies. Just you."

Lennox frowned. "I don't know if I can agree to those terms. If I need to bring in more people, they'll need to be apprised of the situation."

Adria turned away and kept going. "Then, I can't tell you."

Lennox pulled her to a stop. "Adria. Be reasonable."

"I am, Lennox—as much as I can be, given the circumstances. It's you and no one else, or no one at all."

"Except Hawk. Because you can really trust him." Her bodyguard's voice was full of scorn.

"He's the one who figured it out first and told me."

"Figured out what?"

Adria stalked toward the hospital with her mouth clamped tight. She couldn't afford to tell her more unless Lennox agreed to keep it to herself. She couldn't have this blowing back on more people. As it was, she wasn't even sure the band should go to Colombia. What if she brought this to their feet even more than she already had? What if what had happened to Landry...her dad...happened to her friends?

No. She refused to let that happen. She just had to figure out what to do next. The problem was, she was so emotionally and physically exhausted she couldn't think clearly. She needed rest. A reprieve. Time she didn't have if she was going to stop Tati before she hurt anyone else.

CHAPTER SIXTEEN

Ronan

BEFORE I GO TO SLEEP
Performed by The Mills

When Adria walked back into the hospital room, she looked worse than when she'd walked out, and Ronan's chest tightened for the millionth time in just a few days. He might just become a petrified piece of wood soon, frozen in an adrenaline state from which there was no recovery.

She didn't say anything, just went and sat at her father's side. For another hour, they both watched as he slept, looking pale and worn. The doctors were keeping him overnight at a minimum—maybe longer. There was nothing Adria could do for him here tonight, but she was exhausted and needed sleep almost as much as her dad did.

Ronan rose from the chair at her side and pulled her hand into his. "Let's go, Star. You can't do anything else for him tonight."

Her face turned squinty. "Don't tell me what to do, Hollywood."

"I'm not telling you. You know it's the truth. If you expect to be able to perform tomorrow, you need to spend at least a few hours in bed."

Her gaze fell to his lips, and his entire body reacted, electricity coursing through him, but he put a damper on it. He was good at tamping it down. As much as that one kiss had broken open the dams, he also knew he couldn't push past that yet. He had to let her drive the pace of whatever this was blooming again between them, or he'd lose her forever.

She stood up, leaned over to brush her father's hair aside and place a kiss on his forehead, and then headed for the door. Outside the room, she turned to her father's bodyguard, and said, "I want to know if anything changes. With Papá or with any of his men."

"We'll let you know, Ms. Rojas."

When they got to the hotel and the room Zia had arranged for her, a cavalcade of bodyguards waited outside, and Ronan groaned because it meant her friends were waiting for her. Nikki, Leya, and Paisley jumped up from their seats as Adria and Ronan entered the room, hugging her fiercely without a word. The shimmer of black hair and lean bodies only served to remind Ronan of the conversation with Times and Adria about Landry's mistaken identity—how alike they all were when you saw them from behind.

He leaned against a far wall and watched, hoping he could remain invisible until they'd all left, so he could talk to Adria alone again.

"We'll go shopping tomorrow before the concert," Leya said. "Get you some new clothes, but Nikki and I put a few things of ours in the closet for you."

"Thanks," Adria said, sniffing and then extracting herself from their embrace.

Paisley played with her worry ring as she assessed her friend, and her brown eyes flashed with concern. "Do you want to postpone the concert?"

"No."

The door burst open, and Fee stomped in with Asher right behind her. She flung her arms around Adria. "Ads!"

They clung to each other for a second before Fiadh stepped back to look her over just as Paisley had done. She saw what Ronan did but didn't hesitate to say it. "You look tired. Exhausted. We should cancel the show."

Asher's jaw ticked as his eyes met Ronan's over the heads of the Daisies, questions swimming there that Ronan wouldn't be able to answer if his friend asked them aloud.

"No. I just told Paisley I want to do it. It'll keep my mind busy." She looked at Asher. "What's the press saying?"

"Not much. The authorities are keeping a lid on it as part of their ongoing investigation. They've listed one fatality and several injuries, but they haven't announced a target. Are you sure the bomb was left for your dad?" Asher asked.

"Yes," Adria said with a surety that surprised even Ronan, especially given the talk with Times.

"We'll keep an eye on it and cancel the interviews after the concert. With us leaving for Colombia the day after tomorrow, there'll be less likelihood of the media tying it to you even if the Rojas name is mentioned," Asher told her.

The room was silent. Nikki rubbed her temple, Leya played with her bracelets, and Fee scowled while Asher's face remained concerned. Ronan remembered a line from Seneca that said humanity suffers more in imagination than they ever do in reality, and he hoped that wasn't true for these women. Because the visible, real grief they'd lived through was already more than anyone should have had to experience.

"Try to get some sleep," Paisley told Adria. "You can change your mind in the morning if you need to."

Ronan could practically hear Asher groaning because canceling a concert at the last minute wasn't a small thing to accomplish, but he knew Adria well enough to know she wasn't going to. She'd play even if she had cracked ribs and broken fingers.

The band filed out, and Adria headed for the restroom, but Ronan remained. It was Asher who noticed. He hung back from the group, raising an eyebrow and tilting his head for Ronan to join him at the door.

"What's going on?" Asher frowned at him.

"I can't talk about it."

Asher's frown grew. "Why not?"

Ronan stared at his friend, not knowing what else to say. He wanted to tell Asher the whole damn thing. Wanted to tell him how he was having new nightmares. Ones worse than when Asher had been there to wake him from their grasp. These had Adria tied to them. Broken and bloodied. But she'd take off his head if he said anything to Asher, and he couldn't risk the truce they'd established...the fucking kiss they'd shared. He couldn't risk the hope that he might have more with her. Telling her secrets would make all of it shrivel up and disappear.

Asher read something in him that caused him to groan before he asked, "How bad is this fling going to end?"

"Can you call seven years a fling?" he groused, and his friend's eyebrows went up.

"Bullshit. She hates you."

"What's that saying about there being a fine line—"

"Cut the crap, Ronan."

Ronan crossed his arms over his chest. "It's not a fling. She doesn't hate me." At least, he thought that was true. His throat bobbed as he said, "There was a misunderstanding. We're working through it."

Asher rubbed a hand through normally perfectly coifed hair, messing it up in a completely unusual way. "We need you in Los Angeles—that is, if you still want the job."

Ronan nodded. "I want the job. You know I do, and I'll be there, but it's going to have to be after Colombia."

"You're coming with us," he said with a hint of resignation, and it hit Ronan in the chest with an unexpected pain as much as it pissed him off.

"What's the real problem, Ash? You're good enough for Fee, but I'm not good enough for Adria?"

"I'm not good enough for Fiadh. Not by half. Every day I'm trying to keep my brokenness out of our relationship. But not being able to let her go and being worthy of her are totally different issues."

"Adria deserves someone at her side who's there only for her. No one else. Not this damn band or her family. I know what that's like, Ash. We both do. We lived it. We were born with the weight of our family's legacy hovering over us while trying to earn a place in it. Adria...she's just trying to unbury herself from a whole different kind of weight, but it's still hanging on to her. I see her. The real her. I'm not sure anyone—not her friends, not her family, and certainly not you—has ever done that."

Asher's face went from a scowl to a chuckle he didn't even try to hold back. "You've got it bad."

"Fuck you."

Asher shoved his fist into Ronan's shoulder. "Don't screw

it up, because I don't want to have to pick sides between the woman I love and my only real friend."

"We both know I'd be on the first boat out of here if you had to choose."

Asher's face turned serious. "Don't make me."

Ronan didn't respond. He just opened the door and waited until Asher had walked through it before he let it shut in Lennox's glowering face.

The shower was running in the bathroom. Adria's room was the same size as his. Too small for what she was accustomed to now, but when you reserved a room last minute, you got what you got. He grabbed a pillow, kicked off his shoes, and lay down on the tiny loveseat shoved up against the wall beside the bed.

It was going to be uncomfortable as hell, which meant another night of no sleep, but he wasn't leaving her. Not until her sister was behind bars, and GNVL was dismantled. Not until he was sure she was safe.

When she came out, she was in a pair of tiny sleep shorts and a tank, much as she'd been the night he'd gone to see her with the video. Her hair was up in a sloppy bun, tendrils escaping everywhere, and her skin was tinted pink from the shower. It would feel soft and lush under his touch. He longed to run his hands over every inch of it. To embed himself in the other, hotter, sweeter parts of her with his fingers and his tongue. He was an ass for wanting it, especially after the day she'd had—the day they'd all had. But he would never be able to stop his reaction to her.

"What are you doing here?" she asked.

He didn't respond. He didn't need to.

"Ronan...I can't do this right now. I need to at least attempt a few hours of sleep before I have to perform tomorrow night."

"Hence me on the couch," he said.

She didn't respond right away. Instead, she went to the bed, pulled down the covers, and got in. She shut off the light, casting the room into a darkness broken only by the slim opening between the split of the curtains.

"You're going to be sore sleeping there," she said quietly.

"I'll be fine."

In the silence, he could hear the horns from the distant street, as well as the soft inhale and exhale of her a few feet away on the bed. He'd thought she'd fallen asleep until her voice, so quiet it was nothing more than a pained whisper, said, "She told me I'd made my choice. She must have been there. She saw me go after Papá."

He sat up. "What the hell? When?"

"She texted me when I was out with Lennox, who demanded to know what's going on. But I can't tell her if she's not going to keep it to herself—especially without having told my dad," her voice cracked. "It's all a mess."

"You should tell your detail."

"They'll...they'll all think the worst of her."

The faint light was enough for him to make out the shape of her in the bed. She was on her side, facing him, and her eyes were open, glimmering in the semi-darkness.

"I don't know how you can still defend her," he told her honestly.

"She's my baby sister..."

Her voice was clogged with emotions he couldn't stand, but he knew, if he touched her, he'd ignite. He compromised, going to the bed, kneeling beside it, and tucking loose strands of hair behind her ear. He couldn't help her make these decisions. He knew what he wanted her to do, but she had to come to those conclusions on her own. Instead, he tried to distract her.

"You've been holding out on me," he said with a slight tease.

"Yeah?"

"One-forty... You're a genius. Is that how you graduated a year early?" He barely held back the pride he felt for her, because he didn't want her to take it as condescending when all he wanted her to hear was the compliment.

"She's only eleven months younger than me, you know?" she asked, and he was confused by what it had to do with Adria's IQ until she kept going. "If my parents had followed the state rules for kindergarten enrollment at the time, Tati and I would have been in the same grade. I guess Mama didn't want that for either of us, so she had me tested, and they allowed me to start early. The funny thing is, Tatiana is so much smarter than me she probably could have skipped two grades and still outpaced everyone. She could have been like that old show...you know, the one with Neil Patrick Harris as a kid doctor."

"*Doogie Howser*," he said with a small smile, curling his lips.

"Leave it to the Hollywood man to know the name."

She scooted back on the bed and patted the space in front of her. His chest and groin clenched at the same time. He lay down facing her but on top of the covers. A failed attempt to keep something between them besides a couple of scraps of cotton.

"How come you never acted?" she asked.

"Does a single scene in my mom's first *Stiletto* film count?" he said with a wry grin. His eyes had adjusted to the minimal light, so he could see when she rolled hers at him. He gave her a shrug and said, "Not enough talent."

She scoffed. "Please. Half the child actors out there don't know how to act."

"Mom asked me if I wanted to. I think she would have loved to share it with me, but truthfully, I was never interested. When I was on set with them, I was playing with the boom mics and the cameras and ruining takes. I followed around the gaffer and bugged the stunt guys to tell me all their secrets. I'd get my hands dirty with the makeup artists, especially when they were adding blood and guts to the actors. I was always a behind-the-scenes kid, fascinated by all the parts except the acting."

"Did they ever get mad when you ruined takes? I mean, it cost the studio dollars, right?"

"I think some of the actors got frustrated, but they never said anything to my parents who only laughed at my antics. They pretty much gave me free rein."

"That explains your ego." She was quiet for a beat before adding on, "It's nice their careers allowed them to work together so much."

He thought of her parents, living almost separate lives and yet still married. The holes in her psyche the distance had caused.

"It is," he finally answered. "But they've made plenty of films without each other."

"My mom gave up everything after she married my dad. She had the chance to be crowned Miss Colombia, but she fell for Papá and followed his dreams instead. Then, she got pregnant, bam, bam, bam, and for a long time, her world was nothing but babies."

"How old were you when she entered you in your first pageant?" he asked.

"Three. We were still living in Colombia at the time," she responded.

"Why you and not Tatiana?"

She gave a little huff of a laugh. "Honestly, Tati probably

would have done better. She's prettier than me, smarter, and she knew how to say what people wanted to hear way better than I did. The question-and-answer portion was always my weak spot. Mama did enter her a couple of times, but Tatiana absolutely refused to go onstage. There were no tears or tantrums. She just sat down and wouldn't move. Mama would have had to carry her out there."

Adria wiped her eyes, and he realized she'd been crying for a while. He groaned, reaching out and pulling her into his chest. She fisted his T-shirt and tucked her face into the crook of his neck. It brought back their heated kiss in vivid detail. God, did he ache to repeat it.

"I hate that you know all my secrets. And yet...I like it. What does that say about me? About us?"

She looked up, and now her mouth was so close to his that he could practically taste it already. Could feel the warmth of her breath coasting over his face. He clenched his teeth tighter, willing himself to stop staring at the way her lips were parted ever so slightly. Perfect for his tongue to slide between.

"Your secrets are safe with me, Star. Your secrets. Your body. You," he told her.

She pulled back, retreating across the bed so there was space between them again. It felt cold and empty. He wanted her back in his embrace. He wanted to give comfort even if he could provide nothing else.

"You confuse me," she said softly.

"I know."

She smashed an open hand into his chest, saying, "Narcissist."

He laughed, but when he reached for her, she rolled away, turning to face the wall. He watched for a long time, the way her back expanded and contracted with her breath, the way it got slower as she relaxed into sleep. His lids began to droop, and his breathing slowed. His mind was full of the promises he'd made to her, and he vowed to himself they would be true. She'd always be able to trust him with anything and everything she was willing to share.

CHAPTER SEVENTEEN

Tatiana

VIGILANTE SHIT
Performed by Taylor Swift

TATI: He survived! I told you it needed to be bigger.

BLOCKED: It would have brought the entire building down. I don't want the lives of all those souls on my conscience. Your sister would have died with him. Is that what you want?

TATI: Of course not, but she went running after him. Even after I know she watched the video. I'm disgusted with her response.

BLOCKED: Only the clearest of eyes can see the truth. You have abilities others don't. I was fooled by him for years, and your mother is still letting him pull the wool over her eyes.

TATI: That CIA operative met with her. I saw him. She's either working with them or too stupid to understand the consequences.

BLOCKED: I admire your hatred, pequeña, but don't let emotions blind you. We have a plan. Stick to it.

TATI: He will confess his sins for all to hear. Colombia will escape his hold. I will make Tatara-abuela proud. She will not be the only freedom fighter in our family.

BLOCKED: He'll pay. Everything he built will tumble down around him, and we're going to have front-row seats.

CHAPTER EIGHTEEN

Adria

ANTI-HERO
Performed by Taylor Swift

A s Paisley's voice faded away in the stadium, Adria's heart leaped. Her favorite part of the concert, after the song "The Legacy," was her drum solo at the end of "Wild in You," and tonight, she needed it more than ever. She needed to pound out her worries and loss and even the agonizing desire she felt for Ronan. She needed release and escape. So, she lost herself in the beats, the skins, and the rims, spraying the room with a complex polyrhythm that allowed her the creative license she needed. Her body swayed, wrists and arms flying. She went longer than normal, not wanting to stop. But they still had two more songs to give the audience, so she reluctantly brought everything to an abrupt, grinding halt.

The stomping and screaming and clapping of the crowd brought a smile to her face. Maybe her first real one of the day. She pushed back her sweaty hair, knowing she'd be on the big screen, and gave the audience her signature wink that only incited more screams.

She loved this.

Loved the crowd. The songs. The band.

Loved being part of something so unique and different.

The last couple of songs blended together until they arrived at "The Legacy." Even though they'd played it dozens of times now, it still hurt, and with the video playing, it was even harder. Seeing Landry so full of life, smiling, taunting, teasing, laughing, and then serious, fingers flying over the strings of her guitar. Adria missed her with a painful ache deep in her chest.

The idea that she could be dead because of Tatiana... It made her throat close and tears flow as they did many times during this song. But tonight, they were heavier. Harsher. She couldn't control them. They made her drum kit a blur, and it was only thousands of hours of practice that allowed her to finish the song. But she couldn't add her voice to the chorus as she normally did. She couldn't sing, and her friends just picked up the missing chords for her.

Then, the lights went up, and they were bowing and thanking the audience to more thunderous applause, begging for another song. It was addicting...the stage...the crowd...the demands for more. But after the emotional haul that was the last song, they would never be able to do an encore. They left the stage with joined hands, forming a circle and embracing each other backstage. As always, Jonas joined them, arms strong and uplifting, helping to seal them together.

When they finally broke apart, her friends all went off to the men who loved them, except her and Nikki. Her friend flung her arm around Adria and said, "Tough night."

Adria nodded. She tipped her head onto her friend's shoulder. "What if..."

And her friend seemed to know exactly what she meant, because she was vehemently shaking her head, her curls dancing in Adria's face. "No. Stop. Don't go there. Even if, somehow, what happened to Lan is tied up with what's happening now and your dad, it still isn't your fault, Ads. No one will blame you."

She tried to swallow the lump in her throat. Her eyes met Ronan's. He was standing in the shadows, arms crossed. He hadn't worn his ubiquitous beanie in days. She liked him better without it. The beanie had first appeared around the time they'd fallen apart. It had made him look...immature in a way she knew he wasn't. Today, he looked all man. Strong. Vibrant. Radiating charisma. He'd stepped in to be her strength, and she wasn't sure what to do with that—not after years of trying to hate him and ignore the way he made her body pulse.

But now that she'd kissed him again, all her body wanted to do was lose itself completely in his. To forget everything that was going to hell in her world and just revel in the way he made her feel alive and adored. Seen... Enough...

Nikki must have felt Adria and Ronan's locked gaze because a small chuckle escaped before she asked, "You joining the ranks of the lovebirds?"

"No," was her automatic response as she lifted her head and stepped away. But she wasn't sure she believed it, which was almost worse. "But I may be able to burn off some extra energy with him."

Nikki laughed. "So, you don't hate him anymore. What was that even about?"

"A misunderstanding I was too stubborn to see."

Nikki's gaze met hers. "You, stubborn? Never." Adria laughed, but then Nikki turned serious again. "He's got quite the reputation, and the new job with Ravaged Storm Productions—"

"I know. It's not like I'm asking him to put a ring on my finger like Asher did Fee." It wouldn't be wise to sleep with him again. He'd already made his feelings for her clear. He'd already shown exactly what he wanted in Seattle, but she didn't know if she was capable of giving it to him. When they stepped past this moment and returned to their jobs and their real lives, she'd be the one to leave, and she knew what that did to the ones left behind. She couldn't do that to him, even when her body craved him. Deep, hidden parts of her that she'd never let anyone see—like the inside of her heart.

She and Nikki made their way to the dressing rooms, showering and changing, before heading back to the hotel and Paisley and Jonas's penthouse for the after-party. There were no VIPs or press in the room. Asher had kept his promise. Instead, it was just a handful of their crew. It was a relief to know she wouldn't have to wear her smile for much longer. She'd be able to take it off and hang it up with her wink and her sticks.

Adria made herself a plate from the buffet, ignored the alcohol offerings, and downed an entire bottle of water, feeling dehydrated after the exertion onstage. Ronan had accompanied them, which wasn't a surprise, but he didn't hover. When she'd gone shopping with her friends earlier in the day, he'd excused himself to get some work done.

He'd been the one to put space back between them, and she knew it was the right thing. Because if she let them twine themselves together more, he'd ask for everything, and she'd hurt him when she couldn't give it to him. She never wanted him to feel like he wasn't enough for the person he loved to stay. But where once she'd hated him being in the same room, now she found herself missing the closeness they'd shared over the last few days. Missed his legs and arms tucked up against hers. The comfort of his embrace. The touch of his hand as he attempted to soothe her.

After only an hour, Zia took control of the room, reminding them of the schedule for the next day. They were leaving from the private jet terminal at one o'clock for Cadencia.

Adria's stomach flipped. Worry about being in Colombia with the band returned to her. Ronan was right. She needed to tell the detail about what was happening, and she needed to tell her friends as well. She steeled herself to do it on the plane when there was plenty of time to discuss it and fewer ears to hear.

The idea should have relieved her, but it didn't.

She lost any of the relaxation beating on the drums had brought her.

She grabbed another water bottle and headed for the door.

"I'm going to see my dad at the hospital one more time before we leave, so I'll meet you at the airport," she told everyone.

She half-expected Ronan to follow her from the room, and when he didn't, her heart fell to her stomach even though she knew it was better this way. Hadn't she just reminded herself of how much she would hurt him? How much they couldn't be? But when she'd barely gotten to the elevator, and the suite door opened to reveal Ronan, her heart skipped a beat.

He was in another pair of jeans, an old-school *E.T.* T-shirt, and canvas sneakers. He'd trimmed his beard. It was shorter than it had been the last few days, clipped close to his jawline. She wanted to feel the bristles on her lips, her neck, and her inner thighs. Her body clenched tight at the thought.

He didn't say a word as they made their way down to her floor.

Adria could feel the disapproval wafting from Lennox. It had been there all day while she'd shopped with her friends and visited her dad at the hospital. Lennox was still pissed Ronan knew more than she did, or maybe that Adria was trusting him to protect her in a way she wasn't trusting Lennox.

The bodyguard who'd been guarding her room opened it and said, "Room is clear."

Lennox gave him a nod and turned to go, but Adria reached out to stop her, saying, "Tomorrow. On the plane. I'll tell everyone what I know."

Lennox's eyes widened, and then she gave another curt nod before she headed for the elevator. Her shift ended once Adria was secure in her room for the night. Adria felt a twinge of guilt for the long days their detail ran, especially when she wasn't making it any easier.

Adria turned, slipping inside the room with Ronan on her heels. The door had barely closed before he'd pulled her into him. She hesitated just a beat before her arms went around him, and her head rested on his shoulder. Instead of hating him, she hated herself a bit now. Because every time she let him this close, she knew what it did to him. To his hopes about them. She wanted to have that same hope. She wanted to see a future where, somehow, they made it, but she wasn't sure she believed she was capable of staying. And yet, she still didn't have the strength to push him away as he caressed her back in slow, soothing circles.

"I wanted to do that all day," he said, voice deep and growly.

She lifted her head, eyes finding his in the dark, flames zipping back and forth between them. The current was heady and hot, sliding through every inch of her until she felt like she was practically vibrating.

In her platform boots, it took the barest of movements for his lips to descend and take possession of hers. And it was possession. Complete and utter control. Soft and tantalizing at first, pushing gently until her mouth opened, and his tongue invaded. With a groan, he was plundering her, sipping, licking, and her body went limp, sagging into him. He caught her easily, hands gripping her waist with a pressure that was almost too much and yet not enough.

There was something to his kisses...his touch...that she'd never been able to find with anyone else. Something she could never explain. A feeling. As if she'd gone months without seeing the moon, only to find it gliding back into the sky. As if she was herself but somehow also more when he was there.

Those feelings crashed over her with a longing so deep, so severe, it was painful. Sharp and jagged, breaking open all her walls, demanding she pay attention to each one. Like the lyrics from "Wild in You," the emotions were escaping, surrounding her, and holding her hostage but also freeing her at the same time. She just wanted to live in this moment, the consequences be damned. Take this joy and hold on to it while it lasted.

One hand went to her hair, tugging her head back, finding her pulse point and making that his as well. She whimpered when she was not the whimpering type. He growled in return. He released his hold on her hair, fingers sliding under the slouched T-shirt she'd thrown on after the concert. The warmth of his hand lit a fuse along her skin, a burning trail that was sure to ignite.

Just as he went to pull her T-shirt up, there was a movement from farther in the darkened room, the barest rustle of clothing, that had him tearing his lips from hers and pushing her behind him.

A floor lamp came on.

Adria reached for the door, wanting to alert the bodyguard outside as a deep voice—so deep it seemed to vibrate over the space—said, "I just need a word. You don't need to call your team."

Adria looked over Ronan's shoulder to see a man dressed all in black from his military boots to his sweatshirt. The dark clothing helped him blend into the shadows of the room. He was sitting on the love seat, making it look like dollhouse furniture beneath him. His shoulders were impossibly wide, head towering over the sofa top. He had one ankle atop the opposite knee in a pose that seemed relaxed, and yet he felt like a panther, ready to leap at the merest of provocation. The hood on the sweatshirt was up, partly covering his sharp cheekbones, but she saw dark scruff on a square chin, an entirely Egyptian god-like nose, and dark eyes that seemed black over the distance.

"What the hell do you want?" Ronan demanded.

"The same thing you do. Answers."

"I'm calling my detail," Adria said, reaching for her phone. Holden was going to be furious the man had gotten into her room unnoticed. "They've been looking for you."

The man stood in one fluid movement. "You know who I am, then."

193

Ronan scoffed. "We know the name you've given us, but it isn't your real one, is it?"

She blinked, and the man was at the balcony door. She wasn't sure how or when he'd moved. It was as if he'd teleported, apparated, whatever magic you wanted to name it. The curtain blew inward, grazing Angel Carter's shoulder, and she suddenly realized he'd come in that way—fifteen floors up, onto a balcony that was not adjoined to any others. As if he'd scaled the building with his mere hands, and she wondered if he had. Wondered if he was even real.

"The CIA isn't going to find you the answers you seek," Carter's voice spoke quietly into the room. "But I can."

A shiver went up Adria's spine, and Ronan's entire body stiffened.

"Excuse me?" Ronan asked.

"Warren Times is an idiot. The NSA agent...she's interesting. Smart. Savvy. She knows her way around South America. But Times...he's going to trip every alarm the GNVL has laid. I can get you the truth."

"How about telling us the truth about you?" Adria demanded, finally finding her voice. "Did you kill Landry? Why were you at Swan River Pond that day? Who the hell are you, and who do you work for?"

She tried to step forward, but Ronan held her back with an arm across her body.

Angel's eyes barely twitched, but his nostrils flared slightly. "I just need to know when your sister contacts you again."

Adria inhaled sharply. How did this man know so much?

He inclined his head toward the table where a cell phone sat. "My number is there."

He was halfway out the sliding door before his voice came back in. "Only your face will open it. If your detail tries to track it, everything will be wiped. I can help you. I can find who's pulling your sister's strings, treating her like a puppet to be maneuvered across a stage, and I promise you, they'll pay."

"Like you made Ziggy pay?" she asked, voice quivering.

He looked back for a moment, and she swore a fire sparked in his eyes that she could barely see, but it had to have been a figment of her imagination.

Ronan dialed his phone, placing it on speaker.

"Kent," Holden's voice rang through the room.

"Angel Carter is in Adria's room," Ronan said.

Holden cursed. "I'm on my way."

"Tell Kent his security was nearly impossible to break this time. I'm almost impressed. But remind him that he and Asher owe me. This is what I'm asking for as payment. I need to know when your sister contacts you."

The man disappeared out the slider. Ronan sprang toward the balcony, dropping his phone on the bed as Adria turned to rip open the hotel door.

Her bodyguard pushed past her as if an all-call had already been sounded.

"He's gone," Ronan barked, turning back into the room. "He's just fucking gone."

Adria raced to the balcony behind the bodyguard who pointed out into the dark, "There!"

A black form trailed through the night sky with the umbrella of a black parachute above him. His body coasted on the wind, moving toward the trees and the park in the distance.

"He's headed to Memorial Park using base-jumping equipment," the bodyguard yelled into his mic.

The door of the room bounced against the wall as Holden and Lennox bounded into the room, weapons drawn, in nothing more than sweats and bare feet. On seeing just the three of them and hearing the bodyguard's report, Holden slid his gun into his waistband. He sent orders into his mic. "I need a team at Memorial Park, stat. Target, Angel Carter." Then, he whipped out his phone and dialed. "Camp, it's Kent. We've had a Carter sighting in Houston. I've sent a team to try and apprehend him."

For a few minutes, her room was chaos, but with the focus on capturing Angel, no one had even asked what he'd wanted. Why he was there... *I can get you the truth*. But was it anything she'd want to hear? Adria's pulse pounded through her veins like the rudimentary rhythms she'd first been taught to play, left-left-right, right-right-left.

The bodyguard at the door was questioned, but he was adamant he'd cleared the room when he'd heard she was in the elevator on the way down. He was relieved of duty until an investigation could be completed, and Adria's stomach twirled.

She was tired of feeling on edge. Tired of being surprised and having her world turned upside down. She wanted to scream out her frustration. Wanted to rant and rave and tell the entire damn world to leave her alone. Why couldn't she have just that single moment of pleasure she and Ronan had been about to capture?

Maybe this was the universe's way of reminding her of what she'd already told herself over and over tonight. They were both getting attached in ways they couldn't afford. It was likely to end badly, worse than even Seattle had, for both of them.

CHAPTER NINETEEN

Ronan

TEMPT MY TROUBLE
Performed by Bishop Briggs

Ronan's entire body was vibrating with anger. The gall of Carter to show up in her room and then take off again as if it was nothing. As if it was his damn right to slip in and out and make demands. Adria was tense, standing almost rigid while her team swarmed the room. Moments ago, she'd been soft and pliable in his hands, ready to give in, ready to find their way back to each other, even if it was for only a few hours.

He was furious Carter had taken that from them.

Holden took off to the park to search for him with the Secret Service and FBI, but Ronan knew the man wouldn't be found. He was a ghost. Or a demon. Who knew for sure? Each of the Daisies called Adria to check in. They'd been kept to their rooms with their security on high alert, and it felt like one more round of fucking chaos had been added to days filled with them. He hated the out-of-control feeling he had. It made him think too much of being bound in a bathtub.

Instead of having Adria stay there, he helped her pack her things, and they went to his room, followed by Lennox still in sweats with no shoes and a half-dozen bodyguards. Lennox personally cleared Ronan's room, which had no balcony and a window that didn't open. There was no way in except the door.

By the time he and Adria were alone, the heat of their savage kiss in her room had been shoved back behind his anger at Carter, her team, and the entire situation. She changed into another pair of barely-there pajamas, and tonight, he didn't even bother with the couch. Instead, he stripped down to his boxers, slid under the covers, and held them up for her. She eyed it for a few seconds and then joined him, head coming to rest on his bare chest.

He was overwhelmed with memories he had of her like this. Fleeting moments they'd captured over the years that had never been long enough or frequent enough to satisfy his endless need for her. They'd wasted so much time. Days. Hours. Minutes where he could have had her like this with her dark hair splayed across him, muscled torso draped over him, arms surrounding each other.

"I'm scared," she said quietly, body shuddering.

He was too, but he didn't want to say it.

The heat and scent of her swamped him with a heady dose of desire. Need so great he wasn't sure he'd ever find a way to satisfy it. Not even if they spent infinity wrapped in each other. She placed a kiss on his shoulder. Open-mouthed, wet. Hot and hungry, just like him.

He debated. He'd wanted this not even an hour before. When they'd stepped into her room and consumed each other with that heated kiss, he'd been completely on board with them finding their way back to each other. But now, he knew if they did this tonight, it wouldn't be about them. It wouldn't be about finding their way back to each other. It would be about her fear and about holding off thoughts of what was happening to her and her family and the band. He didn't want them losing themselves in each other as a means of putting off anything. Not her worries or his inevitable nightmare that would come tonight. He wanted to have her when he could simply rejoice in every kiss. Every slide of hand. Every desperate moan. When it was the start of something and not a temporary distraction.

He stroked her hair, tangled his fingers in it, and gently pulled back so she was forced to meet his gaze. "Not this way, Star." His voice was thick with desire. Lust. Fucking pure *want*.

"You've taken me every other way, Hollywood. Why not this way?"

"It's different now. I don't want you for a few damn hours while we try and escape our thoughts and our feelings." He hoped to hell she could hear the truth of it. That he wasn't rejecting her but asking for more.

He'd purposefully left the light on in the entry, a weak attempt at holding off his nightmares, but he was glad he had now. It allowed him to see the flood of emotions that came and went over her face with his words. She closed her eyes and then opened them again, pain there he wanted to wipe away until he realized the pain was for him.

"I can't offer you more than a few hours, Ronan. Relationships and me...we don't belong together." He hated she believed that almost as much as he'd hated Carter showing up in her room tonight. He didn't respond as he tried to get a grip on the way his soul was screaming in objection. "I just...

You were right in some ways... It is about my parents. I never want to end up being them," she explained.

He let the words settle him. At least this time she was being honest about it. He responded softly, "I can understand that. But your parents aren't the only model. You have plenty of different examples around you, even now. Look at your friends."

"Paisley and Jonas are joined at the hip. Fee can't leave the room without Asher growling for her. And Holden...he gave up his entire world to be with Leya just like my mom did for my dad. I don't want any of their relationships either," Adria said firmly.

God, he ached to kiss her and prove they could be something different. Something more. But tonight wasn't the night to do it.

He let go of her hair, and she lay her head back down on his chest.

"Go to sleep, Star. We'll figure it out. Not tonight, but we will."

She didn't respond, but she didn't pull away either, and he took it as a win.

♫ ♫ ♫

He couldn't move his hands because they were tied behind his back. His lips were clamped shut with duct tape. His head throbbed. A voice, slimy and thick, saying shitty things scrolled through his brain. He tried to force his eyes open. He tried to see, but he couldn't. Paisley answered, and it sounded as shaky as the tremors reeling through him. *Open your damn eyes*, he screamed to himself, but they didn't respond. A weight shifted on him. Adria... It came to him from nowhere even though he couldn't see. He could smell her. Feel the shape of her. When he finally forced his eyes open, she lay there, slack-mouthed with an unseeing gaze while blood dripped from her throat. He struggled against the vision, the bindings, the weight, and the words the man was whispering.

"Ronan!" Adria's voice called. He couldn't see anything but the god-awful dream. He knew it was a dream. Knew he'd already escaped. Knew Adria had never been there. And still, he was caught in it.

He fought against the hands on his skin.

"Wake up!" Her voice was frantic.

And that was what did it—the fear in her voice. He sat up, heart pounding, body dripping with sweat, automatically reaching for the duct tape that wasn't on his mouth. Adria was sitting cross-legged next to him, worry written all over her face.

He scooted back to lean against the headboard, trying to get his heart rate under control. He snaked his arm around her, drawing her up against him. She lost her balance for a moment and ended up with her legs thrown over his and her upper body aligned with his chest.

"Do you want to talk about it?" she asked, her fingers running a soothing rhythm up over his skin.

"Not really."

"Is it what happened in Albany?" she asked.

He gave a curt nod.

"I think, maybe, I need a break from hotels," he said wryly.

She huffed out a half-laugh and then sobered, saying, "I have them too."

"Nightmares?"

She nodded. "Since I was little. I'm stuck in a wooden box. I can feel it along my shoulders and toes. I can barely lift my hands, and the wood is rough against them, leaving splinters. I can't breathe. It feels like...like being buried alive."

Her breathing grew erratic even thinking about it, and it jerked him from his nightmare into hers. "That's pretty screwed up."

"Vicente and Tati used to wake me, and I'd still be screaming. When I talked to my parents about it, they'd tell me it was just a dream, but it always felt so real." She hesitated. "Recently...I wonder. Sometimes, I get these glimpses of something...as if it's a memory and not a dream."

His heart skittered to a stop before slamming back into action. "You think you were locked in a box?"

Her worried, scared eyes met his, and she gave a careless shrug, one of her graceful ones usually accompanied by her signature wink. All spunk and charisma.

"It's ridiculous. They would have told me...but I just...I don't know."

"Maybe they wouldn't have. Maybe they were hoping you'd forget. I damn sure wish I could. I hate every moment of my fucking memories of that day. Hearing Paisley and knowing there wasn't a damn thing I could do to help her."

Adria ran a finger along the scar at his temple.

"But you did."

His eyes grew wide. "What do you mean?"

"I heard the story, Ronan. You hit the SOS button on your phone. The blaring was the reason Jonas and Trevor knew you were both really in trouble. So, you did help. You saved her and yourself."

"He hasn't even come up for trial yet. Paisley and I are going to have to relive it over and over again."

"I wish he'd taken the plea deal."

"He thinks he's in the right. He thinks he'll convince a jury of it," Ronan said, disgust washing over him.

"There's still time for his lawyer to convince him otherwise."

They sat there, clinging to each other as they tried to let go of memories neither of them wanted.

She propped herself up, gaze meeting his.

"I need you, Ronan. I need the heat and weight of you on me so I can forget everything but the way your hands and mouth make me feel. Forget everything but the sound of you coming undone at my touch."

Every particle in his being ignited, making it impossible to hold back, making his resolve disappear with every desperate syllable she'd uttered. His mouth crashed down on hers. Brutal. Hungry. Determined to make her see, by sheer force of desire and will, that what they were when they were together was bigger than this moment. What they had was something neither of them would ever find again.

He tangled his hand in her hair again, dragging her head back and exposing the long column of her neck that he consumed. Biting, nipping, sucking. She let out a shuddery breath, and he devoured that too, lips taking control of hers, tongue sweeping through her inner recesses, the hidden spots Adria showed so few people.

She moved so she was straddling him while he remained leaning up against the headboard. Their mouths collided again while her fingers slid down his chest, their path leaving a flame that burned, making him ache for more. His hands went under the hem of her camisole, lifting upward, and they broke their kiss long enough for him to pull it completely off and fling it across the room.

He stared for a brief moment, touching the rosy tips he'd thought he'd never see again, before he bent, tongue lavishing one while fingers tugged the other. She moaned, arching into him, and he turned to stone below her.

She dug her nails into his scalp, and the sharp edges only spurred him on.

He inhaled deeply. The scent of her was an addiction, a hit he'd only ever found with her wrapped around him like this.

She ground down on him, and he thought he might lose control right then and there. He picked her up and flipped them so she was underneath him, on her back. He slid his tongue down her belly button, capturing the barbell there, flicking it in his mouth, and she writhed. He smiled against her skin before he continued downward, his mouth leaving a wet trail.

He drew her shorts and underwear over her hips, down over her knees, and then threw them aside. He picked up one graceful foot, kissing the arch, and she let out a shuddery breath and whispered his name in a way that hit him in the chest. He slowly made his way up her leg with his mouth until he got to her inner thigh. His breath coasted over her core, and she shivered. He smiled again, moving to start all over again on her opposite leg. Arch, ankle, calf, knee. Slow, tantalizing kisses he combined with the rasp of his beard that made her gasp and pant, which in turn made him impossibly harder.

This time, when he got to her inner thigh, her fingers found his hair and pushed with pressure. He looked up to find her eyes ablaze as she watched him.

"What do you want, Star?"

"You know."

"Tell me."

She pressed against his head as if to push his mouth closer to the heat of her, and he held back.

"Tell me."

Her eyes narrowed. "I want your mouth, your tongue, your fingers. I want them all on me, inside me."

"Have you ever wanted someone the way you want me, Beauty Queen?"

Her eyes narrowed, fighting it, fighting him, fighting telling him the truth.

He nipped at her thigh, and she gasped.

"Adria?"

She shook her head.

"Say it," he demanded. "Say you've never needed anyone like you need me right now."

He thought he might have pushed too far, because she stilled for a moment, the look on her face turning stubborn before she closed her eyes and said, "I've never wanted anyone like you. Ever."

His heart soared, his dick jumped, his brain left, and he simply gave her what she'd been aching for with his fingers and his tongue. Slow and steady, growing the sweet tension inside her, watching as her muscles contracted, and her eyes fluttered closed. Loving the way her hips thrust against him and her thighs clenched tight.

"*Dios*...that feels so good."

And then, she was over the edge, shaking and convulsing around his fingers. He eked out every last pulse until she went limp, legs softening, hand in his hair stilling.

He planted one more kiss on her bundle of nerves and then eased up to take her mouth. It wasn't the fierce devouring of before. Instead, it was a soft promise. An embrace he wanted to linger in all her secret spots so when she woke in the morning, she'd remember this promise more than the way he'd made her come.

She kissed him back, hands slowly moving over his

shoulders, grabbing his butt, squeezing, and then letting go before easing under the waist of his boxer briefs. His body convulsed almost as brutally as hers had as she gripped him.

"Tell me what you want, Hollywood," she said, the taunt of his words coming back to him, and he couldn't help the chuckle that escaped him.

"As much as I'd love your hand and your mouth on me, I want to be inside you even more. I want to be as deep in you as I can get with your legs wrapped around me, and us doing our best to break the headboard, but I don't have a condom. I wasn't planning this."

"The Player Prince doesn't have an entire carton of them?" she scoffed.

He brushed her hair from her face. "I haven't been with anyone in a long time. There was only one person I craved."

Waves of emotion crossed over her face, and then breathlessly, she asked, "Have you ever been in anyone without protection?"

Just the idea of being inside her with nothing covering him shot liquid heat through him. "No."

"I've never let anyone inside me without one either, and I have a birth control implant. It would be safe."

He groaned, closing his eyes briefly before opening them to meet her gaze. "You're making it really hard for me to say no."

"Good."

She was used to getting her way. Like him. They were both used to it. He'd gotten everything he'd ever wanted in his life—except her. And now, here she was, offering herself, offering to let him slide inside her bare, a sensation he'd never had and ached to experience with her. Instead of giving in, instead of feeling thrilled at the idea, it brought back all the things he'd said before about not wanting this to be a means of escape or a brief interlude.

He'd lost his damn mind in the heat and scent of her. Who could blame him? But the truth remained. He wanted the next time he finally slid home to be a means of showing how much they truly felt for each other. An extension of those emotions that were expressed with fingers and tongues. He wanted every action to be surrounded not with fear and desperation but with an overwhelming sense of love.

Because, fuck, he loved this woman. Had loved her probably since the first time she'd shown up on his parents' *Stilleto* set with the rest of the Daisies. Adria had blown him away. Her poise. Her attitude. Her mouth. Her heart. Her fierceness.

He rolled off her and lay on his back, staring at the ceiling, heart banging so loudly in his chest he was sure she could hear it, sure the entire bed was vibrating with the force of it. What the hell was he going to do?

CHAPTER TWENTY

Adria

BATTLEFIELD
Performed by Lea Michele

A rush of embarrassment flew over Adria. She'd just offered herself up in a way she never had before, and instead of finishing what he'd started by embedding himself inside her, he'd rolled away. Humiliation coated her skin. Not because of what he'd done, but because of what she was doing. He'd been right to stop them. He was the one who was brave and strong, not her. She knew she couldn't give him what he needed, and yet she'd been willing to take what she wanted in this moment anyway.

She went to get up, and he grabbed her hand. She jerked it, trying to escape before she said things that would bruise them both, but he held on tighter. He propped himself up on an elbow, steely eyes meeting hers.

"Don't stomp off. I'm not rejecting you. God, Star...I want that. I want us skin on skin..." His voice was thick with lust, proving his words were true.

"I know." Her chest was achy, and she felt like she might cry, which just added more embarrassment to the moment. How many times had he seen her this way since finding the video of Tatiana?

"I can't go back to the games we played for years—a phone call and a hookup whenever we happen to be in the same town," he said.

"I know," she repeated. Because she did. He wanted the package. The relationship, the home, and family, and she knew if she took those things, she'd break them both in the end.

"Going back to that... It's the same as your parents, don't you see?"

She jerked at his grip again, and this time, he let her go. She scrambled off the bed, searching for her clothes as her insides twisted and turned. She slid into her underwear and shorts, grabbed her tank and pulled it on, but she still didn't turn back to the bed as her mind reeled.

Jueputa. In her determination to not become her parents, had she already become them anyway? Caring about him but never staying long enough to show it? She went to the curtains, drawing them aside and looking out at the lights of the city. You could barely see the stars here. On her family's estate in Cadencia, they appeared so close you could be burned by their flames.

She loved it there, had work that fulfilled her there. Just like her mom did. And that made her stomach crunch. Would she eventually make it her permanent home too? Her family had lived in Colombia until Adria was four. After her father had been kidnapped and held for ransom, he'd insisted on moving them to the States, and Mama had come with them at first. But she didn't like living in California. She missed her family, the estate, and the charity work her family was involved with in Colombia. She spent months there during the pageants' off-season. When Mama was gone, it was just Adria and her siblings and the help in their house in California as her father popped in and out.

But her mother always returned to take Adria back on the circuit. Back then, it had felt like she was the one responsible for holding her family together. She continued with the pageants long after they'd stopped being fun for her. It was Vicente who'd finally told their mother how unhappy Adria was. Mama had looked crushed, and Adria never knew if it was because she hadn't said anything herself or if it was because she could no longer live out her own trampled dreams through her daughter.

With Adria no longer entering the contests, her mom had accepted a job offer with Teen Colombia and was gone even more. Adria had felt like she'd been the one to toss the final brick through the window of her parents' marriage. She'd blamed herself for her siblings losing the last little piece of their mother they'd had. But what if Tati was right? What if it wasn't just Adria giving up the pageants that had caused Mama to run? What if it was their father's affairs?

She shivered.

"Star," his voice was pained. It ripped at her soul because she didn't want to be the reason for it. Not only because she felt like she'd caused enough anguish to the people she cared about but because he deserved to be happy. Because she wanted the joy and passion she had heard in his voice when they'd been together in the past.

She turned to face him, and the open curtain cast him in

a golden glow from the city lights. He was sitting, feet off the edge of the bed, hands clenched to the mattress as if he was preventing himself from coming after her. There was a resigned look on his face, as if he knew she was going to push him away again. It was what she should do. And yet, the idea of doing so sent waves of panic through her.

She'd end up hurting him. She didn't know how to love someone the way he wanted and deserved. All the time. Enough to sacrifice yourself. Her parents hadn't done it for each other or their children. Even as much as she'd loved her siblings, each of them had gone their own way, easily and without hesitation. How was that really loving someone?

"You said you're scared," Ronan said. "I get it. You're afraid not only about what's going on with Tatiana and Carter and the Daisies but about the way I'm stealing in past your locks and barriers."

She gritted her teeth but didn't know how to respond. She was scared. Not just for herself. For him.

When she didn't say anything, he continued, "There's a quote from one of my favorite philosophers, Bertrand Russell, that says, 'To fear love is to fear life, and those who fear life are already three parts dead.' I don't want you to live life as if you are already gone. As if you're living some half-life, accepting less because you think more can only lead to heartache. I don't want that for me either. We both deserve to be drowned in an all-consuming love."

Her breath caught, his words tangling in her chest with the scars of her childhood. What did all-consuming love look like? What did it take to prove you loved someone enough? Was it being there every damn day? Was that what she'd missed from her parents? Simply their presence?

She didn't have the answers. She didn't even know if she

was built to give or take that kind of deep emotion. To be consumed by it. That felt stifling. It felt like being back in a box she couldn't escape from. And because she didn't know enough about herself or what she could give even if she decided she wanted what he offered, she couldn't just accept it. She needed time to figure it out. To figure herself out.

She also didn't want to see him walk away again. The thought of him leaving sliced her already shredded nerves until it felt like she would end up as nothing more than strips of paper ready to blow away in the next breeze. But she had to be brave enough to do just that. Lay her cards on the table and let him go.

"I don't know if I can give you what you're asking...what you deserve. I don't know how to do all-consuming." Every word cost her something, as if she was giving parts of herself away she'd never get back. "It would be selfish of me to let you stay while I attempt to figure it out, because, in the end, I may never be able to give it."

He bounded out of the bed and drew her to him.

"It isn't selfish. It's raw and honest. I'll be just as honest back. I want you to try, and I want to be here while you do. I already see what we can be together. I see the love in you, and I'm greedy enough to want it to be mine."

She wrapped her arms around him, letting her face settle against his chest where his heart stammered out a beat that was almost uncontrollable. She wanted to accept what he was offering, and yet was still unsure if it was fair to either of them.

"You have a big imagination, Hollywood. I'm not sure reality will ever live up to what you've got going on in that director head of yours."

He chuckled, the warmth of his breath coasting over her.

"Then, I'll just have to make a movie to show it to you."

♫ ♫ ♫

Last night, she'd lived in a world of Ronan and possibilities and forgotten briefly the harsh reality of her life. Now, in the light of day, on the way to the hospital to see her father, it all came crashing back in. The disappointment she'd felt in her sister's texts had felt ominous. Goosebumps traveled over her skin, thinking of what that could mean.

She felt uneasy without Ronan with her. She'd become accustomed too easily and too quickly to his stepping in to be her strength when she faltered. But he'd had a few things to take care of this morning before joining her at the airport. He was rearranging interviews, writing sessions, and plans with his parents. It made her feel guilty all over again. He was already making sacrifices, giving up things because he believed there was something in her—in them—she couldn't yet see. She hoped the faith he had in her wouldn't leave him with gaping wounds he'd never be able to repair.

When she walked into her father's hospital room, he was partially dressed with a sling over one shoulder, dictating assignments to his detail. All the fear and trepidation she'd had came bounding back to the surface as she rushed over to her father's side.

"What's going on?"

"I'm going to Colombia," he told her.

"No!" Adria choked out, shaking her head. "That is not a good idea."

Dios. What would Tati do if she found her father there? With their mother?

"I'd never miss you playing in Cadencia for the first time, *mija.* And your mother would never forgive me if I didn't show up for the pageant," he said with a slight tease.

"Papá, you've missed plenty of things before. It's not safe for you."

She hadn't meant to hurt him with her words, but sadness traveled over his face before it disappeared behind a wall of determination. "I need to see Jorge's family in person and make arrangements for his funeral. Then, I'm meeting with a group who can put an end to these GNVL threats once and for all. I will not let them destroy what we have left."

Panic grew, crawling its way through her veins. Her voice was a beg she hadn't used since she was a little girl when she said, "Papá, they tried to kill you."

"They'll wish they'd succeeded. I'm done playing nice. Here"—he waved his hand around the room—"in the United States, I don't have what I need to make them pay!"

Adria's heart stuttered. She stepped closer, whispering so the others couldn't hear, "You mean to use mercenaries? Guerillas? That is not the answer either! You think Mama will never forgive you for not showing up for the pageant, but she really won't if you use the people she despises. Colombia has worked so hard to put our tumultuous past behind us. You can't start what would essentially be yet another gang war."

Her father's eyes were dark and cloudy, and his voice lowered also. "What would you have me do? Quietly pray to your mother's saints while each of you is hurt, wounded, and targeted? They've already taken too much! They took my baby girl!"

His voice cracked with emotions. Fear and sadness overwhelmed her. She looked around the room and gathered every ounce of poise she'd ever had to command the room, "I need to speak to my father alone."

No one budged.

"Now!" she snapped. Lennox and the other Reinard bodyguard who had come with her headed for the door, but her father's men still didn't move a muscle until her father nodded at them. None of them went far, standing outside the room in a sea of black suits and military gear. A wall of defense that wouldn't be enough if her father pricked the beasts alive in Colombia.

Adria sat next to him, grabbed his good hand, and squeezed it tight. She held her breath momentarily, hating what she was going to say and how it would hurt him, but she no longer had a choice. She had to tell him the truth. She inhaled sharply and then said, "I saw Tati."

His eyes flickered, the haunted look coming back briefly. "I told you. I see her too, *mija*. It isn't her."

"No, Papá, you don't understand. I met with Tatiana this week. In a club here in Houston. We talked. We had an actual conversation."

His hand went to his chest, rubbing furiously, and his face paled even further.

"What?! What are you saying?" he croaked.

"She's alive. She's working with them."

He shook his head violently.

"Take me to her!" he demanded.

"I can't... She's gone. To Cadencia."

His fingers were still digging into his chest, and Adria said a prayer that he wouldn't have a heart attack. "What are you saying?!"

"She has this video...of you...having..." Adria's cheeks heated, and she looked away. "Having sex with a woman who isn't Mama. And she says you're working with the CIA. GNVL wants to destroy you for all of it."

When she risked looking back at him, instead of being

pale and lifeless, he was red with fury. "She thinks I cheated on your mother!? You think this too?"

"I didn't say I believed it, Papá, but you're there. Your watch was there..." She trailed off.

"Claudio!" His voice was angry and disappointed all at the same time, his mind clearly going to the same place hers had when she'd seen the recording. For decades, the two of them had worked side by side as brothers and partners before Claudio ruined it all with betrayal.

"He wasn't in California the day this was recorded," she told him.

Her father scoffed. "That's easy enough to manipulate. I can't believe you would think this of me. That Tati..." He took several deep breaths. "It can't be her. This is someone pretending to be her."

Since the moment she'd seen her sister at The Attic, it had felt like she was looking through wax paper at her. A slightly altered reality of the girl she'd grown up with, but there was no doubt it was Tatiana.

"She's alive?" her father said, the pain in his voice so clear it stabbed at Adria's heart.

She could only nod as emotion clogged her throat.

"She let us believe the worst..." He shook his head, closing his eyes against the tears, and it only brought them to the surface of Adria's. But she fought them back.

"I thought maybe you knew..." she said softly.

His eyes opened again. "The things you think of me..." His voice was wounded, and guilt rolled through her because she had let herself consider the worst of him. But she also realized he hadn't denied working with the CIA. And the sad truth was, in some ways, it was easier to believe her father had cheated and sold his soul to the CIA than her sister was doing all of this for nothing. "What have you told your mother? Vicente?"

She shook her head. "Nothing. I needed to try and understand it myself first."

His face turned dark. "Good. Say nothing."

"Papá..."

"Listen, *mija*, now more than ever we need to get her back. Before she does something she can't recover from. Before the authorities are looking for her."

"You mean like setting off a bomb that almost killed you?"

He blanched.

"The CIA and the NSA are already following her," she told him. "They want me to spy on her...to meet with her..." Not to mention that Angel Carter and whoever the hell he worked for wanted the same thing.

"No. Absolutely not! You will not put yourself in their hands, do you understand? I forbid it!" When had her father ever forbidden her anything? When had he been around long enough to do so? Instead, even though her parents had been married, he'd been more like one of those weekend-warrior fathers who offered treats and good times in an attempt to make the most of their moments together.

She swallowed hard, needing to ask the last question before she lost her nerve. "Are you working with them? To undermine the Colombian government?"

He shook his head. "They've sniffed around Earth World for years and even had an employee inserted into our company until I found out and let him go. I would never pit one homeland against the other."

"And yet you're willing to start a war within Colombia. You know that's what will happen if you hire one group to go after another."

He shook his head. "That's different. That's clearing out evil that threatens to destroy everything we love. I am proud of being Colombian. Proud of being an American as well. I don't have to choose one over the other. I can be both."

"Can we?" Adria asked. "I always feel like I'm forced to choose sides. Even going between you and Mama felt the same. I was either Colombian or American, but I was never both."

He squeezed her hand, sadness reappearing. "We thought we were giving you the best of each world."

She bit her cheek so she wouldn't say more, so she wouldn't beg to understand how having neither of them, having tiny moments, was ever supposed to be enough. The silence settled between them for a long moment.

"I don't know what you saw on that video," he told her, "but my heart belongs to your mother. I have never been unfaithful. From the day I saw her onstage, singing at *Fiestas del 11 de noviembre*, I belonged to her. When Claudio introduced us, it was like finding a missing part of myself. Every time we are together, it is the same."

Her heart skipped a beat. His words were too close to thoughts she'd had about Ronan. Too close to the emotions and words Ronan had insisted were true about them. The things he wanted for them. The dreams he could see and that were slowly starting to come into view in front of her. Like a blurry image being re-pixelated.

"How do you do it?" she asked quietly.

"Be apart?"

She nodded.

"Texts and calls and visits. But I'm also comforted knowing she is fulfilled there, surrounded by her family and the girls she's helping. In California, she was only happy when she was guiding you through your contests."

A bitter taste filled her mouth. Maybe if she hadn't been the one to snap the last string tethering her mother to them, she would have stayed. And yet, Adria, her siblings, and her father were Mama's family too. Shouldn't they have been enough for her? Adria would have been miserable if she'd continued on the circuit. Once she'd found the drums, all she'd wanted to do was play them. She hadn't cared about anything but the rhythms beating through her. Maybe they'd all been too selfish, holding on to what they wanted instead of giving in, never sacrificing for those they loved.

It was why she doubted she could do it for Ronan. She didn't know how. She'd never had to before. No one had demanded all-consuming love from her.

"When Vicente started working for you, why didn't you switch places?" she asked him. "Let him handle the work in the States, and you go be with Mama?"

"You might not remember—you were too young—but they took me once." He swallowed, not meeting her gaze, but then he looked back. "I've always been worried they'd come after me again and one of you would be hurt."

Adria's pulse pounded in her veins, the image of a wooden box coming back to her. She wanted to ask about it. To demand he tell her if the nightmares were true. But at the same time, a part of her didn't want to hear the words and be unable to deny it any longer. So, instead, she said, "Are any of us really safe anywhere? They came for us here. Who's to say they won't go for Vicente there? Or Mama?"

Or me again, she couldn't help the thought that stirred.

His chin went up, anger and fire there. "You're right. Which is all the more reason for me to handle this once and for all. I will not stand by and let them harm any of you again. I will not let them use your sister against us."

Her throat bobbed. Worry for him, but also Tatiana, washed over her. "Don't go to Cadencia."

"If that's where she's gone, it gives me even more reason to go," he said firmly. "I will talk sense into her. Convince her of the truth."

She thought again of Tatiana's face at The Attic. The sereneness of her sister. The coldness of her texts. She shivered. She wasn't sure Tati would ever believe anything but what she'd already decided was true. Whoever had fed her sister lies had played right into her sister's scars and her intelligence. But maybe if they presented her with enough facts, she could be saved.

Adria laid her head on his shoulder, and he put an arm around her, squeezing her to him. The weight of the truth and the consequences of their actions was a heavy mantle on her shoulders.

"I need to finish making my plans, *mija*. You're leaving today, correct?"

She lifted her head and nodded. Then, she said, "I still wish you wouldn't go."

"I'll be there tomorrow," his voice was firm. He looked at the collection of bodyguards waiting for them outside the hospital room door. "Do they know?"

"Only Ronan. He was there... He was the one who found Tatiana's message."

Her father's jaw ticked. "You shouldn't tell them. I don't know if you can trust any of them to keep Tatiana out of it."

Her stomach fell. He was still trying to protect her sister, and she didn't blame him, but Adria didn't just have one family to protect. She had The Daisies to consider as well. "I can't have the band in Colombia without the detail knowing enough to take precautions."

He nodded. "But you don't need to tell them it's your sister."

Her chest ached. She didn't know what to do now. She'd been so sure last night. She hated the indecision that crept back inside her.

"I can save her, *mija*."

Could he? Her heart leaped at the idea of having her baby sister back. The Tatiana she'd known and loved. She owed it to her family to at least let him try. Just like Papá had said, they had to reach her before it was too late.

CHAPTER TWENTY-ONE

Ronan

STYLE
Performed by Taylor Swift

TWO DAYS BEFORE

When Adria arrived at the private jet terminal with a V between her brows, her drumsticks twirling, and a heavy silence around her, he immediately wished he'd gone with her to the hospital. He'd told her the truth. He'd needed to put his ducks in a row with Ravaged Storm and his job, but he'd also wanted to call his parents and try to explain what was going on without worrying them. He wasn't sure he'd succeeded. They'd seemed more upset at the end of their call than when they'd started.

"What happened?" he asked quietly, and her eyes darted around to the other band members, their tour team, and the bodyguards. She just shook her head.

Apprehension sifted through him. Was she regretting the tentative step they'd taken the night before? Had something happened that had pulled her back into the shell he'd just broken open? Before he could probe further, they were asked to board the plane, and with the band and some of their crew all in the main cabin with them, there was even less chance of talking.

Adria kept shooting glances in Lennox's direction, and Ronan realized some of her unease was because she'd promised to tell everyone what was happening.

They hadn't been in the air long when Lennox held her to it by saying, "What's really going on, Adria?"

Everyone looked over at where Adria and Ronan were sitting on a couch together. Silence settled down. Adria shot Ronan a look, a warning of some kind, and his stomach twisted. Was she not going to tell them the truth? What the hell had happened at the hospital to change her mind?

"The bombing at my dad's building...the group responsible is *Grupo Nacional Vive Libre* or GNVL."

"They're the same ones who took Tatiana?" Leya's voice was small as she asked.

"But why? I never understood. Your dad's company is changing the world for the better," Nikki insisted.

"They think my dad and Earth World are working with the CIA to undermine the Colombian government," she said. Ronan watched as she showed them her strong and confident face. Just the facts. As if those same words weren't tearing her apart inside.

"How do you know it was them?" Holden asked, dropping the papers he'd been reviewing into a pile on the table and stepping toward them. "My understanding is the FBI and the ATF have barely started their investigation."

"GNVL contacted me."

"Jesus. And you didn't tell me? Any of us?" Holden snapped, shoving his good hand into his pocket while the one he'd barely removed a sling from remained clenched at his side. He was upset, and he had every right to be, but Ronan wasn't going to let him make Adria feel worse than she already did.

"You have no idea what she's been through. So, back off."

Holden shot a glare at Ronan. "What are you even doing here besides getting ready to piss Adria off some more? I thought you said the documentary was done."

"Everybody take a breath," Asher demanded, rising to his feet as well.

"Why don't we let Adria finish what she was trying to tell us," Nikki said, tightening the dual buns that sat on either side of her head. Even after she was done, they looked like they were going to topple down at any second.

Ronan turned back to Adria, watching as her jaw flexed and her nostrils flared, and he realized the truth. She wasn't going to say it was her sister.

"GNVL has made some half-assed threats against me. They said I basically had to choose between my dad and Colombia." Every word was calm, only the way she rotated the two drumsticks in her hand giving away how she really felt.

"Or what?" Paisley asked.

Adria's sticks stopped and started before she finally replied, "I don't know. But we're going to be on their home field. They'll have more resources. I just wanted everyone to know so we can be extra vigilant."

"We shouldn't be going to Colombia at all," Lennox growled.

"Did Carter know all this? Is he working for them?" Holden demanded.

Adria shook her head. "He wanted answers and wanted me to call him if GNVL made contact again. He said you and Asher owed him, and this was what he wanted as payment."

"So, you've seen some of them? You know who they are?" Holden asked. Adria looked down, fidgeting more with her drumsticks, without saying anything. When she glanced back up, she shot a warning at Ronan again. Holden didn't notice as he'd gone back to the stack of papers he'd left on the table. He shuffled through them and came back with one. "Marco and Trevor found a librarian in Boston who saw Carter meeting several times with the same man. She sat down with a sketch artist to give us this. Is this any of the GNVL members you know?"

He handed Adria a paper with a black-and-white artist's rendering of a man. Ronan leaned over to look at it as well. The man was probably in his forties. He looked rough around the edges, and there was a coldness to his eyes that was only emphasized by a scar along his jaw, jagged and raised. Adria shook her head.

"I don't know him."

Nikki caught sight of the paper and reached for it with a shaky hand. "This man was meeting with Carter?"

Holden nodded. "Do you know him?"

Nikki handed the paper back as if it was on fire. "No."

Ronan's instincts screamed something was off. Why would Nikki lie about knowing him? Holden eyed her for a long moment as if he sensed the same thing. "You're sure? It might not be a good drawing. The man was pretty cagey every time they met, and the librarian said he kept his head down. We never got a clear shot of him on any of the cameras."

Nikki shook her head, the buns almost toppling again. "I don't know him."

"Let's get back to GNVL and Carter," Lennox said, bringing everyone's attention back to Adria. "We need to tighten our ranks. No unscheduled stops. The plans for the fiesta should be canceled."

Adria's head whipped to her bodyguard. "We don't have to go to the street fair, but I'm cohosting the pageant with Mama. I can't back out now."

"Definitely no street fair," Holden said. "It's too big of a risk. We couldn't possibly cover you safely."

"What would you have us do, stick to our rooms for five days?" Fiadh complained.

"The estate is plenty big enough for you to be entertained while there," Holden replied dryly. The Rojas's compound was basically a five-star resort, sitting on fifty acres along a private shoreline with equestrian facilities, a fishing pond, two swimming pools, a bowling alley, a theater, and a miniature golf course. There would definitely be plenty to do.

"Being entertained isn't the point. This was Adria's chance to show us her hometown," Fee pushed.

"I agree with Kent," Asher said. "We should stick to the estate and the stadium."

"They're not coming after us, right?" Leya asked, a tremble to her lip as she stared at Holden. He was at her side in two steps, tucking her hand in his, pulling her into his side, and kissing her temple.

"Hopefully, it's just a precaution," he said softly.

"If they came for anyone, it would be me," Adria said quietly, and Ronan's stomach revolted. Had they come for her that day at the pond like Warren Times had insinuated? Mistaking Landry for Adria? When Adria's shoulders tightened, back going rigid, he knew her mind had gone to the same place. She looked at Paisley, and for the first time since starting the conversation, true emotions showed on her face. Regret and sorrow. She swallowed hard and then choked out a pained, "I'm sorry... I think... *Dios*."

Ronan couldn't stop himself from tugging her to him, and everyone's eyes went wide. Surprisingly, she didn't fight him. Instead, she gripped his thigh tightly, pulled herself together, and then started again. "I think—"

"Don't!" Paisley interrupted, her normally quiet voice sharp with grief. "Even if it's true, Ads. Even if they came looking for you and found Lan..." Her throat bobbed. "That isn't on you. You didn't do this to her."

"Even if it's true," Holden said gently, "there's still a lot that doesn't fit. We don't know if it was GNVL at the pond. We have Carter and this man he met with still in the mix."

Fee shook her head. "Angel could have hurt me any of the times we met. He could have left you and Leya on the side of the road, Holden. He could have done something worse to Adria and Ronan last night. I don't understand why he's involved, but I don't think he was the one who killed Landry."

"Unless he botched the job and is now paying penance," Asher said, and Ronan's heart twisted for his friend who'd paid penance for far too long for things he could never change. Ronan was glad Asher had left Wren in the States, because if things went sideways, it would just be one more thing Asher would hold himself responsible for.

"Why kill one Daisy and then save all the others? That doesn't make any sense," Lennox spoke up.

"Carter knows something about what happened. I'm sure of it," Holden said, brushing his hand through his hair and then going back to the table and papers piled there.

Jonas had been sitting with Paisley, his knee bouncing

uncontrollably the whole time, and now he rose to join Holden, looking down at the papers. "What is all this?"

Holden darted a look at the bandmembers as if he was uncomfortable talking about it with them there. "It's the evidence that's been gathered in her case."

Jonas picked up a photo and scoffed, "A feather? The pond was swarming with birds."

"Not now," Holden groused, glancing at Paisley, but she got up and went to the table too, taking the photo from Jonas.

"If not now, when? I have a right to know, Holden. Why is the feather important? What else do you know that no one has shared with us?" She looked so much like Landry right then, standing there demanding answers, one hand on her hip, that it took Ronan's breath away. Landry had said Paisley was hiding everything she could truly be by letting others stand at the front and take the lead, and she'd been right. Paisley had stepped into the light only after her sister was gone, but it seemed wrong that it had to have happened that way.

Holden tipped his head toward the picture she held. "The feather is from a Regina astrapia. It's a type of bird-of-paradise, and the only place on Earth it exists is an island in the Mediterranean called San Fiore. The royal family there has an aviary full of them. There's no way one of the birds could have been at the pond that night as they're kept under lock and key."

"You think someone placed it there as what? A message?" Nikki stuttered out. Her face was pale, and everyone noticed.

Holden gave a curt nod. "But none of us have been able to figure out what it means."

"Isn't that the island you and your stepmom visited last year, Nik?" Leya asked.

Nikki swallowed. "Yes. But we'd never been there before that. My dad never wanted to sail in Europe, so that was the first time Mom and I had ever taken a trip in the Mediterranean."

"I've heard of it also... Damn, it, I can't remember why. Something Torrance told me..." Asher's brows were drawn together. "I'll call him when we land. He'll remember."

"And rub it in how he's the best assistant you've ever had," Fee teased.

"So, this is all of it?" Paisley asked. Her voice shook with anger and frustration. "A sketch of a stranger, a man no one can seem to catch, and a feather? This is really all there is after over two years?"

"We've cleared hundreds of people who were or could have been there as well as many of those who might have had a grievance with Landry and the Daisies. That took time. We also know the knife used was a Yarborough. The tip is broken. It's distinct enough that we'd be able to match it if we found it."

Beside him, Adria's fingers swirled again, her drumsticks moving back into action. "Is that hard to find? A Yarborough?"

"It's exclusively made for and used by the Green Berets, but you can find them on auction sites if you look hard enough," Holden said.

Ronan's eyes found Nikki's, thinking of the man who'd just spent several months teaching him hand-to-hand combat. The man was intense, his military bearing a rudimentary part of him. But Ronan couldn't think of any reason he'd have to hurt Landry, not even if he'd mistaken her for Nikki. When Barry had talked about Nikki, it had been with the same kind of pride and love in his voice as Ronan's parents when they talked about him. And yet, the man had been there that night at the farmhouse.

Nikki rose from the couch, fingers pressed into her temples as if staving off a migraine. "I'm going to go take one of my pills and lie down. I can't... This is all just too much."

Everyone watched as she crossed the room to the door leading to a single bedroom at the back of the plane. When she'd left, Ronan said quietly to the others, "Nikki's friend. The guy who trained me. He's a former Green Beret."

Holden nodded. "I know. He and Nikki's mom had just gotten into town that night. Their story checked out."

"I want to know everything, Holden. I deserve to be told whatever you find as you find it," Paisley said, chin raised.

His eyes flicked to Leya and back. "I just didn't want to hurt any of you more by bringing it up."

"It's never going to hurt less," Fee said. She had tears in her eyes, but they barely obscured the fiery blaze beneath them. "And thinking no one is even trying to find her killer... that's even worse."

"We're trying. I promise," Holden said.

Paisley handed Holden the picture, and then said, "I'm going to go check on Nik."

Ronan thought maybe someone should do more than talk to her. He had an uneasy feeling in his chest, as if there was something they'd all missed but Nikki was starting to see, as if she held all the clues in a box she was afraid to open.

The air was heavy as everyone returned to the activities they'd been doing before Lennox had drawn their attention to Adria. Ronan turned to watch her twirl her drumsticks. She was leaned back on the couch as if she was relaxed, as if the sorrow of the last few minutes hadn't happened at all, but really, he could sense the tension radiating from every pore. He wanted to soothe it away. To kiss it away. To make her forget every bad thing that had happened to her, her family, and the band in the last two years.

Kissing her into oblivion with the others watching wasn't an option. He'd been surprised she'd let him hug her with them looking on. Inch by inch, he was winning her over. Pretty soon, he'd have her convinced of everything he knew was true about them. She'd see what he could see. The life they could have together. He had more hope than he'd ever had since she'd stormed out of the Seattle hotel.

His gaze fell on a stack of board games in a glass-fronted cabinet at the back of the living area. Many of them would be too easy to keep her thoughts distracted for long, but there was a chessboard amongst them.

He went and grabbed it, returned to the couch, and started setting it up on the coffee table.

"What are you doing?" she asked, brow raised.

"Passing the time. Do you know how to play?" he asked.

She leaned forward, helping with the pieces. "*Tío*—Claudio used to play with us when we were little. Vicente and I got bored of it easily, but he and Tatiana would talk opening gambits and strategy for hours."

"I bet, to a mind like hers, it was like candy," Ronan said, shooting a glance to the others and then leaning in. "You didn't tell them."

She scowled, a look he'd grown used to her sending his way over the last few years, but he much preferred her wink and smile. She said quietly, "Papá insisted. He wants a chance to fix things with her."

"You told him."

She nodded. "He denied everything."

"You believe him?"

231

She nodded. "He was so upset...hurt that any of us could think these things of him. He insisted he loved Mama and has been faithful. I can't explain what we saw, Ronan, but it doesn't match with what I know of my father."

She'd chosen the white pieces and made the first move. He countered, not really knowing much about chess strategy, only enough to play.

She looked up at him with a knowing smirk. "That was a really bad move."

He laughed. "It was a pawn. I moved one square."

She winked, the confident, vixen-like wink that did things to his soul he'd never understand but ached to have on repeat over and over again.

"You'll see, Hollywood. I've got you in...no more than fifteen moves."

He chuckled again. "Want to make a bet?"

She raised a brow. "Absolutely."

He leaned in close to her ear, whispering, "I win, and you sleep in my room."

Her gaze drifted to his lips and then back up. "And when I win?"

"*If* you win, I sleep in yours."

She laughed, and it filled his chest with warmth and love. God, he loved her. So damn much. Enough that he was on a plane to Colombia, risking screwing up everything with Ravaged Storm and disappointing his best friend.

"That's ridiculous. You still get what you want either way."

His hand skimmed her thigh. "I usually do."

She swatted him away. "Well, now you've just shot yourself in the foot because *when* I win, you're on your own for tonight."

He let it go, watching as she moved her next piece,

already knowing she was going to win. He'd meant what he'd told her last night. He didn't want them to fall into bed together in a pile of physical need, looking for escape. Even when they'd first started hooking up, he'd rebelled when she'd called what they did simply sex. His soul had already known it was more. Hers did too. She just couldn't see it yet. So maybe it was better if, for the next few nights, he left her on her own. Let her figure out that she already knew everything there was to know about all-consuming love. She just needed to listen to her heart and her soul instead of the fear.

And if, for some reason, she tried to drift away, thinking she didn't have it in her, he'd do exactly what he'd told her. He'd show her every last piece of the love that already beat inside her.

CHAPTER TWENTY-TWO

Adria

I SHALL BELIEVE
Performed by Sheryl Crow

I t had been eight months since she'd been back to *Casa Buganvillas*. As soon as Adria stepped out of the bullet-proof SUV and breathed in the scents of her home, her chest eased ever so slightly. As a child, it had seemed like a resort. A holiday excursion. Whenever they'd visited Mama as kids, Adria and her siblings had spent their days at the pool, riding horses, and competing to be the best at every game possible. It wasn't until after Tati had disappeared and her mother had brought her back to Colombia that she'd finally and truly felt at home here.

Gated and fenced in with tall walls of electrified barbed wire, visitors might think it felt prisonlike, but once you were past the gates and the fences disappeared, it was like being in a wonderland. The heavenly scented bougainvilleas the property was named after grew alongside orchids and sharp-pointed bromeliads. The cascade of brightly colored flowers was a contrast to the dense green of the wide-leafed palms, plumerias, and vine-covered mahogany trees. The wild of the jungle was left untamed until it neared the mansion. There it turned into manicured gardens and koi ponds that were maintained by a dozen landscapers.

"Holy feck," Fiadh said as she stepped out of the Escalade next to Adria, and pride filled her as she looked up at her family's home. It really was stunning.

Ablaze with carefully placed recessed lighting, the ornate façade of *Casa Buganvillas* looked like a famous monument instead of a private mansion. It had been designed by the famous architect who'd redone the government palace in Peru, and he'd used similar floral carvings and festoons here. They dripped over the bronze-colored stones like candle wax, and if you looked closely, you'd find a menagerie of fantastical creatures peeking out from the windows and doors.

"It's like…you're a princess," Leya said.

Adria chuckled. "It's been in Mama's family for a long time."

"I can see why you said there was plenty of room," Paisley laughed.

The ten-foot, gilded front door opened, and her mother and brother stepped out. Adria rushed to them, and they encircled her in their embrace. Her mother was dressed in heels, a fitted skirt, and a silk tank that showed off strong arms and a body that could still walk a runway even at fifty-one. She could pass as Adria's sister with ease instead of her mother. Her eyes were the same bright blue as Adria's whereas Vicente and Tatiana had inherited their father's paler ones.

Her mother pulled back, patting her cheek, and then turned to her friends. "Welcome to *Casa Buganvillas*. It is a pleasure to have you here."

She greeted the band while Vicente looked Adria over. Just like their father, he was tall, black-haired, and light-skinned. A lightweight suit jacket covered his broad shoulders that was too heavy for the oppressive humidity clinging to the air even though the sun had already set. Adria had already broken out in a sweat after standing outside the vehicles for mere minutes. She'd been away too long. Her body was unaccustomed to the muggy air, and yet, it still felt like wrapping herself in a blanket at the end of the day. Home.

Vicente leaned in and said quietly, "You owe me a conversation."

Their eyes locked, and Adria wondered what her father had told him, or if Tati had reached out to him just as she had Adria.

She just nodded.

"Come inside," her mother said, leading the way through the doors.

"*Hey ram*," Leya said as she glanced around the entryway that had taken inspiration from the Versailles Hall of Mirrors. Layered in gold but with hints of red and black, it glimmered in both east and west directions with doors to a multitude of salons and living spaces leading off it. Through an archway with cupids and angels carved above it, a wide white marble staircase was visible, splitting off in two directions to the next level.

A flurry of staff in uniforms appeared, waiting silently to show her friends to their rooms.

"Please go settle in," her mother said with a wave toward the stairs. "Aperitifs will be served at seven thirty in the yellow salon. Any of the staff can show you how to get there. Dinner is at eight. If it's too much after your travels, just ring the bell in your room, and someone will bring you a tray."

Adria almost winced at the formality of it, as if they were the royalty Leya had teased about outside. While her mother wasn't part of any actual nobility, she *was* the only child of one of the wealthiest families on the continent.

As Adria followed her friends and the staff up the staircase, Ronan caught up, leaning in to whisper, "I know you won our bet, but I still don't like being too far away with everything that's going on. How far are our rooms from each other?"

She snorted. "You lost, Hollywood. Fair and square."

"I'm not reneging on our bet, even if you did hustle me. You said your sister was the chess pro," he said with a wry smile.

"No, I said she was better than me."

He was still smiling. A grin that wasn't just his charming Hollywood prince one but, instead, was full of natural affection. It made her resolve weaken. It made her want to give in simply because the last two nights with him at her side had brought her comfort and because she knew they both ached to lose themselves in each other's touch. To lose themselves in the ragged, beautiful escape desire brought from the things following them into the night.

But he'd made it clear he didn't want just sex and release. He wanted more, and until she could offer him everything he saw in his vision, she had to respect that. If she let him in her room, neither of them would. They'd be right back to where they'd been last night with mouths and fingers and skin on skin. So, until she figured out what all-consuming love looked like and if she could give it, she had to go into her room alone.

The problem with that scenario was that if he remained worried about her safety, he wouldn't be able to walk down the hall without her. She reached out and squeezed his hand, saying quietly, "I'm safe here, Ronan. The estate is practically a fortress."

His smile slipped, but he didn't argue, as if he too, knew what would happen if they stayed together again. She headed for her room while a staff member took him down the hall to his. She turned back to see him watching which door she entered. He was only four rooms away from her. Not far. But far enough.

As soon as the door shut behind her, the emptiness hit her immediately—solitude where her thoughts tried to creep in and take hold. She fought running down the hall and bringing Ronan to her. Forced herself to step farther into the room and let the lavender and cornflower colors soothe her.

White furniture trimmed in silver filled the room from the white canopied bed to the intricately carved desk in the corner. It was pretty and feminine. The world normally saw Adria as the edgiest, snarkiest member of the Daisies, but once upon a time, she'd also been a beauty contestant. Here, she felt more like that version of herself than the drummer who preferred Doc Martens and leather.

She headed for the large walk-in closet, immediately shedding the jeans, T-shirt, and boots she'd worn on the plane and pulling on a light cotton dress. It would provide some relief against the heat and humidity, but it was also what her mother would expect her to wear to supper. The top was closely fitted, accenting her breasts before swinging away from her hips to land mid-thigh. It was light blue with silver threads twirling through it like the vines on the mahogany trees outside. She slid her feet into silver sandals that bared her toe rings, and she was thankful that she'd had a pedicure not long ago. The pale-peach color was a tone her mother would approve.

She went through the door to her en suite, the white and platinum fixtures shimmering. She dug in the drawers to find several silver- and diamond-beaded hairpins along with a hair tie that she could pile her hair on top of her head with. After touching up her makeup enough that her mother wouldn't comment, she headed downstairs in search of Vicente.

As much as she was nervous about being alone with her brother, afraid she'd end up spilling her guts, she also needed proof Tatiana was wrong. If she could convince her sister the video wasn't what she thought, maybe it would pick at all the other lies GNVL had filled her with as well.

She found her brother in his office in a wing of the house rarely used by anyone else. He was standing behind a large black desk, tapping through something on his laptop, but he looked up as she entered. "You look tired, *pollita*."

"It's been a long few days," she said in Spanish, making her way over to him and sitting in one of the wingbacks across from him. "Have you heard from Papá today?"

Vicente frowned, slipping into Spanish along with her. "He shouldn't be coming. I don't think it's safe."

She nodded.

"What the hell is happening?" he demanded.

"GNVL was responsible for the attack," she said, guilt overwhelming her for not telling him more. She ached to do so, but her dad had asked her to keep the secret a little longer. If they could convince Tati of the truth, convince her to come home, it would ease the hurt their sister's betrayal would cause both him and their mother.

Her brother's jaw ticked. Frustration obvious on his face.

"I don't understand why they continue to target us when we've done nothing but try to better Colombia. We've even supported causes they've initiated. This feels much more personal."

Adria couldn't look at him. She rose, picking up a picture on his desk of the five of them. She and her siblings were mere teenagers, and the entire family was in riding gear, even Mama. They'd had a picnic down on the sandy beach along the estate's northern edge. It had been a good day—one of their rare moments when both parents had been in the same country at the same time.

The joy of that moment had been almost inexplicable. It had felt like love. But then, Papa had left for Asia, and she and her siblings had been sent back to California for school. The happiness she'd felt in that moment hadn't been enough to last through the first nightmare that had jerked her from her sleep, or the fact it was her sister rather than her parents who were there to comfort her.

She put the frame down, sadness filling her for all of them.

She turned back to her brother. "Would someone be able to access old schedules, travel arrangements, that sort of thing for employees of Earth World from several years ago?" she asked.

Vicente's brows creased. "Either our assistants or accounts payable would have the information. Why?"

"I need to know if Claudio was in California on a certain date."

Vicente's face paled, and he sat down. "You think...you think this is *Tío*?"

She hadn't. She'd only wanted to prove to Tati it wasn't their father in the video. But the idea of Claudio being involved settled in her gut like bad milk. Could he be behind it all? He'd been livid when Vicente had found out about his embezzlement scheme. He'd adamantly denied it, even though the proof had been irrefutable... just like the supposed proof of their father's affair. Instead of getting the authorities involved, Papá had bought out Claudio's stake in Earth World. It had been a way of saving face for all of them and to ensure Earth World's customers wouldn't worry about the company's solvency. *Tío* had walked away a rich man when he should have gone to prison. He should have been grateful.

But maybe he wasn't.

She shook her head. There was nothing to tie this to Claudio, other than a possible video of him having sex in an Earth World Solution's conference room. "I don't know. I don't think so. This...this is something else I need an answer to."

"You're holding back, Adria. Tell me what's going on."

She swallowed hard. "I can't. Not yet."

"If you can't trust me, who the hell can you trust?" His voice was dark and grim in a way Vicente's never was.

"It isn't that I don't trust you. It's more like..."

"You're trying to protect me!" he finished for her. "Just like Tati used to do. I'm the oldest, and yet you both treated me as if I was the youngest, some tiny kid needing to be sheltered. Just because I chose a path that neither of you understood didn't mean I wasn't able to defend myself."

Adria didn't say anything, because it was the truth.

"Remember when Tati punched Nico Jennings?" he asked, and Adria nodded. "I would have taken the hit because I knew he'd be suspended for it, and then I'd get to swoop in and steal his girlfriend out from under him."

"Wasn't his girlfriend Tammy? You did date her, right?"

He grinned. "Yep. And I can tell you, she never regretted

giving up the bully for the pacifist." He waggled his eyebrows. "I wasn't a fumbling idiot. I actually had moves."

"*Dios*, I don't need to hear about your sex life!"

The light moment settled over them just as the gong rang, announcing drinks being served. They both stood automatically, knowing that being late would only upset their mother.

Vicente pulled her arm through his as they walked out of his study. "Give me the dates, and I'll ask Marietta to look them up, but then you need to come clean with why you needed them."

She nodded but didn't promise, because she couldn't.

When they got to the salon, they were the last to arrive. Her band and the men in their lives were all there, except Nikki. It didn't surprise Adria that her friend had decided to stay in her room. If the migraine she'd been fighting on the plane had blossomed into a feral beast, she needed the dark and quiet to help wash it away.

When Ronan's eyes locked on her, Adria's feet stalled. He took her in from top to bottom, a slow smile taking over his face, which brought a curl of heat to her stomach. Electricity zipped across the room between them. She was overwhelmed with the desire to march across the room and kiss him regardless of who was watching. It was almost a compulsion. A need that made her entire being ache to fulfill it.

His brow raised as if he'd read her thoughts.

Vicente leaned in, squeezing her arm. "I don't want to know about your sex life either, *pollita*. Maybe keep the flames to yourself."

Her gaze jerked from Ronan's sexy smile to her brother's grin. If Vicente could read the sexual tension sweeping across the room between them, it meant her friends did as well. She scanned the band's faces. Only Fiadh's eyes danced with merriment as she darted a look between Adria and Ronan. Fee had once sworn she hated Asher as much as Adria had sworn she hated Ronan, so maybe that was why it was Fiadh who saw the truth more than any of the others.

But just like the truth of her sister's betrayal, the truth of what she felt for Ronan could also wound. It could leave marks she'd never be able to take back. She'd been open and honest about it, and he hadn't run. He'd actually doubled down and stayed. He saw her as this brave, resilient creature, whereas she often felt like she was getting through life by hiding.

To fear love is to fear life.

She didn't want to be afraid anymore. She wanted that full life he saw for them, but she didn't know how to cross the divide to get there.

CHAPTER TWENTY-THREE

Adria

BEST THING I NEVER HAD
Performed by Aly Stiles

ONE DAY BEFORE

The next morning, when Adria made her way downstairs, it was with her bag and her sticks in hand. She was ready to go to the arena. To find herself in her drums. To find a beat she could rely on when there were so many things she couldn't.

Mama was already in the morning room with a cup of coffee and a plate of arepas in front of her. She kissed her mother's cheek and went to the buffet to grab her own plate of the stuffed cornmeal pancakes along with some smashed plantains. When she sat down, she poured herself a cup of the best coffee known to humanity from the carafe on the table. She sipped, sighing with pleasure. There was nowhere else in the world that had coffee that tasted like this—like home.

"What time does Papá arrive today?" she asked in Spanish.

"Before the opening ceremony."

The next few days were going to be a blur of activity. After the band rehearsed this morning, she and her mom would be meeting with some of the teens they'd been mentoring. Then, they'd be kicking off the pageant and the festival with the opening ceremonies where The Daisies were playing "Wild in You." The following day, more of the pageant's rounds would take place in the morning and afternoon before the Teen Colombia winner was announced live in the evening. The band's concert would wrap everything up on the last day.

The fact that they'd be so busy was a mixed blessing. She was grateful it would keep her from dwelling on everything happening with her sister, her dad, and even Ronan, but she was also worried about when and where Tati might turn up next. She was worried she wouldn't have what she needed to prove to her sister she was wrong before someone else got hurt.

It was a heavy burden she couldn't shake, and her mother seemed to sense it.

"What are you and your father keeping from me?" Mama asked, raising a brow over her cup as she took a sip.

"You sound like Vicente," Adria said, turning her attention to the food in front of her.

"Adria," she insisted.

When she looked up, her mother's gaze was sad and pained. Adria's heart skipped a beat, and the truth about Tatiana almost burst free. But then her mother's phone rang, and when Adria looked down at the screen, Claudio's name was there.

Her mother didn't answer it, letting it go to voicemail.

"I can't believe you're still in contact with *Tío* after everything that happened," Adria said, annoyed. Vicente's idea that Claudio was behind all of this...it left a sour taste in her mouth. But she had as little proof for that scenario as she did for her father not being the devil her sister believed.

"We don't talk often. Family deserves a chance to be forgiven for their mistakes," her mother said quietly.

"He's not family, Mama. And what he did... He never even acknowledged it was wrong. He just went away mad, as if Papá had somehow injured him."

Her mother tore at the arepa with a fork in a decidedly un-Yesenia-like way. "Our families have been twined together for generations. Claudio has been there for me since I was a little girl. What is that if not family?"

An uncomfortable feeling sat in Adria's gut she couldn't put her finger on. Something about their relationship that was tickling her protective instincts. Was Claudio using Mama like he'd once used Earth World? Had her mother found out about her father's supposed affair and turned to Claudio for comfort?

"Papá and Vicente would not agree with you," she said.

"If your brother did something wrong, would you not forgive him?"

It hit Adria in the chest. It was too close to the truth about Tatiana. Could she forgive Tati for nearly killing their father? For actually killing Jorge? Nothing her sister said about their father could ever justify almost killing him. She couldn't imagine Vicente, with his nonviolent ways, forgiving their sister. Her stomach swam, and the food she'd put in it turned to stone. She pushed the plate away.

"I have to go." She rose, determined to escape. She needed to be behind her drums, losing herself in something that didn't demand she choose. Something that allowed her to just be freely herself without having to wear another layer of skin over the top.

"*Mija*," her mother called. The tender term of endearment wasn't used often by her mother, whereas Papá used it so much it was almost an article. "Why does this upset you so much?"

"I can't talk now, Mama."

Because if she did, she'd tell her everything and then demand her mother give up all her secrets too. How had they all ended up keeping so many from each other? How had they drifted so far apart? Her mother had lied to her when she'd said a handful of pictures would allow you to keep the pieces of the people you loved with you.

She was losing them all. A wave of panic flew through her, and it brought dark wood walls along with it. Fingers scratching, slivers embedding in the pads.

She looked down at her hands, pressing on the scar on her thumb, long and jagged.

She turned, showing it to her mother. "How did I get this?"

Her mom visibly paled. "A riding accident?" It sounded like she'd intended for it to be a statement, but it came out more like a question with an uncertain lilt to the end.

"Mama...my nightmares..."

Paisley and Fiadh entered the room with Leya right behind them.

Her mother looked relieved, and all it did was tighten Adria's stomach further. She'd told Ronan she'd been feeling more and more lately like her nightmare wasn't just a dream. But she'd still wanted to deny it. After her father's reaction the day before and her Mama's now, she could no longer do that. It was real. Even having already suspected it, the harshness of the truth struck her like a blow to her sternum, leaving her breathless.

Why would someone have done that to her? And when?

A shiver ran up her spine, and she couldn't look at her friends. She forced her voice to be normal, but it still had a bite to it when she said, "I'm heading to the arena a little early. I'll meet you there."

Then, she almost ran from the room without waiting for a reply, her feet on the marble a rat-a-tat-tat that sent shivers over her spine. Lennox was near the front door, and Adria told her she was leaving early. Her bodyguard didn't look too happy, but she simply relayed the plan to the rest of the detail and led her outside to one of the waiting vehicles.

The SUV was bulletproof with darkened windows, and the bodyguard in the passenger's seat held a semiautomatic rifle. It sent another swirl of nausea through her at the idea of them needing this much protection. From her sister... From GNVL... From someone who'd stuffed her in a box.

The memories of the dark space hit her stronger than ever. It was as if she'd finally hit play on the entire event, and more and more of it came reeling to life. The little fingers scratching at the wood were bleeding, and she was crying... her face felt puffy and raw from the tears. She remembered her breathing getting shallow and could almost taste the dirty air as she gasped for breath.

Her phone buzzed. She flipped it over to see Ronan's name, and her stomach fell.

RONAN: You left?

She could almost feel his disapproval. He hadn't liked

being four doors down from her last night, and now there'd be miles between them. She almost wished she'd brought him with her. But what could he do? What could he say that would fix this? Nothing.

ADRIA: I needed to leave before I told Mama everything.

RONAN: You should.

No. She shouldn't. How could she? They hadn't told her the truth about her nightmare. She'd been shoved in a box as a little girl! Maybe Tatiana was right. Maybe there was more going on with her family than she'd ever known or wanted to see. Maybe they'd all betrayed each other.

When she didn't respond, he sent her another message.

RONAN: Star. What's going on? Don't shut down on me now.

ADRIA: We'll talk later. Right now, I just need my drums.

She grimaced as soon as she hit send. It sounded like she needed an inanimate object more than she needed him. And in some ways, that was true because he would make her think and talk and feel, and all she wanted to do was get lost.

The crowded streets of Cadencia swirled into view. Surrounded by white-washed buildings that blended with modern high-rises, it was a city that had held on to its past while marching toward a modern future. Street vendors and old markets blended in with new stores. Donkeys pulled carts while electric vehicles drove beside them. All of it called to her in the same way her family's estate did, as if there was a part of her that would only ever be alive when it was here.

The arena was one of the modern marvels recently added to the cityscape. Built near the ocean, the huge glass façade reflected the waves and the sea, the teal of the ocean blending in with the sky. Surrounded by palms and bougainvilleas, the bright-pink flowers contrasted with the blues of the water, turning the entire scene into a vivid abstract painting that sparkled in the sunshine.

They parked near the rear entrance, and Lennox had them wait as the two vehicles trailing them arrived and a sniper got into position on the roof. It felt like overkill. Too much. And yet, it felt like not enough as the images of a wooden box held on to her.

Once the detail was in place, everyone in their SUV got out, hovering around Adria as they made their way into the arena. Her heart pounded furiously until they were inside, but even there, she wasn't sure she felt safe. They made their way down the back corridors to the tunnel leading to the stage. Her drum kit was already put together, and Zia was there, directing the crew as they set up the band's other instruments.

When Adria told her she needed some extra time on the drums, Zia cleared everyone out. Then she hustled off in her lightning-bug-like way to do the million other things she and Jonas did before each show to make sure the concert went off without a hitch.

Adria warmed up with a few old-school rudiments before she quickly lost herself to the more intense patterns. One song blended into the other until they weren't songs but just long rhythms and beats that she loved. Like the waves pounding outside the arena and the thunderstorms that blew through Cadencia almost daily. Like the tapping of hands on a box as her father called her name. That stopped her completely. The arena turned silent as the last vibrations faded away. Sweat dripped down her face and slipped down her back.

Had her father found her? Or had he been there all along?

Her stomach flipped.

A movement in the seats at the top of the stadium caught her eye. A woman was there. Tall, willowy, with long black hair cascading down to her waist. No seventies apparel in sight. Instead, she wore a bright-pink and blue *la pollera colora* with a round-necked blouse that showed off her shoulders. Adria couldn't be a hundred percent sure, but her entire being told her it was Tatiana. How had she gotten into the arena with all their security? The woman took a seat, casually watching the stage. The light shifted through the glass ceiling, and the woman almost disappeared in the glare.

Adria's eyes went to Lennox, her finger on her ear, listening carefully to whatever was being communicated. Adria needed to talk to Tatiana. She had to figure out a way to get up into the stands alone. She rose from her drums and went to the edge of the stage, but the woman was already gone.

Jueputa, had she missed her chance?

Maybe she could still catch her in the tunnels. Adria turned toward the corridor just as the rest of the band came through. Frustration brewed deep inside her. The momentary peace she'd found at the drums was sucked away by the dark memories, her sister, and the fear that there was still worse coming for all of them.

As her friends all moved to their various instruments to tune and finesse them, Adria's eyes landed on Nikki. She looked tired and washed out as she always did after a migraine had gripped her. Stress was a trigger, and it pained Adria to know she was adding to it.

She made her way over to her and asked softly, "You okay, Nik?"

She shrugged. "Yep. You?"

"I'm as good as I can be, given the situation." Adria gave her a half-truth.

"Some days, I feel like..." Her friend stuffed her hands into the pockets of her shorts, looking out into the stadium. "Never mind."

"Nik," Adria's voice was full of concern.

"Seriously, I'm fine." But she wasn't. They stared at each other, both knowing the other was keeping secrets but unwilling to come clean. Just like Adria and her family. She didn't know how to fix it. To fix any of it.

It was Nikki who turned away first, picking up her guitar, closing her eyes and tuning it by ear. Adria watched as the dread she'd felt all morning crept back in stronger than ever.

In many ways, she'd found more of a home with the band than with her own family. And yet, she'd always held something back from them, just like she had with Ronan, because she wasn't used to anyone staying for long. They had all fallen apart when Landry died, almost as if Adria had predicted it. But they'd promised each other not to do it again. Now, she was just terrified that in staying, being together, she was putting them all in danger.

The thought brought more waves of panic.

She had to find Tati.

She had to find her sister and end this before it was too late.

CHAPTER TWENTY-FOUR

Ronan

ROCK BOTTOM
Performed by Hailee Steinfeld

Ronan was frustrated Adria had left without him. He'd put aside everything in his life to come with her, and she'd ducked out instead of talking to him about whatever had spooked her. *I just need my drums.* It bit at him, and he tried not to let it. This was her coping mechanism. This was how she got through everything—by hiding. Behind a calm veneer, behind her drums, behind an attitude that said *I don't need anyone.*

He was antsy, wanting to follow her to the arena, but he was stuck waiting for the rest of the band to go since Adria had taken a number of the vehicles with her. By the time they got in the SUV, he was practically vibrating.

The security at the arena was as tight as Ronan had ever seen it, and yet Holden still didn't look happy as they darted from the cars to a back door. Ronan headed for the stage behind the Daisies, knowing he'd find Adria there even though he couldn't hear the drums she'd said she needed.

Asher's voice calling to him slowed his steps. His friend joined him in two long strides. "We haven't really had a chance to talk. How are you really holding up?"

Ronan gave a careless shrug, turning to continue toward the stage, and Asher kept pace with him. "I'm not the one we need to be worried about."

"Really? Because you look like shit. Have you been having nightmares again?" Asher pressed, and Ronan couldn't meet his friend's eyes because Asher knew him too well for him to lie. He'd had another one last night. The same one with Adria in the bathtub with him. Until this situation with her sister was resolved, he didn't think they'd stop.

Instead of telling his friend any of that, he changed the subject. "Can I ask you something? What do you plan on doing when Tommy gets back?"

The band's actual manager, who Asher had been standing in for, was due out of rehab in January. As president of mergers and acquisitions at RMI, Asher was much more than just the Daisies' record label owner. He had an entire company to run with his father.

"Do about what?" Asher asked, brows furrowing.

"About you and Fee."

"I'll be with her as much as the tour and my schedule allow. Is this what's holding you back from whatever is going on with you and Adria? Your careers?" Asher asked.

It was only part of it, but he didn't feel like telling Asher how he was almost desperate to prove to Adria she knew how to love with all her heart and soul. "You turn snarly the moment Fee's out of the room. How are you going to stand days or weeks apart?"

Asher brushed a hand over his hair, a sure sign Ronan had struck a nerve. "I don't need to be at our corporate headquarters to do my job. I can do it from practically anywhere."

"But what about when you become the chief operating officer?"

"Maybe I won't take the position."

Ronan's heart squeezed tighter at Asher's answer. Ronan didn't want to give up the studio and the dreams he was finally making happen, and he knew Adria wouldn't like it if he did any more than the idea of them spending volumes of time apart. The stage came into view in front of them, and there she was, talking with Nikki.

Her back was straight and face completely composed as always. She was wearing another summer dress that somehow conflicted with the drumsticks in her hand and yet turned her into exactly the person he'd always thought she was beneath her tough layers. Almost as if the dress fit her better than her leather and Doc Martens. As if this was the real Adria. Soft but with a steel back and a rhythm that would leave you breathless.

"Do you really want the job at Ravaged Storm?" Asher asked.

"Yes. I want the fucking job. Stop asking."

Asher chuckled. "Before you tear me limb from limb, I'm only asking because I'm sure there are ways we can work your job around the Daisies' schedule. If I can do it, you can too."

Ronan's heart skittered around in his chest, and he met his friend square in the eyes for the first time. "But the studio is in LA."

"And we have a team there. I'm not saying abandon the ship completely and never show up. I'm just saying it's possible. If you both want it to work, we can make it happen. I want you to have everything you want, Ro."

Ronan swallowed hard over the lump that formed in his throat. "Okay."

"And if you change your mind, I won't hold it against you."

They both stood there, watching as the band started into their first song. The beat of the drums and the pulse of the guitar streamed through the empty stadium, sending music into every corner. The sun was shining through the glass roof of the arena, and it covered the five women in a bright, white halo. Chills rolled over his back. He was so stunned by it he almost forgot to drag his camera out of his bag and capture it on film. But when he did, it caught his breath. They were bright and vibrant and full of life.

He hoped and prayed they could stay that way. That the shadows following them would disappear, chased away by the warmth of the sun.

♫ ♫ ♫

While Adria practiced, Ronan decided to explore the streets near the arena. Hundreds of people were setting up booths for the festival. The colors, sounds, and smells drew his camera into his hand once more. He didn't have to use any of what he filmed for The Painted Daisies documentary, but he could visualize merging some of these new scenes with ones he'd already finished. He wanted the world to see the new pieces of Adria he'd discovered in coming home with her.

As he wandered her city, he found his feet journeying along a side street not far from the arena where a set of empty warehouses sat. It was almost as if his mind, filled with Asher's words, or maybe fate or the universe, were twisting their will into existence because he could imagine turning the warehouses into a sound stage. The area was good. The lighting was good. Maybe they could run an almost exclusively Colombian cast and crew here in addition to the crew in California. His mind whirled with ideas. He'd have to write up a new proposal for Asher. He really needed to hire an assistant to help him.

By the time he returned to the stadium, the band was done practicing, and the stage had filled with beauty contestants. Ronan retreated to seats several rows back and watched as Adria and her mom led the teens through the first rounds of the pageant while a table full of judges watched silently. When the contestants left the stage one last time before the opening ceremony, and the arena started to fill with actual audience members, he made his way to the green room. He hoped to catch Adria before or after she changed and went back onstage because he had a lot to say to her. A lot of thoughts rambling through his mind.

The room was carefully controlled chaos, the Daisies mingling with other Colombian bands performing tonight, contestants, film crew, arena workers, and security. Adria wasn't there, but her father was. He was pacing as he talked on the phone. The arm he was using to hold it was wrapped in a sling while the other moved wildly as he talked in rapid Spanish. Ronan understood the language better than he spoke it, but the pace Salvatore was going made it hard to catch more than a few words. He did hear both Tatiana's and Adria's names.

As Ronan approached, Salvatore hung up, watching him with interest.

"How are you feeling?" Ronan asked with a chin nod toward the sling.

"This is nothing," he said. "Nothing compared to what is going on in here." He pounded on his chest as he stepped closer to Ronan, glanced around, and then lowered his voice until only Ronan could hardly hear it. "Adria says you were there. That you actually saw her."

Ronan nodded.

"Do you believe it was her?" Salvatore whispered, and Ronan could hear the pain and doubt twisted with hope and fear in that handful of words.

"I only met Tatiana once, years ago, when she came on the set of my parents' film with Adria, so I don't know if I'm the right person to ask. What I can say is Adria believes it's her."

Salvatore cursed in Spanish. "I have my people searching for her. I am afraid Adria won't tell me if she makes contact again because she is worried about me. But I need to know." He raised a brow at Ronan, and it was clear what the man was asking, but he wouldn't side with her father over her.

"I won't go against Adria's wishes," Ronan said. "I'm not here for you or Tatiana, or even the other Daisies. I'm here for her. To make sure she's safe and taken care of."

Her father stared at him for a moment, eyes narrowing. "You love her."

"Yes." He hadn't told her yet, but there was no other response he could give. He wouldn't hide it. Not from her or her family or her friends. He'd spent seven years chasing her, catching her fleetingly, and almost losing her. He wasn't going backward now that she'd agreed to take a tiny step forward.

A smile lit up her father's face. "This is good. This is very good. My Adria... She's always had tough skin. Ever since..." He shook his head. "She needs someone to remind her that she has a heart and soul that needs to be used for more than music."

Leya and Fee saw him and started over just as one of Salvatore's bodyguards approached. "Senor Rojas, the gentleman you asked to speak with is here."

Her father turned on his heel to leave, but Ronan caught his arm. He lowered his voice even further, switching to his poor Spanish in case Fee or Leya got close enough to hear the conversation. "She also needs her father. Do you think it's wise to be here tonight?"

Salvatore's eyes widened, but he responded in Spanish as well. "If they are going to come for anyone, it should be me. I can't risk Adria being taken again."

"Again?" Ronan latched on to the word.

"Also," her father corrected in English as if Ronan had misunderstood the word.

But he hadn't. He'd understood it perfectly.

The sickening realization hit him. Adria had suspected her nightmare might have actually happened, and it had. She'd been locked in a box as a child. Trapped. Left alone. Defenseless.

Fuck.

Her father disappeared before he could say anything else. Just as he thought his heart was going to give out, Adria strode into the room, looking confident and sure and wiping away any image he had of her being defenseless. Tonight, she looked even more like the mix of beauty queen and rock star that he'd been pummeled with since arriving in Colombia. She wore a blue leather dress that clung to every curve. The square neckline and tiny straps exposed her muscular shoulders and the soft swell of her breasts.

She was a goddamn masterpiece.

Their eyes met, and they'd taken a single step toward each other when a man with a headset boomed out a fifteen-minute warning. The people who were due onstage first started for the door. Adria gave him a wry grin and headed out.

He followed, pulling her aside before she got too far, determined to get her alone for two seconds. People whirled around them, Lennox raised a brow and stepped back, and Adria gave him a puzzled look.

"I'm due on set," she said.

He grabbed her hand, tracing over the raised skin on her thumb with a gentle finger, thinking of what her father had inadvertently told him. The soft touch made her breath hitch, and their gaze locked again. He imbued his words with every emotion he had swirling through his chest. "You're stunning."

Her eyes flared. "You've seen me in a dress before, Hollywood."

He leaned in to place a kiss on her cheek near her ear, voice lowering, "It isn't the dress, Star. It's you. You're stunning. Brave. Beautiful. Badass."

"That's a lot of 'B' words," she teased.

They hadn't gotten to talk all day, not about why she was upset or why he was now furious and rolling with disgust. But all that seemed to slip away as her eyes dropped to his lips. She turned her head ever so slightly, and their mouths collided. It should have been a sweet kiss, given the crowd and the people surrounding them, but it wasn't. It was wet and hot and desperate, as if she'd been waiting all day for this moment as much as he had.

Lennox cleared her throat next to them. "You'll miss your call."

Adria sighed, brushed her hand over his jaw, and then stepped away.

"Damn, Star," he said quietly.

She smiled and then gave him her signature wink, the one that drove half the world wild. It was sexy and sure, and it was whispering a promise that was only his. Of skin on skin. Of heat and lust.

She whirled on her spiked heels and headed for the stage wings. She looked back over her shoulder and asked, "Are you coming?"

Was there even another answer for him but yes?

He'd just reached her side when she went stiff, her entire body freezing.

His eyes went in the direction hers had and found her mother standing incredibly close to a man who wasn't Salvatore. The moment looked...intimate...heads bent with one of the man's hands on her mother's waist. The man was a similar age to her father, with the same black hair and a tall, broad-shouldered stature her father had once had.

Adria let out a shaky breath and then crossed over to them, anger and purpose in her step.

"What are you doing here?" she demanded.

Yesenia startled, pulling away, but the man didn't remove his hand from her waist. He turned ever so slowly to take in Adria, and the hair on Ronan's neck went up. The man's look was...predatory...perusing her curves in a long, slow glance that made him want to smash the asshole's face.

"Adria. Don't you look beautiful."

She visibly flinched. Ronan was there in a millisecond, hand tangling with hers, staking a claim she could reprimand him for later, but he wasn't letting this man look at her that way without showing him someone would be there to defend her.

Adria looked from her mother back to the man. "Papá will be here any minute. You have to leave."

The man smiled, but it didn't reach his eyes. Those remained cold and calculating. He tugged at the sleeves of his suit jacket, and that was when Ronan saw the watch. The one in the video. If there were only two of them in the world, it made this man her father's old partner.

"Didn't your mother tell you? I am one of the pageant's sponsors this year," Claudio said. The glint in his eyes told Ronan he took pleasure in Adria's shock as she inhaled sharply, swaying a bit on her feet.

"Mama?" Adria said, shaking her head, frustration and a hint of reproach in her tone.

Yesenia was just about to reply when a loud, "What the hell is this?" startled her even more. They all turned to find Salvatore marching toward them, face red, brows drawn tightly together, lips in a solid line.

"Hello, old friend," Claudio said.

Yesenia was at Salvatore's side in a flash, one hand landing on his chest, the other tucked into his arm. "*Cariño*, he just wanted to help."

"No. He doesn't get to help with anything!" Salvatore growled. "That was part of the bargain we struck. Money and silence for his departure from our lives. I will not have him hurting this family again!"

Ronan's heart slammed, his body tensing, wondering if he was going to have to break up a physical fight between two men who should be old enough to know better. To be well past pissing contests. Her father's face was contorted in rage, but Claudio's face was calm, the glint still there. He was enjoying the moment, and it made a shiver go up Ronan's spine.

"I am not the one with the enemies, Sal," Claudio said

casually. "I'm not the one who puts this family at risk. It was your business that got Tatiana kidnapped."

Adria gasped, and Salvatore lunged, swinging a punch with his good hand that landed squarely on Claudio's jaw, but the man barely budged. He'd been prepared for it, provoked it on purpose. Ronan dropped Adria's fingers, stepping up next to the men as the entire sea of people backstage came to a halt, watching the scene. Claudio rubbed his chin, eyes narrowing before his smile returned.

Before he could respond in words or fists, Adria's brother appeared, striding over and calling out, "Enough!" He looked between the two older men. "Violence only begets violence. This is not the answer."

"You knew?" Salvatore turned to his son. "You knew he was sniffing around, and you told me nothing?"

Vicente looked between his parents and sighed. "I thought she told you."

"We have lost so much already!" Yesenia said. Her voice was choked with emotion. "If nothing else, Tatiana's disappearance has taught me life is too short to hold on to petty grievances. To not to be surrounded by loved ones. Claudio and his family are my family."

Salvatore took a startled step back as if she'd struck him.

"*Mi amor,*" she said, reaching for him.

The man with the headset returned, eyes darting between them all. He cleared his throat. "Uh...sorry to interrupt...we're going live in two minutes."

Yesenia put a hand to the V between her brows, a move Ronan had seen Adria do hundreds of times. When he looked over at her, Adria was pale, but her eyes were flashing with anger. She inhaled sharply, and he knew she was going to tell her mother the truth about her sister. Her father knew it as well, because he clipped out an irritated, "Not now, *mija!*"

Salvatore shot a look from Adria to Claudio and back.

She bit her lip, shifting her weight from one foot to the other.

"We need to get onstage," Yesenia said. Then, she looked over at Salvatore. "Please try to understand what it's been like for me. Please try, for me, to heal this rift. Mistakes are meant to be forgiven."

Then, she turned and walked toward the stage with her head held high. The beauty queen, poised and confident again. You'd never know she'd just seen her husband hit a man. You'd never know the turmoil her family had been through in the last few days.

It was another layer of Adria that clicked. It wasn't just her time on the pageant circuit that had taught her how to hide her emotions behind a calm façade. Her mother did it every single day. Love and anger both tucked behind a smooth exterior.

When he chanced a look at Adria, she'd already mimicked her mother's calm, and all he could wonder was how much it cost her to do it.

CHAPTER TWENTY-FIVE

Tatiana

SOMETIMES
Performed by Garbage

TATI: *Everything is in place for tomorrow.*

BLOCKED: *I've hired more men. We'll need triple what we thought to outman their security. It's too tight, even with our surprise.*

TATI: *I can't believe she still defended him.*

BLOCKED: *I told you not to get your hopes up. She's your father's daughter.*

TATI: *And she'll pay for it. Let's just hope he doesn't choose himself over her as he's done with Mama.*

BLOCKED: You must remain detached, Tatiana. You have to see her as merely a pawn we're using to check the king. And if it doesn't work, I need to know you're willing to sacrifice her to win the game.

TATI: Tatara abuela sacrificed her life for Colombia. I may carry the Rojas name because of Papá, but I am a Moreno at heart. I'm prepared to do the same as she did—sacrifice anyone, including myself, to ensure my family and Colombia remain free.

CHAPTER TWENTY-SIX

Adria

WILLOW
Performed by Taylor Swift

Adria was shaking inside, her entire body quivering. Claudio's smug face, her father's anger, and her mother's betrayal all whirled through her. After what *Tío* had done to her father, it seemed impossible Mama had allowed him so close again. This morning, she'd said she talked to him sometimes, but this was different. She'd not only spent time with him, but she'd let him be part of the pageant. How could Mama possibly trust him?

You must choose which side you're on.

Her sister's taunt came back to her, turning her stomach in two.

Was Tatiana even aware of this? Of Claudio sniffing at the door? Her sister had said he wasn't in the States when the sex video had been made, but did that mean she'd found out because she, like their mother, was talking to the man who'd tried to ruin Earth World? It hadn't been just a little bit of money here and there he'd taken. It had been hundreds of thousands of dollars.

It was only years of training that allowed Adria to get through the opening ceremony for the *fiestas* and the first round of the pageant. Just like it was only the hundreds of hours she'd already spent performing "Wild in You" that allowed her to play the song without missing a beat.

She hated that instead of feeling the joy of performing in her country for the first time, she was thinking of all the worst things that had happened to her family—that were still happening to them. She felt like she was being torn apart, the pieces of her that belonged to Mama and Colombia peeling away from the ones that belonged to Papá and America. How was she supposed to merge them back together again? How could she when her sister was standing between the two parts, holding a grenade?

She felt wired. Anxious. Strung tight.

And the crowd seemed to match those feelings—a restless feel to it tonight. The *Fiestas del 11 de noviembre* was known for being almost as wild and unruly as Mardi Gras in New Orleans or Carnaval in Rio de Janeiro, and the ceremony opening the entire weekend's celebrations held the undercurrent of a pot ready to boil over. When the show was over, the audience would pour out of the arena onto the nearby streets filled with booths, street entertainers, and carnival rides. The revelry would only amp up and not simmer down.

She wished she'd had the opportunity to share it with the band like she'd wanted to. The contained chaos. The excitement of the street. Instead, her friends had been shuttled back to *Casa Buganvillas* right after their performance while Adria and her mom wrapped up the show for the night.

By the time it was over and Adria and Ronan got into the last SUV to go home, she was completely drained. He seemed to understand, not forcing her to talk about what had happened between her parents. He simply held her hand, rubbing his finger over the scar on her thumb as he had earlier. As if, somehow, he'd also heard the truth of how she'd gotten the injury. Her throat closed up, but she refused to give in to the tears.

When they walked into the house, there was a loud murmur coming from one of the open salon doors. Her father's deep tone and her mother's lighter one. She hesitated. All she wanted to do was strip off her clothes and bury herself under the covers. She wasn't sure she could handle any more family arguments or revelations.

But before she could disappear up the stairs with Ronan, Vicente emerged from the side hall, heading in the direction of the salon and their parents. His feet stalled on seeing her, and he demanded, "Why did you want to know about Claudio's travel schedule?"

"What did you find out?" she asked.

"He didn't file an expense report for that specific date, but when I discussed it with his old assistant, she had a note in her calendar that said he was in San Francisco."

Adria's heart hammered. San Francisco wasn't LA, but it put him much closer than Cadencia. Was he the one who'd told Tatiana he wasn't there? Was he the one who'd showed her the video and said it was their father? Had he lied to get her on his side? Did it mean he was part of GNVL?

She still couldn't find a way to put all the parts together. Something was missing. But just this was enough to tell Tatiana and prove she didn't know the real truth. If there was even a shred of the sister she'd once known left inside the woman she'd met with, it would be enough to make her curious, to start asking questions.

The conversation in the salon turned louder, and glass shattering had them all sprinting toward the sound.

Her mother was standing beside a sofa table, and on the floor nearby was a broken vase, glass and water and flowers strewn on the marble. Her father was across the room, and his face was the epitome of sadness. He looked almost as bad as he had when Adria had arrived in Houston.

"What's going on?" Vicente demanded.

"It was an accident. Talking with my hands again," Mama said softly, bending to pick it up, and he stopped her.

"I'll call someone to clean it," Vicente said softly.

Silence filled the room. Adria very seriously doubted a mere touch would have sent the heavy vase flying. She shot her father a look, wondering what had really happened. He closed his eyes.

"You are all so willing to think the worst of me," her father said, voice tortured.

"What does that mean?" Vicente asked.

Mama's hand fluttered to her chest, and in that instant, Adria knew she'd seen the video. Her mother thought he'd had an affair, and she'd turned to her old friend for comfort. It made her stomach heave.

Papá waved his hand between her and her mother. "They think I have been sleeping with other women."

Vicente's mouth dropped open before shutting. "Excuse me?"

"There's a video..." Adria said quietly.

Vicente's face hardened, turning to his father. "Of you? And another woman?"

"It's not me." And maybe because he didn't say it with

anger, maybe because he said it with such hurt and sadness, it made Adria believe him more than if he'd protested it violently.

"Claudio was in the United States at the same time," Adria said quietly.

Her mother's eyes widened, her hand going to her chest. "No. He was not."

"He told you this, right?" Adria said, and Mama's face paled.

"You have been taken in by the devil, Yesenia," her father said, turning away and looking out the window into the night.

"He was here when I was crumbling, trying to grieve one daughter while helping the other stay standing. Where were you?" she said, trying to defend herself. Guilt wracked through Adria. Guilt but also anger that Claudio had manipulated them all. She was more certain than ever he was the one pulling Tatiana's strings. He was tearing them apart.

But she could put an end to at least one part of his power tonight.

"She's not dead," Adria said.

Her mother and brother whirled to look at her, startled expressions emitting from them right as her father growled a warning she ignored. It was time. They needed to stop keeping secrets and letting Claudio come between them.

"She sent me a note, and we met in Houston. She's the one who showed me the video of Papá. She thinks..." Adria inhaled a deep breath and kept going. "She thinks it's true, and she believes Earth World is a CIA front trying to undermine the Colombian government. It's why she's working with GNVL."

"*Dios mío*," Vicente said, sitting down on a chair.

271

"We need to find her. We need to reach her before she does more damage," her father said fiercely.

"You knew?" Her mother looked at Papá, hurt and betrayal in her eyes. "You knew and did not tell me?! You let me believe she was dead!"

"No one knew anything until this week," Adria said, her voice cracking as she tried to talk over the well of emotions building inside her.

Her mother paled, connecting the dots and finally understanding. "The bomb..." And then her mother did something Adria couldn't ever remember seeing her do. She doubled over and sobbed, wracking cries that shook her whole body. Not even after Tatiana's disappearance had she seen her mother break like this. She'd cried, been shaken and upset, but she hadn't lost it altogether. Adria's heart broke just a little bit more watching her strong and proud mother collapse.

Adria moved, wrapping her in her arms, desperately trying to hold her up, but unsure if she could because she'd never had to do so before. "Shh. It's okay, Mama."

Her father made to close the distance between them, but her mother put her hand out. "No. I cannot...no." She looked up at Adria. "Take me to my room."

Pain rippled over her father's face, but he didn't move as Adria took her mother by the arm and guided her toward the door. Adria was filled with bitter sorrow for all of them. She wondered if there was ever going to be a day when she wouldn't feel this way again. Where loss and grief, fear and anger, frustration and sadness didn't fill her.

Ronan's brows were drawn together in concern as they neared him. It wasn't just for her. It was for all of them. She could see it in the way his eyes swung around the room, taking in all their faces. As they went by, he stepped in, taking her mother's other arm, and they led her up the stairs to her parents' adjoining suites.

Once there, her mother pushed herself away and went into the bathroom with tears streaming down her face. The click of the door was like a resounding note telling Adria to leave, but she wouldn't. She wouldn't let Mama hide her sadness anymore. Just like she refused to let them continue to keep secrets from each other.

She turned to Ronan, and he pulled her into his arms. A hug that held all the promises he'd been giving her all week long. Promises of staying. Of not leaving her to face the nightmares alone. She couldn't imagine Ronan ever leaving his children the way her parents had left her and her siblings. He wasn't the kind of man to love from afar. He wanted to love up close. To be there.

And maybe that was all it took.

Her family hadn't done that for each other, and look what had happened? The snake had wound its way in and poisoned them all.

But maybe it wasn't too late. Maybe Adria could show them as Ronan was showing her that to really love someone, you had to be there. You had to be willing to sacrifice something, a piece of yourself, so you could keep the most important thing. The love.

She pulled back, rubbing her hand over the curve of his jaw and the soft down of his beard. "I'm going to stay with Mama. I've never... She's never..."

He nodded as if he understood far more than she'd said. As if he'd read every thought.

"I'll be here, Star. Whenever you're ready to talk...or just be held...I'm here."

He kissed her knuckles and walked out the door.

And she almost called him back because she wasn't sure

she could do this. Still wasn't sure she knew how to be the love her family needed.

When her mother came out of the bathroom, she looked surprised to see Adria still there. Adria crossed over to her, grabbed her hand and pulled her to the bed.

"I'm sorry, Mama," she said softly.

"You should have told me," her mother said, hurt dripping through each syllable.

"I should have, but that's not the only thing I'm sorry for. I'm sorry I left you here. I'm sorry you've been alone for so long with no one to show you they loved you. I'm sorry you had to turn to Claudio to find it."

Her mother flushed, looking away and then back. "It isn't like that. I've never been unfaithful to your father, even when Claudio showed me..." Her mother shivered. "But there is no way he is with GNVL. I don't know how Tatiana got tangled up with them."

Adria's chest ached for all of them.

"Claudio was aware of the person the CIA placed inside the company, right? Maybe he told her about it when he lied to her about the video, and she took the leap on her own. I don't know. But I know she's with them. She told me herself."

Tears flooded her mother's eyes, and they brought ones to hers as well.

"GNVL are the ones who took your father all those years ago. She must not know that," Mama said.

Surprise filled Adria. She hadn't known it was the same group, and if she hadn't, she very seriously doubted Tati had. But even if she did, it didn't necessarily mean her sister wasn't with them. Maybe that was the reason she'd joined them. Maybe she'd been so hurt and angry and frustrated that she'd run straight to the group that had already done the most damage to them.

"After the kidnapping, that's when everything first started to fall apart. I hated moving to California, but we couldn't risk them taking any of you again." Her mother brought Adria's hand up, running her fingers over the scar on her thumb much as Ronan had earlier, and Adria bit her cheek to hold the tears in.

"You told me it was just a nightmare."

She nodded. "It was a nightmare, just like when we lost Tatiana. The only blessing was that you didn't remember it. They took your father and you that day, but they let him go so he could get them their money. When we got you back and realized the drugs they'd given you had taken your memories of it away, we thought it was best to let you only relive it once in a while in your dreams instead of every day."

Silence settled down, and then her mother pulled away, tugging down the comforter and fluffing the pillows. "Your father and I... We tried in our own way to forget it also, but every day I stayed in California, I knew why I was there. Every time he came to see me here, he remembered being taken. We couldn't find a place where we could both forget. Maybe we shouldn't have forgotten it at all. Maybe we should have dealt with it differently."

She slid inside the covers, and Adria tucked her in like she'd wished her mother had done with her when she was little. "Do you remember what you told me when I laughed at you for all the family pictures you left in my room?"

Her mother's brows drew together.

"You told me, 'Sometimes your purpose in life means you can't be with the ones you love in the way you want, but it doesn't mean they aren't in your heart and soul. If you keep enough pieces of them with you, you'll feel them even when they aren't there.'"

Mama gave her a watery smile, patting her hand. "Yes. And it's true."

"But maybe..." Adria swallowed, and then continued, "Maybe the most important thing, the most important purpose, is just to be with those who are in your heart. Maybe you shouldn't be keeping pieces of them, but keeping all of them."

Tears fell down her mother's face, and this time, Adria couldn't hold hers back. They joined her mothers, splashing down on their joined hands resting atop the blanket. "If you'd used those kinds of words when you were in Teen Colombia, *mija*, you would have won."

Adria huffed out a half laugh.

Did her mother see that she wasn't talking just about her parents? That she'd meant her and her siblings too?

Mama patted her cheek. "Maybe you're right. Don't make the same mistakes your father and I have made. I think there's a man out there, waiting for you to give him all your pieces."

Dios. Did she want to do that? But if she gave him all of her, how would she be here for her family? Whose life would they choose to sacrifice for one of them to have it all?

"Go. I need my beauty sleep," her mother insisted. "We have a big day ahead of us tomorrow."

She leaned in and kissed her mother's cheek. "I love you, Mama."

"I love you too."

They weren't words they'd ever said often, but Adria was determined to change that. They needed to know the love she felt was there for them in any way they needed it to be. Up close and personal.

CHAPTER TWENTY-SEVEN

Ronan

NOT ALONE
Performed by The Hall Effect

After leaving Adria with her mother, Ronan was too wound up to sleep. The mansion was quiet with all the staff and guests tucked away for the night. He wandered the halls for a bit, but it felt uncomfortable, like peeking into your grandmother's medicine cabinet. So, he found his way outside. Even as late as it was, the humidity hit him like walking through a weighted blanket as he stepped out onto a veranda. The smell of bougainvillea and orchids was almost as heavy as the muggy air itself. Both pressed down, hovering over the gardens and forest that were almost as silent as the house.

He left the mansion behind and wandered down a path lit with old-fashioned lampposts. Eventually, a sound broke through the quiet, water splashing. Not the hard crash of the waves on the shore near the beach, but the soft gurgle of a fountain. He followed the noise and ended up at one of the koi ponds where a stone waterfall trickled into water glowing with the soft, recessed lighting carefully placed in the rocks. Above him, the stars flickered, their natural light barely dimmed by the garden's manmade ones. It was as if they were closer here than anywhere else he'd ever seen them.

There was a wrought-iron bench placed at the perfect angle to watch the path, the bright-orange fish, and the night sky. He sat down, stretching his legs out in front of him and tipping his head onto the back of the seat.

He was angry and frustrated for Adria. For her past and the little girl who'd been locked in a box. For not having parents who were there when the nightmares came. For the threats that were coming at her from a sister who was supposed to love her and a man who had once been family.

His chest tightened. He wanted to pull Adria into his arms and take her away from all of it, but at the same time, he knew exactly why she wouldn't go. Because as much as she insisted she didn't know how to love, how to be enough, she showed it repeatedly. To her sister. To her father. And tonight, he'd seen it up close and personal with her mother.

"What are you doing out here, Hollywood?"

He sat up, eyes finding her in the dimness. She wasn't in the blue leather dress any longer, which was too bad because he'd had some serious ideas about how to get her out of it. Instead, she was in a loose T-shirt and a pair of those cotton sleep shorts that tantalized him almost as much.

He looked behind her, searching the dark for Lennox, and when he didn't see anyone, he growled out, "More importantly, Star, why are you out here without your detail?"

"Like I told you," she said, "I'm safe here. This place is a fortress." She pointed to one of the ornate lampposts back farther along the path. "There are cameras everywhere. People watching constantly. I'm not afraid at *Casa Buganvillas*."

She joined him on the bench, arm pressing into his, and his body flared at the touch. They sat, listening to the water trickle and the occasional rustle of the leaves in a breeze that did nothing to cool the night air. He reached down and tangled their hands together, rubbing her scar again, wanting to tell her that he knew the truth about it—and not.

"Mama finally told me," she said, as if reading his mind. "It really happened. They took me at the same time they took Papá and then used me for ransom."

He pulled her tighter to him, kissing the side of her head as he fought another round of anger and heartache. He wished he could take it away, but he knew nothing would. He could be here for her when the nightmares came. He could listen when she wanted to rant and rave about it. He could hold her hand, and kiss her, and make sure she knew she was loved and safe in that moment. But in the end, she was the only one who could make it through those memories and choose what to do with them.

"You found one of my favorite places on the whole estate, you know," she said, tilting her head onto his shoulder and hooking one of her ankles over his. "I love it here now, but I didn't always. When we came for holidays and vacations, it felt just like that—a place you visit. After Papá moved Earth World to Texas and sold everything in California, I felt sort of rootless. No place I could truly call home. Vicente was at school. Tatiana was in Houston. I needed to be with the band. It was sort of like being a nomad."

"What changed?"

"That awful day," she said quietly. "I'd lost my sister, my friend, and my band, and all I did was sit in Papa's penthouse, feeling like I didn't belong anywhere or to anyone. Mama basically forced me on the plane with her. At first, it was no different here than it had been in Texas." She paused, fingers seeking the scar hidden beneath his hand that was holding hers. He used his thumb to find it for her, pressing into it gently.

She cleared her throat and continued, "I couldn't even play the drums for a while. It was like I'd lost the beat inside me. So, I'd come out to this bench and sit, staring for hours, watching the fish. I'd pretend I was like them, not feeling anything, just swimming in circles. Finally, Mama had enough. She took me to the pageant office and put me to work. Coming and going with her at the same time each day and doing the tasks she assigned, it slowly allowed me to feel like I was breathing again rather than holding it all in. Maybe it was the routine or finally having all of Mama's attention again, or both, but I found my feet once more, and that was when *Casa Buganvillas* truly became a home."

He shifted, pulling her legs into his lap and turning so their chests were aligned and he could look her in the eye. "I'm sorry you went through so much loss."

"The not knowing...it was harder, in many ways, than what happened to Landry. The things I imagined..." Her throat bobbed, and her voice cracked. "Now, knowing she did this to us on purpose, I have this urge to slip back into being that person who sat on this bench, staring at the koi, pretending to feel nothing."

"After Albany, I felt...powerless...humiliated that Zane had gotten the upper hand. It isn't the same as your loss, but I understand fighting to find your way back to yourself—or at least a new version of yourself that takes into account those awful experiences. Part of finding that new normal for me was hiring Barry to train me so I'd never feel that way again." He took a shaky breath and then continued, "With the CIA chasing us, the bombing, and Carter showing up in your room, it triggered those feelings again. But it also made me realize that, no matter how much weight I can lift or how prepared I am, there will always be things I can't control. It isn't the bad situations, but how you get through them that defines you."

"That sounds like one of your philosopher pals again," she teased.

He shrugged. "The strength, power, and courage you—all of the Daisies—show…that's what I'm putting in the documentary. Your pure resilience. You may have been stuck here at the koi pond for a while, but you found your way out. And when this is all said and done, you'll find your way out again. I promise."

She'd been watching him while he'd been talking, eyes locked on his face. Now, she lifted her hand and ran it along his beard, and then she leaned in and kissed him. A soft, almost sweet kiss that matched the beauty-contestant look she'd taken on since arriving. When she pulled back, he grunted out a protest.

She smiled softly, rubbing a soft finger over his lips. "Ever since I stormed out of your hotel room in Seattle, I've been trying to find someone who made me feel like you did. But it would never have been possible." She put her hand on his chest where his heart thudded, increasing its pace with her touch and her words. "It's only *your* soul that will ever talk to mine."

His thumb caressed her pulse point, loving the rhythm it beat out with them tangled this close. "Are you finally listening to what our souls are saying? They've been screaming for years at being apart."

She laughed quietly.

"I don't want to be afraid anymore. Of love. Of living. My parents made so many mistakes. I feel like the biggest one was not keeping each other close. For letting pieces of themselves escape. But I don't know what that means for the lives we've built separately."

"I'm working on some ideas," he said softly. Asher had given him a piece of it today, but he still had some threads to pull together. "Let me prove to you that we can have it all— each other and our big lives and our families."

"There's the Hollywood prince again. Determined to get his way."

"I always do."

She started to say something, but he cut her off, determined to show her with more than words that he meant what he said. He kissed her gently. It was full of tenderness —aching promises being made with the glide of their lips instead of words. He'd hold her to them. He'd remind her every damn day of these vows she'd made at the side of a koi pond without saying a single syllable.

She was the one to break away first, searching his eyes. Then, she untangled herself from him, stood, and held out her hand. He joined her, pulling their fingers together, raising them to his mouth, and placing a kiss on her knuckles.

"I love you," he said softly.

Her eyes widened, but she didn't pull away.

"I know—"

"You don't have to say it back, Star. I didn't say it so you would. I just wanted you to hear it. To know I can be your koi pond, your home, your routine. I can be the one holding you up if you're falling. And when you're not, when you're pounding away on your drums and shining for the world, I can be the one ensuring your light is the brightest it can be."

She shivered at his words, as if they'd landed deep inside her. Then, she smiled at him. "I guess it isn't *just* our souls talking... Your mouth does a pretty good job too. Are you sure you want to keep directing movies? Because I think you have a few good lines to write a script with."

He chuckled and then pulled her down the path the way they'd come.

"My mouth has better plans than words."

She laughed again, the soft noise reverberating through the thick air, joining with the scent of flowers, carving a memory into him that would forever be of this place, of her, and of the oaths they'd made.

♫ ♫ ♫

They'd fallen asleep in her room, tangled together just like they'd been on the bench—her head on his shoulder, hands twined, legs blended together. The sweet moment by the koi pond had followed them inside. It wasn't about sex and desire, it was about promises and forevers, and Ronan wouldn't have traded it for a single orgasm. But he woke the next morning to her alarm going off with a hard-on that was desperately painful.

She pulled away from him to turn it off, and he growled in protest. She got out of the bed but stood staring down at him with a soft smile on her face. She was beautifully mussed in ways that only made his dick harder until he noticed how tired she was. The shadows that still lingered in her eyes. Then, he just wanted to yank her back down and keep her there until it all went away. The worries. The danger. The exhaustion.

"I'll be at the arena all day again."

He hauled himself to his feet, standing in front of her and loving how her eyes lingered over every part of him, including his thighs and the bulge in his boxer briefs.

"Don't leave without me. I'll go shower while you're getting ready," he said and then added on with a grin, "unless you want to save time and shower together?"

Her brow arched. "Somehow, I don't think that would save any time. It would likely make me late."

He tangled his hand in the soft strands of her hair, pulling back gently so her head tipped up and he could put his lips right where they were aching to be. The moment their mouths touched, heat exploded through them. He groaned, deepening the kiss when he'd only meant for it to be a simple *good morning*. She moaned, and it only added to the fire burning through them. His hand went to the small of her back, pressing her into him, angling his head to take her mouth, her tongue, all of her. Aching to find a momentary cure for the incessant hunger growing fiercer with every minute, every sweet promise, every touch that went by.

When his hand slid under her T-shirt, she stepped back instead of coming closer. She smiled, all determination and control he wanted to break. She rubbed her thumb along his lips. "I can't afford for you to tempt me this morning, Hollywood."

"That wasn't temptation, Beauty Queen. It was an appetizer. Just wait until we get to dinner and dessert."

Her pupils dilated, and her thumb came to a complete stop. Then, she inhaled deeply and moved away. At the bathroom door, she looked over her shoulder and said, "You don't need to come with me today. I know you have things to do. You're missing out on a lot of work being here when you hadn't planned to be."

It was true. He had a shit ton to do. But his talk with Asher had given him some ideas. He needed to talk to Nikki's mom, get some more people onboard. They'd make it work.

"I'll bring my laptop with me. I can work at the arena as easily as I can here."

She hesitated.

"Go get ready, Star. And don't you dare leave without me."

"Someday, someone's going to say no to you."

"You already did."

Her eyes flickered with sadness, and he wished he hadn't said it. "That was your one shot. You don't get to say it again."

She laughed. "We'll see."

She went into the bathroom to get ready, and he pulled on his cargo shorts and headed out the door to do the same. As he stepped into the hall, Fee emerged from one of the other bedrooms. She eyed his bare feet and naked chest, and her lips twitched.

"Morning," she said, sliding into step with him.

"Fiadh," he said. "Don't add your warnings to everyone else's. I'm not messing with her. I care about her. I'm not letting anything happen to her on my watch."

To his surprise, she chuckled, finger running along the multiple hoops and studs on her ear. "I was just going to say thank you for taking care of her."

His feet stumbled to a stop, eyes meeting hers. "Yeah?"

She continued past him, twirling around at the steps and looking back. "Just know, if you screw it up, I'm keeping your best friend. We're married. He's mine."

Ronan chuckled. "He told me the same thing."

Her smile curled upward. "Good."

"What are you all doing today while Adria's at the arena?" he asked.

She shrugged. "We'll be there tonight to watch the final show, but we're stuck here during the day. Maybe we'll hit the beach or play mini-golf. I'm pretty sure Holden, Jonas, and Asher think they can beat us Daisies, but they don't know how many rounds we've played over the years while touring."

Ronan chuckled. "Good luck!"

"Don't need it."

She disappeared down the stairs, and he hurried into his room.

After showering and putting on another pair of shorts and a T-shirt to ward off the heat as best as possible, he picked up his camera and headed into the hall. Adria came out of her room at the same time, and his feet stalled. She had on a tiny black dress. The silky material was slashed along her chest, stomach, and thighs, and each cutout was covered in black organza that showed a sexy hint of skin. The hemline danced around her upper thighs, putting her long legs on display. They were smooth and glossy, ending in sky-high, spiky heels with straps that wound up her calf.

Her makeup was thick, ready for the stage and cameras. Heavy shadow coated her eyes, and her dark lashes looked impossibly long. Silver and diamond hooped earrings hung from her ears exposed by the partial updo she'd twisted her hair into. The down part was long and straight, swinging well past her shoulders, with the choppy layers she'd added after Landry's death almost invisible.

The hunger he'd woken with, which had only grown since that first kiss reacquainting them back in Houston, was screaming at him to shove her back into her room, lock the door, and bare her completely...except maybe the shoes. Maybe they could stay.

"Damn, Star, you're enough to kill a man," he said quietly.

She fidgeted with the tangle of necklaces on her chest. They were a mix of silver, diamonds, and black pearls with a handful of lapis lazuli stones that matched her eyes.

"It's too much for daytime," she said. "But they want us to be in the same clothes for the filming today as we would be tonight so they can splice scenes together if they need to."

He nodded, completely understanding. Pulling footage together and then merging it with a live show was a challenge, one he'd never—thankfully—had to do, but he was interested in watching it come together. He also wanted to talk to the director, get his bead on the warehouses and his idea for a local soundstage.

Ronan tugged Adria's hand into his, and they started for the stairs.

"I need a new name for you. A combination of all you really are. Beauty Star?" he teased, and she grimaced. "No, I know. *Reina del rock*."

She snorted. "You're ridiculous."

He smiled. "I'm in love. I'm allowed to be ridiculous. And it absolutely fits you. It's Spanish and regal and perfect."

"I won't answer to it, Hollywood."

"No?" he said, leaning in to place a kiss at the corner of her jaw. "Want to make a bet?"

Heat flooded her eyes, her cheeks flushed, and his chest leaped with joy at having made it happen.

CHAPTER TWENTY-EIGHT

Ronan

CHOKE
Performed by The Hall Effect

THAT DAY

If anyone doubted how much this pageant meant to Adria, just watching her work all day would prove them wrong. Ronan wasn't sure she'd stopped from the time they'd rolled up to the security-packed arena until they were the last ones there. Even her mother had left by the time Adria had retreated to the green room to console the second runner-up who'd taken her loss particularly hard. When the girl finally walked out of the room with her mother in tow, she wasn't quite smiling, but she'd pulled herself together.

Ronan raised a questioning brow as Adria joined him in the corridor, pulling her bag onto her shoulder. She shrugged, saying, "Sometimes, all you need to hear is that you're enough."

He stepped closer, put his hands on her waist, and drew her up against him. "Do you? Need to hear it? Because—"

"I don't know how anyone ever called you the Player Prince. They should have called you the Ridiculous Royal."

He chuckled, and she started to move away, but he stopped her, ignoring her comment and continuing as if she hadn't interrupted him. "Because you're not just enough, Star. You're pretty much the entire universe. My universe."

She stilled, scarred thumb caressing his lips before leaning in to kiss the corner of his mouth. "Take me home, Hollywood. Let's see which nicknames you can get me to respond to."

He grabbed her hand and all but dragged her down the hall. She let out a light laugh.

Lennox joined them with another dozen bodyguards on their heels. Much of the arena had shifted into darkness by the time they made their way through the dimly lit corridors to the back entrance. At the door, Lennox suddenly halted, pushing Adria farther backward into the hall as she listened in on her earpiece.

"Repeat?" The bodyguard's face turned dark. She drew her gun. "Roof, repeat?"

The heavy door slammed open, smacking Lennox in the head and sending her to the ground, weapon traveling across the cement floor. A sea of heavily armed and muscled men swarmed into the arena. They were dressed in black clothes outlined with skeleton bones, masks hiding their real faces behind grisly images with blank eyes and white lines. Ronan's heart stopped and started, adrenaline roaring through his veins as he placed himself between Adria and the men.

Outside the still-open door, gunfire lit up the night, the sounds and flashes resounding through the corridor like cracks of lightning and the boom of thunder. Lennox dragged herself to her feet and jumped between Ronan and Adria. She swung a powerful right into the chin of the closest skeleton man. His head bounced back, but he still jabbed back, barely missing Lennox's chin.

Ronan's body finally clicked into motion. He jerked his camera off his chest, smashing it into the nose of another assailant as he approached. The man stumbled back before rushing forward again. Ronan dropped his broken camera to the ground, lowering his stance as he'd been taught. Fury welled, fueling him as he used every bit of training he'd received to keep the man from reaching Adria.

Chaos consumed the corridor. Adria's security team engaged with row after row of assailants. Fists collided with chests and faces, and the sickening sound of bodies colliding filled the air. As her team sent one skeleton man to the ground, another dozen would emerge from the bowels of the arena like shadows emerging from the walls. Demons swarming from hell.

Every time Ronan laid a man out, two more came at him until there were three swinging at him at the same time. His heart skittered as his fist slammed into the face of the nearest one, and he twirled, aiming his foot into the chest of the next. It pulled him too far away from Adria, and from his peripheral, he watched with pride and fear as she swung her bag like a weapon, hitting another masked man in the head.

It was with a terrifying clarity he realized just how outnumbered they were. Not by a few, but by hundreds. He'd promised himself he'd never be taken again. Never. And he proved his point by slamming fist after fist into the men coming after them until his knuckles were cracked open and bleeding. He was unable to see the damage he did to them behind their creepy skeleton masks, but his body felt every inch of it. His legs were swept out from under him as five more assailants surrounded him, binding his arms and legs, and flipping him onto his stomach. A heavy booted foot landed at the base of his spine.

Dark memories tried to take hold as he bucked in an attempt to dislodge the arms and feet holding him down. They jammed his face into the floor, and he tried in vain to keep his eyes on Adria. She had three men reaching for her as she kicked and swung. It was as if they were afraid to hurt her in a way they hadn't been with Ronan and the others.

Gunfire roared through the space, and his heart fell as Adria ducked. Lennox twisted the wrist of one of their assailants, turning the weapon he'd just discharged toward his partners, and four went down.

"Behind you!" he shouted, but it was already too late. Lennox was tackled to the ground, head colliding with the cement. The crack of it hitting was almost inhuman, and her face contorted in pain. She was overrun with men pinning her in place.

Ronan had lost sight of Adria, and a new wave of panic sent his heart rate spiraling. He tried again to heave the hefty weight of the booted foot from his spine, ramming his shoulder into the leg of his attacker.

"Adria!" he screamed her name, desperately searching for her.

"Ronan!" she cried, fear spiraling through the syllables.

He twisted his head in the direction of her voice and saw four men hauling her down the corridor as she kicked out. Her hands were behind her back, and the sexy dress had risen. Terror coated her face.

With a strength he didn't know he possessed, Ronan let out an animalistic roar and tossed the men off him. He ran after her, shoulder slamming into people as they tried to block him. He wouldn't go quietly into the night. Not again.

Suddenly, he was yanked backward by two enormous men, and a rifle was pointed into his face by a third. His stomach flipped nastily, memories of a weapon that had knocked him out filling him.

"I *will* kill you," Ronan growled, struggling futilely, hating the powerlessness that threatened to overwhelm him.

"Do I shoot him?" the man holding the rifle called out.

The sound of heavy breathing and the scent of blood and sweat filled the corridor as a quiet voice at the end of the hall rose over the noise of the brawl to say, "Just leave him with the others. He's not why we're here."

His eyes landed on Tatiana, who wore a black dress like Adria, except hers covered her body from neck to ankle. She was just as tall as her sister and almost as beautiful, but her face was pale in the shadowed corridor. Her long hair swung around her face and trailed down to her waist. She looked like a phantom. Like Satan's wife or sister. As if she'd risen from the fiery depths just like the hundreds of men she was commanding.

The men holding Adria drew up next to her sister, and Adria struggled viciously again, biting the hand that covered her mouth. The man cussed.

"Don't do this, Tati. Don't," Adria cried out.

"You chose poorly, sister," Tatiana said. "Sacrifices have to be made for Colombia. Abuela Salomé made them, and now, so shall we."

Ronan lashed out again, kicking at the gun pointed in his direction. The man was unprepared, and it went clattering to the ground. He smashed his elbow into the face of one of the men behind him before slamming his head back into the nose of the other, and then he broke into a sprint again, aiming for Adria and her sister. His feet only stalled when Tatiana pointed a pistol at Adria's head.

"Stop," Tati said. "Stop or I'll just end it all here."

"No!" he howled as Adria went deathly still.

Tatiana's head tilted sideways, a curious look on her face as she took him in, panting and bloodied. Desperate. "You love her. Does she love you?"

Tatiana shifted the gun in his direction, and Adria fought against the arms banding her. "Stop, Tati! Stop! I'll do whatever. Go wherever!"

Ronan's heart tore in half. Adria hadn't said the words to him yet, but her actions had screamed the love she felt, just as they did now. He took another step toward the sisters.

Her sister laughed softly. "You do. Wow. This is surprising." Tatiana tilted her head the opposite way, considering Ronan. "Why don't you come along for the ride, then? Maybe you'll be useful after all."

More men surrounded him. An endless sea of them.

He may have sworn he'd never be taken, but he also knew he'd die in this corridor if he continued to fight. And if he did, he couldn't be there for Adria. If he went with her, perhaps there'd be a chance for them to escape. So, he did the one thing he'd said he'd never do again—he dropped his fists to his sides and allowed two of the men to pin his arms behind him.

Nausea rolled through him, but he gritted his teeth and snarled, "I'll come if you promise to keep that gun trained on me and not her."

Tatiana laughed, and it sounded soulless.

"You're not in a position to bargain."

Then, she turned and headed back into the darkened arena. The men holding Adria pulled her along behind her sister, and Ronan went willingly. He would go with her. He would follow her until there was nothing left of him to do so.

Tatiana strode purposefully into a storage room and lifted a door that had been perfectly concealed in the concrete floor where a metal ladder appeared below it. She headed down into a dark space lit by a single lantern. The walls appeared to be made of dirt, as if they'd collapse at any second. Adria struggled again, and Tatiana turned back, pointing the gun in her direction from below. "Dear sister, please don't be such a trial. Either we knock you out and bring you, or you can come on your own."

"I'm not going with you!" Adria cried. Tatiana shrugged, and the man behind her slammed the butt of his gun into Adria's temple.

"Adria!" Ronan screamed as her body crumpled, barely held up by skeleton arms. Bile hit his throat as memories of his own body doing the same crawled through him.

One of the men tossed Adria over his shoulder and descended the ladder. Ronan followed them, desperate to get his hands on Adria. To hold her. To put his body between her and the others. The swarm of skeleton men trailed after them before the heavy cement door in the floor was swung shut with a resounding thud. The tunnel they were in turned black and dank, lit by only the lantern Tatiana now held aloft. The smell of wet earth surrounded them and a salty hint of the sea.

They'd only gone several hundred yards before another door appeared. Tatiana opened it with a large metal key, and they emerged onto the beach below the arena. The soft lull of the waves on the sand gleamed beneath the full moon, and the heat of the tropics landed on him like a heavy mantle.

Tatiana looked over her shoulder, taking Ronan in again. "Cover him."

A black mask descended on his head, zip ties bound his wrists, and he frantically fought for control beneath the thick cotton. Too many memories. Too many feelings of helplessness. He barely forced it all back, keeping his focus on Adria, listening for her and the heavy breathing of the man who carried her.

He needed his wits about him. Needed them not just for himself, but for her.

Once upon a time, he'd helped Paisley escape using his phone.

He'd succeed again. He had to. There was no other option, because he'd be damned if he lost Adria after just getting her back.

CHAPTER TWENTY-NINE

Adria

I CAN'T SAVE YOU FROM MYSELF
Performed by Aly Stiles

Adria's head was throbbing violently. She raised a hand to try and soothe her aching temple and hit something solid. Something that prevented her from reaching her face. Her heart skittered to a stop. Her entire body tensed. No. No, no, no, no, no. Nausea rolled through her as she gingerly lifted her hand again only to collide once again with wood.

She sobbed.

Panic settled in. She squirmed. Bare toes striking wood. Elbows hitting it. Even her head butted against it, causing pain to swirl through it once more.

"Let me out!" she screamed.

She fought. Banged and kicked as best she could as tears rolled down her face.

It was pitch black in the box.

No light.

And then a voice. Soft and deep. Soothing.

"Adria?!"

Relief and joy flew through her. "Ronan?!"

"I'm here, Star. I'm here."

"Get me out of here. Get me out!"

It sounded like a choked sob escaped him. "I can't. I'm tied up. I have a hood over my face, and I can't see. Where are you at?"

Terror flooded her veins, making every part of her go limp before her hands pounded again against the wood, pummeling the planks like she did her drums. Over and over and over. She heard a crack. Nothing gave way completely, but she was rewarded with a sliver of light. Instead of helping, it increased the fear crawling through her as it showcased the box even more. It was barely big enough for her body. Someone had removed her shoes. Her dress was still there. Her underwear... *Gracias a Dios.*

"Fuck! Star. Where are you?" Ronan's voice roaring through an empty space brought her back. She cried, choked ugly tears that tore through her.

"Adria! Fucking talk to me!" His voice was full of anger and fear.

"I-I'm i-in a box."

He swore a string of curse words, and she could hear him attempting to move. The shuffling of clothing. She tried to gain control. Tried to hold back the gasps and pants. She wasn't alone! She was in a horrible place, but she wasn't alone. He was there. He had come willingly after swearing he'd never be taken again. Hadn't he told her he'd die before being taken hostage again? And yet, here he was...with her.

"Ron-n-nan," her voice cracked over the tears as her teeth chattered and chills rolled over her repeatedly.

"I'm here," he said, cold fury in his voice.

"P-please...don't stop talking. If I know y-you're there—" She choked again on more sobs.

"I'm here, Star. I'm here, and we're going to get out of this."

"Do you have your ph-phone?" she asked, hope blooming. He could save them. Someone would hear the SOS just as Trevor and Jonas had heard it when Paisley was taken.

"It was in my pocket, but it's gone now. I'm trying to find something to cut the zip ties with."

Her heart lurched again. They were both living their worst nightmares. Her in a box. Him zip-tied and captured all over again. How could this happen? How could Tatiana do this to them...to her? Did her sister know that this had happened to Adria before? Had she been there? They had to have been teeny-tiny kids. Her pulse pounded, her stomach swirling.

"T-talk to me," she begged. "D-did you see where they took us before they covered your face?"

"I think we're in a basement of some sort. I've heard a lot of feet above us, and there's been voices, but I haven't been able to make out what they're saying." His voice was a mere whisper, and she realized he didn't want their captors to hear them. "We were taken out of the arena using that underground tunnel. It ended at the beach. They put a hood on me and put us in a boat. We weren't in it for long, maybe fifteen minutes at the most, before we were unloaded on a dock of some sort. They walked us across asphalt, and then dirt, into a building with heavy sliding doors. I was forced down a set of stairs. I couldn't tell what they'd done to you..." his voice cracked, stopping for a few seconds as if he was trying to regain control. "I'm on the ground. The walls are brick, and the floor is cement. There'll be something I can rip the ties with."

Determination took over his voice, and it helped calm her, until she looked about her again. It was like she was in a casket...but even a casket would be larger than this. *Dios.* Tears trailed down her cheeks.

"H-how long?" she asked.

"I'm not sure. An hour, maybe."

Her ears picked up a sound just as Ronan uttered, "Shh."

Something metal and heavy, a twist of a lock maybe, and then a door was opened, banging against a wall. Footsteps on cement, like dress shoes rather than boots, and there was more than one pair.

"You shouldn't have brought him," a deep voice said in Spanish, and a shudder went up Adria's spine.

"It was either shoot him there or potentially use him. I'm sure the Hawks will send us quite a hefty ransom to free him. And if Ads doesn't cooperate, we can use him to force her," Tatiana's voice said coldly, also in Spanish.

Adria wanted to scream at her sister. Wanted to cry and sob and maybe even hit her. But instead, she bit down on her lip. Let them think she was still knocked out.

"But he knows who you are," her uncle said.

"I'll just disappear again. I did it before."

Silence greeted that response, and Adria could imagine Claudio's face, brows drawn together in thought. Sometimes, her uncle had stared at her for so long she was afraid her skin would melt. It had been uncomfortable, as if he was expecting her to say something poignant. Something specific.

"Do you have a way to contact his parents?" he asked.

"I have his phone. We'll just unlock it with his face, shall we." Tatiana almost sounded joyful and disgust rolled through Adria.

She heard the shuffling of cloth.

"Your pretty face got beat up a bit. Sorry about that," she said in English, sounding not the slightest bit remorseful. "But maybe it will encourage Mommy and Daddy to pay a bit more."

Adria's heart twisted. He'd have more nightmares added to the vicious ones he already experienced all because of her. No...not her...her sister. Her family. People who were supposed to love and protect her.

The anger that rolled through her at that thought was better than the panic and fear.

"I'll send this picture and a text to them, and then I'll call Papá," her sister said, returning to Spanish.

"Wait for me before you contact him. I want to hear what he says."

Footsteps headed away and then stopped. Her sister said, "Don't kill him, *Tío*. We need him alive if we're going to get the ransom."

The door slammed shut.

A moment later, a tapping rolled over the box. Fingernails along the wood above her face, and she instinctively jerked backward, the noise giving her away.

A soft chuckle burst through the air before he said in Spanish, "Ah, so she is awake."

Adria didn't respond.

"Do you remember this game, *niña*? I've wondered for so long if you did."

The fury that had momentarily stabilized her disappeared with another wave of panic as the tapping continued. In her nightmares, she'd thought maybe she'd been the one making the noise, trying to get out of the box, but instead, the incessant tap-tap-tap was coming from him.

"No comment? For a few years, I worried you'd eventually remember who'd taken you."

"Wh-why did you?" she finally couldn't help asking.

"You weren't supposed to be with your father that day. But you were always such a daddy's girl. It ended up working to my benefit. Of course, he didn't know it was me. I got to console him, beg him to do as your captors had requested to make sure you were set free. Then, I convinced him if he stayed away, you'd all be safe. And it worked. After that, if he came to Colombia, it was for short spurts. Mini vacations. Never enough time to see what I was doing. Never enough time to stop me. And then, he sent Vicente here in his place." Tap-rat-a-tat-tap.

"V-vicente caught you stealing."

"I would have expected it out of Tatiana or even you, but who would have thought that meek-mannered Vicente would ever have the intelligence, or the balls, to stand up to me?"

"What did you do to my sister?"

He chuckled again, the tapping turning into a dance. "She's been so much more fun to play with than you. All you did that day was scream. I had to use the Rohypnol I'd planned to give your father, but I misjudged the dose. I hadn't been prepared to give it to a child. That's why you don't remember it, I think."

Adria fought back another wave of nausea at the calm in her uncle's voice. Instead, she did what she could to shake him. "She's smarter than you. Tati will figure it out—what you did before and how you're using her now."

"Will she? I left her all the cookie crumbs and let her follow them herself. She thinks she discovered this, that we joined GNVL together." His voice was full of humor. "But I've been preparing for this for much longer than she could imagine."

"But I know now," Adria said.

"Yes, you do. But it doesn't matter. None of you will make it out alive this time. Not your father, not you, not even dear little Tati who's been so helpful. Vicente will be so overcome with grief he'll commit suicide, and then...then everything will be the way it was always supposed to have been. I will have what is rightfully mine."

"Mama," Adria breathed out, the picture of him tangled with her mother the day before slammed into her.

"Salvatore stole her from me. After decades, it was time for Yesenia's family and mine to truly be joined. She was so much younger than me that I knew I had to wait. And I did, patiently watching as she blossomed into an amazing beauty queen. And then, he swooped in and stole her. Whisked her right off her feet. But I will be there while she grieves. I'll be there, showing her it wasn't me who stole from the company, but Tatiana all along. The little genius who had a penchant for rescuing her homeland, funneling it into GNVL. A crusader saving Colombia from the evil, villainous United States government."

Ronan had been quiet for so long Adria had started to get worried, but she heard movement from his direction now. A movement that caused her uncle's tapping to still momentarily.

"You won't get your money if we're all dead," Ronan's deep voice spoke in Spanish.

Her uncle laughed, and the rat-a-tat-tat resumed. "Smart boy, keeping your knowledge of our language to yourself. You should have kept it a while longer. But I suppose it doesn't matter. I don't care about your parents' money.

Yesenia has enough to last us a lifetime. And when we sell Earth World—because how could we keep it after all that we've been through?—we'll have even more."

"Did your cronies kill Landry Kim by mistake, thinking it was Adria?" Ronan asked the question Adria dreaded. She caught her lip, holding her breath, aching to know the truth but afraid of hearing it.

"I did wonder myself, but I was told no. Tatiana didn't want Adria dead then. She wanted her sister to join her cause. So smart, and yet so blind in this one area. She loved you the most, I think, *niña*."

Adria shifted again in the box, and as she did, she noticed that it wobbled for the first time. As if all her pounding and movements had shifted it to an edge. Her uncle tapped the wood one more time and then walked away, shoes snapping on the cement.

"I had to give up our game too soon when you were little, *niña*. Let's see how long it takes for you to break this time. I'm curious if you'll hold out longer than the others. But everyone breaks at some point."

The scuffle of feet was followed by the thud of bodies colliding together.

A loud slam as something hit a wall. Heavy breathing. A groan that sounded like her uncle. She prayed violently. She prayed for Ronan to be safe. For her to get out of the damn box. For no one to die. Not Tati. Not her father.

Adria jammed her shoulder into the side of the box, and it tilted again. She slammed into it harder, willing it to fall. The sounds of Ronan and her uncle fighting surrounded her. The box moved again, and then finally, it tipped, tumbling onto the ground with a loud snap. She was on her stomach, the cracked seam where the light had seeped in no longer visible, and the darkness descended again. She tried to push upward or sideways, but the weight of the box on top of her was too much.

A loud noise came from above them. Like thunder or a thousand feet pounding on the floor. Shots. Shouts. Hope sent a hot trail of tears down her face. She wanted out of the damn box. She heaved her body again, and the box rolled to the side. The crack became visible once more. It was wider now. She could see out of it into a room lit with a single bulb hanging from the ceiling. Ronan had his hands on Claudio's neck, strangling him.

"Ronan!" she screamed his name, but he didn't budge.

She shoved her hands against the cracking wood. Pushed with her bare feet at the bottom, feeling a sliver slide into her big toe that sent pain ratcheting through her. She'd have another scar, one that would match the one on her thumb. She pounded on the failing wood, fighting, struggling, refusing to give up.

The hammer of boots seemed to be coming from all around them.

With another vicious shove, the box split apart, and as she spilled from its recesses, her leg caught on a jagged piece, tearing into her flesh. She inhaled deeply, the dank smell of oil and sea in the basement like heaven. Her eyes landed on Ronan and Claudio. Near them was a pistol that had dropped in the fight.

She scrambled to her feet, lurching for the weapon, raising it at the two men, and with a command she didn't feel, she said, "It's over! Stop!"

And even though she had the gun, Ronan still didn't let go. His face was dark. An avenging angel focused with deadly intent on Claudio's purple face. A new terror filled her. The idea of Ronan living for the rest of his life with the knowledge that he'd killed someone.

The door burst open, revealing Holden followed by a wave of men and women. Some wore the uniform of their security detail, some the suits of the Secret Service, and some the uniform of the National Police. Adria's entire body sagged with relief, and she barely caught herself on the wall.

Guns were directed at the two men struggling, and Holden's voice barreled through the room, "We've got this, Ronan. The police are here."

Even then, Ronan held on. Claudio gasped, clawing at the viselike grip Ronan had on his neck. Holden strode across the room and had to fight to get Ronan to release him. Claudio sank to the ground, inhaling sharply, his own hands replacing Ronan's as the purple faded from his cheeks. Ronan's gaze, full of hate, was still focused on the man who'd taken everything from her family. Holden tapped Ronan on the shoulder and said, "Go take care of Adria."

Ronan finally looked away, eyes settling on her. His face was dirty, bloodied, and bruised, and his hands were cut and swollen. He took two steps toward her and then another. Finally, she was in his arms. The gun in her hand clattered to the ground, and she clung to him, overwhelmed with relief and sadness. They were safe. They were safe, but at what cost? Tati... Claudio... Their sanity... Neither of them would ever sleep dreamless again. Nightmares would always follow them.

CHAPTER THIRTY

Ronan

PEACE
Performed by Taylor Swift

She smelled like sweat and blood and fear as she clung to him, and it pissed him off that it covered her natural scent. It made the hatred in Ronan's chest swell again. Made him want to go back and finish what he'd almost accomplished in ending her uncle's life. As if she could sense it, her arms tightened around him.

He kissed her temple where a black bruise and swelling were developing, and he hated that as much as the fear and terror she'd been through. He stepped back slightly, taking in the rest of her. The sheer organza of her dress was ripped in several places, her hair was scattered and tangled, and her face was pale. When he saw the blood on her legs, he dropped to his knees.

"You're hurt," he barked. Her hand went to his hair,

306

fisting it, tugging as if to make him rise, but he ignored it and gently wiped at the cut on her calf with his T-shirt.

"It's just a scratch. Let me see you." She pulled harder, and he looked up at her. Tears filled his eyes. God...she was okay. She was okay physically, but would either of them ever be okay again mentally?

He clambered to his feet and yanked her to him, kissing her. It wasn't soft and tender like it should have been after what they'd been through. It was rough and savage. Full of the loathing and fear they'd both felt. When he'd seen the box they'd put her in...he'd almost lost it. Thank God he'd found the screw on the wall by the rusty sink. Thank God he'd been able to snap the bindings. His wrists were screaming at him, but he didn't care. She was here. Their lips were touching.

She pulled back, wild eyes going around the room, taking in the men who were pulling her uncle to his feet and drawing him from the room.

She squirmed away from him, running to the door, "Tatiana!"

Ronan exchanged a brief look with Holden before they both raced after her. There was a single set of stairs that led up and out of the dark basement. Adria was already at the top, eyes searching the sea of people in the warehouse by the time he caught up to her.

Only a handful of men in their skeleton costumes were in the room. They were spread out along the walls as police officers stood over them with rifles. The dozen or so assailants who were left was nothing compared to the hordes that had attacked them. A mere drop in the sand. Where had they all gone? All he knew was the authorities in the room outnumbered the assailants this time.

Adria whipped around, glaring at Holden. "Where is she?!"

Holden's face was confused. "Your sister? Tatiana? She was here?"

Ronan's stomach fell, twisting and turning.

Adria listed sideways, and Ronan rushed forward to catch her.

"She was working with Claudio," Ronan said firmly. Adria stiffened next to him, but he wasn't holding back anymore. Everyone needed to know.

Warren Times strolled in the large roll-up doors, looking just like he had in Houston. A businessman with a briefcase tucked into his hands. He searched the room. When his eyes landed on Adria and Ronan, he strode through the maze of bodies to them.

Holden put his hand out, stopping him. "Who the hell are you?"

"Warren Times. CIA."

Holden glared. "Of course. What the hell do you want?"

A man in the garb of the Colombian military joined them. He stuck his hand out and shook Times's hand. "Good to see you again, Times."

"We capture them?" Times asked.

"There's no *we* about it," Ronan barked. "You weren't anywhere to be seen, asshole."

Times just raised a brow. "Who do you think told them where to find you?"

"But you weren't there to prevent it from happening!"

"Somebody better start explaining what the hell's going on!" Holden commanded.

Times ignored everyone, gaze settling on Adria. "She's gone?"

Adria looked around the room again, took a shaky breath, and then nodded.

For one of the first times, an emotion appeared on Times's face, irritation or anger maybe. Then, his eyes landed on Claudio as they dragged him up the stairs. "We'll need a crack at him," he said, not to Holden but to the Colombian soldier.

Ronan looked at the handful of skeleton men in the warehouse that they'd rounded up. "This isn't even a tenth of the ones who attacked us at the arena."

The knowledge settled heavily over them, but no one responded.

"Where's Lennox?" Adria asked Holden.

"At the hospital. She has a fractured wrist and a concussion, but she'll be okay."

"Did anyone else get hurt..." she trailed off, unable to finish it.

"Everyone's alive, some with injuries, but everyone made it through," Holden assured her.

Relief flooded Adria's face. A feeling Ronan felt as well. He didn't want her to live with yet another death on her conscience. It was bad enough she would always wonder if she'd been responsible for Landry in some way.

"Get us the hell out of here," Ronan said, meeting Holden's gaze with a firm one.

"You'll both need to answer some questions," the Colombian soldier said.

"You can send someone to *Casa Buganvillas* tomorrow," Holden told the man. He pressed a finger to his ear and said, "We're coming out. Have the cars ready."

As he started to lead them out of the warehouse, Adria winced. Ronan took one look at her bare feet and swept her up in his arms. She started to protest but then just relaxed into him, arms going around his neck. They followed Holden into the parking lot where dozens of cars had surrounded the warehouse. Some had official lights strobing through the night sky. Some were dark and unmarked. The orange glow from the streetlights lining the wharf cast a strangely tinted shadow over the world, making it more nightmarish than reality.

They weaved through the vehicles as their security detail took up the rear. At their SUVs, Holden held the door open for them, and Ronan placed Adria inside before joining her. He pulled her legs into his lap, eyeing the cut and then her feet in the darkness.

"Where else are you hurt, Star?" he asked, voice still gritty and dark. The anger and frustration lurking inside were emotions he wasn't sure he'd ever be able to be rid of again. They'd follow him for the rest of his life, peeking out when he least expected it, traumatizing them both repeatedly. He hated it. But he hated more that she was hurt.

"I think I have a cut on my toe, but it's nothing. Not compared to you," she said, hand landing on his cheek. He suddenly realized it throbbed mercilessly. It wasn't just his face that ached. His chest and ribs felt like he'd been rolled down a hill. His knuckles were split and bloodied. But it all faded with her there next to him.

He inhaled, trying to let the truth settle over him. They were safe.

They drove through the streets, and he caught glimpses of the festival still going at full steam. Music and lights and waves of people, a revelry that added another dream-like feel to the entire night. A chaotic air stirred unpleasantly in his gut, and it was a relief when they made it to the outskirts of town and the dark foliage took over.

"You knew she was alive?" Holden demanded, turning to

face them from the front seat. "On the plane, I could tell you were holding back. Your sister was the GNVL member who'd made contact?"

"Leave it be," Ronan warned.

Adria put a hand on his arm, and the warmth sank into him. It did little to ease the turning inside him. The fear. He wasn't sure how he'd ever let her go again. How he'd ever stand having her out of his sight. Damn his job. Who needed a job? Certainly not him. He had enough in his trust accounts for him and his children to do nothing and still have money left. But he also knew Adria would hate it if he gave up anything for her...for them. He couldn't think about it at the moment. He'd fight that battle another day. Right now, he'd do whatever it took to stay at her side.

As they pulled up to the door of the mansion, it opened, and Adria's parents emerged, looking disheveled and panicked. Adria scrambled from the vehicle, running into their arms. They surrounded her in a hug, and Ronan heard Adria sob again. It twisted in his chest as he moved toward them, heart in his throat, determined to ease her sadness.

Holden's hand landed on his shoulder again, slowing Ronan's steps. "Let them have a minute."

Ronan ground his teeth but then turned to look him in the eye. "Thank you for coming for us."

"It shouldn't have happened at all," Holden replied, and Ronan could hear the bitter disappointment in his voice. The failure.

"They outnumbered us, Kent. By at least a hundred. There was no way any of you could have expected it, and no way you could have prevented it without an army behind you."

"Maybe that's what they need."

The band appeared on the steps behind Adria's family.

Leya's eyes found Holden's, and tears filled them. The man left Ronan to pull his fiancée to him. Everyone seemed to take turns hugging Adria while Ronan watched, chest still tight and full of emotions he wanted to purge but knew would cling to him for a long time. As everyone moved into the gilded hallway, Asher strode over to him, embracing him in strong arms and pounding on his back.

"I'm glad you're okay." His friend's voice was thick with relief and sadness.

For a second, Ronan let himself savor being held. Strong arms. Strong friendship. This man had sat with him through nights when the nightmares wouldn't let go, just like he'd been there for Asher after Nova had nearly killed Wren. They may not have been blood, but they were brothers. If Asher had ever done what Tatiana had to her family, it would have unraveled Ronan. Shredded his heart and soul. He couldn't imagine what Adria and her family were going through.

Back at the warehouse, Adria had gone running up the stairs, searching desperately for her sister, even after knowing what had happened. If that wasn't all-consuming, unconditional love, he didn't know what else was. Adria had to see it. Had to know she was so damn full of love it was tumbling out of her. He moved away from Asher, searching for Adria and finding her with his eyes again.

"Let's get you cleaned up," Yesenia said to Adria with a shaky voice.

The band didn't look like they were ready to let her go, but Adria hugged them all one more time individually, and then took her mom's hand and started up the stairs. She was halfway up when she looked down, gaze finding his.

"Will someone look after Ronan's injuries, please?" she asked.

All the Daisies turned to take him in as if for the first time, scanning him, eyes widening, and he realized he must look more of a mess than he felt.

"Feck," Fiadh breathed out. She and Asher exchanged a look.

"I got it," Asher said to Adria.

"I don't need anyone babysitting me," he snipped.

"Let him help...for me?" Adria begged softly. His jaw clenched, but he nodded, watching with reluctance as she disappeared up around the landing with her mother, fighting every urge to sprint up after her.

One of the staff showed up with a first aid kit, and Asher took it from the man, jerking his head toward the stairs. Ronan followed, but it suddenly felt like he was moving in quicksand. The adrenaline had fled from his veins as the feeling of safety and being loved hit him in the chest. And that was when he thought of his parents. His feet stalled completely as a new dread washed over him.

"Fuck."

"What?" Asher demanded, eyes narrowing as he searched the area for danger.

"Give me your phone," Ronan commanded.

"What?"

"Damn it, Ash, your phone. She was going to send a ransom note to my parents. They need to know I'm okay." Ronan's stomach twirled, thinking of the desperation his parents must be feeling.

"I already told them," his friend said gently, and another wave of relief went through him. "They called me as soon as they got the ransom demand. I've been keeping them apprised, and they found out almost as soon as I did that you were safe. But I wouldn't be surprised if they show up in Cadencia tomorrow to see for themselves you're okay."

His friend's lips twisted with a hint of humor Ronan couldn't feel.

Instead, he finished hauling his body up the stairs and into his room. He left Asher in the bedroom to head straight for the shower, determined to lose the sweat and fear and blood clinging to him. He shed his clothes and stood under the stream of scalding water for what felt like an hour. His eyelids closed even though he was standing. He needed sleep. He needed Star. The fucking box she'd been locked in appeared in his head again, and his eyes popped back open. As soon as Tatiana had ripped the mask from his head, and his eyes had landed on it, he'd been overwhelmed again with powerlessness. Fury.

He washed vigorously, as if scouring his body could rid him of these new horrific memories that would be added to his existing nightmares. His body was a chaotic mess of bruises. They covered his torso, his arms, and his legs. His knuckles were broken and raw, and the soap and water stung them. He leaned a palm on the shower wall, breath raspy, trying to inhale and yet feeling as if there was duct tape on his mouth all over again.

The mask hadn't been quite the same, and yet it had still restricted his airflow, stopped him from getting the full lungful he'd needed.

The bathroom door opened. "I just need a minute, Ash."

No response. He turned his head slightly, and Adria was there, stepping inside the steamy room, coming toward the shower. Her hair was wet but combed straight. She had on a loose T-shirt that landed below her hips where a pair of sleep shorts barely peeked out. She looked like heaven... until he saw the haunted look in her eyes.

He turned the water off, opened the door, and reached for her. His wet body surrounded her, drenching her dry clothes. They just clung to each other. Her face in the crook of his neck. His in her hair. It was over. They were safe. But Tatiana was still out there, and their healing would take months...years...decades. The only thing that eased the stabbing pain that thought brought him was the idea of not having to do it alone.

Asher had been there for him after Albany. Even his parents and the therapist he'd seen. But none of them had been there every single night. Hadn't been able to be there when the shadows reached out at unexpected moments, triggered by who knew what. But now, he and Adria would have each other. Because he wasn't spending a night without her. Not a single one. Not for a long time. If ever again.

She pulled back, and he grunted his disapproval.

"Let's get your hands wrapped," she said.

Her eyes scanned his body, taking in every single mark and hesitating ever so slightly over the part of him that was very aware of her standing next to him in barely anything while he was completely naked. He let her guide him to the counter and the vanity stool. He sat, and she kneeled in front of him with the first aid kit Asher had brought up. She took a roll of gauze and carefully wrapped it around his knuckles.

She wouldn't meet his gaze while she worked. Finally, when it was taped off, he pulled her chin upward. Emotions swam in those lapis seas. Deep. Heavy. He leaned down and kissed her. This one was soft and tender like the one earlier should have been. It was full of gratitude. Relief. Love.

She broke the kiss, rising and pulling his hand into hers. Then, she drew him out of the bathroom. Asher was nowhere to be seen as she moved him toward the bed. She climbed in, and he started to follow but stopped when he caught sight of her bandages—one on her leg and another around her big toe. She also had her share of bruises on her hands, arms, and legs from struggling against their attackers...maybe from fighting her way out of the damn box.

Tears filled his eyes as first his fingers and then his mouth slid over each bandage and each bruise. He whispered prayers to the universe as he went, begging it to allow her to heal. Forget. Stop the pain.

She tugged on his shoulders, and he came down, half on and half off her. Her mouth found his. Hungry. Needy. Maybe it was what they needed, simply to fuck away the memories. To make sure neither of them spent even one moment thinking of what had happened...what could have happened. But he still didn't want the first time they were together after years apart to be this way...an escape from trauma.

Maybe she finally felt the same way, because after a long, savage kiss, she pushed him so he was on his back, and then she curled up into his side with her head on his chest. His arm secured her to him, and their feet tangled together, the bandage on her toe skimming his calf and reminding him again of what they'd been through tonight.

"She was right, you know. I love you," she whispered, and his heart spun happily for the first time in what felt like years.

"I know," he said and was rewarded with a little huff before he continued. "Your actions proved it, Star, long before your sister said it."

"I hate that she got to say the words first. That she took them from me."

He drew her chin up again, gaze meeting hers. "Say it again, right now, with our eyes locked, our bodies linked, and our souls the only ones listening, and it will be our first time. Nothing before will matter because this will be the time we both believe it."

She swallowed hard, easing herself up slightly, hand cupping his jaw, rubbing over the bristles of his beard, and sending waves of desire through him. "Ronan Xavier Hawk, I love you. I've loved you since that first kiss in the corridor at your parents' film set. I loved you even when I hated you. I love you even when I don't know how to show you it or how—" He cut her off with a finger to her mouth.

"You're wrong, *reina del rock*. You know exactly how to love. Endlessly with devotion and forgiveness."

She stared at him, tears filling her eyes. "What do we do now?"

"We don't have to figure it out tonight. I love you. You love me. Let that be enough for this moment."

She kissed him softly and then set her head back on his chest. "You're right. It *is* enough."

He hadn't thought he'd sleep. He'd thought if he did, the nightmares would find him. But wrapped with her warmth, her skin against his, and the I love yous the last thing they uttered, he did. Deep. Dreamless. With hope settling into every crevice of his being.

CHAPTER THIRTY-ONE

Adria

SURVIVORS
Performed by Selena Gomez

When Adria woke, she panicked. Not because it was dark or because she felt like she was in a box, but because the bed was empty. Ronan wasn't there. Then, she heard the toilet flush and the sink run in the en suite, and her heartbeat slowed.

She was surprised she'd slept. Surprised neither of them had woken with nightmares chasing them. But maybe it was pure exhaustion. Pure exhaustion and love.

Her heart flipped at the thought. Through everything that happened, that tiny knowledge was able to spark joy through her soul.

She loved him. He loved her.

But then doubt settled over her again. It didn't change the fact that to be together someone would have to give up everything or let time and space slowly poison their relationship like it had with her parents. And it certainly didn't change the fact Tatiana was still out there, ready to come for them again.

The bathroom door opened, and Adria was disappointed to see his defined and cut body with those delectable thighs hidden beneath a layer of clothes—jeans and a T-shirt that would probably be too hot for the humidity. But she wondered if he'd put them on to hide some of the black-and-blue marks on his skin even though the ones on his face glared at her. The bandages she'd carefully wrapped on his hands the night before were gone, and his bruised and torn knuckles were visible over the distance.

He came to the side of the bed, sitting on it and leaning down to kiss her tenderly.

"You're dressed already?" she said, her voice husky with sleep, or maybe it was just raw from the screaming she'd done inside the damn box...pounding on it. Her eyes closed and then opened again, concentrating on the handsome man in front of her instead of the dark space. Ronan had risked his life to follow her down that tunnel. It filled her heart and sent chills up her spine at the same time. She didn't want him to sacrifice anything else for her. Not his body. Not his soul. Not his job.

"It's ten," Ronan said. "Fee came by earlier. Everyone is wondering if you feel like continuing with the concert today."

She sat up, surprised it was so late. She glanced toward the windows, but the light was hidden behind blackout curtains. Her stomach tightened at the thought of going back to the arena. It would be terrifying, but she couldn't let her sister and her uncle stop her from living, from sharing her music with her people. Her friends had come all this way with her. They'd damn well play. "I'm going."

She eased out of the covers, slipping onto his lap, and he grunted in surprise, hands settling on her waist. Then, she kissed him, open-mouthed and hungry, tasting the toothpaste on his lips and the heady essence that was simply Ronan, begging him to respond. And he did, taking command, tongue sweeping over hers, and sending shivers of delight over her body. His hands shifted to her butt cheeks, pushing their cores closer together, and she smiled at the feel of his erection pressed into her through his jeans. She ground down, and he groaned. He bit and nipped at her, cursing softly. And while the kiss was passionate and intense, it was also something more. A deep, unfathomable claiming. As if all their past lives had finally come together again while the swirl of the future stood before them. Only Ronan had ever made her feel so much from a single kiss. As if it was much more than bodies and need. It truly was their souls talking, just like she'd told him.

A knock on the door had them pulling apart, but their eyes were connected, and somewhere inside, so were their hearts. Love drifted between them, surrounding them like cotton candy around the center cone. Soft and sweet. But it would stick. It would hold on. She had to believe that it would.

"Ads? You in there?" It was Paisley's soft voice.

Adria smiled, rubbing her hand over Ronan's beard and loving the spike of it against her palm, wanting to feel the same coarseness all over her. She hated that her responsibilities kept her from doing just that—losing herself in him for days.

She stood and went to the door. On the other side, Paisley's brows were drawn together, finger on her star-shaped birthmark by her eye, pushing at it. Relief coasted over her face on seeing Adria. "Hey."

"Morning. I'm just headed to my room to get ready. Just give me a few minutes."

Paisley didn't even really acknowledge it, worry replacing the relief as she asked, "Do you have the phone Angel left you in Houston?"

Trepidation dripped through Adria's veins. "It's in my luggage. Why?"

Paisley whirled around, racing toward Adria's bedroom, and her heart slammed back into action, a staccato beat she was tired of feeling. She ran after her, knowing without having to turn that Ronan had followed also.

Inside Adria's closet, Paisley searched through Adria's luggage. Adria's pulse picked up again.

"Paise, tell me what's wrong."

Her friend came up with the phone Angel had left. She didn't respond right away. Instead, she crossed the room to hand it to Adria before saying, "He texted me. He said...he said to have you check the phone he'd given you."

Adria inhaled sharply at the same time as Ronan let out an angry, "What?"

"How do you know it was him?" Adria asked through tight lips and an even tighter heart.

"He sent a picture of himself to prove it. Jonas took my phone to Holden, and I came to get you."

Adria's hands trembled as she used her face and her thumb to unlock the phone. The battery was almost dead, but there was enough juice left to see there were several unread text messages. She opened the app, and her heart thudded at a blocked number. There were words that blurred in front of her and a video that was nothing but a black screen with a play button hovering there like some kind of omen. Another chill went up her spine. This one was a premonition she wouldn't like what she saw.

Ronan had crossed over to her, and he pulled her into his chest, arm going around her waist while he looked over her shoulder.

BLOCKED: It's up to you now. Tell me what you want.

She hit play and almost vomited. It was a coffin made of a shiny, dark wood. A hand reached out and pulled open the top portion, revealing Tatiana's face. Adria gasped. Her sister's eyes were open, fury cascading from them. She had a piece of duct tape over her mouth, and her hands were on her chest, prayerlike, bound together by the same tape.

"What the fuck?" Ronan growled.

Angel's deep voice came over the video. "Tatiana insists she wasn't involved with Landry's death. I'm pretty sure I believe her. I'm good at getting what I want from people."

Her sister moved on the video, squirming as if to try and sit up, and he simply closed the lid. Adria's stomach lurched, tears rolling down her cheeks.

Angel's hand tapped on the coffin much like her uncle had done to her in the box, a rat-a-tat-tat that had her heartbeat stopping. Her breath left her body. Dark thoughts and dark memories sucked her into their hold. Then, Angel spoke again. "It's up to you, Adria. Does she live or does she die? Your choice. Tell me to set her free, and I will. Tell me to hand her over to the police and the CIA, and I will. Or tell me to leave her to the death she and Claudio had planned for you."

Dios. How long ago had he sent the video? She looked at the time stamp and saw it had been over thirty minutes. Had Tatiana run out of air in that amount of time? Was she already gone? A sob escaped her.

She tried to type but the phone kept slipping out of her

sweaty palms. Ronan grabbed it, surrounding her hands with his. "Star. Tell me. Tell me what you need."

"*Dios*, call him! Text him! She can't die. She can't!" Her voice was pained and tortured. She'd never wish that on her sister. Never. Not even after everything she'd done. Her mother's words from before about Claudio came back to her. She might not be able to forgive her sister for everything, but she'd never want her to die.

Ronan tapped out the text *Let her go!* Then, he tried to call, but as the number was blocked, it was impossible.

Adria grabbed the phone back from him and copied the text Ronan had already sent, repeating it over and over.

ADRIA: LET HER GO!

ADRIA: LET HER GO!

ADRIA: LET HER GO!

Relief filled her when she eventually got a response.

BLOCKED: Shall I drop her off with the police?

Tatiana would go to prison, but she'd be alive. She wouldn't be able to hurt them again, but she'd be arrested for kidnapping, attempted murder, murder, and the bombing. She'd also be out of her uncle's clutches. Adria and their family would be able to see her, explain to her that Claudio had used her...try to reason with her.

ADRIA: Make sure she gets to the station safely. Not a bruise or a cut.

There was no response. Adria pushed away from Ronan, pacing the room as he and Paisley watched. A knock was followed by her door opening. Holden, Lennox, and Asher piled into the room. Lennox had a cast on her left arm, and her face looked as bad as Ronan's, but she was dressed in the black garb of their detail, with her gun at her waist. Guilt ate at Adria. Her bodyguard should have been on her way home. She should have been resting, not here still trying to protect Adria.

"Did you get it? What did he want?" Holden demanded.

It was Ronan who explained. Shock rolled over their faces. Holden immediately put his phone to his ear and stepped outside into the hall. She couldn't stand the waiting. Doing nothing. It would drive her insane, so she went to her closet, gathered some clothes, and then headed into the bathroom.

She dressed in cutoff shorts, a flowy blue tank, and sandals. Not quite the rock star or the beauty queen, but some weird mix of them both, maybe more the *reina del rock* Ronan had insisted she was. Her hair was a disaster, so she just piled it into a messy ponytail, and then spent a mere minute on her makeup. Nothing could hide the dark shadows under her eyes or the bruise on her temple.

It would have to do.

When she walked out of the bathroom, only Ronan was there. He wrapped her in a hug, and they just stood, comforting each other once again.

"Have we heard anything?" she asked.

He shook his head. "Let's go find out."

When they got down to the salon, it was filled with the band, her family, and more of their detail. Everyone's face was grim.

"What?" she croaked out, emotions clogging her throat. *Please, let Tati be alive.*

It was her dad who answered. "He dropped her off on the station steps in Cadencia, tied up with duct tape. They've moved her to an interrogation room. Your mother and I are going there now, but if you don't want to come, we'll understand."

She stood there, her pulse racing. Did she want to see her sister? Did she want to know why she'd done what she'd done? Did it really matter? Then, her gaze landed on Vicente, and all she could see was his red-rimmed eyes and the haunted look on his face.

"Together. We'll go together." As her family moved toward the door, Adria looked back at her friends, and said, "I'll meet you at the arena?"

"Feck that, we're coming with you," Fee said.

Holden shook his head. "I don't think that's a good idea. They'll never let all of us in. We'll just be a distraction."

No one looked like they agreed, but Adria just hugged them and repeated her words about seeing them later.

"If you need us, call us. We'll come no matter who the hell thinks there are too many people in the room," Nikki said gruffly.

Adria nodded and then followed her family out to the SUV with Ronan's hand wrapped tightly in hers. The number of vehicles that drove with them made it look like a presidential convoy, and it all felt like *too little, too late*. The silence in the car was almost unbearable. The weight of grief and guilt hung over all of them.

But at least they were all safe.

Even Tatiana.

CHAPTER THIRTY-TWO

Adria

LEST WE FORGET
Performed by The Brothers Bright w/ Levi Lowrey

At the police station, they waited for two hours before one of the officers came out to tell them they could see her sister. They all rose, but the man shook his head. "She says she'll only speak to her siblings."

Both her parents paled, and Adria wanted to scream at her sister all over again for wounding them one more time. For throwing yet another dagger. For two seconds, she debated walking away, but then she threw her shoulders back, squeezed Ronan's hand, and followed her brother.

Tatiana was shackled to the floor. Her face was red and raw from where the duct tape had been pulled off. She should have looked sad and defeated, but instead, her shoulders were back just like Adria's, and her eyes were full of fire.

"How could you, Tati?" Vicente said, pain in every syllable.

"How could I? How could you sit back and allow our homeland to be run by puppets? How could you stand by while our family slowly disappeared? Like always, I was the one who stood up for us."

"He lied to you," Adria said, voice shaking. "It was Claudio in the video, Tati. We proved it. We have his travel receipts. We know it was him. He did all of this just to get Mama. He hated Papá because he felt like Papá stole her from him."

Tatiana's eyes narrowed, and her lips flattened.

"He kidnapped me and Papá when I was little. Did you know that?"

"What?" It was Vicente who said the words, shock traveling through the air.

"My nightmares. They were real. He put me in a box just like he did yesterday. He wasn't going to let any of us live, Tatiana. None of us. Not even you. He wanted us all out of the way."

"No, you're lying."

"I've never lied to you," Adria said. "Not once. Why would I start now? If you don't believe me, I can bring Ronan in here. He heard him say the same thing."

She could see her words struck a nerve in her sister.

"How did he even pull you into any of this?" Vicente growled. "How could you trust him at all after how he stole from us?"

She pulled her handcuffed arms back to her chest, shifting uncomfortably. She got a look in her eye Adria had seen many times. It was her sister's genius mind whirling through all the scenarios. After a moment, she leaned in. "Papá lied about that. It's actually Papá who took the money.

I saw the money trail." Vicente was shaking his head, disgusted.

"No, I found the money trail. Me. Did you even think to ask me about it? Like Adria said, we've always told each other the truth!"

Tatiana's face blanked out, as if she was pulling herself further and further away. Her voice was calm when she spoke again. "Did you know *Abuela* Salomé was a freedom fighter? *Tío* gave me her journal. She fought in the *La Violencia*, working against the United States, who were secretly trying to influence the outcome and put their puppets in place. She lost her life because of it. She was murdered by people working with the U.S. And it's happening all over again. I know Earth World works with the CIA."

"Papá said when he found out they'd placed a person in our office here, he fired the man," Adria said.

Tatiana shifted uncomfortably. "It doesn't matter. My sacrifice, all of our sacrifices are worth it if we can ensure a free Colombia."

Adria's heart twisted and turned. Her sister was gone. This person...she was someone else. She may not have been kidnapped, but she'd still been stolen from them.

"I'm done." Vicente stood and went to the door. "You killed people, Tatiana. Jorge... he didn't deserve what happened to him. He'd done nothing but look after us, after our father. Do you even care what you put us through? What we thought? How we imagined you beaten, raped, dead? And not once since we walked in have you shown an ounce of remorse for that. For putting people you loved through this."

"Love," Tatiana scoffed. "Our family doesn't know how to love."

Vicente slammed out of the room without comment. Adria stood on shaky legs with her heart constricting. Her sister's words were so close to the ones she'd told Ronan. She'd believed her family loved each other, but just not enough. Not enough to stay or enough to sacrifice their own desires or be there when the worst came. But her mother had been there when she'd lost her way, had gotten Adria back on her feet. Her parents had moved out of Colombia after she'd been kidnapped as a girl, sacrificing their life there to make sure their kids would be okay. Her father had paid a million-dollar ransom without thought or hesitation in order to get his daughter back. He'd risked himself by showing back up in Colombia to try and save Tati once he'd known what had happened.

"You're wrong. Just because how we lived wasn't conventional, wasn't some perfect family sitcom, there was still love there. And guess what? I still love you. Will always love you. And maybe, someday, I will even forgive you for putting us through some of the worst days of our lives. But that isn't today. Not while you sit there without a shred of remorse. While you sit there and say some cause was worth killing me for. Me, Tati. Your sister. Your *familia*. Your flesh and blood. The person who would have done anything for you."

Tatiana scoffed. "Yeah, right. You ran away with your little band to play rock star, and I was left alone in a new city with a father who was never there. Claudio was the only one who saw what I needed."

Adria's stomach twisted with guilt. "If I'd known you needed me, Tati, I would have dropped everything to come. All you had to do was say the word."

And she realized it was the truth. She would have given up the band—the one thing she thought she'd never give up —to go to her sister. She thought she didn't know how to love enough, but she'd loved her sister enough to sacrifice everything.

Their eyes met, and for a moment, they were just Tati and Adria again. Two little kids who'd shared their dreams of changing the world with music and medicine. And then, her sister disappeared again, and the cold person she'd become settled over her.

"Go. Just go. I didn't need you then, and I don't need you now."

The words were a direct conflict with the pained admission moments ago, and it tore at Adria all over again because, in the words, she heard her sister's fear. She heard the little girl who'd held her hand and cried because she had no friends. So, Adria swallowed back all her hurt and anger to repeat, "I love you," adding on, "we've got a lawyer coming for you, and I'll help you however I can. I'll be back to see you soon."

Then, she walked out the door. Guilt would tear at her for the rest of her life. She'd always wonder if she could have saved her sister if she'd noticed her crumbling. But she hadn't, and she couldn't change that. But she could try and be better going forward. She could promise to love her friends, her family, and Ronan so much they would never doubt she'd be there for them.

She could make the greater sacrifice.

If she was willing to make the greatest sacrifice for Tati, she could do that for Ronan too. She could do that for all of them.

When she went out into the main station, her father had his arms around both her brother and her mother. She rushed to them, and they hugged each other tightly. As she stepped back, Ronan moved to grab her hand, holding her up when she thought she might fall, just like he promised.

She turned her head to tell him everything. That she loved him. That she'd give up anything to be at his side. But her words bled away as Claudio emerged. He was surrounded on one side by a police officer and on the other by a man in a suit carrying a briefcase. She knew the moment her father saw him too, because he was a blur, barreling toward Claudio.

"I will kill you for what you've done!"

But before he could reach him, there was a loud crack of glass shattering, and Claudio's entire body jerked backward. A hole appeared in his forehead, blood spattering from the wound and spraying over the face of the lawyer next to him.

Screams rent the air.

Adria's heart slammed into her chest, and then their bodyguards basically threw all of them to the ground, shielding them with their own bodies. When no more shots followed, their team scrambled them to their feet, shoving them all into an interrogation room with no windows and one door. Her parents and Ronan demanded to know what was happening, but they were left alone in the room while the detail figured out what had happened.

She was shaking. She could see it. She watched as her hands wavered and her legs quivered, and yet she couldn't actually feel it. She was numb. Ronan jerked her into his embrace, and her face went to his chest, arms surrounding his waist. And there was the heat. The life. The love she needed.

"What the hell just happened?" Vicente demanded. "Papá?"

She pulled back from Ronan enough to see her father's face. It looked haggard. Shocked. He shook his head, pulling her mother back close just like Ronan was holding her. Her mother was crying. She seemed to have aged overnight in ways she hadn't in a decade, and Adria's heart ached.

"No. I said the words just now, Vicente, and I don't feel sorry he's gone, but I didn't arrange this. How could I have? I had no idea where they were holding him."

He seemed to be telling the truth.

But she remembered in Texas the fierceness with which he'd insisted on ending this once and for all. She'd known he was going to hire mercenaries...

Whether or not he'd have Claudio's death hanging over him, Adria was glad it was over. The man they'd called uncle could no longer hurt them. He couldn't even manipulate her sister anymore. They had miles to go before any of them would be okay again, but they were safe, and they had each other.

CHAPTER THIRTY-THREE

Ronan

FALSE GOD
Performed by Taylor Swift

T he car was silent on the way back to the *Casa Buganvillas* except for the sound of her mom's tears. Adria had told him the other night that she'd never seen her mother like this, not even after Tatiana's disappearance, and yet now she seemed to have completely crumbled. Maybe it was because she felt responsible for letting Claudio back into their lives. Maybe it was because they'd all let each other drift too far apart.

Adria was feeling guilt for that same reason. He could feel it bubbling from her. But he didn't know how they could have foreseen one man's evil and stopped it. Ronan had been in the room with evil one too many times now, and he knew there was no logic to it. No reason. No way to predict it.

When they got back to the estate, Adria's dad took her mom upstairs to lie down, but Vicente joined them in the salon where the rest of their friends were waiting.

After having explained what had happened, it was Fiadh who asked what had crossed his mind on the way back. "Do you think it was Angel who fired the shot?"

They all looked at each other. No one could say for sure. The man seemed to be looking out for the Daisies in ways no one could truly approve of, working under some kind of vigilante code that was sure to backfire on him at some point. Someone would catch up with the man. Someone would eventually hold him accountable.

A bustle of noise in the entryway turned into a couple bursting into the room. It took Ronan a second too long to realize it was his parents. His mom was in a forties-style summer dress with bright-yellow pumps, and his father was in a linen shirt and pants as if he was ready to step into a riverboat along the Nile. They looked like a classic movie come to life.

He strode across the room, and before anyone said another word, they were hugging him. Sadness and relief wound through him. He felt like shit for making them worry again. For having a son who'd ended up tied up by a madman twice in one year. After Albany, he'd gotten on a plane back to LA before they could come to him. But this time, he'd had no plans to leave Colombia until Adria was ready.

When he pulled back, his mom had tears running down her face.

"What happened to your casting call?" he demanded.

She patted his cheek. "You know better than that. You'll always come first. Our family will always come first."

At her words, he darted a glance at Adria, and he could

see they'd hit her in the chest. Her family had gone so long without putting each other first. But it wasn't too late to fix it. He stepped away from his parents to grab her hand and pull her toward them.

"Mom, Dad, you remember Adria Rojas?"

Adria didn't even let them greet her before she uttered quietly, "I'm so sorry. I'm so sorry we put Ronan in danger again."

His mom wiped at more tears, and his dad turned serious eyes to her. "We're glad all of you ended up coming home safe. Ronan, you, and your friends have all had quite a year. Let's make sure we don't have any more excitement, shall we?"

"Dad," Ronan's voice was a warning growl, but Adria just huffed out a half laugh.

He introduced his parents to the rest of the gang, and they all visited quietly until it was time for the band to get ready for the concert.

"You're really sure you're up for this?" Paisley asked her, and Adria nodded her head.

"I've always wanted to play here. The one song we did for the pageant isn't enough. I want my people to hear the entire album. To hear what we did for Landry...for all of us." Her words were quiet and sure, and Ronan's chest expanded with pride and love.

Everyone went to the concert, even his parents and Adria's family. As they waited backstage for the Daisies to go on, he grew antsy. Not because of the fear that had hovered around them for days, but because he wanted to take her home where they could finally lose themselves in each other. He had words and promises he needed to discuss with her.

He had a lifetime to build, and instead, they'd be at the

concert for hours. He watched from the sidelines as she slowly turned herself back into the rock-star Adria he knew. Confident. Sure. Drumsticks twirling in her hands. He watched as their mothers visited and their fathers debated the quality of the whiskey in their glasses, as if they'd been friends their entire lives. Maybe it was another sign that they belonged—how well their parents got on.

When the Daisies took the stage, he lost himself in the music he'd heard dozens of times now. He itched to have his video camera. He didn't regret using it as a weapon the night before, but he missed having it as he watched Adria pounding away on her drums with thousands of people watching her in awe. Screams filled the arena the longer her solo rolled on. Her eyes were closed, her muscles flexed, and her hair swung wildly. She was a beautiful vision of resilience and fucking talent.

She was magnificent.

Magical.

A damn goddess.

He was so lost in watching her that it wasn't until her drums went silent at the end of her solo and the audience had erupted that Ronan realized Asher and Jonas had come to stand on either side of him.

"Welcome to the club," Jonas said as the band started into the second-to-last song of the evening.

Ronan frowned at him. "Excuse me?"

Jonas's green eyes flashed, and a smirk appeared on his lips. "Asher, Holden, and I are upstanding members of the Daisies Ultimate Fan Club. Welcome aboard."

Ronan didn't think anything about this was funny, but Asher's huff of a laugh eased the tightness in his chest. "As Jonas said when I joined, let me buy you a drink, and we can commiserate over how fucked up it was to watch the woman you love being attacked, and how you'll never, ever feel like you can keep them safe when they're in the public eye all the damn time."

Hell, it was exactly how he felt. He'd never feel like she was safe enough. Not with a thousand men guarding her. He glanced from Asher to Jonas, clenching his jaw. "Will it ever get easier?"

"Hasn't for me yet," Jonas said with a careless shrug.

"Believe it or not, having Holden on board helps. He keeps us abreast of what's going on, and I trust the man. He's gotten further than anyone on Landry's murder...and Angel Carter," Asher said solemnly.

"But the man still showed up and did what none of our security could," Ronan said, stomach tightening as he thought about Carter, Tatiana in the coffin, and the bullet hole in Claudio's head.

"I can't approve of his methods," Asher said. "But I do know he's been on our side more than not. I don't trust him. He has his own reasons for tracking Landry's killer, but I believe that's exactly what he's doing."

Concern flew through Ronan. "What else does Holden know that he didn't share on the plane?"

"Not anything, really. Reinard thinks Carter is part of a secret society called the *Cavalieri d'Oro*. They've been working in Europe for longer than the Knights Templar, but we don't know why the group is interested in what happened to Landry," Asher explained.

A chill ran up Ronan's back. "So, it's not over. Whatever has been following them around...it's still out there?"

Neither of the men answered, a tension wafting between them. Adria had just been through more trauma than anyone should be expected to go through in a lifetime, and yet, there was still a door open, letting the shadows that lingered around them in.

"So, do you still want the job?" Asher asked quietly, for the third time in almost as many days.

Ronan didn't answer with an instant reply as he had before. "I need to talk with Adria first."

Asher clapped him on the back, and they all watched as silence settled down over the arena before Paisley started into "The Legacy." Her voice wavered a little, and the other band members immediately chimed in, picking up the threads that were missed as they always did.

A knot in his throat emerged that he could barely breathe around.

In some ways, it felt like what had happened to Landry was meant to happen in order for each of the Daisies to find the life that was waiting for them. Asher and Fiadh would certainly never have gotten together. Paisley wouldn't have become the force she was now. Their lives had been pulled together, woven tighter by Landry's death. It felt wrong and yet beautiful. Meaningful.

He had a few more things to change about the documentary. It wasn't ready yet. He needed to hold off for a little longer because he had a strange premonition that before it was done, he'd have more to say about all of them. More to show the world.

Another round of chills wafted over him.

"I'm going to postpone the documentary a little longer," Ronan said to Asher.

Their eyes met for several seconds, his friend's jaw ticking, but then Asher gave a curt nod. "Maybe that's for the best."

The audience went nuts as the last chords drifted away

in the arena. Screams and stomps and clapping. The Daisies' names were chanted in the air, and the five women held hands, took a bow, and made their way offstage. They formed the huddle they did every night after performing. A circle of grief and loss but also hope and love. It was beautiful. Jonas was there in two strides of his long feet, surrounding the women also.

Ronan took a step toward the huddle, and Asher held him back. "Just wait. She'll come to you."

The circle broke, and Fee came running toward Asher. He swept her up in his arms, kissing her on the lips, holding on tight. Leya's eyes scanned the stage, and she drifted on dancer-like feet to Holden who pulled her to him. Paisley and Jonas were already linked, hands twined. It left Nikki and Adria standing there together. Adria had her arm tangled with her friend's, and she dragged Nikki with her over to Ronan.

He was finally able to put his arm around her. He leaned in and placed a kiss on her cheek, and her body stilled, breath held for a moment before she let it out.

Nikki's eyes flashed with amusement.

"And...'another one bites the dust,'" Nikki sang out, and the Queen lyrics seemed entirely inappropriate and appropriate at the same time. She was still smiling as she started walking away.

"Nik," Adria called, and her friend turned back. "This doesn't change anything. I'll always be your wingwoman."

Nikki's eyes flashed for a moment with sadness or loneliness, but it was gone so fast Ronan almost thought he'd been mistaken.

"I know," she said before heading toward the dressing rooms.

Ronan and Adria stared for a moment, and then her

hand slipped to his neck, drawing his head down, and their lips met. A kiss that was full of longing and promises and love. So much damn love he thought his heart might explode with the amount of it.

She pulled back, saying, "I'm not staying for the after-party."

It was being held in one of the club-level rooms at the arena, and Ronan had figured they'd be there for several more hours.

"You're not?" he said, heartbeat picking up.

"No. I already spent plenty of time with the press this weekend. I told Paisley and Asher I needed to go home tonight. I'm done." Her blue eyes glimmered with intensity, a meaning in them he understood, an offer she was making. One he'd refused several times now in the last few days, but he didn't want to turn down again.

"Let's go home," he said quietly.

They stayed at the arena only long enough for her to grab her things and to let their families know they were heading out. Then, they were striding out to the SUVs with the detail in tow. In the back seat, his hand slid up her leather-clad leg, dangerously close to the juncture at her core, and it reminded him of the ride they'd taken almost three years ago. The one that had ended with them naked in his hotel room until he'd stupidly brought out a piece of paper to have her sign.

Maybe it reminded Adria of it too, because she tightened under his touch ever so slightly. Then, she leaned in and pulled his mouth to hers. The kiss was hot, needy, and intense as it always was when they were joined like this. Two meteors heading toward the same spot on the Earth's surface. Ready to collide with an eruption that would leave them obliterated. Turn them into a new crater that would define the rest of their lives.

It took too long to get to the estate. Too long to jog up the stairs. Too long for the door to be closed and clothes to be shed. But then, it was just him and her and bare skin. He dipped her backward onto the bed, lips trailing down from the corner of her ear and jaw, over her collarbone. The heat and sweat and tantalizing scent of her after she'd spent hours onstage was a heady, pheromone-induced aphrodisiac. His hand tweaked one rosy peak, and his mouth surrounded the other. She gasped, fingers curling into his hair, nails biting into his scalp. God, he loved it. The sounds, smell, and the feel of her under him.

He moved lower, trailing wet kisses over her stomach, playing with the barbell there. "Ronan," she moaned.

He smiled, loving that she'd always responded to his touch this way from the very first time they'd done this dance. He moved lower, fingers and mouth slipping through her heat, and she swore softly in Spanish. A delightfully indecent chant that had his dick hardening to an almost painful level. But he needed to watch her come apart before he embedded himself inside her.

His tongue twisted, palm sliding over her sensitive parts, fingers circling.

"*Dios*...I need you...in me," she told him, and her eyes were so dark with lust and longing it almost made him lose focus.

"Come for me first, Star," he muttered, the movements of his hands and mouth picking up pace.

Her lashes fluttered shut, her body arched, her breath gasping, and then she fell apart, trembling and convulsing around him as he watched. The beauty of that moment was his and his alone. The way she became something else, something more than just the rock star or the beauty queen, even more than the *reina del rock*. It was like she was bathed in a shimmery glow, as if the magic of her homeland was infused in her body, and when she broke apart, the light leaked through all her veins and crevices.

He eased his way back up her body, taking her mouth and devouring it. Her hands went to his hips, pulling him closer, and when he looked down, the emotions in her eyes almost had him coming without ever having been inside her.

"You sure you want this?" He had the presence of mind to ask, and he wondered if she understood he meant more than just his body inside hers bare.

She nibbled on his bottom lip and then broke the kiss as her hands tugged at his hips, bringing him even closer. "I've never wanted anything more in my entire life, Hollywood. Nothing. Not even my drums."

He groaned, dropping his forehead to her shoulder while he regained his control. Then, he looked back into her face, needing to see every expression as he eased into her. Her lids fluttered again before opening to watch, as if she was as fascinated by him as he was with her. He'd missed this. Missed sliding into her with those beautiful eyes staring at him. Missed the connection that went far beyond their bodies.

Another deep groan escaped him as he pulled back and then thrust in again, bottoming out. God, he could stay just like this forever. Her, him, joined in the deepest, closest way two humans could be. But she didn't let him, demanding more until they were both moving again. The pace was slow and yet desperate, a slow roll along her rim, easing into a crescendo, until there was nothing left to do but chase the high that would come with the exhilarating release. The magnificent ending. Her body tightened, trembling, and she sang his name as she let go, and he joined her, leaving everything inside her. Hoping it would brand her just as much as she'd branded him with every inch of her heart and soul.

CHAPTER THIRTY-FOUR

Adria

LABYRINTH
Performed by Taylor Swift

She woke to the roll of a tongue along the small of her back. The sheet was piled around her waist. A warm hand was already sliding under it, squeezing her cheek. Her entire body lit up, as it always had every time they'd come together like this.

Her eyes fluttered open, and she looked over her shoulder to see Ronan's steely eyes heated, full of longing and lust and love, and her heart felt like it doubled in size. Like she wasn't going to be able to keep it inside her chest if it grew any more.

She went to roll over, and he stopped her with a palm to her back. "Not yet. I'm not finished with this side." His voice was thick with sleep and desire.

His hands and mouth massaged and caressed every inch of her shoulders, her back, her ass. A slow and torturous offensive that was the opposite of the fast and furious she wanted after spending days...years...missing this. Missing him.

Finally, he flipped her over, but then he began the same leisurely, sensual exploration of the front of her. She ran her hands down his chiseled stomach, grabbing the one piece of him that was clearly as desperate to be inside her as she was to have him.

He tsked and moved away, sitting on his heels, running his gaze over her instead of his hands.

"Ronan," she growled.

"You've been torturing me for years, *reina del rock*. This is just repayment."

Then, he leaned back down and started nibbling the tender spot at the juncture of her jaw and ear before trailing wet kisses down over her collarbone, soft fingers barely fluttering over her peaks that were aching for him.

Every time she tried to touch him or speed things up, he moved away, withdrawing her hands and his. Wells of desire, frustration, and raw need grew inside her. When he did it for the fourth time, she finally pushed him off her and rolled out of the bed, taking the sheet with her and wrapping it around her body. He laughed, and went to grab her, but she stepped back.

"No, Hollywood. You ran out of time. You moved too slow."

He pounced, catching the end of the sheet and dragging her back to him. He sat on the bed with her between his legs. "We're never going to run out of time, Star. Never again. You and me...we're forever. We're going to spend the rest of our lives drowning each other in love, remember?"

She froze for a minute. "Even a week ago, your words would have left me feeling trapped. Caged." Something close to fear flickered in his eyes, and she pushed on, needing him to hear the rest before he assumed the worst. "But I see it now. Our love. It's the stable ground we can jump from. It gives us the safety we need to soar and a home to land in. Our love is freedom, not a cage."

His throat bobbed. "We both thought I'd need to show you what love looked like, Star, but instead, you're showing me."

She dropped the sheet and straddled him, bringing her heat right down on top of him. "Let me show you again."

His eyes dilated, nostrils flaring. She glided the heat of her over him until he bottomed out, and her walls trembled. The torturous, slow seduction he'd put her through had made her hungry and ready. Their bodies moved together, the high pulling at them, tugging them toward the peak. He rolled them over so she was on her back, and she lost any control she had, crying out, chanting his name as her entire being convulsed, and stars flashed before her eyes. He went over the edge after her, and they lay there, joined in the most delightful of ways, while they tried to catch their breath.

He tucked a strand of her hair behind her ear, fingers sliding down her arm.

"You drive me crazy, Star. You always have. The first time we were together, I was young and stupid enough not to understand what it meant. That you were a gift the gods were giving me. That you were mine, and I was yours. It took you walking out that day for me to understand it. But you're the only woman I want. The only person I need at my side."

She swallowed hard, caressing his jaw, thumb landing on his lips that were slightly red from the ferocity of their kisses. She didn't take her eyes off him as she let out a shaky breath and dove into the conversation she'd been avoiding. "We need to talk." He nodded and started to say something, but she cut him off, getting the words out in a rush. "I need to finish the tour. But then...but then... I can tell the band I quit."

He stared at her for a long moment. His voice was low, guttural, almost pained as he asked, "What?"

"Just what I said. My dad says he's moving back to Colombia. My parents finally realized being apart isn't working for them. I don't want that for us. I want to be with you. Even if it means making sacrifices."

He leaned in and kissed her. It was a tender kiss, almost like the one they'd shared by the koi pond. Soft. Reverent. Full of the love he'd expressed that night. He pulled back, and his eyes were watery. "That's the most beautiful thing anyone has ever said to me, Star. Knowing that you'd give it up..." His throat bobbed, but then he pulled himself back together, eyes narrowing. "But no one is making those kinds of sacrifices. We don't need to. We can get everything we want."

She bit her cheek, trying not to cry. "How?"

"Asher and I agreed. Any movies I decide to direct myself...we'll plan filming around your tour and recording schedule. When you're on the road, I'll go with you. I can do almost everything virtually while running the studio. Nikki's mom has agreed to travel with us as my assistant. If I need to do casting calls or meet with directors or film crew, they can come to me wherever I'm at. It'll make me a bit of a diva, but soon, everyone will see that no matter where I'm at, I work as hard as them. And when I'm behind the camera, I'll really be able to prove it."

She stared at him, letting what he was saying settle into her chest.

"What about our families?" she asked. "Your parents... mine... They need us."

"If you're not on tour or recording, and I'm not filming, we can split the time between LA and Cadencia. I've already put the bug in Asher's mind about building a soundstage here. I want to recruit some local screenwriters and directors. Maybe we'll make some entirely Colombian-based movies."

That feeling, as if her heart was going to continue to grow and grow until it didn't fit into her chest, filled her again. Could they do this? Have everything? It seemed impossible. Too perfect.

"I have to admit," Ronan said, running a hand over her arm as her silence continued, "this isn't the response I was hoping for."

She leaned up and kissed him, hard and fierce, with all the promises they'd been making since the koi pond. Maybe before. Maybe since she was eighteen and had been swept away by Quentin Hawk's all-too-handsome son.

"I love it. I love you. But if...if it ever gets to be too much, we have to promise to talk about it. To not give up and let the distance fill in between us." She'd never survive it if she ended up losing him like she felt she'd lost her family. She was trying to find her way back to them, but she couldn't do that with Ronan. Not after giving him all of her pieces to keep.

His hand trailed over her. "I can't see any reason it would ever become a problem for me. We get each other and the careers we both wanted. But maybe, when we have kids, we can talk again."

She laughed softly. "Kids?"

"I want the whole thing with you, Star. The fairy tale. A

white wedding, a couple of houses, kids. But I can wait. I'm a patient man."

"You are not patient. You move so fast I can barely catch my breath."

"Hmm. Seems to me...about ten minutes ago, you were complaining I was going way too slow."

His hands and mouth dragged down her body, and every nerve ending came alive.

"That's just because I'm greedy for your love just like you said you were for mine. I want all of you. Every last piece. They all belong to me," she said fiercely.

"It's all yours, Star."

She let herself get lost in his touch, knowing he was losing himself back. Overcome with the feeling that when they were joined like this, it was the only place she felt completely and absolutely herself. Not the rock star. Not the beauty queen. Not anyone but Adria. A woman who was cherished and adored by one man.

You're my entire universe, he'd said.

She'd spend the rest of her life making sure he knew he was hers as well.

EPILOGUE

Ronan

YOU'RE STILL THE ONE
Performed by The Mills

"Cut!" Ronan called, and the entire set went silent for a moment. Everyone's breath was held, waiting to see if he'd want them to do another take. But he knew in his heart it was done. They'd finished the film. It was perfect. Better than *The Secrets Inside Us*. Better than anything he'd ever made. He looked over at Gemma, who was grinning. She knew it too. They looked back out to where her husband, the lead actor, stood waiting for his next direction before Ronan's gaze was drawn to Adria's face. Her blue eyes were shimmering with tears. She knew it too.

"And that's a wrap!" he called out.

A cheer erupted over the set. Goosebumps went up his spine.

The entire cast and crew could feel it. This was an Academy-Award-winning film. They were going to win Oscars. And if they didn't, all of Hollywood would be griping about it, knowing it should have happened. Maybe it made him a cocky bastard, but he believed in what they'd done that much.

"Champagne is ready in the back room!" Adria shouted.

More cheers as everyone dropped what they were doing and headed that way. Ronan stepped out from behind the camera where he'd spent the morning making sure everything he wanted was captured on film. Adria met him, wrapped her arms around his neck, and kissed him.

It wasn't PG, but it wasn't exactly X-rated either. It was heated and hot and full of the love and pride she felt for him. That they felt for each other. Over two years into this relationship, and they were still going strong and steady. As corny as it was, they were the solid ground under each other's feet and the wings that lifted each other up when they needed it. Adria had been right. Their love was freedom, not a cage.

"How did you know to have the champagne ready?" he asked.

She smiled and winked at him. He traced her brow with one finger as she responded, "I knew because I saw what you were doing and felt it." She pressed a hand to his chest. "In here. Like I always feel it when you've accomplished what you wanted."

"Yeah? Can you feel"—he tugged her hips against his— "what I want to accomplish right now?"

She laughed. "Yes, but you need to go say something to the crew before we disappear into your trailer."

"The trailer isn't going to cut it today. There's no way I could keep it from rocking, and we don't need it posted on social media again."

She drew him toward the room at the back of the restaurant they'd been using as a makeshift green room. "Then, you better hurry because I'm not sure I can make it all the way back to the hotel."

He chuckled. "It's literally a five-minute walk, *reina del rock*."

"Do you know what we could do to each other in five minutes?"

God, yes. He did.

His feet picked up the pace. The crew was waiting. Someone handed him a glass of champagne, and he said some words he'd never remember. Then, he told them all to go celebrate. To spend their last two nights on San Fiore, relaxing and celebrating. The movie would pick up the expense even though they were done filming.

More cheers.

Then, he was drawing Adria from the room and out onto the colorful, tiled street outside the restaurant where they'd spent the last five days with their trailers in the lot next door. The tangy salt and floral scent of the island hit him as it had every single time they'd come here, like it was yet another place he could call home. It was embedded in his soul in some way. The beauty of the island and the pride of its people made it the perfect place for the closing scenes of the movie.

They made their way along the quay to the hotel, Lennox following at a distance with two other bodyguards. While the threat to the Daisies had died away with the people and groups coming after them having all been stopped and Landry's killer having been found, their careers required some sort of security to ensure they remained safe. Sometimes, it was from well-meaning fans, and sometimes from creeps who thought they had a right to invade their personal space.

The hotel came into view, and Ronan's chest squeezed. It was one of the most picturesque places he'd ever seen. Embedded into the hillside like the mansions of Capri but glistening with gold-flecked marble, it was the perfect neutral to the explosion of flowers that surrounded it. Plants climbed up the walls and were embedded in enormous stone urns, draping from every balustrade and balcony.

With Adria's hand still in his, they bounded up the enormous stone steps at the front, slipping through the elegant lobby and out the back doors to where a handful of villas were arranged around a large pool with gemstones lining the bottom in a colorful mosaic.

At the door of their villa, he turned to their bodyguards. "We're in for the rest of the day. Make sure we aren't disturbed."

As the door shut behind him, Adria turned around, crossed her arms over her chest, and said, "Nikki is coming by later."

"I'm sure she has a million other things to do," he said. He picked her up, and her legs surrounded his waist, and then he kissed her like he'd wanted to do at the set. Deep and slow, licking into her corners, filling her up until it felt like they'd both come home.

He carried her up the marble and wrought-iron staircase to the white-and-gold bedroom on the second floor where French doors overlooked a balcony literally hanging over the sand.

He'd already stripped her of her little white shorts and tank top before they'd taken two steps into the room. She returned the favor, pulling off his T-shirt and unbuttoning the cargo shorts he'd worn to try and avoid the heat of the day. Once they were both naked, they just stared for a moment, taking in each muscle, each scar, each piece that made the other who they were before they collided together and became something different. Something more.

Then, they were on the huge canopied bed, the sheer curtains blowing around them in the breeze from the open windows. The scent of the sea and the flowers wafting in over them adding to the heady, dreamlike experience. Every touch and every sound was amplified. Every taste of her skin on his lips and tongue a revelation he'd never get tired of finding. Soon, they were both panting, a deep hunger tuning out every other thought and every other sense. Their bodies moved in a beautiful rhythm they continued to perfect the more they were together. Like a movie or a song that only got better the more you watched and listened to it. Souls that wouldn't ever get weary of the other. She was better than any sunrise or sunset he'd ever experienced. Better than any award. Better than breathing.

When they'd peaked and fallen over, landing in the beautiful tranquility of release, they lay tangled together, and the room slowly came back into focus. The ocean outside the doors crashed along the shore. The sound of seabirds and laughter from the beach trickled through the room. He was at peace.

She pulled away, and he started to drag her back, but she laughed. "I'm going to the bathroom, Hollywood, not the other side of the world."

He grunted but let her go.

His eyes drifted shut while she was gone. Once, a long time ago, he'd imagined a morning spent like this, with a balcony overlooking the sea and the smell of coffee, vanilla, and flowers cascading over them. And now, he had it. With the film done, they could spend the next few days just enjoying each other's bodies and hearts and souls.

"Ronan," she called. He opened his eyes, and his heart caught at the sight she made. Her black hair was a tangled web around her face and shoulders, sliding over her breasts that he was displeased to see she'd covered with his T-shirt. He sat up, hands immediately going to the hemline and pulling it up, but she swatted him away.

"Stop," she said, pushing him back against the headboard and straddling him.

Then, she put a box on his chest. A small, square, velvet box. The kind he was supposed to give to her.

"What's this?" His voice was gruff, a mix of emotions pooling inside him.

"I guess you'll have to open it to find out," she said with her signature wink.

He did, inhaling when he saw a pair of rings inside. Simple bands of silver and gold twined together with a handful of lapis lazuli stones embedded along the curve.

"Once, you told me you wanted the whole shebang. A white wedding, a house, kids, each other. We're just missing a couple of those things. I know you were biding your time, waiting for me to be ready, and I want you to know I am. Marry me, Hollywood. Make me the queen of your personal kingdom."

He put a hand behind her head, drawing her close and kissing her fiercely. "You already rule my life and my heart, *reina del rock*. But I'll happily slip these rings on our fingers and claim you in front of the world so no one ever forgets it. I love you."

"I know," she said with a smirk.

He closed the box with a snap, setting it on the bedside table, and then flipped her over, pulling the shirt from her body. "You know, do you? Maybe I want to show it to you anyway. Maybe I won't stop loving you until I've drowned you in it. Until every last corner of your soul is mine."

"All of the pieces are already yours, Hollywood. They always were. It just took me a while to give up my fear and really, truly live."

♫ ♫ ♫

I hope you loved Adria and Ronan's second-chance romance as much as I loved writing it and that you're on the edge of your seat with a list of possible suspects as we move on to the final book in the series. In case you missed it before, you can catch some exclusive scenes from each of the Daisies' perspectives, including Landry's, in the bonus material, *Swan River*. It also gives you a hint at what's to come with the final Daisy to take to the page, Nikki Rani. You can get it for FREE with a newsletter sign-up:

https://www.twsspub.com/bonus/pdbm

MESSAGE FROM THE AUTHOR

Thank you for taking the time to read the fourth book in *The Painted Daisies* series inspired by Taylor Swift's "False God." I hope you loved the way Adria and Ronan found their way back to each other and overcame fear to find love. I hope each moment of their story combined with the mix of music leaves you with memories you'll think about every time you hear one of these songs from now on.

Blue Marguerite is the fourth book in a connected, stand-alone series. While each couple will have their own suspense plot line and their own happily ever after, you'll need to read the entire series to find out just what happened that day at Swan River Pond with Landry. The good news is the entire series is out now and you can get the final book, *Royal Haze*, now.

If you go searching for the town of Cadencia in Colombia, you'll be looking a long time as it's my own made-up little world. I combined aspects of many cities along the Gulf coast to make it a little bit of paradise. There were a million things I would have liked to share about the heritage and culture of Colombia in this story, but alas, there was only so much space on the page. I hope you take some time to learn on your own about the beautiful people who live there.

If you like talking about music, books, and just what it takes to get us through this wild ride called life as much as I do, maybe you should join my Facebook readers' group, LJ's Music & Stories and join the conversations there today. Hopefully, the group can help *YOU* through your life in some small way.

Regardless if you join or not, I'd love for you to tell me what you thought of the book by reaching out to me personally. I'd be honored if you took the time to leave a review on BookBub, Amazon, and/or Goodreads, but even more than that, I hope you enjoyed it enough to tell a friend about it.

If you still can't get enough (ha!), you could also sign up for my newsletter where you'll receive music-inspired scenes weekly and be entered into a giveaway each month for a chance at a signed paperback by yours truly. Plus, you'll be able to keep tabs on all my stories, including fun facts about The Painted Daisies and more.

Finally, I just wanted to say that my wish for you is a healthy and happy journey. May you live life resiliently, with hope and love leading the way!

ACKNOWLEDGMENTS

I'm so very grateful for every single person who has helped me on this book journey. If you're reading these words, you *ARE* one of those people. I wouldn't be an author if people like you didn't decide to read the stories I crafted, so THANK YOU!

In addition to my lovely readers, I'd be ridiculous not to thank these extra folks who've made this journey possible for me:

My husband, who means more to me than I can explain in one or a thousand sentences, and who has never, ever let me give up on this dream, doing everything he could to make it come true, and then CHEERING from the rooftops at my tiniest success. Here's to you being a "Kept Man" someday, my love.

Our child, Evyn, owner of Evans Editing, who remains my harshest and kindest critic. Thank you for helping me shape my stories and reading this one a million and one times until I got it right.

The folks at That's What She Said Publishing, who took a gamble on me, this wild idea I had for a series, and then were determined to see the best in all of it even when I chewed my lips to smithereens, worrying that it would fail.

My sister, Kelly, who made sure I hit the publish button the very first time and reads my crappy first drafts and still loves my stories anyway.

My parents and my father-in-law, who are my biggest fans and bring my books to the strangest places, telling everyone they know (and don't know) about my stories.

The beautiful Liss Montoya who took the time out of her busy life to make sure that I represented Colombia and Adria's heritage with grace and respect. I'm forever grateful to you for reading with kindness and correcting my mistakes, and for teaching me the most interesting curse words I've ever learned!

The talented Emily Wittig, who made the perfect covers for this heart-wrenching series.

Jenn at Jenn Lockwood Editing Services, who is always patient with my gazillion missing commas, my hatred of the semicolon, and scattered deadlines.

Karen Hrdlicka, who ensures the final versions of my books are beautiful and reminds me hyphens aren't always optional. You're a beautiful soul.

To the entire group of beautiful humans in LJ's Music & Stories who love and support me, I can't say enough how deeply grateful I am for each and every one of you.

To the host of bloggers who have shared my stories, become dear friends, and continue to make me feel like a rock star every day, thank you, thank you, thank you!

To a host of authors, including Stephanie Rose, Kathryn Nolan, Lucy Score, Erika Kelly, Hannah Blake, Annie Dyer, and AM Johnson, who have shown me that dear friends are more important than any paralyzing moment in this wild publishing world, MWAH!

To all my ARC readers who have become sweet friends, thanks for knowing just what to say to scare away my writer insecurities.

And I can't leave without a special thanks to Leisa C. and

Rachel R. for being two of the biggest cheerleaders I could ever hope to have on this wild ride called life.

I love you all!

ABOUT THE AUTHOR

Award-winning author, LJ Evans, lives in Northern California with her husband, child, and the terrors called cats. She's been writing, almost as a compulsion, since she was a little girl and will often pull the car over to write when a song lyric strikes her. A former first-grade teacher, she now spends her free time reading and writing, as well as binge-watching original shows like *Ted Lasso, Wednesday, Veronica Mars,* and *Stranger Things.*

If you ask her the one thing she won't do, it's pretty much anything that involves dirt—sports, gardening, or otherwise. But she loves to write about all of those things, and her first published heroine was pretty much involved with dirt on a daily basis, which is exactly why LJ loves fiction novels—the characters can be everything you're not and still make their way into your heart.

Her novels have won multiple awards including *CHARMING AND THE CHERRY BLOSSOM,* which was *Writer's Digest's* Self-Published E-book Romance of the Year in 2021. For more information about LJ, check out any of these sites:

For more information about LJ, check out any of these sites:
Website: www.ljevansbooks.com
Facebook Reader Group: LJ's Music & Stories
Goodreads: www.goodreads.com/author/show/16738629.
L_J_Evans

facebook.com/ljevansbooks

twitter.com/ljevansbooks

instagram.com/ljevansbooks

amazon.com/LJ-Evans/e/B071R365YK

bookbub.com/authors/lj-evans

tiktok.com/@ljevansbooks

pinterest.com/ljevansbooks

OTHER TITLES BY LJ EVANS

Disguised as Love — Cruz & Raisa

THE PAINTED DAISIES

Sweet Memory

Green Jewel

Cherry Brandy

Blue Marguerite

Royal Haze